MISS MORISSA

Books by Mari Sandoz published by the UNP

bridge owner's office. Henry Clarke was not there, but she saw him on his star-faced bay at the toll shack. She pushed past the men who would hold her back and stopped before Clarke, forgetting that he was her father's employer, knowing only that he was in command here.

"It seems to me you might have the humanity to take down that terrible thing hanging at the bridge, no matter who is guilty of the crime," she burst out, speaking over-loud to cover the weakness of her emotion.

The bridge builder turned to look down upon her, his long gauntleted hands settling to the saddle horn, his reddish beard glowing in the sun. After a long time of silent, remote appraisal he spoke. "I am sorry that I must deny a beautiful woman anything—"

"Shall we put it on a basis of humanity, Mr. Clarke?" Morissa insisted firmly.

"Yes, oh, yes, Miss Morissa," the man said, the preoccupations of the day already back upon him. "It is that—a humane act, keeping the owls away by nailing up an example—"

"But this is sinful, or, if sin is a word of no meaning here, let us say it is unlawful—"

"Yes, unlawful, Miss Morissa. But have you heard of the murder of the Metz family, up the trail in the Hills?"

"What pertinency could that have here?—that massacre by Indians, by savages?"

"By Indians for gold dust? That's all that was taken, Miss Morissa. No clothing, no food, not even the gun they had or the cartridges. Persimmon Bill's gang of roadagents have already made their brags all around about it. Even the arrows and moccasin tracks they left all over the place are old tricks."

For a moment Morissa was nonplused. "I still don't see what that has to do with this—" she objected finally.

"My child, there were at least twenty thousand people around here within five, ten miles last night. Fortunes in money on this side, and in gold dust on the other, all without a sheriff or police or court. No law for the protection of property or of life, and perhaps a hundred Persimmon Bills among us, ready for murder. That's why the man is hanging there—because we have no law except the gun and the rope."

"But what did this man do?" Morissa still persisted.

"That, my dear, cannot be put into words today, but you might notice that there is not one known outlaw left here this morning, no Persimmons, no Dunc Blackburn, not even Fly Speck Billy. Now if you will excuse me, I hope to get the bridge opened by noon."

Angry and humiliated, Morissa Kirk strode away, pushing through the crowd to the stage station. There she bought space on the coach that would start back to Sidney in two, three hours. Then she hurried

17

as fast as she could across the bottoms to the little soddy so gray and sad beside Robin's standing wagons. Inside she began to throw her clothing, her belongings, back into the little pressed-metal trunk, all the garments that had once been so carefully folded for another, a happier journey. One moment she stopped to wonder how Tris Polk would look upon this hanging at the bridge, but only for a moment, then she stuffed in the last of her petticoats and jammed the lid down.

It did not matter to Morissa Kirk now that she had no plans. Certainly she could not return to the practice she gave up so gaily for her wedding. No, it must be somewhere new, still in the West, Kansas perhaps, or in Colorado along the mountains, but not so far beyond the law next time, not where she need look upon this mortal humiliation that man can put upon his kind.

And in her horror and anger she forgot her patient in the wagon. Before she thought of him there was a sound of hoofs galloping towards her door, a shouting, "Hey! Lady Doc! Hey!" and of horses stopped in mid-run, a man off, pounding properly but urgently at the jamb of the open door.

Quickly Morissa Kirk wiped the wet from her cheeks and went out into the sunlight.

"I'm from Polk's beef herd down river a couple miles. Man with a party of gold seekers near us been knifed," the sunburnt cowboy said, motioning to the extra horse he led. "Bleeding bad, about gone—"

Morissa snatched up her black bag and, with her hair still in the heavy braid, she swung into the saddle, knee about the horn, holding on as she followed the man spurring ahead around the thickest of the crowd. When they neared the party a knot of men in black came from the wagons to meet the doctor and then drew together, their bearded faces darkening at her approach.

"No—not a woman doctoress!" one shouted, with a Pennsylvania Dutch accent. "This we want not."

"No! We hold not with females working spells!" the others agreed angrily.

"But at least let me look at the man," Morissa pleaded with them. "I've been told he's dying. Let me see him; perhaps I can tell you what to do—"

"No! No!" they said sternly, gathering in a dark wall around the fire where the man apparently lay.

"You damn fools! Doc saved a life here yesterday," the cowboy said angrily. "She fetched a man back who was drowned sure as hell!"

But the dusty group only drew nearer to each other, seeming even more determined and afraid, muttering in their own language, making secret gestures and signs among themselves.

"Ignorant bigots!" Morissa wanted to cry against them, but she held

18

herself to an inner raging that made her tremble. Plainly there was no use waiting, so she turned back to her horse, mounted as he whirled from her blowing skirts. She let him start off in a shying run, leaning forward in the saddle to steady her bag, her braid snapping out behind her.

"I had no idea, Doc," the cowboy apologized when he caught up. "I'm from over in Wyoming myself. We don't see things that way. Women got the vote there years ago—"

Back at the soddy the young doctor sank down in the duskiness of her sun-blinded eyes, still shaking with anger. Not that she hadn't met this attitude before, both in medical school and in her practice, but here it was a direct, a desperate and perhaps a fatal thing—not just a preference for a male doctor but a preference of none at all to a woman, even of letting a man die.

As she sat despondently on the cot Morissa recalled the words of a slight, earnest young army surgeon named Walter Reed. He had given up a good position in New York and stopped on his way to an Arizona post to speak to a group of young doctors. "I suggest that you go to the frontier," he had told them. "Your patients will be the young, with the ills of youth and a new country. Epidemics, appalling accidents and violence." He spoke of the two frontiers of medicine: the laboratory for research against such scourges as diphtheria, typhoid, and the yellow fever that swept up from the South every summer to kill tens of thousands; the other the West, where the ills of a whole region would be administered to by strong young hands like those he saw before him, or perhaps by none at all. "Too often there are only the grieving to watch the sick tonight, and many are dying entirely alone—"

Yet just now, she, Dr. Morissa Kirk, had been ready to sit beside such a one with the little that her hands could offer. And what would it matter to the man, dead or alive, that the doctor had been a woman?

But the stage taking her back to Sidney and away would soon be leaving. She must dress, try to eat something. Wearily she combed her long hair in the doorway, the sun running like fire over its moving darkness, her eyes touched by the same golden flame, and the dash of freckles already seeding her short nose. With the hair pinned up, her bangs smooth, she looked through the covered tin cans back of Robin's little two-holed stove: flour for flapjacks, tea, smoked side meat, dried peaches, apples, and white beans.

Almost as soon as the smoke curled up around the stovepipe oven and out into the sun there was a tap at the door. A hairy, gray little man in a dusty frock coat and bare feet stood there, with a lidded old pail in one hand and a willow withe of dressed fish in the other.

"Good morning, fair one!" he announced. "I am the laughing cavalier!" Setting his pail down he slapped his chest as he bowed, and

19

with a slender, scar-twisted hand held up the four big trout. "May I offer these piscatorial prizes to milady?"

"Fresh?" Morissa asked, trying to sound suspicious but having to laugh in spite of her mood.

"Very fresh. Caught and dressed this morning by Wilmer D. Q.— for DeQuincey—Jones. Named by a sweet mother who recited from 'Dream Fugue' at her wedding, and a lovely sight she must have been, so fair and bemused. But time a-wastes. May I suggest a genteel barter? Two of these most excellent fish for bread or the wherewith to accompany the other two—"

Morissa had to be amused at this foolishness. "I think," she said, "I've traded for fish with some of your cousins back in Mercer County, Missouri." But she did add a little more flour to the biscuits and got out Robin's big spider to fry the trout. Some of the delicate white flesh, juicy and tender, might make a change for her patient too. In the meantime the little man sat with his back against the door jamb, the tails of his coat turned up out of the dust, his eye carefully on his old axle-grease bucket while he talked, as though to his first listener in a long time.

He had heard over at the Water Holes station that there was a young doctoress among them here, a lovely young daughter of Aesculapius. He himself was an adherent of Hahnemann. "I am a firm believer in the homeopathic dose, as a firelet is known to kill a great burning prairie if judiciously employed. Or a small nip in the morning cures the excesses of the night," he said, clearing his catarrhal throat.

When Morissa was ready for the trout he interrupted himself. "Ah, Miss, honor me by discarding not one head of these beautiful fish. The cheek of the noble trout is a most delectable tidbit, fit for the Immortals—"

Morissa nodded her sober appreciation, grateful for this diversion of her thoughts from the immediate, from herself. A wee bush is indeed better than nae hiding at all, she told herself.

When the man reached to take the tin plate of trout and brown biscuits from her, Morissa asked about the peculiar gnarl of flesh on both the back and palm of his right hand. "How did you get that scar?"

Coyly the man hid his hand under the plate. "Indian arrow," he said modestly. "A lovely Sioux maiden fled her irate father with me. We were overtaken. An arrow clove my hand, felled me, and she, thinking me dead, threw herself over a cliff."

"Oh, nonsense, Mr. DeQuincey Jones!" Morissa protested.

"I swear it by our sacred love! The place is called Lover's Leap, off yonder southward from the Wild Cat Mountains."

"You find Lover's Leaps everywhere. My grandmother once wrote me

20

of a famous one in Scotland. What I meant was that no arrow through the hand ever *felled* you, as you call it."

"Ah, fair lady—the red demons had poisoned it, curare, you know," he said, as he licked the last bit of meat from a fish skeleton and threw it over his shoulder toward the road, leaving the four fried heads in a neat row on his plate by the side of the biscuit.

"Curare?" Morissa started to scoff, but the lope of a horse interrupted her. It was Robin, shouting, "Fish Head! You son of a gun! It didn't take you long to smell out a meal!"

So the little man slipped the biscuit and the fish heads into his pocket and shuffled away.

Robin looked around the bare soddy, with the girl's pretties all packed away, her diploma gone. He grieved for the young doctor whose mother he had married long ago, and he yearned to ease the misery and anger he saw lying deep within her now, to protect her from more impulsive mistakes. "The bridge will open around twelve or one," he announced grandly, "and a man's gone up to the horse herd for Jackie to come to see it, and visit a little with his sister. I thought he'd better come before your fame spreads so's you won't have time for us—" he said, laughing as he scratched his beard a little and nodded in the direction Fish Head had gone.

"Ah, Robbie, you sing a mighty pretty song to catch a crow!" the girl replied.

"Aye, it is true nothing can enter the closed fist, my girl," the man said. This admirer had come all of twenty miles to see her and Fish Head was a man of parts, with a silk hat in that old axle-grease bucket, ready for the most formal occasion. He had been a flashy figure in the early days of the U.P., a railroad card sharp. Usually stopped off at Ogallala when the Texas trail herds were due, the drivers loose with most of the summer's pay burning their pants. But when Fish tried to clean out a lot of Mexicans one of them pulled an old greaser trick on him, flipped a knife through his hand, and when they got the blade loose from the table underneath, there was an ace of spades, split and bloody, under his palm. The tendons were cut, left the nimble fingers stiff as sticks. "Now he claims he's headed for Deadwood but wants to wait out the Indian scare—"

Morissa nodded without looking up from her own idle hand and so Robin had to drop it. He was needed at his grading crew, working to ripen the new bridge fill, strengthen it to stand up under the heavy wheels of the afternoon.

"Been better if we had a little rain on it," he added, and finally left, for Morissa seemed to have nothing to tell him.

After Robin was gone she went to her patient and rolled up a side of

21

the old wagon canvas to let in a little May sun. Although the man had taken a fair nourishment, he looked gray as death in the sharp light, his heart only a furtive, reluctant little beat for all the digitalis the young doctor dared administer.

"I am leaving orders you must go down to Sidney tomorrow, where you can be more comfortable, indoors, and with better food and care," she said as she counted the pulse against her watch.

Tom Reeder lifted himself in protest, his gaunt cheeks suddenly flushed. "I'll be robbed and throwed out the window," he exclaimed hoarsely.

A wagon hurrying up outside saved her from arguing with the sick man. It was two men from the Pennsylvania party. Firmly they stood together beside their horses, their black hats squarely on their heads. They had come to ask about medicines to be bought for bleeding and the easing of pain.

Morissa felt the anger come up in her throat again. Bleeding, easing pain, after all this delay!

"You are inhuman men," she said to them. "You are letting a fellow creature suffer for a bigoted whim!"

But in a moment she was ashamed. Bustling her bag together she climbed into the wagon unasked, unpermitted, and motioned them to hurry. When they got her through all the crowd and back to the man stretched on a blanket, he was already white as death, the eyes glazed. She laid her head to his bloody breast, felt for the pulse that was gone, and folded the limp hands.

"Who did this? Who stabbed him?" she asked, and as she had expected, she was not told.

It was very late when she could start back, too late even by wagon, unless the Sidney coach was long delayed. Afoot she headed straight for the soddy, almost two miles away, leaving the men standing there, as she cut through a little gully free from campers because it was too steep for wheel or horse, and full of leafing rose brush. Suddenly a small black bird with white on the wings rose into the air, singing all the way, a trilling so clear and sweet it stopped the heart. And as he slanted down, still singing, another arose, and then a third almost at her feet, and when they were gone into the light spring wind, Morissa Kirk stood still and for the second time today she had a wetness on her cheek.

Then, with sudden resolution she hurried on, for now there was work to do, the murders to report to the sheriff at Sidney, as the ethical doctor must even in this region with no court or law. As she wove her way through the crowd she heard the rattle of impatient harness, the snort and stomp of faunching horses, and a call from the stage office for "Morissa Kirk! Dr. Morissa Kirk!" until they probably let someone else have her place. At the driver's whoop the coach came through behind the escort of horsebackers and hurried away toward Sidney and the railroad. The dust of it spread over the long line waiting for the bridge to open and over Robin Thomas, come to stand where he could see who got on the stage, and then slip away.

Morissa pushed in at Clarke's big store and saloon and then out again, elbowing her way with her black bag, ignoring the importunes for another kind of succor. Finally at Etty's she found a little cache of Indian trade goods in a lean-to off the gambling rooms. There was not much for her in the place, crowded with trail wares. The floor lay piled with barrels of hardtack and twist tobacco and stacks of grease buckets and cartridge cases; shovels, gold pans and horse collars hung from the low ceiling; cheap soogans and work boots and pants jammed the shelves. But there was a bolt of red calico under a lot of Indian goods, dusty and pushed aside because very few Indians traveled the route since the buffalo herds vanished.

"—Not that we're looking for Indians in particular, with most of the bucks on the prod," a clerk called Eddie said when Morissa got him diverted from his brags about the gold he would dig as soon as he raised a grub stake. While he talked she looked the material over, turkey red with a small black and yellow figure. She pulled a couple of threads from the cut edge and chewed them to test the color. Over the acrid taste of the dye she noticed the man, only a boy, perhaps not twenty, with hair as fair as a child's, his innocent, long-fringed eyes all over her, bold as a roadagent.

She bought sixteen yards, enough to curtain a dressing corner and a closet nook for her wardrobe. With a smooth two-foot board from a packing box, well-planed, and with few knots, she went back to the soddy, carefully turning her face from the bridge and the lonely figure still hanging there. Yet all the anger and sorrow swept back over her and she wanted to fling herself on Robin's cot and lose it all in sleep, like a hurt infant retreating to his mother's warmth and softness. Or get into one of the grader's wagons and whip away to Sidney and the railroad, with the curtains for the soddy left uncut, unsewn.

Contemptuously Morissa Kirk reminded herself that it was the young colt, the wind, and the unbedded maid, who run this way and that. The wind and the colt she could not control but the unbedded maid she could certainly put to work. Yet even in this she wavered between the two sides of her nature, the feminine and the practical: whether to start with the curtain for her finery or with her doctor's sign announcing her presence. She remembered a quip from medical school: Any jackass who can drive one nail can hang out a shingle against the patient but a shingle against the rain takes the ability to drive two nails.

23

Before she had settled her vacillation there was a hoarse shout outside and a boot kick at her door. A man stood in the sunlight, blood all down his pants, the right hand bound up in a hasty, blood-soaked shirttail. "Got it caught under some shifting mine machinery when a wagon started to go over, upset—"

It must have been very painful, but the man refused the morphine or even a drink of whisky. "Just fix 'er up anyway, Doc," he said, and when Morissa still hesitated, he shouted, "Goddamn it, woman, fix 'er up so's I'll have something left to pull a trigger with!"

Morissa soaked away the blood in a pan of warm water with carbolic acid, lanced the accumulated clottings pocketed through the crushed flesh, and trimmed away the dead tissue. Then she set the broken bones as well as she could although the hand was swollen and dark as a blood stomach. The man never made a sound and when the bones were lightly splinted, the fingers wrapped separately in vaseline-soaked gauze, she comforted him. "—You certainly are one man who is fitted to this raw country!"

But she had to warn him that there was still blood poisoning, gangrene, and lockjaw to think about. "You better get close to a hospital," Morissa started to say, but the man suddenly turned green under his stubbled beard and she got the washpan to him just in time.

"I didn't go to puke before a lady," he stammered miserably afterward.

When the man was gone the doctor thought about the purifying effect of courage on the beholder. After the man's fortitude she could sit here in fair contentment and run up the curtains, although the stitches would have grieved her mother. "You take more care sewing up a patient than a hem," she had complained sadly a few days before she died. "And it's the patient's stitches that are the temporary ones."

Morissa had managed to laugh a little then, knowing there was no arguing with a dedicated housekeeper. But these curtains were also intended as temporary. She was busying her hands with these little tasks to shut out the picture of a man hanging at the bridge, and of an ivory-white satin wedding gown that she would never wear.

She ran a string through the curtain and hung it along the wall on stakes driven into the sod, half of it under her garments to protect them from the rooty earth, half over them. Then she lifted her gold-shot rose brocade from the trunk where she had packed it only a couple of hours ago, the reseda green dress, too, and the rest, turned them inside out and hung them carefully, wondering when she would ever wear such raiment here. Yet there were some very handsome men in the region, men of elegant bearing who would not be deprived of the opportunity to make their graceful bows over a lady's hand. Tris Polk, for instance, the rancher named Martin on the Sidney coach yesterday, and the

24

bridge builder himself. She must order a full-length mirror immediately, for who could seem a lady without one?

But that was for tomorrow. Now she penciled the letters DR. KIRK on the board she got at the store, blackened them in solid with shoe polish and tacked the sign up on the door outside. Later her brother might cut out the letters, so the sign could hang in the window with a light behind it, as clear by night as by day. Somehow the most desperate medical emergencies of life, like so many of its sorrows, and its ecstasies too, seemed to come in the time of darkness.

Standing before her sign Morissa realized that for the second time in two days she had committed herself to a life here, where no sheriff shadowed the murderer or the lyncher, where the gun on the nail in reach of her cot was to be her sole protection—that and such wit as she might have inherited from her Grandmother Kirk. But it would be a long, long life without the man she was to have married Wednesday.

Suddenly Morissa was crying, overwhelmed in it as in the waters of the Platte flood. Yet even this could not be a thing of privacy here, not with the sound of more hoofs already at her doorstep—a rider leading a horse with a sidesaddle, a handsome white-stockinged black.

Morissa wiped her face like a rueful child and rose slowly to go to the door. It was Tris Polk, slicked up as for a dance, his hat in his hand, the sun bright on his thick black hair.

"Come see the bridge opening, Dr. Kirk," he called. "I brought you Cimarron to ride since you seem to like him so well."

III

At CLARKE'S SUGGESTION, MORISSA AND TRIS POLK CROSSED THE bridge afoot before the official opening, following their horses led over by a station hand. They made a fine tall pair for the idle watchers, the young doctor elegant in a riding habit of her favorite green, the long skirt held off the rough planks as she walked beside the rancher, smooth-shaven and browned, handsome in his black flannel shirt with belly-tan Stetson and chaps, his spurred heels loud on the bridge. Yet Morissa remembered to keep her eyes turned from the place where the man might still be hanging, her face quiet but remote.

"Looks like the lady doc's gonna give that Gilda over to Johnson's a run fer Polk there," one of the loafers told the rest, the dark faces about him grinning in anticipation.

On the rise north of the river Morissa and the rancher sat their horses to watch the great run up the trail. The bridge stood empty under the windy May sky, empty and ready—sixty-one long, many-footed segments, low and flat, with the saw-toothed railing along the sides to prevent the fractious and the incompetent from ending up in the river. It was a one-way road of planking over the broad prairie stream, connecting the two dark queues of waiting travelers, the shorter reaching back from the bridge to the north, the other stretching away across the wide bottoms of the Platte, the far end lost in the blue haze toward Sidney. And many of the bigger freight outfits and the beef herds were still scattered up and down the river, camp unbroken.

"We don't hope to get our herd across today, or even late tomorrow," Tris Polk told Morissa. "This is a gold rush—"

Finally Henry Clarke rode his horse through the crowd at the south entrance and fired one pistol shot into the air. The toll arm flew up, and before the smoke began to drift away into the sunlight, his pony express rider was thundering over the bridge and on northward, carrying government mail for the troops at the Sioux agency posts, and illegally on to Custer City and Deadwood Gulch more than two hundred miles away, almost a hundred and fifty of those miles through Indian country, where no white man had a right to be.

Next there were the four stagecoaches gleaming in the sun, their six-horse teams running, followed by the rumbling of heavier wheels. But the first wagons were not gold seekers going north to the Hills, or eager Indian-fighting troops. It was a party of forty-five miners going south, back from the Black Hills in disgust, saying this gold rush was all a hoax, another Western big-wind.

Custer City was a deserted ghost camp since the Deadwood strike, and those who scrabbled off to the gulch found only very poor panning, with about as much color as a pinch of gold dust thrown on a blizzard wind. A man could make as much digging ditches back East, or graves.

So Clarke hurried them across to get them out of the country. Everybody turned from them as from a contamination, only Fish Head drinking the little whisky they tried to set up. Their voices were not to be heard above the bright call of gold or its warmth imagined in every pocket. Everybody here knew of Tom Reeder's heavy box and the gold belt that almost drowned him, and some had seen the yard-long watch chain of nuggets that Bone Eye Newcomb, the card sharp, wore when he hurried through to Sidney two weeks ago; but nobody knew that he had been run out of Deadwood for selling gold-washed pebbles, or that he had only enough yellow dust to color a few bricks for the Eastern trade. Yet they would have hurried just as fast, Morissa suspected. Somehow their hurry seemed less to gold than from something, from something that followed as close upon their trail as the pursuing dust.

26

With the Westerner's reluctance to ask questions beyond perhaps "What name you travelin' under?" Tris Polk made no inquiries of Morissa but kept up a little talk about the last few weeks here, while he waited to cross with his beef herd, overdue for meat at Deadwood. He spoke quietly, and with long silences, for he was apparently no loose-mouth or banterer but more like someone older than his twenty-six or seven years—a man who had accepted responsibility for others when very young.

Etty came riding out toward the bridge to watch, his old beaver cap pulled down even on this warming day. Tris spoke of him. Ettier, Etty, was one of the real old-timers. Seems he came up the Missouri in his fourteenth year, only a boy, as most of the mountain men did. He must be over sixty now, Tris thought, and had three sets of Indian relatives in different tribes. Etty was a genuine fur brigade man.

"But he looks so small, and without that old cap his bald head pushes up like a mushroom growing through a gray tangle of hair and beard—as absurd and defenseless."

Tris laughed, his teeth very white in the brown face. "Most of the mountain men looked like that, I guess. Seems they were mostly small men, too, usually shorter than you are. I remember Kit Carson, probably no more than five foot two or three."

Morissa nodded skeptically as she glanced at the tall cattleman beside her and thought of all the others like him that she had seen these two days—long men, looking even longer in their narrow-legged chaps, their tall hats and high-heeled boots.

When the special travelers were over the bridge, the line from the south started to move up and the two watched in silence as the throb of the bridge rose from a rumble to a pounding roar, until Morissa's horse began to prance his elegant white feet and to faunch at the bit, eager, it seemed, to join this rush to the Hills.

Once the rancher spoke sharply to Cimarron. "The black was your own choice yesterday, Miss Morissa," he apologized.

The girl nodded, her bangs shining under her narrow hat. She had seen the keenness of this horse, his sensitivity to his rider, and as she toyed with his eagerness, the weight of the morning began to slip from her until she, too, could scarcely resist the pull of this vast gold hunger there below them, the excitement of it making Cimarron crow-hop, throw his fine head. But suddenly he stopped, looked northeastward, ears up. A little knot of Indians was watching from a rise, their horses motionless, the sun glancing from a rifle barrel or two. Men began pointing that way and the Indians turned and were gone, leaving a spreading puff of blue smoke and the sound of one lone rifle shot behind.

Morissa looked anxiously towards Tris. "Just some of the wilder Sioux bucks," he said. "They claim all the land from the Platte north, including this knob where we're standing, but they can't keep the gold seekers out; nothing can. The United States Army failed at it last summer."

A long time the girl watched the empty knoll where the Indians had been and didn't ask about a possible attack on the bridge. Then suddenly it occurred to her that young Jackie was off north there, with Robin's herd. She looked around for Robin, but he seemed very busy at the new bridge approach.

"I don't think he's worried about the Sioux just now," Tris comforted. For a moment Morissa was surprised. Of course everybody would know everybody's business here, but she couldn't decide how much of the rancher's words were mere reassurance for a nervous city woman's usual dread of Indians.

The light wagons that carried the spill-over of passengers from the coaches to the Black Hills were followed by a hundred other fast outfits, mules and horses. Many of the latter, perhaps wild mustangs only a few weeks ago, had never heard the thunder of their own hoofs on hollow planking, or smelled roily water running underneath. They reared back, so that some had to be led over by Clarke's men, even blindfolded, or dragged across by one of Robin's sturdy old teams of scraper mares. Perhaps it was the man still hanging there, the dead owl that was to scare off his kind. . . .

As the afternoon lengthened the noise increased and the exuberant whooping and pistol shots too, particularly when Madame Volanda, one of Denver's vice queens, came through. She had chartered a big street omnibus and had it modeled into a beautiful boudoir. Through the many lace-touched windows, all could see Volanda and four, five handsome sporting men sitting elegantly inside as they passed. Behind her came ten wagons gaudy as a circus parade, the canvas rolled up on the bows, carrying her girls with all their finery and mirrors, and furniture, and the gambling devices. The girls were in satins and blowing plumes, smiling and bowing like ladies of a court. But as soon as they were across the canvas of the wagons was let down.

"—Perhaps so the girls can finish their daytime sleep before night," Morissa laughed.

The rancher beside her nodded a little and busied himself retying his lariat strings, and the girl suddenly realized that she was a lady-woman to this man, a *Godey's Lady's Book* woman, even though she had swum the river on his horse yesterday and was a doctor of men. It reminded her of some of her patients, particularly Allston—

But Allston Hoyt was now a man to be thrust from her mind, and the bridge opening was a fine show and apparently a paying one. Five dollars for the earlier places per wagon with driver and team, whether

28

horses, mules, or oxen, two dollars for the later, and always fifty cents for each extra animal or man. Enough gold was clinking into the till over there to draw any roadagent still around after last night. But the money went right to the toll shack, into the padlocked steel box that was forged to the bridge bolts. No outlaw gang could rush it away with less than the new dynamite, even if they got past the Winchester-armed guards, doubled since the hanging.

"Who was he—the dead man?" Morissa managed to ask, her voice tight and small, so intense that her horse began to faunch again.

"Let's say nobody knows his name," Tris said, putting out a hand to Cimarron's tossing black neck, the touch so gentle it seemed almost a caress for the girl in the sidesaddle. "You must not grieve yourself."

The man, Tris told the young doctor, was one of the outlaws from Robbers Roost over in Wyoming, on the Cheyenne trail to the Black Hills, and far from the sheriff there too. They worked the stages hard, sometimes holding up as many as two, three a week, particularly on down trips. Maybe they wanted to keep the gold coming through their wild country, and make some return for the protection they got from the Cheyenne officials by blasting the bridge of the Sidney gold trail here. The Sidney route would be tough competition for Cheyenne, with a shorter railroad haul, the trail itself much shorter and over open country, easier and safer both from outlaws and blizzard snows. But the man with the dynamite last night dropped it and got away in the fading moon. All those who seemed ready for half a dozen holdups, from Clarke's place to Etty's, got away too, in the confusion.

"Then this man here isn't even the one with the dynamite?" Morissa demanded, color rising in her face.

"No, just the man standing guard for him with a Winchester—" the rancher admitted. But that didn't matter. Where there was no law there could be no common bedding ground for outlaws and honest men. " 'You run with horse thieves you hang for a horse thief' is an old rule on the frontier."

"I think it's savagery, and you're siding with the savages!" the girl retorted angrily.

"Maybe, but this is still wild country, Miss Kirk, and on the trails danger makes money for the stages and the big hauling outfits. Discourages lone travelers and small freighters. It makes jobs for the gunmen riding protection, too, and it will until we get law here. No outsider and few small parties would dare try the Cheyenne trail to the Hills alone, unprotected. So long as people are robbed, the gunmen will sit up sassy as rattlesnakes on our doorstep, and we have to walk around 'em."

"And sooner or later some will turn out to be in cahoots with the robbers," Tris finally added, when it seemed something more must be said.

But Morissa Kirk only turned her head from the rancher, her soft bangs tossing a little on the wind. She did not trust her voice or its certain betrayal of her anger.

When the long wagons of mine machinery and equipment started to come up, she watched Robin climb over his green fills to see how they held up under the heavy wheels and the clumsy sideslip of the extended running gears. He had reinforced the abutment with crisscross willow mats and chunks of sandrock scattered like nuts in a coarse pudding, but the scrapers had not finished until long after sunup.

Morissa noticed some men, probably the Pennsylvanians, walking behind a wagon that separated from the crowd south of the river and moved to a little rise. Then for a while the bright sun glinted on working shovels, and afterward they turned around and joined the long string of the waiting. When they passed up the trail they were sitting stiffly on the boards laid across the wagon, dark as dusty crows in their black. One of them ducked his head in reluctant recognition to Morissa and brought the determination of anger to her once more.

As though there had been no silence between them, Tris spoke apologetically of the reception the doctor had received from the men, particularly after one of his cowboys took her there. "You would strike many rough spots like that here, Miss Morissa," he said, slipping into the first name without noticing it. "But with the bridge about done, Robin will be pulling out soon, and you'll be gone—" He left it open, his voice trailing off.

The girl knew the storm-gray eyes were intent upon her and felt a foolish warmth creep into her cheeks. "I haven't heard Robin's plans yet, he's been so busy," she evaded, recalling, in her Scottish heart, that a crooked answer merits no straight question, as Grandmother Kirk would have said.

Her evasion got a Western reply, silence, and so Morissa occupied herself with the hypnotic movement of the people funneling slowly through the narrow passage that was the bridge and then whipping away up the trail as though the gold were just over the first rise. She thought of the other hopeful trails once through this valley. The Mormons had fled persecution up the north bank here, almost at Cimarron's impatient feet. On the other side of the river, up past Chimney Rock and Scotts Bluff standing against the western horizon was the rutted trail of the Overlanders, those who were tolled West by earlier dreams of gold, and the homeseekers on the way to Oregon and the rolling western seas.

But now much of the south river bottoms was closed to every passing wheel or hoof, although it was all free land, public domain. Robin had told her about the Coad brothers, with ranch buildings at the foot of

Scotts Bluff. They had wired the gap between the bluff and the Wild Cat range to the south of it, and all the passes through the Wild Cats, down the twenty miles to Chimney Rock, that curious needle that pricked the whitish sky. They held all that broad valley, the only opening the eastern one between the Chimney and the river, and that they closed even tighter by gun-packing line riders ready to shoot. Coad's Kingdom, Robin called it, and no man could enter. Nobody camped up there even in this crowded time except their own beef herds and freight outfits.

One of Tris's cowboys interrupted Morissa's thoughts. He came from the beef camp with a can of coffee, tin cups, and a hot raisin pie in a dutch oven that he carried carefully in a gunny sack. They spread their slickers and made a little picnic of it there on the knoll beside a patch of wild yellow sweetpeas, their fragrance so heavy that the butterflies clung dizzily to the glowing spikes of bloom.

"I guess I let my mind fly off with the geese there a while—" Morissa apologized. "I was thinking about the emigrants who used to come up the trails along the river, and the valley off west."

"You certainly can quit the country without moving an inch," the rancher said ruefully. "Do you like what you see around here?"

"Oh, I do!" Morissa replied, speaking with the enthusiasm and sudden identity of the homeseeker in a new region. "Robin told me last winter that all the time he worked on the U.P. grade out to Utah he felt that they missed the finest region, the one with the most promise—the North Platte valley."

"Well, there is better grass than this along the Platte here, Miss Morissa, and for water you don't need a river so big you can scarcely swim it for months hand running."

"But look at the crops that will grow here."

"Crops! A city young lady like you thinking about crops—! Even the grass burns up clear to the bogs here in July. Not enough rain."

"Not enough rain with all the water running past? Irrigate!"

But this the rancher beside her seemed not to hear. Instead he watched the curve of her brows that were like the wings of a river swallow, and talked about getting up a big picnic. "You can't leave us here without seeing the valley from the top of Scotts Bluff. A rep from a British financial syndicate's around, looking for a ranch. He brought his new wife, a London actress, and a whole spread of house men and maids. I'd like to get up a picnic for them on the bluff, if you'll come."

"It sounds fine," Morissa said, "but you know there's always a chance that I'll be called away the last minute. A doctor can't be too definite in her promises—"

"A doctor? —How about the woman?" Tris Polk asked, his eyes

searching the girl's flushed face until she wanted to shout a defense against him, cry out the pain and hurt the woman had endured for being a woman, but she was silent.

It was well Morissa had her little black bag tied to her saddle. First it was a broken tooth to be pulled, the jaw fat and shining, and then injuries and dosings, one after another, until she was so weary she was relieved when Robin signaled to them. Their horses prancing side by side, Morissa and Tris Polk fell in behind the down stagecoach coming in from Deadwood, a couple of arrows still sticking in the side, sent after the coach as it passed a small party of Indians just below the agency.

Toward sundown Jackie rode in from the horse herds. He had seen no Indians but was full of excitement over his sister's visit here, and over the live young antelope he brought rolled in a gunny sack and tied across the back of his saddle like a slicker, hoofs hanging down on one side, big-eared head on the other. The soft brown eyes were glazed with terror but the trembling nose reached out to sniff at Morissa's hand, the tongue eagerly sucking at her little finger.

"Oh dear, starving! But what will we feed it, with no milk cow?"

"Mare's milk's better, the men tell me," Jackie said matter-of-factly as he slid his long length from the saddle. Morissa saw with joy how much he looked like their slight, earnest-faced mother, almost as though she lived again in the bearding youth, and yet how much like Robin he was in the strength of his body, and in his quiet manner.

Avoiding the kiss Morissa might have given him, he grinned, untied the antelope and set it down, to stagger stiffly around them and the horse, the shy, lovely head reaching out, the tongue searching. Before Jackie came into the soddy he rode off for one of the wet mares in the grader herd and brought her and the colt into the corral. With the sun slanting between low thunderheads over him he milked enough for one of the nippled bottles from Morissa's emergency case, and together they taught the baby antelope to drink.

That night the little creature slept inside because there was lightning in the west and it would surely get wet in the rain, although Jack laughed aloud at the idea. "Oh, Sis! They always stay out—"

"But he might wander off, with those dogs around Etty's, and still so much commotion around," Morissa insisted.

That was true. Although thousands had passed over the bridge, the planks rumbled with hoof and wheel far into the moonlight, the slow bull trains plodding over to camp with at least that much of a start in the morning. Some said that Clarke took in twenty thousand dollars this one afternoon. Morissa believed it—and all from a bridge that had cost him nothing beyond his effort, his time, and his faith for almost two years. The material and labor were donated or paid for by the railroads and the businessmen of Sidney, Omaha and points east. There was one certainty: None of the money came from the upper Missouri river towns or from Cheyenne, all competitors of the Sidney-Black Hills gold trail.

By now the side of the bridge was clear in the moonlight Morissa knew, the man hanging there finally gone, buried beside the one from the Pennsylvania party, who had died with his boots on too—both at peace. Anxious to shake off such thoughts, Morissa went out for a last look at her patient in the wagon. He was almost as pale and weak as when she first pumped air into his reviving lungs yesterday.

The young doctor hated to admit this, for without Reeder her work here didn't add up to much. One patient was lost by default, beyond all help except the easing of pain, even if she had been permitted to touch him. She had sewed back an ear half torn off in a waller fight, lanced two carbuncles, pulled the rotten bicuspid, dressed one crushed hand and one mule-tromped foot, quieted a running drunk, revived three fainters overcome by the crush and excitement, doled out salts, calomel, and itch ointment, and a tin of crab salve. A woman came for the salve and the young doctor measured it out with her customary gravity, although she was certain this was a barroom joke, plotted, perhaps, by the pretty, boyish youth over at the breed's store, the boy called Eddie Ellis. Yet when she looked at the woman more closely Morissa had decided it was no joke.

And now it was night, with lightning in the west flickering swift as the eye's blink. In the bowed wagon Morissa stooped to look down at Tom Reeder, awake, his face anxious, his pulse like a feeble watch deep under cotton wool.

"You ain't gonna ship me out—" he said slowly, his pale eyes deep-pupiled from the darkness.

Yes, Sidney would be better, and he could be taken to Omaha by train if necessary, to a good hospital.

"You can't go do that to a man, ma'am," he murmured weakly, as though talking in a half dream. Here in her father's wire corral, with everybody knowing the gold wasn't on him, he felt safer. Outside—

"I am a very sick man—" he mumbled over and over.

"That's just it," the doctor finally answered. "You are very sick and not improving. I can't even feed you right."

But he did feel stronger already, he pleaded. It was always expecting to be robbed, filled full of holes any minute, that wore a man down. He had made a strike up to Alder Gulch in Montana, ten years back, and sold out for twenty thousand, then was creased alongside the head by a bullet out of a brush patch, robbed and left for dead. Last year he was cleaned out again by the big break in silver at Virginia City over in

Nevada, when Comstock himself lost maybe forty-two millions in a week. That wasn't done with no gun but he was just as busted. This time he planned to fix it so's nobody'd know. He went in rags around Deadwood Gulch, wore gunny sacks and wire for shoes in thirty-five below zero, and lived on the rent of his old team now and then—poor as a camp robber sitting on a stump, and talking poor-mouth just as loud.

Lucky his claim looked bad, out in a bare pocket of rock with no timber around to cover any snoopers come to stick a dirty nose into his panning, for the pocket had trapped a lot of nuggets amongst the gravel. He took out a whole palmful the morning of his strike, shining like a girl's pretties in the sun. He covered the strike over fast with his old blankets and shoveled his placer dumps on top. Every day he scooped out a few pans from underneath, all winter and spring when it wasn't frozen too hard, until the pocket played out, stripped clear down to bedrock.

"It took a lot of ponderin', with claim jumpers and holdups thick as buzzards around a buffalo kill," he said, looking up at the girl in the lantern light.

By then he had been feeling so poorly he couldn't straighten up, and on top of everything that pain had come in his middle, here under his ribs, a hole with a gnawin' like a mouse. He was afraid of the doctors at Deadwood; paying them with gold would give him away, and then there was that talking gas and ether they used on a man. Finally got so he couldn't keep anything on his stomach any more, and a chance come to hitch in with Pratt's freight outfit and some a them Sunday miners leaving the Hills. Altogether they were too strong for most roadagents but there were a dozen men right in the outfit as would cut a man's throat for a pinch of color. So he couldn't wait for the bridge to open, not with thieves sneaking around his wagon of nights, and his stomach too bad for fried side meat and pan bread.

"Well, I don't know about Alder Gulch or the silver," Morissa admitted, "but I know you have gold here, enough to keep you all your life, if you get it to a bank."

Slowly the man turned his cavernous eyes towards her. "I got no truck with banks. They folded up on me back in '57. I'll leave my stuff right in that little box over to the stage station," he said, and Morissa couldn't remind him that even Clarke's place was not invulnerable now that the outlaws were using dynamite to make way for their Winchesters.

"Try to rest tonight and don't forget that it's the fox with the sly nose that puts his foot in the trap—" the young doctor said gaily.

When she was back in the soddy she took down Robin's gun belt from the peg and looked at it a long, long time in her lap, touching the pistol grip cautiously, drawing the gun from the holster out upon her knee.

She was sitting like that when Robin and Jackie passed on their way to their bunks.

"That's a fine new Peacemaker you got there," the boy said, and together they showed Morissa something of the gun's working. "Yes, I did get it special at Clarke's store here," Robin admitted. "Tomorrow Jack'll show you the fine points of pistoleering."

Now for the first time the girl looked up, surprised that a sixteen-year-old should know anything about the gunman's craft. Seen this way, Robin's concern that Jack was being drawn to the professional killer did not seem absurd at all.

But the target shooting had to be put off, for later in the night it began to sprinkle. Slowly, grayly, the rain fell, on and off, for almost a week. At the bridge the hoofs and wheels passed steadily, the rumble subdued as water softened the planks. But almost everything else stopped, the cleanup around the bridge and the camp, even the beef herds that should be heading north to the Indians or the Hills.

Morissa was glad to have her family together this little time, particularly now, with the clouds running in gloomy windrows against the Wild Cat Mountains whenever the rain lifted enough to see. The soaked ground gave Robin an excuse not to pull out to the small grading jobs Clarke wanted finished up along the trail north. Morissa tried to get reacquainted with the young stranger who was her half-brother, but usually he was over talking to his friend Eddie Ellis clerking at the bridge. When she could she sloshed along the bottoms in gum boots with Jackie, taking up willow and cottonwood seedlings to plant around Robin's soddy.

"Temporary-like?" the boy asked slyly. "People been asking, like that Gilda Ross who maybe's got an eye on Polk."

"Well, if I'm temporary, I hope the trees will last—" Morissa replied, as she selected another new-leafed whip of cottonwood for Jackie's spade and then watched a couple of antelope coming down a little spring draw north of the river.

Back at the soddy they met Robin riding in from the stage station, with a roll of mail, mostly the Sidney and Omaha papers and a couple of medical catalogues. He riffled through them. "Here's something for you!" he said, and threw a patent-medicine circular over to Morissa. Only when he had said it, and saw her look, like a sun's ray striking Chimney Rock and gone as swiftly did he realize what he had done.

When the rain came down too hard the three worked inside the soddy, padding the tops of the nail kegs with worn soogans covered with pieces of old buffalo robe. Morissa and Jackie put up shelves all around under the roof, boards laid on stakes driven into the sod wall, while Robin carved out the DR. KIRK in Morissa's window sign, and added a

35

little staff twined with the double serpent for decoration. "Folks will go to thinking you're a sure-nuff snake doctor, with that caduceus—" he laughed.

The rain didn't stop men from riding up for a word with Robin or Jack. Eddie Ellis came too, and turned out to be as bold-eyed here as at Etty's or Clarke's, wherever he was needed. He was only around the bridge until the rush was done and then he would return to keeping the books for the Indian agent up at Red Cloud. He still talked big of making a gold strike.

Generally the visitors refused to sit down, apologetic about their hats and slickers that dripped dark patches on the dirt floor, but some stayed for a cup of coffee and a sniff of the haunch of venison Robin had brought in for a slow pot roast with wild garlic, or a boil with noodles in the old army kettle. They talked a little, but mostly they came to sneak glances at the new lady doc, who seemed like any girl, only not flirtylike, one of the men told Jack.

"She—your sis, she don't go makin' eyes under them bangs like most good lookers would—" meaning most of those he had seen.

"Oh, I don't know," Robin teased when Jack told this before his blushing sister. "Seems to me she's got that rancher, Polk, hangin' around pretty close—"

"He won't be for long, not when he hears about—about me," Morissa replied hotly and went out to look at her patient, feeling very childish and ashamed.

The first day of rain three Indian families came through on their way down to their relatives in Indian Territory, where they hoped there might be more to eat than at Red Cloud Agency up the trail there a ways. One of the children was very sick and old Etty came riding over with the father, a tall, silent Indian, to ask the doctor to come very quickly. "He say it is the disease of the little red spots and the son will die like his mother if you will not come— But there is nothing for pay."

Morissa hurried her essentials together and rode out, the rain loud on her slicker as the squeeging hoofs of the horses splattered mud. She stooped under the tipi flap into the duskiness around a handful of red coals, the baby on a ragged blanket beside the fire, unmoving, burning with fever. Morissa had never been closer to an Indian than at a circus, and with the darkness and the brown skin, it was only the smell and the degree of collapse that told her the father's diagnosis was correct—a severe case of measles, with, from the chest indications, serious complications.

There was little that Morissa could do except work on the fever and hope to get a little strength into the small boy. She administered a febrifuge, oiled the poor withered skin, sponged the child with cool

36

water and then rolled him in a moist towel. Now and then she tried to get the boy to swallow a little warm mare's milk taken from the antelope's ration, or a little skimmed venison broth with the rice strained out.

And while she watched and worked, sitting awkwardly on the ground, an old Indian woman was squatting on the other side of the fire hole, wailing her mournful medicine songs, the black eyes hot and angry upon the white doctor, the firelight flashing on the long butcher knife at her waist as she swayed.

It was a hard, long night, but toward morning the child seemed a little easier, and so Morissa went home but returned several times during the day and for most of the night. By the second morning the small boy slept, the skin less like a piece of weathered old rabbit leather, and two days later he was hungry.

Before the sky cleared the Indians moved, their tipi poles dragging the mud behind the horses. But the boy's father stayed back, looking after them, and then he and Etty rode over to Morissa's soddy. Slowly the Indian dismounted and tied his oddly spotted gray horse to the corral fence. There, through old Etty, he made a little talk: "The white man has taken our land, our homes, our buffalo, and given us only hunger and the sicknesses to kill our people. But you are not like these others. You are a healing woman. You have given me back my son—."

Then he drew his blanket from the horse and, with it folded over his arm, he strode away in spite of Morissa's protests that he must not do this, old Etty unheeding, too, riding his shaggy pony at the moccasins of the father.

Morissa looked after the Indians with the sadness deep within her laid bare by their need, their dignified and desperate gratitude. In a little while they would be gone, as so many who were here would be, never remaining long enough to be anything of themselves to anyone, certainly not to Morissa Kirk. But that was true of the doctor anywhere.

Before an hour passed, a dozen men had ridden over to look at the doctor's new horse, with the spotted hindquarters that were like a light brocaded drapery thrown over him, the tail thin, the eyes light, and the head magnificent as from an old Grecian frieze.

"An Appaloosa, and a damn good one," they said.

"That horse is one of the finest of the breed developed by the Nez Perces up north," Robin agreed. "He will carry you a hundred miles day after day and stand up to graze afterward. But we'll have to teach him to let you mount on the white man side, not the Indian with a bow in the hand. And to stand with the reins down, so you won't be left if there's no hitchin' post."

Tris Polk rode in through the rain and was as complimentary. "A fine-

37

looking twosome you'll make when you get that horse fed up and curried a little," he said, as he looked at the tall, straight girl in Jackie's slicker, her sun-tanning skin tawny and glowing. "I have a silver-mounted side-saddle back in Texas, ordered as a gift for Empress Carlotta of Mexico from a Texas saddler. It was never delivered because the revolution came and she never got back. Ride it for me on the Appaloosa in the Walker horse show they're planning. With your green habit and that horse—Carlotta's court could have seen nothing finer."

The young doctor smiled to this, thanking the man for his pretty words, but drawing away within herself. Robin moved his scraper-horny hands uneasily as he watched, and if he thought of Allston Hoyt and the unworn wedding dress he gave no notice of it.

As soon as Robin Thomas was finished with the work up the trail he was taking his grading outfit east to a new railroad line heading out towards the Black Hills, but still many years away. "We'll be living in tents and shacks, far ahead of settlements," he told Morissa. "Maybe we'll have a boxcar now and then, but nothing much for doctoring, unless you find a place you like and settle to wait for it to grow."

"Oh, I guess right here is as good as any," Morissa said as she mulled up a little ointment in the mortar in her lap.

"But we'll both be-gone—"

Yes, she understood that, but she would stay as long as she could, or a doctor was needed. She had decided she would like to file on a piece of land up from the bridge, on the north side; take in that lone cotton-wood where the antelope come down.

"Oh, Clarke will probably have that covered by a filing," Robin said, a little relieved. "He's expecting a town when the railroad comes through."

Morissa tossed her head like a colt smelling the first snow in the air, her motion lifting the darkish bangs from her forehead that was still white above her tanning, reddened cheeks. "I diagnosed that much from what I've been hearing, from Tris Polk and the rest," she said. "But they must know that the railroad will bring the settlers thick as ants to a sorghum boiling."

"That won't happen here for years—"

"Maybe Mr. Clarke doesn't think it will be years. At least I don't. I have to have patients. In the meantime I'll file on the best place I can get near the bridge and the trail, but that little creek and the draw where the tree stands would make a good place for a dam to irrigate a garden patch."

"Oh, I couldn't advise that, Morissa," the father said soberly, pretending to be concerned with the draft of his pipestem. "There'll be trouble if you grow garden truck here for the homeseekers to see, even a shirt-

38

tail patch. The ranchers have killers on the payroll, to keep the range clear. One of the men working for the government surveyor sent over north of the river to put down section corners was hung by the Boslers, just for a hint."

But Morissa was not listening. "Maybe I'll take up a tree claim too, running along the north and west of the homestead for winter shelter," she added.

"Oh, Daughter!" Robin protested. "I can understand your shrinking back, hiding yourself, particularly just now, with not even a letter, but your plan here is suicidal."

"Suicidal—" the young woman repeated after him, but as though facing the word for the first time, her arms gone slack in her lap on each side of the old mortar, her face suddenly blighted, and once more Robin thought of the day he stood behind her mother as she told the twelve-year-old Morissa that the girl's poor-farm days were done forever. There had been no joy in the young face, only a frozen standing away from them both, as though she could not choose the good, as though it could not be for her, was somehow not fitting.

IV

AND THEN THE LETTER CAME. IT WAS AFTER THE LAST OF THOSE waiting for the bridge were gone north, and most of those who had catered to them—the whisky and woman tents and wagons, and the professional gamblers except Johnson and his big blonde with an eye for Tris Polk.

Although there was always a crowd of night campers at the bridge, enough to crowd Clarke's and Etty's, Morissa found the evenings long, with no one except Tom Reeder in the wagon out there. Sometimes the loneliness was sharp as the howl of the coyotes, but continuous, and pushing in like the shadows of the lantern on the dirt floor and the rooty sod walls. Only the red calico curtains and the cut-glass scent bottles seemed of a woman's life.

Morissa received the letter from the hand of young Eddie Ellis, coming to bring it to her from the stage station. She accepted it as for a stranger and then went slowly along the weeding bottoms to the shade of her soddy. There she sat on her nail-keg stool among the flourishing young willows and cottonwoods, with the spreading young portulacas blooming about her feet. She laid the letter on her knee, the rectangle creamy white against the dark blue of her skirt, the address bold in black broadstroke.

At last she had to open it. There was one paragraph:

My Dearest:

I was pained and grieved by your inconsiderate disappearance, and it took me some days to discover your probable hiding place, which I abstracted from the Omaha offices of Henry Clarke, Esq. Come back, Morissa, my child. It is true that the discovery of your shadowed parentage distresses my family beyond reconciliation, but I assure you that the unhappy circumstance of the gap between our stations need be no obstacle to our love.

As ever, ob'd'tly,
Allston

Her eyes ran over it again, selecting the words she would see: "—no obstacle to our love." The broad ink strokes seemed to lift themselves from the paper, and she could not hold back the tears. She would fly to her trunk, pack it swiftly, perhaps in time to catch the down coach for Sidney today.

But then she had to consider the sentence more carefully, all of it, the part that spoke of bridging "the gap between our stations" too. So there was a gap to be bridged. And nowhere was there any mention of marriage or a return of his mother's ring to her hand.

Slowly Morissa looked back over the life that had made the gap, back to her earliest recollection of waiting for her young mother to return from her work as a hired girl, worn out, white. Later when the mother sickened, Morissa was put out with a dozen other children at an unhappy sort of poor-farm, but Lorna Kirk, barely twenty-one, could not face putting her five-year-old into a foundling home for adoption. And at the little Missouri crossroads school the shameful term "woods colt" was spoken openly before Issy, Morissa, the meaning of the phrase eagerly explained to her in words from which the girl could only flee into work. At school she learned envy, too, particularly of one pupil who was never called by a nickname or anything less than her whole name: Martha Jane. It was said that *her* mother was not one to soil her white hands with work. Instead she rode the Princeton region on a fine Kentucky mare and spent the money her husband's family sent willingly so long as the youngest son kept his wife far away, out of sight of God-fearing people. But even if this was true, and Mrs. Canary really had come from a water-front dive in Cincinnati, she was legally married, and so her Martha Jane could speak out Morissa's shame boldly before all the school. Shaking back the curls from her pert, pretty face, and smoothening the wine-colored velvet of her dress she sang the words:

40

> Issy over the ocean,
> Issy over the sea,
> Issy's a bastard kid,
> > She can't catch me.
> > One, two, three—

skipping her red-handled rope to its beat.

But as soon as Martha Jane's breasts began to push at her velvet bodice she followed her mother to the gay young soldiers, gayer because they might soon be dead, whether from Johnny Reb or a bushwhacker. After that their two good saddlers were often tied to the hitchracks at Princeton, and on the shady hotel piazza the mother and her precocious twelve-year-old flirted with drummers and spies, anyone with flash and gold. Or they could be seen flying over the country roads in fast rigs while the meek husband cared for the younger children at home.

All this time Morissa was at the poor-farm. She helped milk, churn, slop the hogs and then plodded to school barefoot, with a chunk of cornbread and sorghum wrapped in newspaper or in cornshucks when the paper failed.

Then the pale, sickened Lorna Kirk married Robin Thomas, a road worker, a grader. He bedded her down comfortably in his covered wagon and took her West. Four hens rode in the straw of his scraper tied beneath the wagon, and a milk cow followed at the tailboard. In this way they would have the eggs and milk Robin believed his wife must have to live. But it was a precarious venture, with little hope of work, and so Morissa had to be left behind. During this lonesome, deserted time she withdrew deeper into work; in the late evenings that were her own she lost herself in her school books and in dreaming over the letters that came back, telling of a lovely wild country, and later of the worrisome time before a brother was born, and then the slow gathering of strength, until one day they were back, her own mother there beside her, with the quiet, bearded Robin, and the four-year-old Jackie clinging to his trouser leg. At first Morissa dared not trust their words, feeling unfit for the new family, but after a few days she put on the new shoes they brought her and went with them, slowly believing the kindness that could lie in the calloused hands of this sunburnt man as he cared for his ailing wife, and the prideful look that could live in his eyes as he considered his family.

"You must get some schooling," he had told the girl. "Good steel rusts a lot faster than old stove iron if it ain't used."

But he couldn't help much with all her mother's illness. Morissa managed to pass the teachers examination and at fifteen she was teaching a nearby school, with boys who towered over her using Martha

Jane's taunts against her. Hurt, and proud, she turned her back on her first beau without explanation or more than secret tears. She studied, and saved every penny because she must learn all she could about this consumption that had gnawed at her mother's breast so many years. But Lorna Kirk could not wait, and after the funeral Robin helped her serious, big-eyed daughter get to Philadelphia. There she won her medical degree and then went back farther west to set up a little practice, out near Omaha, and to leave the words of Martha Jane behind her forever.

She met Allston Hoyt by answering an emergency call to a by-road and found him on the ground beside his scattered and broken buggy, apparently dying from a runaway of his flashy roadsters. She stemmed the flow of blood there, kept the man warm and alive until his coachman came with the ambulance. Afterward, at the big white house high above the river, she directed the nursing and told him that he must now always be careful. It was a heart attack that had brought on the runaway, she thought; his own failing hand on the stern lines over his fiery matched blacks.

But even after he went back to his office he kept sending the carriage for Morissa, although she told him of her Scottish grandmother's saying: "A cold needs a cook fully as much as a doctor—" and the heart a serene brow more than the chemist's potions.

A serene brow? For that sudden prescription he would need discipline, Allston Hoyt argued. He was still a young man, barely forty in spite of the silvery touches at his temples. He must be taught how to live.

"Don't worry too much," Morissa finally told him. "Heart patients who don't die of the first attack have a way of burying most of their friends and relatives—" making this vigorous to cover her own growing concern for him, and for herself.

But he kept calling her to him at the pillared house on the rise above the Missouri until it became a joke between them. Then one afternoon he led her out upon the terrace overlooking the river, the bottoms golden in cottonwoods, the maples and oaks reddening against the bluffs. He talked a long time, going back, back. Immediately after college he had to take over the family's investment firm because his father, too, suffered from a heart condition. The panic of the fifties ended and he went West to recoup their fortune in the boom that followed the transcontinental railroad, and he had built up the business in spite of war and the crash of Black Friday. Then this illness struck at him on a side road, before there had been time to live, to be a human being. And now in his first leisure, no, idleness, he had fallen in love, wholly in love with his doctor.

"—Come with me. I'll take you to Scotland on our honeymoon.

42

We'll look up your grandmother's people and perhaps locate some of mine," he urged, and his brown eyes were very dark against the pallor of his sudden emotion.

It was then that Morissa should have spoken, but she was suddenly like a spring hillside in sun-shot rain, with such a softness, such a glistening happiness that she could know nothing else. When she left she walked in the western wind that trembled the fall leaves, and on her finger was the fine old diamond that had belonged to Allston Hoyt's mother.

The plans went well and pleasantly all the winter, although Morissa would not give up her practice and still made the rounds of the river bottom shacks, where smallpox and diphtheria were like the Plague of London. Robin couldn't come home from the bridge grading for the formal post-Easter announcement dinner at the Western Empire Hotel, but he wrote he would certainly be there to judge her May trousseau, largely purchased with his money.

Then suddenly Allston's sister had sent the coach for Morissa. The fragilely elegant woman poured her a cup of tea in her handsome green parlor, with the long, white-dressed windows and the pale gold upholstery. Speaking calmly, objectively, Alicia Hoyt asked Morissa her father's name, and when the girl replied that it was Robin Ralston Thomas, the woman shook her head gently.

"My dear, I mean your own father—" she said.

Now Morissa had to remember all she had hoped was forgotten in her busy life—the unhappiness of her child-mother, the taunts at school and later in her own classroom.

"My hobby is genealogy," the woman explained. "Allston wanted to make you a gift of your family tree to carry along to Scotland, as a guide in your travels to your ancestral seat. Despite much careful search I can find only one use of the name Kirk by your mother—*Miss* Lorna Kirk —up to her marriage to Robin Thomas."

So it was done, swift as a surgeon's knife, and, given such circumstances, it was the kindest way, Morissa realized. She could have said that Robin Thomas knew all this and yet married her mother, and made a beloved daughter of the bastard child. But a railroad grader, no matter how fine and good, was not an Allston or a Hoyt.

As she rose to go Alicia offered her the jeweled bottle of smelling salts from her little stand. "I shall not offend you with my expressions of sympathy. Dear Allston is prostrated, and thought this would be kinder, coming from one of your own sex—"

Morissa thanked the woman and went away. Dismissing the coachman outside of the grounds, she walked the five-mile distance toward the city, walked it along the bluffs of the Missouri and saw nothing at all about her, not the swift spring that ran in new grass along the rutted road, or the pale cloudy green of the wooded river valley below, nor the boats and barges that worked their way slowly up the gray flood and were passed so gaily by the down-bent craft. She saw nothing at all until suddenly a broken-backed bullsnake struggled to drag its useless length out of the rut at her feet. Morissa Kirk looked down at the injured creature and with the swift blow of a rock she flattened the head, and then with two sticks she rolled the twisting length off into the grass, where the dumb writhing could wear out its necessity in the good way, alone.

Afterward she stopped at her office only long enough to pick up her pill bag and went down through the river bottom shacks, seeing to their needs for one last time. In two days she was on her way West, to Robin and Jackie and the North Platte valley where no one asked a man's origins or his past, no more than the "What name you travelin' under?" she had often heard since.

And now there was this letter from Allston Hoyt, thick creamy paper lying on her knee. But almost as though from her memory of the crippled creature in the road that day, a call of "Snake! Snake bite!" brought Morissa out of herself. A man was spurring up to the soddy and shouting this over and over until he slid from his lathered horse. "They's bringing a kid what's been rattlesnake bit!"

Morissa ran around to the door, the letter left to blow forgotten where it slipped from her lap. A heavy work mare was galloping ponderously in from the bridge, a man riding her bareback carrying something, a child in a pink dress. Close behind him came a woman astride another old mare, bareback, too, whipping the man's horse along ahead of her and then her own, riding bent forward and whipping, whipping.

The young doctor was already inside, reaching for boiled scalpel and knife, for a stimulant. She flipped open the handiest book, her Hartshorne, to "Snake bite," and slapped a pane of glass over it, angry that she was so inexperienced in this situation. She had never even seen a case of rattlesnake bite, and already the child was being carried through her low doorway. The little girl was about six, curiously stiff and awkward, stuporous with the smell of raw alcohol about her. Morissa had her laid on the cot and made a swift examination. One of the legs was hugely swollen below a handkerchief tourniquet twisted with a wagon bolt, tight enough for gangrene. A big cud of chewing tobacco was tied over the wound above the ankle, hacked but ragged and shallow. That and a drink of corn likker was all they knew, the gaunt woman sobbed.

"How much corn liquor?" Morissa asked. Even Hartshorne seemed doubtful about whisky, but he had nothing much to offer, particularly this long after the biting.

"All the corn we had, about half a cup—"

The doctor's lips tightened. "Make coffee," she ordered the woman,

44

and tried to give the child a small tablet. But she could not swallow, so Morissa loosened the tourniquet a little and slashed into the wound, making it deep and wide, squeezing it. Only black clots and a yellow oozing came, and the doctor ran her slender steel up along the vein as along a fish's belly, and down into the foot too, clearing out the thickened blood both ways until a weak bleeding started. Then she stood back brushing the hair from her cheeks with her sleeve. There should be something more to do but Morissa Kirk, M.D., did not know what or where to look.

"How big was the snake?" she finally asked.

"It was big as my wrist, bigger—" the woman cried, holding up a brown, work-gnarled arm. But the gesture and her anger were both turned against her husband. "—Bringin' a woman and a child to such a country!"

In the morning, while blackbirds sang along the marshy ground, Morissa helped bury the small girl. Most of the night the child had lain quiet and remote, never conscious, and the doctor couldn't be certain when the pulse finally died whether it was from alcohol or venom. She brought out a white cashmere shawl that had never been worn and wrapped the child in it. The mother stood dry-eyed with her back against the window, looking with clenched lips down upon the father as he squatted on a nail-keg stool, his head in his hands.

"She ain't even no doll baby to be buried with!" the mother cried when one of Etty's men drove up with a little pine coffin hammered together like a feed box, but white with drying kalsomine under the armful of the sweet-scented golden banner that Fish Head had gathered.

Quickly Morissa rolled up a finger towel, tied it tight for the neck and sewed on two shoe buttons for eyes, red yarn for lips, and made a swaddling blanket from a pretty blue handkerchief. Then she tucked it into the child's arm and folded the corner of the white shawl down over the quiet face. Lorette, old Etty's breed wife, heavy with child, joined Morissa and the parents as they followed the coffin to the knoll beside the new mounds of the Pennsylvanian and the hanged man. There Lorette knelt beside the grave, crossing herself within her blanket, perhaps thinking of her own two small ones buried here, while Morissa stood with the gaunt mother and the father and read a little from her white wedding prayer book. Old Fish Head was there too, with his tall hat from the axle-grease bucket held elegantly over his heart, the wind lifting the thin gray hair, water running from his rheumy eyes. The curious little antelope had followed very close at first, but now he stood off a ways, big ears erect, looking, with animal instinct remaining aloof from death.

Then they went back down in the wagon, silent, the anger between

45

the parents something that was cold and dead, the link that had perhaps bound them broken. Morissa hurried to her neglected patient, fed him, gathered up her laundry whipping in the wind behind the soddy since yesterday, and lay down to catch a little belated sleep for the night's long vigil. She did not wait to see if the parents went back up the trail, still heading on for gold, or if that too was meaningless now. Not until the antelope came to waken her toward evening, nuzzling the doorknob and the screen of the open window, did Morissa recall the letter from Allston Hoyt. Tear-blinded, she looked all through the little house for it, and finally recalled that it had been in her lap outside when a man came shouting "Snake bite!"

So she tucked up her skirts and ran all around the house, looking carefully through her young plants, through the little woodpile, among the few wagons left in the grader's corral, and then all over the bottoms, back and forth, first down the wind and then in carefully widening circles everywhere, even along the edge of the muddy riverbank, the antelope at her heels, bumping her every time she stopped to look. Finally when the late darkness came Morissa went with the lantern to ask at the station if a letter had been picked up, and to the whisky stores and Etty's Lorette. But no one had seen it.

Slowly she returned to the soddy, stopping at the lighted window to look at the cut-out sign: DR. KIRK. Even if she kept on letting children die in her arms, it was plain that there was nothing else ahead for her. Gently she pushed the little antelope away from the door and went inside.

There was a tremendous electric storm that night, the sky an angry violet-rose, shot with blazing, jagged bolts, the earth shaking with the roar and crash that knocked bits of sod from between the roof boards to the cot and the floor. Morissa had caught up the young antelope, suddenly shy and wild with his animal foreboding, and now, as the thunder grew, the little creature stood squeezed into a corner, the mild eyes that were turned back toward the lamp and Morissa bleaching with terror at the louder crashes, the sensitive skin shivering.

Around one o'clock, when it seemed that the rain must begin at last, more than just the scattering of big drops that rattled like bird-shot against the window, there was a running outside and a shout at the door. It was one of the men from a big herd that came up out of Texas a week ago, the beef steers thin-flanked, with spreading horns and still wild as deer. They had been held up north in the sandhills since then, to fatten a little. Tonight they went crazy in the electric storm. Sid Martin, the owner, helped try to turn the stampeding herd. His horse stepped in a badger hole and it looked like Martin's neck was broke.

"But he's alive?"

"Yeh—was when I left."

46

"Oh, I hope nobody tries to move him! Hurry out to the pasture and get my Appaloosa—"

"I brong you a horse—them 'Poolusas is nervous in storms—"

"But yours won't be woman-broke—"

"You better get into some a Robin's work pants, and I fetched you a pair a chaps to hold off the rain, 'n spurs. This ain't the night for no lady sidesaddlin'—"

So Morissa slipped into Jackie's levis, recalling the first time she saw Sid Martin, on the stagecoach that brought her up from Sidney. With her medical bag and some extras rolled in an oilskin behind the saddle, and with her slicker buckled high, they started into the rain turned to silver sheets by the lightning until everything was shut out. It was lucky that she rode astride, as she had the work mares of the poor-farm in her childhood, for a hundred times the horses plunged over banks, slipped, stumbled into badger and prairie-dog holes, or side-jumped as some wild thing flushed before them. A hundred times Morissa would have been off if she were riding sidesaddle. But the man ahead kept spurring on, while the young doctor steadied the jump of her medical case with an anxious hand. Then it began to hail, the horses plunging and rearing like wild creatures as they fought to turn their backs to the storm, and now Morissa discovered one purpose of the roweled spurs and the cruel bit that so often brought blood from the cowboy's horse. But she thought of the man with his neck broken, and spurred on, too, trying to keep the lean rump of the bay ahead within sight in the hail and rain.

It was clearing for dawn when they suddenly came out on a broad flat ringed in by low hills, the hail white as snow over everything in the morning light.

"The herd'll be scattered to hell 'n' gone. Take weeks to get a fair lot of 'em together. But at least they ain't dead at the foot of some bluff up here like they would be on some ranges. Ain't a canyon or a bluff within two hundred miles east, so far as I know," the cowboy called back to Morissa.

As they neared the trail wagons drawn up close together out in the flat, a wrangler came walking awkwardly to meet them, his boots crunching the hail. "Yeh," he said, taking the horses, "he's alive. We pulled the wagons up on both sides of him and spread a tarp to keep off the hail, but it's been damn cold for a hurt man—"

Morissa stooped under the canvas to look down at Sid Martin in the light of the morning lantern. He was conscious, turning only his pain-filled eyes to the young woman, his gaunt face gray.

Without moving him at all, the young doctor seated herself behind the man's head and slid her fingers gently, very gently, along under his neck until she found a displacement, what seemed an appalling displacement, so she gave him a stiff dose of morphine. "You've been amazingly courageous not to move all this time, but maybe I'll have to hurt you, and even the slightest jerk—"

From the man's eyes she knew he understood, had known from the first, and she blessed the knowledge of anatomy these men of the out-doors learned, their perception. When Sid Martin seemed to doze, she went to work, very carefully, remembering how tender the spinal cord was, recalling the pulpiness of the gray-white mass even in autopsies—much of it soft as a custard. A thousand times this morning she wished that she were old in experience, double her twenty-four years, triple them if it would give her the skill to save this man's life. Every second she feared for the stopped heart that would mean she had crushed or broken the cord, for all her care. And every bit of gain must be held with her numbing hands until she gathered control and force enough to apply the next gentle, steady little pull on the head, always toward her—not the tiniest fraction of an inch to one side or the other—until there could be space enough to clear the cord, realign the vertebrae.

Once the cook touched her shoulder and held a tin cup of hot coffee to her lips with his hairy hands. She shook the sweat from her face and looked about, amazed to see the sun high as her head, the hail all gone from the pounded earth except in the draws that were like the white patches running up the flanks of a calico-dun. She swallowed the coffee gratefully, awkwardly, while she steadied the man's head, but he seemed to be coming out of the opiate. Quickly she had the cook administer a little more morphia, and nodded the watching men to her. "Get me some heavy leather, any stiff, heavy leather. Maybe saddle skirts—"

They brought a couple of leather skirts from the gear wagon, and an empty flour sack to make a pattern under her direction. Their boss must have a cast to hold the break in place, but it couldn't be tight as a plaster cast on a leg, or of anything that would shrink to cut off his breath, or that would break, if he wasn't to die.

So, while she held the head and the man slept, almost relaxed now, they cut the skirts to fit the pattern a couple of the cowboys had managed to make around her hands. They joined the pieces with copper rivets from the cook's ditty box and made a lacing up the side with rawhide strings, a tongue underneath for firmness. Then they eased the leather brace around the man, digging earth away under the neck and shoulders because they dared not lift him. By the time Sid Martin was awakening, he was in a neck-and-shoulder boot, stiff as sole-leather. He was laced into it, with no give sideways and none forward or back, except directly down from the chin where side pads of cotton pre-vented choking. But the sides arched up against the jaws solid as iron to prevent turning the head.

Now Morissa stretched the ache from her knees while she waited,

48

and slowly Sid Martin became aware of those watching him, all his help here except the two gone to locate the stampeding herd. He tried to move and was held down by an arm across his chest, saw it was a young woman and smiled a little as in a dream. But gradually he remembered.

A long time he seemed to be taking stock of himself. "My hands and feet don't seem to be so numb," he said slowly, and the doctor nodded. And as he grasped the extent of the leather brace, he grinned. "Think you got me trapped fer sure, don't you, Doc, Miss Doc Morissa—" he said, but the strain on his face showed that he understood.

There was still the problem of other injuries, internal ones, and the long rough distance back without a trail for wheel or pony drag. After he relaxed a little from the first realization, Morissa went over him carefully, searching out any bruise, any sore and tender spot internally, but she found nothing else. So she settled to a late dinner of fried beef, sore-thumb bread, and canned peaches, wondering how long she dared remain here, with Tom Reeder alone and unfed at the bridge, and no telling what other emergencies might come up. She needed a nurse there and a little hospital, even if only two rooms. Perhaps Robin would build one before he went to his next job. A soddy with four, five rooms for now, she thought, a little amused that it had grown so fast from the two rooms of just a moment ago. There would be a long space with rods for division curtains, and a lot of windows for geraniums and sunlight. The house should be built with a sheltered south alcove to sun any young patients, children that she would have to send on to Sidney now.

"You pull me out a this, Doc, and you sign your own ticket—" Sid Martin said, cautiously trying to ease the stiffness from his legs.

"Maybe you'll feel different when your neck's in one piece again— and it may be more in one piece than you think. I look for a section stiff as a plank—"

"Stiff, hell! —Excuse me, but it was limber as a wet saddle string when I tried to get up last night."

"I think the doc here needs her a good team and buggy," the cowpuncher who had come for Morissa suggested.

She laughed at the absurd fee and sat a while, comfortable, warm, and happy and good in the silence of the lean, sunburnt men who had no itching need to talk and keep talking. After a while they got up, bit off their cuds, and worked them into juicing as they climbed their horses. Suddenly she remembered that she hadn't thought of Allston Hoyt or the lost letter for a long time, not since a cowboy rode shouting out of the storm last night.

But perhaps Morissa would not need a team and buggy or even the sidesaddle Robin ordered sent up from Sidney; she would not want the

49

house here, with her trees and flowers growing so well from the rain that followed the hailstorm. Late one afternoon while Morissa was out beyond the bridge picking a bucket of mushrooms from a witches' ring, a large and bedraggled party of a hundred fifty or more came down from Deadwood. The news had been brought in by horsebackers who ran into them up the trail and hurried back to cry the alarm and, in the way of men, share all bad tidings gladly.

"The Black Hills are busted!" they shouted. "The gold's played out!"

The bridge dwellers were well accustomed to rumors by now, particularly alarms of Indian uprisings and the mines running dry. But this seemed serious.

"Looks like somebody's shure 'nough tapped hell with a two-foot auger this time," the bridge tender said, and spit off over the railing as the delapidated wagons came toward the river. Everybody was out to watch as they stopped on the far side, and their captain, a recent candidate for state governor, came over to see his friend Clarke.

Yes, it was true, the mines were done, he said, speaking quietly. Played out. They had tried to stay on, hoping, and now many were flat broke, without enough left to pay their toll. "—If you can't see your way clear to let us cross, Henry, we'll have to go down on the other side—"

"But that's around a hundred thirty miles over old washed-out trail—" Clarke protested.

So he let them all across, but it was a gloomy night in the valley of the North Platte. Robin Thomas came down from his grading in the White River country to talk to Clarke about it, and then made a turn around the whisky stores and roadhouses and a few of the bigger freight outfits. This was not like the stampeders on opening day. This time nobody stood away from the men. While there seemed few professional miners in the party, they were plainly not the usual Sunday gold seekers, afraid to bend the back over pick and shovel. Perhaps Tom Reeder had found the last good pocket, or, as some of the party slyly suggested, obtained his gold in other ways. Nobody knew of a one-man placer strike that big, and keeping it secret sounded fishy as a mud hen, but there were plenty of holdups and mine robbers around.

After a while, when enough whisky had been set up to them, a couple dozen of the party went over to Morissa Kirk's and demanded to see this man Reeder. At first the young doctor stood against the ragged, half-drunken crowd at the wagon step, Robin's Colt hanging at her slim hip, but when there were angry murmurings and threats she moved inside and let them line up for a look into the lantern-lit wagon, one after another. She sat beside Tom Reeder while they did this, the man's pale, frightened eyes turning to her hand, steady on the grip of the revolver that he knew she had never fired at a man, and then back to the flushed dark-bearded faces looking in, the lantern light reddening their eyes.

Afterward she sent the men away with short, cold words, and went back into the wagon where her patient was shaking as from the ague under the buffalo robe.

"Fools!—all a lot of fools! Both gold and the failure to obtain it seem to work the same," she said, and when Reeder once more refused her demand that he be moved to Sidney, she admitted that he might be better off here while this exaggerated terror possessed him. Here he seemed to trust at least one person.

All this time Morissa had her own kind of shaking ague. She had not replied to Allston's lost letter and when no further message came she tried to keep herself from sending him her address, or making a dozen other approaches that she hoped would not betray their intention, like an antelope hunter's deceptive round-about pursuit, for how was Allston to know that his letter had ever reached her? And who could say what change the days might have made in his attitude, in him, even since he wrote?

But in her calmer moments she tore up the telegrams and the notes she wrote him, notes that did not refer to the letter, passed it off as a joke, pretended to misunderstand his meaning, or told a half-truth, that the letter had been lost to her. She tore them all up, for Allston Hoyt was no antelope to be stalked so foolishly.

And now, if the gold at the end of the Sidney trail was done, she must really pack up and start over again, the third time in her three years out of medical school. Carrying the hollowness of this within her, she walked out past the guards into the darkness of the bridge and stood on the silent center of it a long time, leaning over the water, over the murmur, the sweet, cool smell of it, and heard the frogs, the chatter of ducks, and the thumping of a shitepoke off in a marshy spot somewhere.

V

MORISSA HAD NEVER SEEN SO FLOWERY A REGION, OR ONE SO fragrant. First there were the Easter daisies, bright soon after the snow, and then came the sweetness of the sand lilies, the golden banner, purple sweetpeas, and the wild plums and chokecherries. Great patches of violets stretched along the bottoms, followed by a scattering of blue tulip gentians, and higher up, clumps of blue beardtongue and tangles of wild roses. Later the gravelly knolls carpeted themselves in the purple, white, and cerise of loco peas, and the ridges beyond carried the waxy white spikes of yuccas and the yellow and flame of cactus bloom.

With all this tapestry of color it seemed sad that the isolated ranches stood so bare. Perhaps a cottonwood shimmered beside the watering place or the windmill; dusty horseweeds, sunflowers, and stinking bee-plant pushed in thick upon the corrals. Without a woman at the log and sod shacks, there was not a planted flower for two hundred miles up and down the river except at Etty's stockade and now at Robin's old soddy.

The willows Morissa set out were shooting up fast and the little cottonwoods rustled over the morning carpet of portulacas. When she first came, Etty's Lorette had beckoned the young doctor into her garden plot. There she thrust her spade into the patch of volunteers that sprouted thick as some fleshy russet fur from last year's bed of moss roses. She lifted a sod of them for Morissa's apron. "You can pull 'part," the heavy-bodied young woman had suggested.

Now a month later the seedlings had spread into a mat of color under the long morning shadows. There was a gay sun chair too that Robin made from a cut-down salt barrel, covered, back and all, with a spotted cowhide. He made a bumbershoot to stand over it from a similar hide spread over an old buggy wheel, with scallops hanging down all around the edge.

By now the cowboys had taken to stopping in. "Could I trouble you for the borry of a match?" one might say, and Morissa would offer the box, smiling at the man's sheepish grin. "I thought you all kept to chewing tobacco on the range, with the fire hazard—"

"Yes, ma'am, but when I comes off it, I likes to roll me a prairie burner—"

Then perhaps the man would squat on his heels at the door awhile, his horse standing with patient reins dragging. Sometimes he might say as many as five words to the antelope nosing along the yard fence while Morissa kneaded bread sponge or folded powders. Finally the man would reseat his old Stetson, swing into the saddle and lope away, the heels of his horse kicking up dust as measured as volleys of bullets hitting the earth.

Sometimes Lorette came, moving ponderously across the bottoms from Etty's stockade, to throw her Sioux blanket back from her neat braids and sit awhile with Morissa. Etty had run several whisky and billiard saloons along the early trails but she preferred it here at the ancient Indian crossing. Her French father had sent her East to a Sisters school for a few years and she could read and write and embroider, too, Morissa discovered, her silken work lovely as delicate paint strokes. But now she was heavy with child, her fifth, only two left alive

52

by diphtheria. Although Lorette had returned to the blanket, she asked, in her soft Indian way, about Morissa's hats, and about a good school for her girls when they grew older. "Their father he say they must be same like white—" she murmured wistfully.

"And they will be very pretty, as they are already," Morissa agreed, thinking of their soft dusky brown hair, the oval of their French faces. Lorette looked modestly down and seemed pleased, but with the sadness of a woman whose husband would have his daughters depart from her ways and her station for his; doubly humiliating, Morissa knew, to the Sioux in Lorette, where a man customarily left his people for his wife's.

The young doctor tried to make her neighbor feel welcome, weary as she was for a woman's face among so many men. Then one day while Lorette was there, Etty rode in with a deer across his saddle. The woman sprang up so fast she dropped a teacup and fled for the stockade without the mannerly apology she had been taught. The next day she held her blanket close about her head when Morissa came for some string to train her morning glories. She turned her eyes down, without greeting, but it was plain that her face was bruised and swollen.

Two evenings later Etty came riding over and Morissa went uneasily to the door, expecting some complaint. He was excited but because his wife's time had come and none of the medicine women were around to help. "I think maybe the baby she come backward, like the colt sometime—"

That night Morissa learned how silent a woman of Indian blood could be in pain. But Lorette was strong and patient and young. By morning Etty had a son, his first, and Morissa went home to drop to her cot without undressing. She still did not know why the Frenchman had beaten his wife, whether because she was visiting the doctor when he came home or for some more private reason, perhaps out of male resentment against the prolonged self-containment that pregnancy was. But Morissa realized now that she must move cautiously here.

Before nine in the morning a man from Sid Martin stopped by. "The boss was rarin' to get on a horse couple days after you was up, but he's been gettin' yellow as them old puff balls since. Out a his head all last night."

Morissa rubbed her eyes wearily, trying to wake up. "Any pain, maybe under the ribs somewhere?"

"No, guess not, but his head's a bustin', he says."

So the doctor put her saddlebags on the Appaloosa and started out. "Just keep due north, anglin' off east a mite—You can't miss it," the cowboy had called back as he rode on toward Sidney. That "anglin' off" direction for her first trip alone into the vast, undifferentiated country of the sandhills made Morissa uneasy, but with Robin's little compass

53

she held the Appaloosa from following what seemed a far bunch of wild horses but might be Indians, the men hanging on the far side to avoid detection. Sid Martin did look bad inside his worn leather neck brace—gaunt, yellow, with a slow pulse, whether from an injury in his fall or from gallstones or infective jaundice she couldn't decide in a moment. She gave him a mild liver dose and a diuretic and had the cook make up a blanc-mange flavored with the vanilla she brought. The patient seemed improved by the time she had to start back. "Feed him like a sick man, not fried beef and beans," she ordered.

"Graveyard stew?" the cook asked uneasily through his whiskers.

Morissa nodded. "Yes, if you can get the milk," and wrote out a diet and dosing list. "And better take him out of here."

She felt so worn that she could scarcely climb into the sidesaddle. Yet she had to hurry to get out of the hills before dark. Several times she caught herself dozing in the hot afternoon sun. She pulled herself up firm and erect for a while, watching the occasional antelope spring from his resting, looking back over his white rump as he ran, and once she raised a deer in a pocket of buckbrush. Yet it seemed only a moment until she was nodding again, even with the Appaloosa's swinging gait.

> Sit it slow and stand it fast,
> Makes both man and horse to last,

she sang to herself, trying to keep awake with the jingling advice for the trot Robin gave young Jackie with his first pony. But still her head drooped, sagged lower and lower, until suddenly she felt a great jerk and seemed to be flying through the air. When she came down she hit head first, so hard it seemed her skull crushed in like a hollow pumpkin.

A long time afterward Morissa Kirk began to come out of a deep darkness, her stomach retching. With bursting head she held herself together as well as she could and gradually her eyes cleared until she could see grass before her face and thought suddenly of the rattlesnakes. But when she tried to sit up everything spun around and she was sick again.

Afterward she tried to think. The throbbing head and periodic vomiting meant concussion. She had been thrown by her horse out in the open sandhills, far from any trail. Only Martin's men knew where she had been and they wouldn't discover that she was missing for a long, long time. Miserably she wondered once more what she was doing in such a wilderness, when people needed doctors everywhere, and when there was even Allston Hoyt and his letter assuring her that her birth need be no obstacle, at least to their love. Tears from another sickness ran over her cheeks.

When she could, she tried out her back, her arms, and legs. Apparently nothing was seriously hurt except her head, with the recurring nausea like a dark storm rolling out of the horizon to shake her until she lay limp and exhausted in the grass, counting to time the intervals, to gauge the injury.

In her clearer moments she tried to plan what must be done. Slowly she lifted herself to an elbow, holding her reeling head when she must. There was something nearby and when her eyes focused she saw it was the Appaloosa, quietly grazing. She must have taken the knotted reins with her when she went over his head, probably in a side jump or a stumble. Now, reins down, he was waiting as Robin had trained him, and suddenly she understood the deep and trusting affection of the cowman for his horse.

But night was coming and she did not dare go near the Appaloosa yet, the retching sure to frighten him, send him off into the hills out of her reach, even if he did not get in with the wild horses or was lost to the Indians. So she drew herself together upon her quivering stomach as an ailing child would. With her hair loose to spread about her, and the denim riding skirt drawn up around her shoulders against the chill, too, she managed to sleep a little between the intervals of sickness. Coyotes howled along the hills, with the thin yip of pups somewhere close by, and an occasional long-drawn-out howl from a prairie wolf. When dawn finally came she was shaking with cold, her throat raw and dry, a lump like a rounded plateau on the left side of her aching head.

Weak and stiff she tried to sit up and finally she stood, bent over, yet on her feet. The Appaloosa was nowhere in sight. Slowly she moved to a higher knob, stooping to the sickness when she must. But the morning hills seemed empty, bare except for a grazing antelope and a prairie chicken calling to her young, at least a dozen of them, all standing innocent and open, staring at the woman on the hillside. Morissa tried to whistle and then called "Appaloosa!" At the first sound the young chickens were gone, the prairie hen fluttering along the grass tops to toll danger away. But there was no sign of the horse, probably driven by thirst to some far pond or creek, or gone.

Finally, when Morissa thought to try a loud Indian whoop, a head lifted from a low place, a gray head, ears erect. The horse came no closer but it was a comfort that he was there, with the saddle in place, even when he started to move on, slowly, holding his jaw sideways to avoid the dragging reins. Morissa started toward him, stumbling, crawling, the grass cutting her palms, but hurrying in spite of her fear of rattlesnakes, stopping only a moment once to braid her hair out of her eyes, for with the sun the Appaloosa's thirst would grow. He snorted a little as she approached across what seemed a wild horse trail, but he only drew back a step or two and waited as her hand crept toward the reins at his feet. Then he came to rub his nose against the girl's stooping shoulder, nickering softly.

She pulled herself up with the stirrup and tightened the girth as well as she could. Making herself speak quietly, steadily, "Whoa, 'Paloosa, whoa, boy—" she went up along the stirrup leather, choking back the waves of nausea, until at last she was mounted.

It was old Etty, out for a little fresh meat, who saw the Appaloosa coming slowly down a long slope toward the Platte. The doctor was leaning low over his neck, her disheveled hair hanging down into the thick mane of the horse that the girl had twisted around her wrist to keep from falling off when the dark waves of sickness broke over her. So Etty brought Morissa Kirk in, leading the horse, people running out across the bridge to see, the antelope along behind, all recognizing the Appaloosa from far off.

By morning Morissa felt better, still weak, with a headache, but probably without permanent damage. Beside her sat Lorette, silent.

"You should be home and in bed!" the doctor scolded.

"It is now the third day," Lorette said cheerfully, and went to make a cup of tea. "A man he come from the Sid Martin," she called over the singing kettle. "He say Sid be better."

So Morissa drank her tea and turned her face to the wall to sleep. But first she should write a note to be sent to Robin: "Your training showed up well. Appaloosa did not leave me."

Early Sunday morning Tris Polk tied his horse to a yard post and walked up between the flower beds, come to take Morissa to watch Bill Tillow, the wild horse catcher, handle some of his stock. "We don't commonly take Eastern women to see these bronch bustings. They don't understand it's a fight to the death between the man and the horse— But you're not so cold-footed," he said.

Now he spoke of her accident. "We've been worried about you. I heard clear up at Deadwood that you were left hurt out on the prairie," he said as he walked beside the girl to the Appaloosa, not looking at her, making the words quiet ones, as though about someone else.

They met Robin and Jackie coming down the trail. In their Western way they made no fuss, but Robin saw the yellowish stain left at the girl's temple, and a pallor that remained from her fall. "A day in the sun will be good for all of us," he said heartily, and was caught up in the absurdity of his tongue by the laughter in the sunburnt faces.

They had brought Eddie Ellis along. He was back working at Red Cloud Agency since the bridge rush was over. Even in the dust of the trail Ed's blue eyes looked like those of a man just in out of the rain, or a long-lashed child smiling through tears, but a child with full, aggressive lips barely shadowed by beard.

Together the little party headed eastward, around a great plot of bull-tongue cactus with hundreds of blossoms large as cupped hands, greenish-yellow satin, with dusty bumblebees buzzing drowsily. A couple of young antelope huddled in the middle of the patch, the ears so nearly the shape and size of the cactus tongues that only Tris could have noticed them. Although Jack and Eddie rode up very near, the little creatures just scrooched closer to the earth, remaining by instinct where no soft-padded animal—coyote, wolf, or mountain lion—would brave the inch-long spines of the cactus.

"We better hurry or we'll miss too much," Tris called to the boys. The horse catchers had only a small herd of wild stuff in the canyon corral they put up lately. The big herds were farther off north, up around the Box Butte country, part of the million or so of this very adaptive animal scattered over the West, all growing out of a few stable-fed Spanish stock. The horses were fast, tough, pawing the snow for winter feed, afraid of nothing except mountain lions in timber or rocky country where they could drop to the defenseless backs—no problem on the open prairies.

Morissa nodded thoughtfully. "Something like that's happening to us Americans out here," she said, as she looked at the man riding beside her, the fine ease of the long body in the saddle, the lean narrow hips, the lean face, and the difference in color and cut of raiment here. As usual, except when working cattle, Tris wore light fawn-colored chaps and hat, with dark trousers and shirt, blue today, and a yellow silk muffler knotted at the nape of his neck. It went well with Morissa's yellow shirtwaist that pointed up the golden lights of the sun in her hair and in the hazel of her eyes. Against Tris's skin, burned Indian-dark, the yellow made his eyes darker, gave them a hint of fire somewhere behind the deep and living smoke. But always the eyes were aloof, and for just a moment Morissa caught herself wondering what passion would bring to them and had to turn her burning face away, feeling the man's presence beside her as though his hand were cupped on her yielding shoulder. Angrily she reminded herself of what she was, how one man had received it. So the young doctor's eyes found a refuge in the three riding ahead, Eddie on a fast horse, always a step out in front of the others.

"He seems to know where the corral is located," she said, to make talk.

"Oh, Ellis would know, even though the corral's just built," Tris replied, almost angrily. "The horse-thief trail from the Indian herds crosses there, leading off down through the wilder breaks to the Platte."

Morissa nodded, recalling the trail vaguely from the morning after her fall, but then grew uneasy as she realized the man's resentment and his apparent meaning, with Jackie a close friend of Eddie's. "Oh, Ed probably saw the corral while out hunting sometime," she said reasonably, without convincing herself.

Tris rode silently beside her until there was a shouting and they turned to follow Robin's pointing gauntlet. But instead of the horse corral it was a bunch of range steers, with an old buffalo bull fighting them off, fighting off their curiosity as well as their anger. The bull was ragged, with reddish patches of wool hanging everywhere, his thin tail switching as he made furious little charges this way and that, his small eyes lost in the curling mat of his forehead, angry froth dripping from his jaws.

"Is he mad, rabic?"

"Oh, I don't think so. Just fighting—"

"Somebody'll get him inside of a week, the meat old and stringy as rawhide," Robin said. "Dry weather and heat probably drove him out of hiding in the breaks for water."

Finally Eddie led them around the side of a bluff overlooking the narrow neck of a rocky, brushy box canyon filled with dust. The wild horses, about fifty, had been driven inside the long arms of a trap corral that was joined to the high sandstone canyon, the lower opening closed by a pole and brush wall and gate, built high as a man could reach—high enough so the mustangs couldn't get a nose over or they would be climbing them like cats. They were circling away from bow-legged Bill Tillow in the center of the corral. He spread his loop this way and that, the horses trying to keep their heads back behind others, all of them trying to hide except one bold mare, bright as a red fox, taking the lone, unprotected front as the roper waited his chance, the horse he wanted sensing it as they circled, keeping back against the corral wall.

Suddenly they got the scent of newcomers and stopped, heads lifted that way. Morissa held in her Appaloosa to look down on them, through the lifting dust—bays, grays, sorrels, and buckskins, a blue smoke, a black or two, and the clouded white of calicos and paints. The powerful necks were raised high, the manes falling thick and long, their tails reaching the ground.

At a switch of the rope they ran again. This time the loop snaked out and an iron gray was suddenly left behind as the rest broke from him. Bill threw a dally around the short snubbing post in the center of the corral; the gray hit the end of the rope and went over.

Morissa gasped. "Oh, he'll break every bone!" she cried.

"You'll get used to seeing them do that—" Tris said, laughing gently. Still, the girl felt foolish, a tenderfoot, and yet horses did injure themselves. But the gray was up immediately and already knew how he could ease his choking breath. At the first little pull of the rope he took a step toward the man and, because the slack was gone immediately, he took another, and again another, his nostrils round as funnels, blood flecking the foam on the wind, his whitish eyes enraged, but his feet obedient.

"Sure looks like the booger's gone against a rope before," Tris said to the men at the gate. They nodded, their eyes sneaking shy looks under their curled, dusty hatbrims to the young woman and her Appaloosa.

Slowly Bill worked the horse in, until the gray made a great lunge to escape the nearing smell of man and the cutting rope, and as he went down again, the dappled body rocking in the dust, Hank dropped from the fence and was on the neck with a knee. A hand turned up the flaring nose while with the other he eased the rope on the windpipe a little. In the meantime Bill threw a breaker W on his legs, so even a child's jerk on the strings, the rope, could bring the horse to his knees.

"Won't those hard falls injure him?" Morissa asked, still the doctor, still the uneasy woman.

"Little danger, Miss Morissa. They're tougher than you think. And it's certainly better than letting a horse get away or kill a man, accidentally or deliberate. Now and then there is a killer among them, a horse that'll make straight for you, paw you down."

With a hackamore hitch around the gray's snorting nose to relieve the choke of the loop, Hank grabbed his W string and let the horse up. The gray stood a moment, shaking, and then he tried a kick against the ropes. He was jerked down, and then again, but when he scrabbled back up the second time he lifted his head toward the hackamore man as in curiosity, in friendliness, testing the wind with a rolling lip. No one moved, the wild herd squeezed off in a corner watching. Now slowly Bill began his soft, coaxing horse talk as he started down the rope, his voice quiet but firm. "Whoa there, you boogerin' son of a gun, whoa there, whoa—" moving his hands very slowly along the rope, "Whoa—"

Once the horse looked around to the string man behind him and then instead of drawing up close like a folding accordion to get as far as possible from the approaching hand, he took a step forward. "Oh, so you know what I want, you little booger—" Bill said, approving, and pulled at the rope a little. To this the horse reared back, and was brought to his knees by a jerk on the W. When he got up he looked around to Hank once more and then took a meekish step forward to the next pull. Then Bill turned his back and, drawing on the rope, walked slowly away, the gray following—the horse from the wild herd leading almost as well as a work mare.

"Why, it's amazing—what that man can do with a horse!" Morissa exclaimed.

Tris lifted his hat and shook his thick hair into the wind. "Yes.

59

Probably won't be another in the whole lot learn to lead like that and not make at least one good try to get away, or get his man." Cupping his hand to his mouth he called out to Bill: "You better look for a brand or rope burn on that horse. He's got away somewheres and gone wild."

The men in the corral grinned and Bill spit into the dust. "Aimin' to put your brand on 'im, Polk?" he asked. "We ain't found no saddle sign but I kinda thought all along he's smelled rope before."

At noon they had beanhole beans with sowbelly thick in them, dutch oven biscuits and coffee, followed by a sack of raisin bunches from Tris's saddlebags for a little sweetening, although the horse outfit had all put half a finger of sugar into their coffee for that. But they ate the raisins anyway, crunching the seeds and talking horse in short, terse phrases. A big herd hung out up around Snake Creek flats someplace. Lot a dark bays among them, good buggy horses for the Deadwood market. They'd get 'em, at least when the snow got deep.

Afterward Tris and Morissa went to sit on a high rocky bank far above the corral wall while Bill and Hank saddled the gray. The horse blew himself up against the girth, but he hadn't been hard to get the leather on after he smelled it, or to mount. He moved out around the corral in an easy jaunt, Bill holding the broncho's head up with a close bit, keeping his spurs turned out.

"Why don't you give him his head, let him go to it outside?" Jackie called out.

"There ain't no good hazin' horse amongst us, an' we ain't here to make runaways or outlaws. What we gotta do is make 'em lead a little, and take hobbles without breakin' a leg. They do the bustin' down to the corrals at Sidney. We're the catchers—" Bill said, as he cheeked the gray and stepped off into the dust.

"Heck, I'll ride him out in the open if you're 'fraid!"

Morissa heard her brother in surprise, and shook her head to him, "Never put your arm out farther than you can draw it back—" she advised. But Jack wouldn't show that he heard.

"Don't let that gray fool you, son," Hank advised. "He ain't just strayed outa somebody's ridin' string. He knows a rope damn well, but he ain't got no saddle marks an' cal'lates not to have none—"

"Why don't Tris here ride 'im?" Eddie Ellis suggested, looking up toward the two on the bank. "He's got somebody to show off to—" But stubbornly Jackie still insisted on his prior claim, until Robin promised that he could go down to the breaking corrals at Sidney sometime to try it.

"Just let me know the day—" Jack told the men at the gate. "Just let me know!"

But Eddie was persistent too. "Why don't you ride 'im, Tris? Ground's soft here, and you got your doc along—"

"Oh, this is my Sunday off," Morissa interrupted. But she felt the antagonism towards Tris, and so she turned her attention to him, leaving the boys without an audience.

The next horse caught was a zebra-legged buckskin that fought the rope all the way, and when he was saddled on the ground, with Hank astride him and the blind snapped off, he went up into the air again and again.

"Look at that belly full a bedsprings!" Robin said, laughing, but it was just straight hard bucking and suddenly he quit. Hank slipped off and wiped the sweat out of his hat band. Technically the horse had been ridden.

But next the rope settled on a fine fox sorrel mare, around five or six, well-fleshed, alert, powerful. She hit the end of the rope going away and somersaulted, shaking the ground. She was up immediately, her eyes red, her lips drawn back, and fast as a cat she charged upon Bill, her forehoofs flailing out for him. He jerked the rope to take up the slack at the dally, to get beyond the mare's reach. But the rope had got crossed against the pull, and the loop that Hank snapped out for a foot missed too. Bill fled for the gate and rolled under it just as the mare was upon him, hitting the solid poles a thunderous crack that echoed in the narrow box canyon. By now Hank was at the rope around the snubbing post to release it, draw up the slack, but the mustang turned on him, her sides heaving, her teeth bared like a snarling wolf's, and he ran, too, the men at the gate flapping their hats to draw the angry mare's attention, and chunking her with clods.

"Whew, a born outlaw!" Tris called to Jack. "Ride that one for us!" and smiled to Morissa's anxious protest.

But the young doctor thought she saw something else in the mare, something wild and incorruptible that brought a smarting to Morissa's eyes, and anger running through the breast, anger against the rope too, and the tormenting humans. Yet the men came from all sides upon the fox mare now, and got the rope solid to the snubbing post once more, only this time she would not go against it. Instead she fought the rope, snapped her jaws on it, struck at it for the enemy it was, and fought off the men bringing more ropes, fought panting and foam-flecked, her sides heaving, her hoofs like lightning in the dusty heat. And when Hank finally snagged a hind leg and she felt the pull there, too, she made one final attempt to break free. She reared, going up into the air, up in a great flying, pawing leap, and then came down forward on her head, her neck folded under, and lay still, the spurts of dust spreading in the air and settling slowly about her.

61

"That's too bad," Tris exclaimed into the silence. "What a saddler she would have made!"

"Oh, no!" Morissa cried out, the tautness in her arms a paining.

"She could have been gentled with a bucket of oats, and a patient, affectionate hand," the man said quietly.

But Morissa wanted to cry out against this also. Such brightness, such wild spirit was not to be betrayed, not to the saddle, the rope, and the bit and spur.

As the men dragged the dusty carcass of the mare out with their saddle horses, young Morissa Kirk turned her face away, looking up around the quietness of the canyon rim. But there, against the pale sky, were three riders standing close together, watching. Something strange about them made them fit into the doctor's sorrow about the mare, a free wildness that could not be bound, and only when they whirled and were gone, the sun glinting on their rifles, did Morissa realize what she had seen. "Indians!" she cried, pointing to the empty skyline.

"Looking for horses," Tris said, as he started away, running awkwardly in his boot heels toward the Appaloosa grazing on a picket rope. The horse catchers spurred out to round up their riding stock and then they divided, swinging around the canyon both ways to flush the skulking Indians.

"May be too many for us to stand off, if they aren't gone already," Robin said uneasily. "They want horses mighty bad—thieves got too many. Besides, they're restless about all the whites coming in. We better ride."

Mounted, the visitors swung off down the mouth of the canyon and out upon open prairie to avoid a possible ambush. "The Indians may be following the horse-thief trail," Tris said, looking over toward Jack and Eddie Ellis riding close together but hurrying, too, headed for the Sidney trail and down it through the evening sunlight until Robin knew that Morissa and Tris should be safe enough, probably seldom be out of sight of travelers or trail camps. Then the others turned back north. Morissa looked after them, somehow uneasy about her brother, with the Ellis boy so much, and yet glad that he had found a friend.

The lanterns were already lit on the bridge ends when the two reached the valley of the Platte, and the campfires scattered along the stream seemed peaceful and undisturbed in the dusk. Morissa's head felt sore again from the fall last week and her back was stiff after the long ride in the sidesaddle today. She wanted to accustom the people here to seeing her ride astride, forked, so much safer and easier, but she had larger ventures in mind for the future and so must make the little conformities now.

At the soddy Tris helped her off and for a second it seemed he would kiss her, but he gave her the opportunity to turn her face away without seeming to, with no words needed, no notice of it at all.

"All day I've thought about you hurt up in those hills alone," he said gruffly, and swung into his saddle.

Morissa went to the wagon to see her patient but she stopped outside to look into the darkness after Tris. She thought about the wild horses that had fought the rope so hard, and about the dead mare, red as a fox.

The big picnic for the visiting Britisher, Harry McApp, had to be put off because he broke his foot in a runaway, but the Walkers were giving a reception for him and some American financial and packing-house representatives at Sidney, Tris told Morissa. "It won't be as much fun for you as the picnic but a better chance to see you look pretty."

Morissa wondered about her sunburnt face above the whiteness of her throat and shoulders, like the face of some remote gypsy ancestor peering through, but she was not one to plaster her skin with whiting. So the next few times she was out in the hills alone she slipped her shirtwaist down in the sun, carefully avoiding blisters, although the golden quality of her skin, evidently a gift from a non-Scottish father, she thought ruefully, did make burning less likely.

When Tris came for her at the hotel in Sidney her reward was in his eyes as he saw the smooth, tawny shoulders above the handsome gold-shot reseda gown of summer taffeta. It brought out the golden flecks in her eyes, and the shining glint in her dark bangs and in the brows that were like bronzed swallow wings.

"Marry me—" Tris Polk said softly. "Marry me tonight at the post here."

Morissa tried to laugh. "Why, of course, darling, but shall we look in on the Walker reception first? There is a financier and a packer for your attention, a broken foot for mine," turning it aside as lightly as she could. And when Tris started to protest his seriousness, she put her hand through his arm and drew him along. "Choose a Sunday maid and ye'll hae a Sunday wife—" she warned him. "You better see me in a kitchen apron sometime—"

The evening was a gay one. "Our ladies here are as lovely as any in New York or Paris or even Chicago," a white-haired meat packer said to Morissa, and he sounded surprised, although the women were almost all city-bred, three from Britain, including the tiny, whimsical doll-like actress, Grace Enders. Gowned in heaven-blue satin with a train stiff and elegant as a bluebird's tail, she fluttered a moment beside her Harry's chair and crutch, and then was away.

Even the warehouse where the reception was held, for lack of larger banquet space in the raw border town, had a kind of grandeur. Partitions had been knocked out to make a long, spacious room and a platform dance floor was laid upon the hard-packed earth. Buffalo, grizzly, mountain-lion and goat skins covered most of the log walls, with ranch gear—fine silver-mounted guns, saddles, bridles and spurs—hung against the skins, relieved by the color of handsome Indian blankets, beadwork, and warbonnets. Spaced along the walls were buffalo-horn candle holders, like clustered upright, light-bearing cornucopias. There were silver candlesticks for the long tables of planks laid across empty barrels and covered by the Walker family napery, with bowls of blue penstemon and waxy yucca blooms, and the gleam of Walker cut glass and silver. There was champagne on ice in flower-banked lard buckets, and the meats varied from trout to bear, through young antelope, beaver tail, grouse, and quail. Under the talk and the pleasant sound of the tables a string quartet from Omaha played chamber music.

The evening began as gayly as Morissa's engagement dinner that Allston Hoyt had arranged, with even more compliments, although these were from a different people. The whole occasion was planned, she suspected, to sell ranches or ranch shares to the syndicate represented by Harry McApp. As Morissa looked over the tables she thought about her plans to take up a homestead, become a despised settler, and then she recalled a few words, half-heard words McApp had said to Clarke, with Forson, the meat packer, beside him. "Slaughterhouses near the herds, that's the best way. If you had a railroad at your bridge—"

So, if Clarke had the railroad there might be a packing house at the bridge, Morissa thought. But she had been inattentive to the young Englishman at her left and must bring herself back. It was easy enough. There were half a dozen men for every woman here tonight and it was the first fun she had had since that afternoon with Alicia Hoyt, the afternoon that sent her here rather than to McApp's own Scotland.

The dancing later was a lovely sight. Cantwell Walker, sunburnt as from India against the whiteness of his linen, led the grand march with the tiny blue-gowned Grace Enders. But many eyes followed the tall pair that was the Texas cowman Tris Polk and the handsome, even elegant young woman who claimed to be a doctor and had come so mysteriously to bury herself in the wilds of the north valley for a little summer while. Yevette, the dark-eyed young daughter of the Chicago packer, was attracted to the romantic Texan, or told to seem attracted, Morissa couldn't decide which. Still, with a blond young Englishman from McApp's entourage happy to bow over the hand of a wilderness doctor, Morissa was content until Tris came brusquely with her velvet wrap to take her away.

It was late, even for Sidney, but the saloons and the dance halls were still open, full of bearded freighters, trail drivers, gold seekers and neat blue-clad troopers from Sidney Barracks, troopers waiting for the Indian wars. No one here seemed depressed by the rumors that the Hills were played out, unless that was behind the two gold bricks put to gleam in the bright, lamp-lit window of the bank plain for all to see but protected by sturdy, hand-forged iron bars.

Tris and Morissa edged through the crowd. "There are three guards with sawed-off shotguns watching through slits in the curtain, they tell me," he said. He spoke softly, but some of the men around turned their heads and one slipped away into the crowd. "Cut Lip Johnson," Tris whispered to Morissa. "Wyoming outlaw."

So they moved on through the milling street, slowly, like two sightseers, Morissa holding her skirts above the rough planking and the dusty earth walks beyond. "It's been a lovely evening," she said afterward, speaking a little sadly into the silence between them, but when Tris drew her gently toward him, it was her cheek she turned to the cattleman.

The next day she wasn't on the stagecoach headed up the gold trail when he went to see her off. Instead she had taken the train east to the land office and filed on the homestead and preemption. The quarter she wanted as a timberclaim was covered and she selected another—altogether 480 acres of her own. A month ago the North Platte valley had been a temporary refuge, a haven in desperation because Robin was there. But now he was gone, and all that was left to her anywhere was a government claim, the first settler to push in north of the river.

Suicidal, Robin had called it, and yet perhaps that was what she sought; certainly it was suicide for her career that had been so well launched only a month ago. Even now she could return to Omaha where she had been invited to join the rising medical group—the first woman so honored. Only two years out of medical school and she already had professional standing there. What if she was a woman rejected, did life stop for that?

Or was this suicide what she really wanted—and to make the guilty knowledge of his part in it an eternal accusation to Allston Hoyt? Was it, too, at the bottom of her attitude toward Tris Polk? That she was drawn to him as a man much more than to Allston would have been clear to any doctor with a patient named Morissa Kirk, yet she was choosing a lone homestead in the wilderness instead of a good life in Texas as Mrs. Polk, or in Sidney, or at the least, on Tris's ranch down along the railroad.

But Allston was something far beyond the physical to her, and in a moment she was broken into incoherence by even this thinnest edge of thought. With her handkerchief to her lips she fled from the land office, but the papers of her entry were clutched tightly in her hand.

On the way back to Sidney Morissa tried to plan. She knew she must live on her new land to hold it, and next spring plant the ten acres of trees on the timberclaim. There would be the garden, chickens, and some milk cows to add to the seven head of cattle from doctor fees that she had running with Clarke's herd now.

But the cattlemen would not like this settling north of the river, or her fencing and irrigation. One of the first to be disturbed would be the Boslers, with their claim to a hundred and fifty miles of the north river front for their forty, fifty thousand head of stock. "That's an empire too big to fight," Robin had warned Morissa. Their hired hands had pinned a crude sign, HORSE THIEF, to the chest of the surveyor's helper they hanged at Sidney. Everybody said it was to scare his employer out of their free-land holdings. Turned out that the surveyor was an old Indian fighter and a pretty knotty piece of pitch pine. He immediately hired another man off the street, equipped him with a good rifle and finished the survey through all the Bosler range. But things like the hanging were to warn settlers off the free land up there, and now that the effect was plainly wearing off, it could happen again any time.

"You mean they might hang me?" Morissa had scoffed.

"Not so long as you're in good with Clarke and Tris Polk—"

"So—! I have to keep in good with them. And if they should find out something that destroys their respect for me?"

"Well, be better if they didn't. Rope don't care whose neck it stretches," Robin had said, laughing, pretending it was only an abstract rope. Yet he was compelled to say it, knowing too that Jackie must teach his sister something about the new Colt so she would be willing to carry it.

Their talk that day had been interrupted by a soft tap on the door, almost as though one of Etty's dogs had come nosing. It was Fish Head, the grease bucket containing his silk hat hanging from his arm, the little man looking very crestfallen to find Robin there. The father laughed. How could one think of necks stretched and proficiency with Colt's Peacemaker while barefoot old Fish Head stood on the doorstep?

VI

ON HER RETURN FROM THE LAND OFFICE MORISSA KIRK FOUND Sidney stirred by something besides gold rumors. General Crook had met the hostile Sioux up in Montana and whipped them.

"Yeah, the report says he whipped 'em, but I see he's withdrawed to his camp. That don't look like no victory to me," Morissa heard one of the old Indian fighters from Sidney Barracks tell the crowd at the stage station. They listened attentively, for they were waiting on the coach from the Hills, already long overdue. Not only did the gold trail pass within whooping distance of Red Cloud Agency but the entire region from south of there to Canada, including all the Black Hills, was legally Indian country, where no white man had the legal right to go. Those wilder northern Indians under Crazy Horse claimed the land clear to the Platte and the bridge and planned to hold it.

Morissa said nothing of her homestead north of the river. She knew that the Indians harried the Cheyenne trail to Deadwood, not over fifty miles west of Clarke's bridge, driving off horses and mules in spite of the Winchester guards and the troops, the Indians almost as troublesome as the outlaws.

When the coach finally came in, the passengers from Red Cloud said that the Indians had kept the agency awake with their victory dances the last two nights. They claimed Crazy Horse whipped the pants off General Crook and they ought to know. Crazy Horse was a nephew of Chief Red Cloud, and old Red's son was in the fight.

"Here we're feeding them dirty loafin' Indians and their young bucks off killin' our troops!" the station master complained.

Yes, and this morning the last of the young warriors vanished from the agency like fog before the sun. One party followed the stagecoach halfway to the Platte bridge and then cut in ahead, blocking the trail. The woman passenger was pushed down to the floor for protection but the driver was an old friend of Red Cloud's and so the Indians parted, the warriors sitting their horses on both sides of the trail, blankets drawn up to their angry eyes as the coach galloped through. Then they whirled off northwest towards the Yellowstone country. But the escape still had some of the passengers feeling their scalps uneasily.

"You better settle in town awhile," the station manager advised Morissa. "You're the only white woman for two hundred miles along the Platte. Be bad when the Indians strike."

For a moment she felt weak and afraid, with only the Peacemaker on the sod wall against the silent moccasin in the night, the tomahawk, the knife, and the bark of the rifle. "No," she answered slowly. "I'm the only doctor for those two hundred miles," and handed her valises up.

Guards were shifted from the gold coach to ride the regular north stage, empty today except for two ranchers hurrying to their beef herds, and Morissa Kirk. The other spaces had all been canceled, and for the next month. One of the special guards, the shotguns, riding inside said he was from the Cheyenne trail, but between the bloody Sioux and the roadagents, the stages there had stopped running by June. Only the largest freight outfits with troop escort could get through, everything else shifted to the Sidney trail, which ran east of Robbers Roost and the Indians that headed north to the hostiles.

With Crook's large army defeated, the hungry agency Sioux, still something like ten thousand, including many old warriors, were buzzing like angry hornets and not over a hundred twenty miles from Sidney, only eighty from the hated Clarke bridge that brought so many gold-hungry whites running into the Indian's Black Hills unprotected. With the help of the northern hostiles they might certainly feel powerful enough to throw all the whites out of the region, including those of Deadwood itself, all the ten, fifteen thousand people, women and children, too, jammed into a pitch-pine gulch, ready for the fire stick and the scalp knife.

The hurrying stage was met by Henry Clarke and his bookkeeper, Gwinn, near Courthouse Rock, Winchesters across their saddles, field-glasses in their hands. They had caught no Indian sign, no signal, although several of Lorette's relatives had slipped in for ammunition before going north. Clarke had wired Washington for troops to protect the bridge, although he was an old friend of the Sioux and usually more worried about white outlaws. "This time it won't do much good to hang up a dead owl," he told Morissa, stroking the dust from his beard and smiling. "Not against a Sioux war."

Fortunately Gwinn, who had cared for Tom Reeder in the wagon while Morissa was away, had avoided the questions about the strange silence at the bridge, and not a wagon crossing. Two days later a small dusty guard of troops came to pitch their tents at the north approach. The government had three armies out up north and was pushing the contractors to hurry some of their deficient deliveries to the hungry agencies, particularly Bosler, already under investigation for beef frauds.

The next day, a prairie scorcher with the temperature above 100, Morissa had to go up the trail to set a broken leg and help get the man down. She strapped on her Colt and as a special precaution she rode awhile beside a bull train going to Red Cloud and was almost overcome by the stink of it.

"Salt pork fer them Sioux," the whackers called to her. "An' you better keep your gun oiled up, ma'am. That there braid a yourn'd look mighty good hangin' to some buck's belt."

Two ambulances of Army officers out to inspect the situation at Red Cloud Agency came through, and young Lieutenant Larman from the bridge was ordered to join their mounted escort. This looked like a good opportunity to get past the Sioux for a farewell Fourth of July excursion to Deadwood, Robin decided. It might be the last if the mines really were played out or, as likely, the hostile Indians eluded the troops up north and struck toward the settlements. Clarke was going up to strengthen the defenses of his stage stations and get his pony express established to the Black Hills mining camps. He sent tents and bed linen ahead for the guests and took Gwinn, the bookkeeper, along to ride the back of the special coach while a guard from the gold runs who had fought Indians sat up beside the driver, rifle across his knees. Jack and Robin would be horseback and Tris too. Morissa felt a little guilty that she hadn't told the rancher about her homestead, although she realized that sticking the feathers of explanation on a buzzard's neck plainly would make no eagle of forthrightness of him, or her. But Tris was bringing his Chicago guests along, the packer Hurley Forson, his vivacious daughter Yevette and her chaperon, her Aunt Clara, a fiery old feminist. While it didn't look like the time for a tenderfoot outing, Morissa knew it must be important to Tris and probably Clarke, too, and even Robin—a matter of large Eastern and British investments if the Indian scare could be discounted. This outing, if successful, seemed the way to do it. So she hired Charley Adams, a field nurse in the Civil War, from the bridge guard to look after her two patients, and tried to keep Tom Reeder from uneasiness. Even the antelope sensed something and ran back and forth at the garden fence while Morissa packed.

The coach with the horsebackers following rumbled over the bridge soon after sunrise, close behind the two prairie ambulances of officers and the escort of bluecoats riding in double file ahead and behind. They swung off northward on the empty trail, with the meadowlarks still singing in the morning cool. But soon the heat drove the birds to pant in the shade of weeds or brush on the yellowed prairie as it did most of the larger game, although on a short cut an occasional antelope whistled, turning up the white of his rump as he ran, and then circled back in curiosity. There were almost no travelers and few freight outfits on the trail. Those few were very long, with mounted guards, rifles across their saddles, hurrying essential goods through while they could. Several horsebackers passed Clarke's party, hoping good horseflesh would get them away in case of an Indian attack. Even these carried rifles now, almost no one trusting to the more ornamental Colt.

But no one in Clarke's coach mentioned the rumors, or any other unpleasantness. They saw no Indians up close except at a little huddle of tipis along the brushy White River bottoms, where two old men were out smoking beside the evening trail, and some lean dogs barked. Even Aunt Clara, worn to silence by the heat and the long rough road, was ready for her bed when supper was done. Morissa dropped off wondering that Eddie Ellis wasn't down to visit with Jack, his dew-lashed blue eyes following her or certainly the handsome Yevette, young and bold-eyed too.

In the morning Lieutenant Larman came galloping down from the agency on a fresh horse, eager as a hungry man drawn to a coffee cooking. He had a nice six-day leave and could go all the way to Deadwood, and his young face flushed with pleasure as Yevette Forson cried, "Oh, Lieutenant, then you can keep us safe!"

Although Morissa suspected that he might be sent as protection, neither Robin nor even Clarke seemed uneasy, and now with five good shots in addition to the guard riding the box—six, counting Morissa who had been practicing at targets—they were probably safe enough. Four were on horseback, Jackie with his Colt, the rest, too, and with rifles or carbines ready in the scabbards. The station keeper said there had been no Indian troubles up ahead in almost a week, and only an occasional brush with petty horse thieves and roadagents, usually close in to the Hills. The eighteen-year-old Yevette shuddered, and tied on her swathing of red veil, for the sun was really trying to a delicate complexion, didn't Morissa think so, particularly to a fair skin—looking critically through the layers of chiffon at the doctor's brown cheeks.

As the sun climbed hot and clear, Yevette kept up a mild, veil-eyed flirtation with the Lieutenant riding alongside, and with Gwinnie up behind and Jack and Tris, too, giving Morissa an occasional sweet and tolerant glance. She did not notice the strange badland formations that lay on both sides of the trail. From a distance the naked reaches of earth looked like the palms of mammoth dying hands, cupped, yellowish, and withered. Upon approach the witherings became gullied canyons, bluffs, and buttes, with hundreds of little pinnacles and toadstool formations that rose stark from the water-torn slopes, the sun bright as on snow, still and oven-hot on the coach, shining on no other moving thing.

Finally they were out upon the high table with a ridge rising dark in the northwest, so blue-dark that Morissa knew it was the Black Hills, although to the left the yellow prairie still shimmered in mirage lakes, with little dry-land whirlwinds zigzagging idly across the plain, lifting bits of grass and leaves and then letting them drift. Far ahead the trail climbed over the rise of the prairie swells, a long bull train and the occasional faster travel like rows of crawling black specks. Inside the jolting coach the weary newcomers began to doze, their heads pillowed against each other in the heat and dust. Clarke let down the canvas curtain toward the afternoon sun, and settled back too, smiling companionably to Morissa as he closed his eyes for a little rest until the next change of teams.

But suddenly half a dozen horsebackers rose up behind a low ridge to the left, moving parallel to the coach, little more than their heads showing—hatted heads, not Indians, unless they were disguised. The guard leaned down toward the window and spoke quietly, pointing. Clarke peered out beside the curtain. Morissa looked, too, and gripped her hands tight, for already Robin and the Lieutenant were turning down along a dry creek bed between the men and the coach. She tried to see Jackie, somewhere behind, but Tris came hurrying up. He held his horse as close as he could beside the flying wheels and silently handed his belt and holster in to Morissa. Their hands touch a moment, their eyes met.

"Be careful—" the young doctor whispered, her throat tight. But in a moment she calmed, and moving softly so none would be awakened, she drew the cartridge belt about her narrow waist and set the pistol ready under her hand. Outside, Tris balanced his rifle across the saddle and fell back to plan with Jackie. Morissa could see the boy now, riding without apparent concern over the coming attack, his hand resting at his holster the only sign, and she marveled at her earlier doubts about a gun for a sixteen-year-old in this wild country.

By now the driver was easing his six horses into a clattering run, gradually, without seeming to, but the men were spurring up, too, rising higher into sight, sending a couple of bullets into the trail before the coach, and apparently heading for a place where the ridge dipped toward a timbered creek and met the trail at a twisting, brushy crossing. The violent jolt and lurch of the coach had jerked Aunt Clara awake, too. She stared around with sleep-bloated, frightened eyes and grabbed at her brother and the others, all bracing themselves as they could. Then she took Yevette's hand to comfort the girl, but when the guard sent a bullet to spurt a warning reply over the riding men she cried out at the thunder of the Winchester over her head. The packer stretched his thick neck, suddenly no longer red, to look out, too, and then peered back into Clarke's face. Cursing softly, he tried to reassure the old woman. "Just blowing up a little powder, my dear. Fourth of July, you know."

The next bullet, from Gwinnie's rifle, hit a little closer to the riders coming much faster now, sure to cut the coach off at the crossing. Then Robin started to use his rifle against them, firing from down in the dry bed, the bullets sending up warning puffs of earth and dust before the horses but almost under their feet now. The men swung out a little from this rising fire and then Morissa realized that they probably had accomplices at the crossing and planned to strike the trail beyond there, cut off the stage's escape.

Robin and Lieutenant Larman sent them a few more shots while Tris and Jack cut in past the rocking coach for the creek. Then suddenly a rider rose out of a gully and charged for the crossing. There was a quick movement in the brush before the coach, a shaking and plunging, and Morissa saw Tris stop, lift his rifle and shoot. Smoke puffed out blue and he spurred ahead to Jackie's shout. She closed her eyes a second for courage and then drew the heavy Colt and steadied it against the edge of the swaying window, waiting for the first highwayman to step out into the road. As she braced herself for this killing, the driver sent the

71

coach plunging down toward the creek close upon Tris and Jack. The top-heavy vehicle swayed dangerously to left and then right as it took the turn and dip into the timber and the broad muddy crossing. Yevette sobbed in fright against Clarke's shoulder and Aunt Clara was thrown against Morissa and her gun, and prayed aloud as dirty water splashed in over them and bullets whistled past.

But the driver did not stop. Feet braced, he cut right and left with his whip, skillfully holding his six galloping horses together, and so the coach righted itself and was up on the far bank with a lurch. There was more running in the brush, but no command to halt came, and no bullets. Then the coach was out on the bottoms and the horses settled into a lathered panting trot, up in plain sight of a big freight outfit barely half a mile away.

Behind them the pursuing riders had stopped and were bunched together, apparently looking, while a man afoot near the crossing emptied his futile pistol after the stage, one spent bullet striking the body like a sharp hailstone. Gwinnie picked it out of the wood and tossed it in to Clarke. Aunt Clara cried out when he put the mushroomed pellet, still hot, into her palm.

"Did you see Tris drop the horse of the outlaw that was beating us to the crossing?" Gwinnie called out. "But that stray cow running through the brush sure had me scared—"

Morissa laughed in foolish relief. By now the roadagents seemed discouraged. They headed into the creek bed and up toward the dark canyons of the Hills that looked near enough to touch. Morissa sighed. The next time roadagents or Indians appeared, at least those in the coach wouldn't be such frightened tenderfeet.

But Forson the packer was still busy. Wiping a handkerchief over his sun-blistered face he tried to quiet his sister's demand that she be taken right back to her private car down on the tracks at Sidney. Now finally Yevette was excited enough to forget the sun. With her veil thrown back she leaned out to thank the Lieutenant. Oh, he was so *splendid*, so *brave*. Jackie, too, was riding taller as he came up to look in on Morissa. "We'd a give it to 'em!" he said, slapping his gun, his boy-face gaunt with excitement, so strained and taut with it that Morissa wanted to cry.

"Perhaps it was somebody who saw us around Red Cloud station last night," Clarke said quietly, stroking his reddish beard. "Or one of those outfits usually after fatter game, before the Indians and the troops got so thick around the Robbers Roost that the stages quit running through there. Dunc Blackburn perhaps, but more likely Fly Speck Billy's gang. If we had been easier picking there'd been trouble. That's the indisputable advantage of our prairie route," Clarke told Forson, with his persuasive businessman's way. "Only a few spots are fit for daytime holdups on this trail. But that outfit worked mighty fast if it was this special coach they were after."

The way he said it, with a little unmirthful laughing in his thick beard, made Morissa look after the men, recalling something that seemed familiar in the way one of them rode. Clarke's laugh suggested it, but perhaps he meant her protest over the man hanged at the bridge that first day and was enjoying these few shots in her direction. Or was it Clarke they were after, now that the Indians could be blamed? Then Morissa remembered something else—that Jack had asked last week if Eddie Ellis could come along, so Ed must have known and through him perhaps Fly Speck or any of half a dozen other roadagents hiding out among Red Cloud's Indians. Then Robin came up and asked a quiet question of Clarke: "You think they were a little easy to drive off—?" looking under his palm all around the prairie and back toward the Sioux agency.

Uneasy, Morissa settled herself to quiet the aunt. She poured a little camphor into a handkerchief and cooled the woman's brow. Yevette needed no easing. She had a hero.

They got through by taking every man who could be spared from the stage stations and so, with five armed guards, they pulled into the packed and noisy gulch of Deadwood as the last sun left the timbered peaks. The gold town was in deep shadow, lights glowing suddenly here and there from the log and slab and canvas structures jammed along both sides of the little Main Street, scarcely wide enough for the bull trains to pass the fast evening carriages of the fancy women. The street was really choked where the placer mine in the middle of it narrowed the moving streams, the crowded horses tangling in their fright at the pop of firecrackers that sometimes were pistol shots, the creaking bull outfits plodding on.

The gulch walls climbed steeply from the string town, shacks leaning one over the other far up on each side. Robin had arranged for a two-room log house many rough steps above the noise of the town, but more private than the bunk-rowed hotels. The girls and Aunt Clara had the larger room, with a stove to take off the mountain chill and to heat bath water for the tub that was a whisky barrel sawed in half and set behind a sheet hung across a corner.

Yevette complained, wondering how she would manage without a maid for the evening toilette. But she did very well, chattering about her brave lieutenant all the time as she kohled her eyes behind Aunt Clara's back, skillfully setting off their handsome darkness and the whiteness of her skin, although it was pinkened a little by the wind, even through the veil.

Aunt Clara managed to forget her alarm at the popping firecrackers and ate well of the hurried dinner brought in. Then they went down to the crowded, door-lit street and into the Golden Belle. The Belle was a log theater and dance hall, with a bar, gambling tables, a stage, and twenty curtained boxes across the back behind the audience. Two of the boxes were opened together, the cots removed, and chairs brought, and the curtains looped back for a view of the stage for Tris and his party, the rancher's amused face confirming what Morissa suspected—that these were the cribs of the girls working the place.

The crowd was largely muddy-booted miners and other hopefuls, so like those waiting at the bridge the day Morissa first came. They pushed in and out under the smoky lanterns, milled around the bar and the gambling tables with the gold scales still busy weighing dust. Morissa noticed that Huff Johnson was at one, and making a good showing. The sleeves of his snowy white shirt were turned back from his delicate wrists, his black brocade vest buttoned close about his narrow waist, his mustache elegantly trimmed. But he had a new granite stare for Tris Polk, contrasted to the warmth of Gilda Ross's gay words, and Morissa knew why Huff had moved away from the bridge and why Tris Polk had taken so long to deliver his beef herd at Deadwood. She realized that in these Victorian times to let such conduct be known might seem reprehensible, and an insult to her, when Tris had asked her to marry him so recently. Perhaps it was part of him as a Texan—like the young medical student from Georgia who argued so hotly that the slave girl was an indispensable part of a gentleman's education, and the preservation of Southern womanhood.

As the crowd grew, Robin noticed a few army deserters around, troopers who had guarded the railroad tracks against the Indians. They told him that half a company had deserted General Custer last month on his march west to the Yellowstone. The gold pan looked a lot better than the scalping Sioux.

Henry Clarke was greeted by an old acquaintance, too, the blond-bearded, loud-voiced General Dawson, who came into Deadwood when there was only down timber in the gulch. He was showing some bankers and mine financiers around and Clarke took Forson over to join them. If the mines were done, certainly nobody here at the Golden Belle was admitting it.

"Everybody's got to be seen here at the Belle at least once an evening," Robin said. "Even the sheriff, who knows the gun's still the law." Many of the more flamboyant men and women were from the other houses along the gulch, the elaborately gowned women with their pomaded escorts beside them, like Madame Volanda who had crossed the bridge with her girls that first day. Wild Bill Hickok was there, too, at a corner table, his shining hair tumbling over his shoulders. A dozen smooth-fingered gunmen strolled through the crowd, and a scattering of roadagents, even Fly Speck Billy. Speck gave it the final touch for Morissa—the whole crowd not very different from that around the bridge before the opening, except that here they were not waiting to cross over to anywhere; here they had reached such destination as there was.

The Golden Belle had a small orchestra, and a square piano of carved rosewood on the little stage for the variety acts. The program included a farce playette, a little minstrel troupe, and the Flora-Dora Trio, three plump and close-laced dancing girls in bare shoulders and hip-length black stockings that would have shocked Aunt Clara if she hadn't been dozing, her charge, Yevette, concerned with her lieutenant.

The last act was by a dark, foreign-looking accompanist, very indifferent at the piano, and a pale blond singer, pretty in a sad and worn way. Her light voice was almost lost in the celebrating and pistol shots and the noise of the crowd drifting past. A quiet, gray-haired man pushed through to the stage and in the midst of the spatter of applause, lifted a gun and fired twice, missing both times. The accompanist ducked behind the piano, but the shots and the smoke were barely noticed by anyone except the owner. He came flailing through from the bar, shouting "Don't shoot my piano! Don't hurt my fine instrument!"

There was one more shot, this time from the accompanist. The gray man held himself very erect a moment and then sagged to the floor as the crowd parted around him. The singer cried out and ran to him. "Oh, my darling, my darling—" she sobbed as the man lifted a hand to touch her.

"Stop him," the wounded man pleaded weakly of the faces looking curiously down upon him. "He stole my wife. Don't let him get away—"

By now Morissa found herself there too. Automatically she had elbowed forward, with Tris steadying her. "He's about gone—"

The accompanist was brought down by two bearded miners and held there facing the singer across the man he had shot, the warm pistol forgotten in his hand until it was taken from him.

A long time the wounded husband stared up at him. "Bring a priest—" he urged weakly of the silenced crowd. "Marry them—"

So, with Tris there beside her, Morissa had to see the husband die, the killer be pushed up beside the dazed and silent woman, hear a priest speak the words: "Do you take—" the voice quiet but addressed to the sunburnt and bearded crowd and their scattering of women—all hushed for the moment. Afterward a man from the orchestra sprang up on the stage and began Mendelssohn's Wedding March. Then he remembered the dead man almost at his feet and let his hands sink, the piano die. Without seeming to move, the crowd parted for the newly married, let them walk down the soiled, smoky path toward the door.

Morissa gripped her nails into her palms. At least her mother had been spared this indignity to the betrayed, this final violation of the spirit. But the young doctor knew she must shake off this morbid and sickly preoccupation, must not keep running down this worn path like a mouse in a wagon rut.

It was very late when Morissa got Aunt Clara quieted enough for sleep. "Is there no law?" she demanded over and over. She made a real fuss when she discovered that there was no lock on the door. "No locks anywhere around, ma'am," Tris laughed when Morissa called him to ease the old woman's mind. "No petty crimes here in the West. We rob 'em in the open, or kill 'em, as you see, but that's all."

Speechless, the woman tried to move the washstand against the door. Tris did it, and piled the chairs and the tub there too, and climbed out the window that was held in place by one big nail. Afterward Morissa heard him start down the long steps to the town. She thought of Gilda Ross, and the jealous eyes and itchy trigger finger of Huff Johnson.

Next morning all of Clarke's party was out in time for the Centennial Independence Day celebration, with bunting, whipping banners and rifle salutes, the orchestra from the Golden Belle a band for the hour. General Dawson, his long blond hair and beard blowing in the wind, read the Declaration of Independence and electioneered a little for Hayes. "A gr-r-reat Republican for a gr-r-reat nation beginning her second hundred years!" he shouted over the sunburnt faces turned up to him, his voice thrown back in echo from the gulch walls.

There were some answering shouts for Tilden from the jobless, but nobody could vote here in the Indian country anyway, and so the general read a memorialization to Congress: "We petition that august body for speedy and prompt action in extinguishing the Indian title to the country we are occupying and improving—"

Morisa watched the crowd line up to sign the petition, mostly men, more under their twenties than over them, and everybody signing the great roll of paper, even the Chinese, Negroes, and old Swill Barrel Johnny, a brother in spirit to Fish Head of the Platte bridge. "Twenty-five thousand people around here," a loud-mouth offered easily, "but likely we won't need that petition. Custer'll wipe out them red devils up north and they won't be givin' us no more hot powder."

As the crowd moved off to wet their gullets, Tris led his party over to see the new Black Hills jewelry. The clerk thrust aside a lot of idle lookers from the little showcase and helped everybody get a souvenir of Deadwood. When Morissa shook her head to Tris, he urged her gently. "—Just a remembrance of a pleasant outing," saying it sadly, with something autumnal in his voice, something final, and the girl wondered if he might be joining Forson's packing firm, or taking up with Gilda Ross for good.

So she selected a ring: a greenish vine to circle the little finger, with a bunch of reddish grapes and a handsome green gold leaf. Afterward Robin took the Lieutenant and Yevette and Jackie to see the gold bricks in the bank window and then to pan a little gold dust for themselves at a friend's diggings. The rest went with Tris along Main Street, Morissa beside him in a white dress, with a ruffled rose and gold parasol that made her eyes browner, her flushed cheeks ruddy as a child's under the sun boiling down into the narrow and crowded gulch. At Number 10 Saloon a woman in a bedraggled dress leaning against the wall stopped them as they tried to push past. "Well, if it ain't Trish Polk, you old son of a gun!" she shouted thickly. "How's about buyin' a lady a drink?" So, to the amusement of the Chicago packer and the increasing delicacy of his sister's thin lips, Tris introduced the woman.

"The famous Calamity Jane," he told them, "well known around Sidney, Cheyenne and Deadwood Gulch—"

But when he spoke Morissa's name, Calamity leaned closer and with the occasional acuteness of the drunk, recalled something from long ago. "Kirk? You say Morisha Kirk?" she cried. With a staggering step forward she held out a small, dirty hand. "Why you growed up real nice, you little bastard!"

Once more the hated word was like a slap across the face to the young doctor, her angry flush plain to everyone in the bright mountain sunlight, and with everybody watching, for Calamity Jane was on the howl and had her grab hooks in some city dudes. Grinning in expectation, they stood around to savor the mortification Calamity could cause by her sodden, dissolute face, the unkempt hair, the voice like a roaring bull elk's.

Encouraged by so much attention she tried to hold it, extend it. Wavering a little she began a childhood chant, swaying as she tried a jumping step and had to grab for the saloon wall. But she still held out one hand to detain Tris and his friends. "*You* remember it, Issy Kirk, jumping rope, don't you?" she demanded of Morissa, and began again: "Ish—Issy over the ocean, Issy over the sea—" laughing very hard at her joke.

"You met Dr. Kirk before?" Tris interrupted, trying to draw the woman aside, to relieve Morissa's mortification and ease his guests away.

Calamity stopped. "Doc? Did he say *doc?*" she shouted. "So you're a dealin' in corn plasters an' snake oil stead teachin' school like you was plannin' back in Missouri?"

Now it was up to Morissa. "Yes, sometimes I can cure corns," she managed to say pleasantly enough, "although I haven't had much practice handling the snakes—" and was immediately ashamed of the poor joke, the unprofessional taunt.

But the crowd roared. "Calamity knows about them there snakes all right!" some one yelled, and Jane joined in the laughing, happy to be part of it on any terms.

So Tris slipped her a gold piece and moved his friends away, and later, on a grassy spot up the placer-roiled little creek, the talk turned to Calamity. Evidently the Canary family really had gone West when they left the Princeton region, Morissa said, thinking about the pert, pretty Martha Jane in the red velvet bodices that she had envied so much in her childhood, when she was the barefoot, poor-farm child. Now Martha Jane was this sodden, unfortunate creature in an ugly little gulch town surrounded by mountains that were gophered through by the gold-hungry—a broken, miserable woman at twenty-six.

Once the young doctor wanted to jump up and run to find her, tell her that there were cures for this illness, to come down to the bridge and she, a genuine doctor, would care for her. But instead Morissa sat demure with her white ruffles spread about her and listened to Tris tell his guests the newspaper tales about Calamity sneaking in among Crook's soldiers and scouting for him, when she was really found drunk among his mule skinners and sent right back. There was a story, too, that she saved a colonel's life, when all the colonel ever heard of her was that she might have been one of the predatory women he drove from his camp.

It was an excellent occasion for Aunt Clara's stern little lectures on the new Women's Christian Temperance Union and the need for woman suffrage. "Give us the weapon and we will banish the Demon Rum!" she cried with her best elocutionist's gestures, but not at their most effective from a seat on a rotten old log beside a creek in Deadwood Gulch, the elocutionist's nose peeling from sunburn.

Tris nodded and exchanged a grin with the packer and Morissa.

"Clara's been a good mother to Yevette since my wife died," Hurley Forson told the young doctor afterward, "but she does coddle her notions."

Morissa smiled in preoccupation. Everybody coddled a notion or two of his own, an illusion, good or bad, but today one that had tinged all her values since childhood had been shaken, brought down, and somehow the fall of Martha Jane Canary left an ugly place, like an oak's fall that suddenly exposed all the sad, stunted growth within its shadow, naked and mean, as naked and mean in this fall as if the oak had been genuine.

It was Gwinnie hurrying out with a carriage to fetch them that broke up the outing. It seemed more than just the prearranged conveyance to a gay early supper before a big evening, and so it turned out. The young man managed a word with Tris, and later the rancher came, serious-faced, to speak low to Morissa.

Trouble, he said. A rider from the Red Cloud stage station came to warn Clarke that the Indians claimed Custer's whole regiment was wiped out up in the Yellowstone country. Already a couple of Seventh Cavalry carbines taken up there had been sneaked in to the agency Sioux.

"Wiped out?" Morissa whispered. "You mean killed?"

"Yes, claim every man was killed by the Sioux. We better try to get back down while we can. No telling when the Indians decide to strike our bridge and cut the trail running right past their noses. There may be raids all over as soon as the northern warriors start the victory dancing at the agencies and whip them all to a bloody pitch. Besides, when the news gets out here there'll be panic—these tenderfeet stampeding like longhorns in a thunderstorm, and we have to keep you and the Forsons out of that."

"Does the Army know?" Morissa asked, looking over to the dapper young Lieutenant Larman with Yevette.

"Rumors, probably, but if there was more, the Lieutenant would be on his way back to the bridge hard as he could ride."

The party made a short evening of it, not going to hear the English troupe's *Mikado*, as they had planned. Because Yevette got an hour alone with her lieutenant in the mountain moonlight she was happy. Aunt Clara began to snore softly at the supper table. "It's the mountain air," the doctor consoled her and put the old woman to bed for a nap and then did not waken her. It was late when Morissa heard the men come in, Tris after the others.

They started back at dawn the next morning. The dusty, rutted little main street of Deadwood Gulch was almost empty except for that placer mine set in the middle, and the trash, papers, and bunting from the celebration scattered around. Here and there a drunk was sleeping in the gray dust, and two who would never awaken were laid out beside a saloon. In an hour the wagons, the long bull trains, would be moving through the narrow street, and all the jam of a boom that still seemed alive. But in an hour or a day the Custer news would explode like the caches of mine dynamite hidden around the gulch.

The driver hurried them out past the last scattered diggings and stump land, past a man sitting on a rock with a rifle across his knee, guarding a little hole in the ground, probably something like the one where Tom Reeder made his strike. For a moment Morissa thought of him, but Tom was safe at the bridge, his gold in the station, or so it was five days ago.

She wondered, too, about the scare stories of the Indians. Were the Sioux really powerful enough to throw all the whites out of their treaty grounds if they tried? The frontier would run red, as some predicted, and many innocent ones on both sides would die.

Although no one had told Aunt Clara anything, or Yevette, unless the grave-faced young Lieutenant knew, the two were silent, uncomplaining, their weary heads nodding with the jerk of the coach. Morissa was very tired too, and the ammunition belt very heavy about her waist, the last cartridge loop filled, her mind numb with the bald final instructions from Clarke and the extra guards, and Hurley Forson, too, in case the coach was ambushed, overrun. This time there would be no stops for sleep. Somehow they must endure the drive straight through as on the regular stage run, with horses and men changed regularly, everything changed except the coach and the passengers. If it seemed best they could hide out in the bluffs and badlands and then go past Red Cloud Agency in darkness, both Robin and Clarke certain that the Indians wouldn't attack at night. They had an old, old notion that night fighting was bad luck, perhaps because the dew stretched the bowstrings and softened their moccasin soles. But it would not soften the hoofs of their war ponies, or the blast of the Winchesters smuggled to them the last year under the freight loads going through, paid for by pony herds they later claimed were stolen. Or the new weapons taken from Custer's men. No one in the coach unless it was the Forson women thought of the roadagents now.

Once Morissa looked around to the riders that included all the family she had—Robin and Jackie, yes, and Tris, too, and then to these people inside the stagecoach, all so vulnerable to lead and fire and the scalping knife. Then she pillowed her head on her arm and dozed off, not awakening to the jolt or jerk of the hurrying coach.

VII

THE WEARY TRAVELERS LOOKED DOWN INTO THE NORTH PLATTE valley, serene, an eagle turning slowly against the far windy sky, several big freight outfits camped below the bridge, and a trail herd pulling in from the south, like a string of brown ants moving under their dust and hurrying faster as they smelled the water. Even Aunt Clara relaxed a little, easing her aching old bones as well as she could. And as Morissa saw the bridge standing so quietly over the rising sand bars, with three horsebackers, an Indian and his two women, fording the shallow stream from Etty's and plodding away northward, she wanted to laugh at the promise Hurley Forson had extracted from her as they left Deadwood— to save the last three shells from her cartridge belt for his daughter, his sister, and herself. They had come down the whole trail and seen no Indian except a few more old men sitting out beside the road smoking; one of them lifted his left hand in greeting, or perhaps in protest as the fast coach spread its dust over them.

True, there were troops out everywhere now, a whole army sent to head off the Indians slipping away north, many stationed where the old lodgepole trail to the north crossed near the Robbers Roost country. But probably the earlier discontinuance of the Cheyenne stagecoaches had already driven men like Dunc Blackburn away to the Sidney trail. If it was really his outfit that followed Clarke's special coach, they were lucky as weasels in a hen coop to get away.

But there was some of the panic that Tris Polk had foreseen when the news of Custer's fight got out. In a diffused form it spread over the entire region from Texas to the Milk River and the Cannonball. In the Hills and down the trail a lot of dispossessed roadagents, general hide-outs from the law, and a few discouraged miners and scouts organized the Montana Volunteers, to join General Crook, they said, but perhaps mainly to show off around Deadwood, where, forgetting that they were all trespassers on Indian lands, a committee had posted a bounty of $125 each for Indian scalps. Buffalo Bill Cody heard about the Volunteers and hurried up the trail to join them for the publicity. He stopped at Clarke's, talking big in words he had learned from his New York manager. He handed out photographs of himself in beaded buckskin, and for once Morissa saw a man who was as handsome as he was pictured.

And up in Deadwood flour was selling at fifty cents a pound.

The Custer annihilation affected the north valley, too, as Morissa had discovered when their coach rolled to a stop at Clarke's. Tom Reeder had pulled on his pants and quit the place. As soon as he heard about the Custer fight he bought another horse from Etty, got his gold at the stage station and with old Fish Head to drive, he started for Sidney and the railroad.

Morissa had stretched at her weariness from the long trip. "Why, the old dead beat! So he jumped his doctor bill?" she said, humoring the station hands in what she considered their little joke. "I guess two months was all of our tame company he could stand."

But the man was actually gone. He had left a note and a package with the station master for the doc. The note was written with a lead bullet on a paper sack:

im taken my stuff an pullen
out and im taken the antlop so
i won be lonsom tom reeder

The package was a little rawhide bag. Morissa poured the contents out into her palm—gold nuggets, looking curiously like warm and shining beans, mostly with the same bent shape only a great deal heavier.

"Oh, he'll get killed for his gold sure," Morissa exclaimed as though of a child. "He probably never got to Sidney."

But Clarke's old station hand shook his head and unloaded his cud into the sandbox. "Oh, I guess he's made it all right, Miss Morissy," he said as he wiped his yellow mustache. "Tom, he sent his treasure box down by stage, expressed it straight to the bank."

A rueful smile pulled at Morissa's wind-chapped lips. "So he could look after himself very well, the malingerer!"

But it was wise for him to go. Reeder was a sick man and now he could get the care that might help keep him alive a while longer. She would miss the antelope, although he had grown large enough to jump the fence into the yard and the flowers.

Before Morissa could get to bed, a cowboy rode up, speaking apologetically. A man was took sick with typhoid down at Redington's on Pumpkin Seed Creek, south of the Wild Cat range.

"Oh, I just can't go now," Morissa protested wearily. "Not without some sleep. We've come straight through from Deadwood. I'm just not fit to care for a patient."

"He's took pretty bad, ma'am, mebby dyin'—" the cowboy said slowly. "Them Sidney docs won't come; got typhoid down there, too, an' afraid of Indians. We borried us a wagon from Clarke's; got it ready with a bedroll spread in it. Mebby you could catch you a little sleep on the road."

So Morissa tried to shake the pall of weariness from her. "Give me half an hour to clean up and get my pill sack together—"

Two days later Morissa had the man in her soddy, working to lower the fever and keep a little soft but nourishing food in him. She tried the less drastic of the new remedies for disinfecting the intestinal tract, afraid of the caustic carbolic dosages.

While Charley Adams sat beside the sick man, Morissa had gone over the bridge and with a plat in her hand that she unrolled here and there, she sought out the almost obliterated government corners of her land. Then she decided on the site of her new home, on the second bottom, well out of reach of such floods as the one that welcomed her first day here, yet not too deep to water. There she set the stakes for the house, in the V made by the river and the trail—two streams that crossed, the

82

stream of water and the stream of man. Here she would put down her roots and, she hoped, grow like the occasional towering cottonwood of the region. But some grew into stunted, curious dwarfs that never reached beyond three, four feet, and there seemed no accounting for why a tree here became the one or the other.

The next morning Robin set his breaking plow into the virgin earth for the home of the first settler north of the river. He cut the sod in a low place where it was still moist enough this hot July to roll flat from the breaker bottom, although a little too low for the tightest mat of rooting. Even so, Morissa didn't plan to use this house for the thirty, forty years that a good sod building would stand up.

As Robin's plow turned the dark strips, smooth and shining, blackbirds followed close at his dragging whip, gobbling up bugs and worms. His sweating men cut the sod into manageable lengths with their spades, stacked the slabs carefully on the platformed wagon gears, and then laid them like long dark bricks on a foundation of stone from the Wild Cats. It would be a long building, set directly across the line between Morissa's preemption and homestead, to serve as residence first for the one and then for the other.

"It don't take long to get onto the tricks of any trade, I guess—" Robin said.

"The land is good, and I intend to have as much as anyone else would get—" the girl said firmly, and Robin remembered that her great grandfather had stolen the wife he wanted, carried her off to the Highlands, and kept her shut up until she learned to love him enough to reload his guns as he held off the brothers come for her.

In two days the door casings of Morissa's house stood up stark as play entrances to an imaginary dwelling. Wide double-window spaces were set in, with deep ledges for sunny winter seats, and for pots of flowers to brighten the dark months. Long, straight pines were dragged out of the Wild Cats and hauled in on extended wagons for the ridge poles, and for the stable and the windmill tower later.

But long before the last rattlesnake seemed gone from the gentle slope, and the walls were high as a branding corral, visitors showed up, to hunch with forearms crossed on their saddle horns and perhaps spit a little tobacco juice into the yellowing grass.

"Pretty big spread you puttin' up here, ma'am," one said to Morissa. "Plannin' to marry you a ready-made family?"

"Oh, I don't know. The house won't be as big as the one up the river at Coads', I hear. But I can always add on if I need the room."

"Who's gonna stand off the Indians?"

"They'll get more guns and everything by attacking the trail station and the ranches than me. Besides, the troops are stationed on my side of the river—"

Sometimes a cowpuncher would get out his makin's, sift the tobacco into the pinched paper, and lick it thoughtfully. "Plannin' on runnin' cattle?"

"Yes, some," the girl usually said to this query. She had ten cows, or twelve—whatever the number happened to be, and planned to get more, since cattle were easier for patients to come by here than money. But she would need all this space to care for the sick. "No telling when there'll be a typhoid epidemic with the water problem so serious all along the trail. Besides the victims of Indian raids."

When the visitors spurred away, they usually left a hazy sense of unfriendliness behind, like the thin smoking of dust raised by their dogloping horses in the summer heat. Morissa realized that this unfriendliness would grow when the ten acres were broken out for her treeclaim next spring, and her little irrigation ditch was started.

Then the new Centennial Model Winchester rifle came. Robin opened the box casually. "Guess maybe I better leave this here with you, if you persist in staying," he said, as though the gun hadn't been ordered for Morissa. And once more he saw the firmness come to the chin of his stepdaughter, just as the day he asked their doctor to tell her how difficult her life would be as a female sawbones.

He had known she would stay, at least for a while, and so he settled his hat closer to his shaggy gray hair and went to lay out a target, clearing a square yard of sand on the slope of a ridge where the heavy .45–70 bullets could bury themselves, not kill stock or perhaps a man far beyond the reach of sound. Then he showed Morissa how to use the new rifle and got Jackie to challenge her every few days. At first the gun left her shaken, not the recoil against her shoulder or the thunder in her ears, but the thought that she was practicing for murder. Yet she would soon be alone here, with helpless patients in her sole care, and so she kept on, until it became almost a game. Although the target was only two hundred yards at first, men came from the saloons to watch this young city woman with a ribbon on the heavy braid down her back kick up the sand every shot. Then they hurried back to throw down a few fast drinks.

Morissa had a team and top buggy now, sent up by Sid Martin. He was no longer yellow as a Deadwood Chinaman, he wrote, but still fighting the saddle skirts around his neck instead of riding them. Otherwise he was doing all right for a man who ought to be dead, except that his whiskers itched like the mange inside that leather. Maybe he had sand fleas.

One of the ranch hands brought the buggy to the doctor's yard gate, untied his saddle horse from alongside the team and left the outfit there, the buggy and harness shining new under the thin dust, the bays standing with their ears up as Morissa came out and shying a little from her blowing calico skirts. But the mare reached out a soft, inquiring nose to the low words Morissa made for her.

"This is ridiculous overpayment," she said to the man as she rubbed the velvety little gully under the mare's jaw. But he made it clear he wasn't sent for conversation. He handed Morissa the letter from inside his shirt, swung into the saddle, and set his spurs.

Nellie and Kiowa were four-year-olds, the gelding a little too faunching and flighty, but perhaps he would quiet down, or could be replaced by one better fitted for a doctor who dozed off returning from night calls. Besides Morissa found him an amusing horse. He might pass an old tarp flapping against a thistle without lifting an ear and then plunge sideways, snorting and rearing, at any hoptoad that blinked in his path. And it was as well that he was an engrossment, for Morissa needed something to laugh at, something to arouse a little of the Scottish humor her Grandmother Kirk was said to possess.

She missed Robin and Jackie very much, even though some of the grading crew still worked around her place, fencing a pasture, digging a well with a tight curbing against the thirsty gophers and field mice, even snakes who would only die in its depths. They threw a little dam across the thread of creek that probably roared with water in the springtime, and laid out a ditch down to her yard. Morissa knew she wouldn't get much water this year unless there was a cloudburst, but she wanted to utilize the plow and scraper crew while she had them.

Robin was gone to look over his new job before moving down, and Jackie was visiting with Eddie Ellis up at Red Cloud among the surly Indians. But what disturbed Morissa was word that the boys were seen with the outlaws hiding around the agency. She thought of Grandmother Kirk. "A kinsman is part of your body but a foster brother is a piece of your heart," she once wrote to the girl at the poor-farm, hoping to comfort this child that she could never acknowledge. Now the granddaughter knew what she had meant, with Jackie half kinsman and half beloved foster brother.

Perhaps Morissa was alone too much, with the stream of travel past her new place thinned to a dry wash, the typhoid patient improving, the man with the broken leg up on crutches and gone to Sidney. Tris Polk had not stopped in since she crossed to the north side of the river and even Etty's small daughters drew back with something more than shyness when she approached. Then the young doctor lost another patient, her first here north of the river, and never really hers. Yet somehow it put as much defeat upon her heart as the little girl with the snake bite. As Dr. Aiken at medical school once told her: "Perhaps women make bad physicians. Their emotions involve them in the simplest physicking."

85

Morissa had been to a beef camp down the river to see about a man thrown when his cutting horse hit a wet spot. On the way home she passed a covered wagon drawn up near the bridge, a woman out in the shade, the baby in her lap choking and blue—perhaps whooping cough. Morissa stopped the shying Appaloosa, handed the reins to the man standing futilely by and unhooked her saddle pill bag.

But the woman lifted her voice against her coming. "No female doser will work her spell on my son!"

Ashamed that she had thrust herself so unprofessionally into this rebuff, Morissa swung back into her saddle, shouting instructions to the father as she let out her prancing horse. Next morning she found the man at her door with his hat between his hands, asking that she come to say a few words at the burying. "—The missus is sayin' may-like you got you some book larnin'," he stammered. "Seein's you set yourself up a-dosin'."

Yes, enough book learning to bury her son now that he was dead, Morissa wanted to cry out. But she went. Standing beside the mother she read once more from the little bridal prayer book and wished that she had another white cashmere shawl to wrap about a child, another bit of her trousseau turned to some purpose. But the day would come when she had a row of small beds in her sod house and a glassed-in space where sick children could grow strong, and sad ones happy—hoping somehow to discover them in time to restore them to health, to laughter, and to wonder.

People around the bridge and the trail workers all knew that Tris Polk had not tied his horse at Morissa's gate since Robin cut the first sod north of the river. Gradually the story of Calamity Jane's school days with the young doctor, and who could tell what later association, sifted down from Deadwood. The men repeated it, letting it spread like a well-thrown loop, scratching their beards appreciatively, speculatively, or resetting their hats to their eyes.

"Yeh, things is clearing off a little," the Bosler wagon boss said in one of the whisky stores. "Might have known she was settin' up in Calamity's business over there, a young woman wanting to bunk alone like that—"

Some of the more speculative went beyond listening; they wandered over when they were around the bridge. But apparently acquaintance with Calamity didn't mean professional sisterhood, for they came back looking mighty sheepish. One who had primed his courage a little too much before he went complained the doc pulled a gun on him. "One of them new Winchester's with a slug like your thumb—"

Most of those who lived at the bridge shook their heads knowingly for another reason. With Robin gone, the city girl would soon be clearing out too. Not even the roughest old widowwoman was willing to come into the region as cook, if any ranch would have a woman. Certainly the lady doc would go flying East before the first puff of blizzard wind, her new sod walls left as a rubbing place for the lousy longhorns.

But for the present Morissa Kirk seemed to be making a great busyness of her move into the new house, bringing her barrel chair with its wheel bumbershoot, and her flowers and shrubs, laying out the new yard and gardens for next year. Besides, Lt. Wilbert Larman was turning his young eyes in all their blue seriousness toward Morissa now that Yevette Forson and Tris both seemed gone. Wilbert understood about caste from his West Point training, he told Robin on the Deadwood trip, and knew how far out of reach a millionaire packer's daughter was to a poor shavetail.

One weekend Morissa went to a post dance down at Camp Sidney with him. Wilbert had educated feet, as Sid Martin called them, and she would have had a good time except that she saw Tris Polk riding through a side street early in the evening. He was going somewhere in a hurry sitting the white-stockinged Cimarron with the ease to break the heart.

But the Lieutenant was still a boy and with him she need not be a woman, only a laughing girl. Saturday nights they usually looked in at Etty's roadhouse for a while, watching Lorette's breed relatives from the trail stations and up around Red Cloud. The girls were creatures of flying grace in the square dances, the reels, and the polkas and in the Canadian steps that they taught the lonely men with much hilarity and fun. There were usually two or three white women who had stopped in off the trail, generally showing the wear of Deadwood or similar places. Once Morissa noticed a very childish plump and pretty blond girl dancing with Eddie Ellis, but a little unsteadily and tiring much too soon. Although a schottische left her panting, her face red and perspiration-streaked, her eyes still turned to the pack of men along the walls and looking in the doors and windows.

"She's after one of the tenderfoot bridge hands that Clarke fetched West," Eddie whispered to Morissa in a promenade. "Seems she's carryin' his bastard—"

Anger came up in Morissa's flushed face. "Don't defile the innocent unborn with that name!" she said hotly, and the baffled twenty-year-old could only say, "You're sure a looker when you're mad," and finish the dance in silence, his baby-lashed eyes searching out Morissa's, until she wondered in exasperation how she got herself into such a situation, with boys like Wilbert and Eddie hanging around when there were so many men in the country, not only Tris Polk, but dozens of others.

The next morning someone came for Morissa. The yellow-haired girl had taken on too much of Etty's red-eye last night and now she was behind the station outhouse among the tansy with her wrists cut. But when Morissa reached the bloodied spot the girl was gone. It was Fish Head who found her, crawled away behind a stunted willow clump at the river's edge, face down in the clear shallow water that washed her long pale hair out full length, like some lovely golden sea growth moving restlessly over the sand. As Morissa had suspected, the girl was pregnant; not over fifteen or sixteen years old and already in her seventh month under the cruel lacings. In her little bag was a gay note to her father, saying she was going away to make her fortune singing and dancing at Deadwood, and she would return with a pocket full of gold; he would see.

Within five of the hot July days the father was at the bridge, a tall graying man in black. It was too late; the girl had been buried over on the knoll, with only Etty's Lorette to mourn and tell her beads. But the father had anticipated that and brought an embalmer so his child could be returned to the family plot. He spoke angrily of the violence of this dreadful and lawless country, where a man's guileless young daughter could be killed and none brought to justice, and when Morissa finally made him listen to the truth and its circumstances, he rose up in anger.

"You are traducing an old and honorable name, madam!"

But later she saw him with his head in his hands beside the river while the undertaker worked in a little tent set up at the graveside. Her heart was heavy for the father, and for his lovely child. There seemed no limit to the misery a man might be willing to trade for a moment's gratification. She wondered why her mother had no word of anger for the one who seduced her. "Ah, the urgent lover is soon gone with the geese—" she once said, and never more than that.

The new rifle hung on Morissa's wall, but she seldom used it unless coyote or wolf came too close to her half-dozen white hens. Guns here had many purposes besides the hunt: on the range against a coyote or gray wolf attacking new calves, against a charging longhorn, or in a stampede; socially they served as decoration and equalization, and as protection or aggression for men who had enemies or planned to have them. Morissa kept her guns ready for Indians and holdups and other lawlessness, but she couldn't take the roadagents too seriously, even though their preying had stopped the Cheyenne coaches entirely for weeks at a time and left men dead in the dust of the trail. She always thought of roadagents in terms of Fly Speck Billy with his small-boy face, so curiously spattered by the dark freckles, although Robin had reminded her that such men could be the coldest of killers.

Morissa had moved into her new place before it was half finished, and although her sign hung above the door, a small vigil light behind it through the dark hours, the large kalsomined hospital room seemed bare as a barn. The bunks were usually empty and the swinging coal-oil lamp over the operating table had been lit only once. Even Fish Head did not seem to be hungry any more, at least not hungry enough for her cooking. The young doctor wondered if she was being quarantined, lone-corraled, since no one came near her, not for so much as Epsom salts or toothache killer. And Tris Polk—how much of his avoidance grew out of her move across the river, how much from Calamity Jane and her "You little bastard—?"

Then one afternoon a stagecoach left the road to the bridge and came thundering to her door, swaying crazily, the horses galloping heavily and uncontrolled. One fell in the harness, the rest stood with dropped heads, sides bellowing, lathered, and as Morissa ran out, the driver toppled toward her from the box. She caught him, eased him to the grass, her hands slick and sticky from the bleeding under an arm. Dried blood was splattered like brown paint down the side of the yellow coach, and inside four of the five passengers were wounded, and Owen, the guard on their Black Hills outing, too, with a thigh shattered and torn. Apparently somebody had got wind of the unscheduled run, for the stage was held up by a gang of masked men opposite a high rocky point. The driver refused to stop and while Owen, riding guard up in front, winged one of the roadagents, two passengers followed his orders and threw out the iron strongbox to divert the others. But the box was plainly too light, empty, and the thieves left it and came spurring up around the coach. While Owen picked off three of their horses, the driver was shot, and the guard himself was left clinging to the high seat, his broken leg pounding helplessly against the side of the thundering coach until they could stop to get him inside.

Later there was talk of a treasure shipment hidden in a worn carpet-bag lined with buffalo leather, so heavy with gold it required two strong men to lift it out. But Morissa didn't see this. She called for Charley Adams from the bridge troops to help her work with the patients. Together they got the driver's bleeding stopped, and started after the bullet and the bone fragments in Owen's thigh. Although the splintered femur had punched out through a jagged hole big as two fists, the artery was untouched or there would have been a dead man inside when the coach reached the valley. True, the patient might still die, but in her three months beside this trail Morissa Kirk had discovered something of the toughness and the resilience of these people. So she showed the grizzled old army nurse what she wanted done with the ether, then, expert from much field practice, he spread the wound while the doctor gently probed its welling depths for bone sliver and bullet. Finally they cleansed the wound with carbolic acid solution, drew the leg out straight and long as the other, and packed and stitched the wound, leaving it deep-tubed and open at the two ends. Because this would need constant

89

observation, Morissa had Clarke's blacksmith make a sort of iron frame from wagon rods over a temporary open cast, fastened the leg securely against slip or shift, and slung it up with a pulley and sandbag.

Afterward, when they were out of their bloody cover aprons and resting a moment in the shade, the old soldier shook his head. "I seen Dr. Mary Walker time or two, but I never seen her work. All I can say, ma'am, is I never expected to see no woman doc get mixed in no job like this—"

Morissa smiled wearily, pushing the trailing hair off her hot neck. "Perhaps I didn't either. I've never been faced with a bullet-shattered femur that had been banging against a galloping stagecoach before. But you take what comes here, and I guess this isn't too different from repairing a splintered chair leg, except if we're lucky this will grow together, even with the slivers that are missing—"

The wounds of the others were all comparatively minor. Only the woman with a bullet through the tendons of the neck, was really in pain. A little morphia would get all but Owen and the driver to Sidney, and so the bullet-pocked coach went on, one of the women spreading her old-fashioned crinolined skirts over the carpetbag with the gold again.

Several times this bad first week the guard's fever went very high, and angry red streaks began to move along the blood vessels. Morissa thought seriously of amputating the leg, but she clung to it as desperately as the patient now, the severance a personal mutilation in a land where the cripple was indeed a misfit. She worked with cold packs, she and Charley Adams, in two-hour shifts. It brought a little talk from the casual freighters and beef herd men. Maybe the Kirk woman was like Calamity Jane after all, with a soldier openly moved in over there. But the young doctor was too concerned to know. She gave her patient febrifuges and finally, in desperation, when the man was delirious and wasting, she tried a thick dark tea made from the silver sage weed that Lorette said the Sioux used for fever and blood poisoning. At least the tea was bitter enough to seem medicinal, and in a convalescent patient it ought to arouse a wolfish appetite. At best this was a sort of final gesture, for by then the patient was too weak and exhausted for the amputation.

Somehow they kept Owen alive through those first weeks. Then suddenly he began to take notice. "Still got me in one piece, eh Doc?" he asked weakly one day as Morissa examined the scant discharge from the tubes, sniffing it, testing it for grit between her fingers. Now the man began to eat, and to sleep. The swelling loosened and the wound began to drain and stink. Finally the doctor put a solid cast inside the iron frame and got the patient ready for Sidney, nearer to his friends.

Henry Clarke stood beside Morissa as the wagon took the guard away.

"I have been withholding my objections to your move across the river, my dear, hoping that you would get discouraged and leave for a more salutary location without my intercession," he said, speaking with stiff formality. "I am still certain there will be serious trouble if you remain. However, I must express my gratitude to you, not as to the daughter of a trusted employee but to an excellent physician."

Morissa felt herself blushing over the forced little speech and tried to thank the man as she looked after the wagon with misted eyes, wanting to tell Henry Clarke that she appreciated something of his accomplishments for the West, for the homeseeker, including the seven bridges much like the one here that he had built over the frontier, built against all odds. Some of these odds she could at least name now.

As soon as the troops along the Cheyenne trail went to join General Crook on the Yellowstone the roadagents began to work it again. After two guards were killed and three passengers shot, orders went out that the gold would come down in an armored coach, a treasure vault on wheels, with no passengers except guards inside and out, half a dozen armed riders far out in every direction. The regular coaches were to submit to search, everybody get out, hands in the air, women and all.

But Henry Clarke would not have his passengers down in the dust to be mauled by ruffians. "Seems we were overconfident," he told Morissa ruefully, pulling at his fine beard. "And my men paid with their blood. Next time I plan to leave the holdups bleeding."

He went East immediately and hunted out a pair of treasure guards who wouldn't be in cahoots with the roadagents, at least for a while. In addition he nailed a piece of rope neatly tied into a noose outside of each stage station, and was heard to say in the saloons up around Red Cloud Agency that his bridge had sixty-one spans, each one as hungry for a man dancing at the end of a rope as the night before the grand opening.

Clarke brought back something else, too, a beautifully chased belt watch for Morissa, a repeater with a sweet-toned little bell for the second hand, too, one that rang to a finger's pressure after one minute.

"No telling when you'll be caught without a light," he said, and when the girl tried to thank him he waved the words curtly away. "I won't have my men killed. Owen would be dead if you hadn't been here. Now he's alive and with a good serviceable leg. We'll have no polite soft-talk!"

To Morissa it seemed time for firmness, too, with the attack on their stage and the killing they saw at Deadwood, the murderer untried. Now there was word that the gunman, Wild Bill Hickok, had been shot down, killed in Deadwood's Number 10 Saloon with a bullet in his back, aces and eights in his hand.

The stage driver who told the story at Clarke's one night had seen Wild Bill laid out handsome, with dark-faced men gathering along the street to string the murderer up. But just then a Mexican bullwhacker came spurring into town with an Indian head under his arm. It was half-dried and stinking, but certainly Indian, the long braids flying—one of a vanguard of the killers of Custer come to attack Deadwood.

A hat was passed through the roaring, milling crowd now doubly concerned with their cartridge belts. Around $70 in gold dust was gathered, although the posted bounty was $125. Anyway, some said the whacker had merely cut off the warrior's head after the freight boss shot him among the stock. Still it was of an Indian with a scalp, and killed very close to them here. The gulch hurried to man the defense.

"So they lets the cold-blooded murderer get away, with Wild Bill layin' there dead?" one of the Hill-bound passengers demanded.

"Well, Indians are Indians, and there's no shortage of gunmen—" Clarke said casually from his desk behind the counter. "Bill's name was posted up in Cheyenne last winter, heading the list of a dozen or so undesirables warned to get out of town. Claimed he was a roadagent and professional killer. Bill slit the list from the wall with his skinning knife and stayed awhile, but a gunman can expect to get a dose of lead sooner or later—"

"Mebby Bill wouldn't use his gun fer you!" a bar loafer shouted.

Clarke ignored him. "It's this Indian bounty that I don't like, this paying for human scalps. I had hoped we were beyond that kind of savagery—" The bridge builder didn't look toward Morissa as he said this, but he knew she had overheard the story, particularly about the scalp and the bounty, from the way she pushed her mail together and hurried out, half-blind. Some day she would do something desperate in one of these dark and terrible moods—something destructive, like a wild mustang that could not accept the rope.

Morissa ran with her lantern, over the dark bridge and to her lonely place. She didn't look into her bundle of new medical books and her magazines, or even the letters. She sat with her hands clutched tightly in her lap, more alone than she had ever felt in all her life.

Lieutenant Larman took Morissa through the new blockhouse on the little built-up island joined to Clarke's bridge. Of native pine, it was erected as a warning and a protection against redmen and white who would attack this crossing. The second story, square too, but larger, was set diagonally upon the first, giving the gun slits complete command of any approaching enemy. So the new Camp Clarke stood, like a sort of thick, shaggy head lifted to look both ways over the long bridge.

92

"At the first sign of danger you're to hurry in here, and bring your pill sack and instruments, in case we have to stand a siege—" the young lieutenant said, laughing, but underneath there was a deep seriousness. Morissa knew that his orders were sound, yet any attempt at an attack would certainly cut her off at once.

No one knew where Crazy Horse and his great force of hostile Sioux were, and this, with the disturbing rumors from the mines, kept the travel past Morissa's place down for weeks. Then suddenly there was a new gold strike in the Deadwood region, several, but in the more difficult business of hard-rock lodes, the richest one the Homestake, optimistically labeled the most promising gold mine in the world, with a Bolthoff Ball Pulverizer set to go into operation there before winter. The movement to Deadwood quickened once more, with the curious urgency of the gold-hungry, like ants running before the breath of winter. This was no business for the pick and gold pan, but much of the new heavy mine machinery needed now went in on the Kearney trail that started far down the Platte and cut across the sandhills and the rise called Pine Ridge, toward Deadwood. The route was very long but it saved expensive railroad freight and was mostly through open prairie, long-grassed for the bull trains, the work-gaunted oxen no temptation to the roadagent or the buffalo-sweetened tooth of the Sioux.

This shift that cut down the hauling on the Sidney gold trail and the tariff at the bridge brought other changes past Morissa's door. There were fewer poor men with gold pans, more speculators and businessmen, some with families of small children, and maple dressers and square pianos for something more permanent than the swift, hot flash of the placer boom. Sturdy hard-rock miners came in, and the gamblers and the fancy women were less tawdry and less receptive to the charm of Fish Head. So he moved back to the bridge, but with no news of Tom Reeder since he left the man at the post hospital at Sidney. The young antelope had vanished almost at once, probably into some empty frying pan. A lot of trash was coming in down there, old Fish said disapprovingly.

Morissa fed him young grouse with fresh bread for the gravy and a dish of lettuce from her little garden. He hung around to comment on the sights he had seen as he wiped the tall hat he always brought out for the passing coaches.

"It is becoming most effete up in the Hills," he said. "I must find some less decadent camp, some Eldorado more worthy a true prospector's talents—"

"You haven't the footwear for winter around Deadwood," Morissa teased. "Not where it goes down to thirty below zero, as all our friends up there could tell you." But if she thought she might hear news of Tris Polk, she was disappointed.

93

"Ah, I am a lover of nature, an attentive swain to all her changing moods—" was all he answered.

But whatever Fish Head thought about Deadwood, many remembered uneasily that every dollar of gold taken from the earth up there was still the legal property of the Indians. So another conference for the purchase of the Black Hills was arranged.

Long before the conference date the bridge carried travelers headed to Red Cloud Agency, many of them contractors of pants and blankets, of sugar, coffee, and beef, and of wagons, plows, and hoes. Morissa sat on her Appaloosa beyond the bridge a ways as the army ambulances with the commission passed, and the fast rigs of the contractors. She recalled the stink of the salt pork going to the Indians earlier in the summer, and wondered what they could hope to receive now.

"All gathering like buzzards to the kill—" Robin said sourly, perhaps because he had returned to go up, too, hoping for a little work there after a while. The council must turn out better than last year. There had been an hour or two then when none of the commission to buy the Hills, not even the generals, hoped to get out alive, so angry were the young warriors at this talk of selling their country. But this year the wild young Sioux were away north with Crazy Horse and wouldn't be riding around the outskirts of the conference painted and stripped to the breechclout, waving their rifles and crying for blood. This time the conference would meet inside the agency stockade, with bayoneted troops all around, and cannon.

Morissa went up with Sid Martin. If he was to make anything out of his cattle he had to see about beef contracts. With this horse collar that she kept on him, he felt safer with his doctor along. So Morissa took a wild ride in Sid Martin's top buggy behind a team of calico bronchs that he managed by half-standing at the dashboard, herding them along in the general direction with whip and line. Morissa's little velvet hat was over her nose one minute and flying back the next, but the doubletrees held and they got there, the horses lathered white, eyes still rolling for something to send them off again.

"I did a better job on your neck than I realized," Morissa said ruefully as she took Sid Martin's hand to step from the buggy.

There was a post dance that night, and the next day she went down to the Sioux conference with the men. The stockade was full, mostly with whites, for no Indian except the chiefs and headmen was permitted inside. The commissioners talked a long time, and then one blanketed Sioux after another rose from their council circle on the floor, the oratory interrupted by many "Hous!" of approval from the rest. They talked but they would not sign for the sale, and so the third day all visitors were sent out and the gates of the stockade bolted. There

94

the chiefs must remain until they did sign, and their families, their women and children outside, would get no flour or meat, nothing at all until the pen was touched. It was a difficult time for Chief Red Cloud. Only ten years ago he was powerful enough to force the Army out of the Bozeman trail forts that were set up to protect another gold rush through the Indian country promised to his people so long as grass shall grow and water flow.

But his people were trapped on this little island, this little agency in the shadow of the soldier cannon and the hunger the white man brought. With his face like the eternal granite of the Hills the chief arose, drew his blanket about him and led the row of silent men to the table where the white paper lay, and that night the keening of women along White River was as for a great man dead.

Morissa heard them and had no response for Sid Martin's elation that now there would be really fat contracts from the money the Indians got for the Black Hills. There would be contracts unless the Senate reneged and decided to pay the Sioux nothing for the sale, now that Crook's army was safe in Deadwood.

"I wonder if I am becoming an Indian lover—" Morissa said on the way home.

"It don't matter now, with the Hills bought up. But Indian lovers been run out of the country—"

"Like settlers?" Morissa asked slowly.

For a moment the cattleman looked at the girl beside him, turning his whole body, his head still so firmly held in her brown leather collar. "Ahh, Miss Morissa, I can't see you goin' on living there on that open range, like some rustler building up a spread with rope and running iron. —But I ain't like some," he added thoughtfully. "If you really wanted to live there, I'd be just the man to humor you."

Morissa had to laugh this away, and said no more about land or Indians. After the wild team had taken Sid across the bridge and on south, she went to the station for her mail. There were a lot of freighters gathered for some visiting in the whisky store. They looked in her direction under their dusty hats, saying something about Sid Martin among themselves. Maybe he was cutting out both Tris Polk and the Lieutenant—

So the young doctor gathered up her mail and hurried out and across the bridge that stood over the gold-touched river of evening. Not until she got inside the door and had her lamp lit did she notice a thin packet among the letters. Inside was a birthday hand card from Allston Hoyt, the hand carved from thin ivory and holding a silken bouquet of fall flowers. There was nothing to indicate the sender except the bold broadstroke of her address, not a word added to the greeting, not even

95

his name. Yet it was a kindness and Morissa's throat tightened as she touched the lovely satin asters. But suddenly she recalled how he knew her birthdate—from the genealogical search his sister had made.

With one swift motion of her strong fingers she tried to rip the card in two, but it did not tear like paper would, only cracked into slivers of ivory in her hand.

VIII

THEN ONE NIGHT THE GRAY CAT CAME SCRATCHING AT THE DOOR and crawled with frosted whiskers under the cover at Morissa's breast. In the morning there was a white rime over all the river valley, and as the sun climbed the morning glories at the window let their leaves droop, cooked, and the portulacas that she had moved were as though scalded with the teakettle. But it was a fine golden fall, the upland tawny and red-clumped where the prairie rosebushes sat close to the earth. The buckbrush browned, too, the berries waxen white, the deer leaping from the patches to stand off against the hillside and look as Morissa rode by.

The rifle was as certainly in her scabbard or across her buggy bed now as her pill sack went along—always on longer trips during the Indian scare, but even on short rides since one early morning when she came driving back from another typhoid patient down at Redington's. She had been idling along through a rocky pass as dawn cleared, looking off toward the shadowy plum thickets where she got a bushel for preserves last week, and wondered about the wild grapes.

Suddenly the horses had reared, lunged sideways, and snapped the tongue off. The next jump drove the broken end of the tongue into the ground and shot the buggy up into the air. It went over forward, throwing Morissa clear. The horses kicked the doubletrees to pieces and bolted back down the rutted trail, with the doctor still clinging to the lines, dragged face down through chuck holes and stones and brush, battered and torn. In danger of losing her eyes, even her life, and with just sense enough to squeeze her lids tight and turn her head to the side, she hung on, her arms ripped and her face and throat, too, until it seemed she could not let go any more and would certainly be destroyed. But finally the horses began to slow a little and then they stopped, blowing, worn out. A long time Morissa could only lie still and when she managed to collect herself she was afraid of scaring the team into another runaway. At last she stumbled to her feet, bleeding everywhere it seemed, pounded, skinned, and lacerated, but without broken bones. She got the horses quieted, Nellie first and then Kiowa, and tied securely to separate pines, still panting, lathered, and nervous as she had never seen them before.

Back at the buggy she found her rifle that had been flung out, and her medical bag, too, with only a few vials broken. Then she looked around for something that could have frightened the bays so. She found it in a soft spot of earth where the horses had bolted—the pad mark of a big cat, the track larger than her hand. Swiftly she looked all around and up to the rocks above her. There, on a ledge over the road and not fifty feet away, a mountain lion watched her lazily, the long tawny body half-raised but still slack, relaxed.

Slowly the girl started to retreat, moving backward, an inch, two, always in the direction of the buggy and the rifle. The cat watched without alarm or anger or much interest, blinking like an indolent sleepy yellow tom. The rising sun that touched the rocks above him moved down, sharpening the gold of the magnificent head and the tensing shoulders. But at last the girl's exploring foot found the buggy wheel and then her hand touched the cold steel of the rifle.

As she drew the gun up carefully, slowly, to aim, the lion seemed to sense what this was and rose, still easily, however, without apparent menace or alarm. But it seemed that he whirled just as she pulled the trigger, leaping as the shot roared out, and started up the bluff face. Then he was gone, Morissa too inexperienced to know if the leap was from the bullet. With the rifle clutched by the grip she scrambled up the ledge as well as she could in her stiffness, only vaguely recalling the danger from a wounded lion. But she slowed when she saw fresh drops of blood curling dry sand about themselves, small, bright inside, probably from the lung. She followed more cautiously now, but through brush and pine needles she lost the trail, so she returned to the buggy.

By notching the broken pieces of the tongue to hold the wire always in the buggy box with her spade and the lantern, she spliced the tongue together, reinforced by the light strips of steel she carried for emergency splints. Then she went to kick earth carefully over the cat tracks, hoping the scent would be gone by now. With Nellie, the quieter of the bays, she pulled the buggy back up on its crazy wheels, hitched up and then led the nervous team through the pass. Finally she climbed ·in, so sore she could scarcely lift her foot to the step. By the time she reached the bridge she was in serious pain even through the morphia she had to take. When the man came to lift the toll arm he took one look at her and dropped it back down.

"Miss Morissy!" he exclaimed, and called out, "Hey, Help! Doc's been hurt!" as he got her out and into the stage station. There he brought coffee and a washbasin as the few early customers trooped in curiously from the bar.

Not until she saw their faces did Morissa realize how she must look, her face bloody and dirt-caked, skinned and torn, the sleeves ripped from her bleeding arms. Only her cap and the stout denim of the jumper she always wore on cool night drives had saved her head, her throat, her breast from being stripped to the bone. Before she was done with the story the young men around were faunching to start after the lion, but the old hunters like Etty advised a little wait. Let him stiffen from his wound, at least until they could get trail dogs from that Englishman visiting over at the Tanner ranch.

It was nearing noon when Allan Barrow rode in. He looked at Morissa's bandages in reserved astonishment. He called his dogs up— liver-spotted, little more than a good mouthful each for the lion—and with Etty and Lieutenant Larman led the hunters out, enough rifles and ammunition along for an Indian uprising.

Morissa had to turn back before they got half a mile out and wait for their return toward evening, with the mountain lion across the back of Etty's pack mare. The wounded cat hadn't gone far, only a couple of miles before he crawled under a big rock. Good thing Morissa didn't catch up with him. A gut-shot lion was bad as a grizzly.

Allan Barrow had a traveling photographer take a picture of Morissa standing over the dead lion with her Winchester. She had removed some of the bandages but she still looked like the victim of a mauling.

"This will make my good relatives realize they have exiled me to a very wild and dangerous wilderness," Allan said in satisfaction.

Afterward he had a long table set up at Clarke's for the hunters and Morissa. The next day the young doctor wondered at herself. She had acted as proud and show-offy as a ten-year-old with his first 'possum. Maybe it was the wine with the venison. But she would have a nice rug for her fireplace and the Britisher was taking her to Tanner's dance, if her face wasn't too scabby.

Three days later Tris Polk came, driving a handsome yellow-wheeled buggy with white-stockinged blacks, the kind of horses he liked. "Same stock as Cimarron, fine and showy," he said, "but you know the old saying, 'Four white feet, feed 'em to the crows.'"

Morissa laughed as easily as she could with her healing face and the hurt of the man's absence, and her own foolish and undeniable joy at seeing him again, even if the buggy was purchased for Gilda Ross. They looked the new team over together, the beautiful heads and flaring nostrils, the large luminous eyes with fire burning there—almost like Arabians, Tris said, but a hand and a half taller. The white-tasseled buggy bridles were certainly grand on them.

They talked about Morissa's runaway with her team, about what was going on around Sidney and the trail, the news from Deadwood and about the Philadelphia Centennial celebration, the World's Fair, that Tris had hoped to take in while he was in Chicago with the Forsons. Then there was the Presidential campaign too—anything except the mention of Morissa's move to the north of the river to a homestead and her start in what looked like a pretty permanent settler layout plunk in the middle of the cattle country.

"I hear you patched up Owen's shattered leg fine, and have Sid Martin planning to ride in the fall roundup."

Morissa raised her hands in despair. "You Western men! Sid will probably get his head snapped off again, and live through that too. Next time I'll wire him together. From now on I'm going to nail all the broken bones together—"

So they talked, a little awkwardly, mostly of impersonalities, and in the afternoon they drove out to the Wild Cat range where Morissa shot the lion. Through Tris's spyglass they saw a bighorn sheep far up on the gray bluffs with her young standing behind her, and farther off two rams, their great curling horns like a vague darkness over their heads.

"Proud, noble creatures, aren't they?" Morissa said, a choke in her throat as the rams turned and leapt over a crevasse, stopped against the sky a moment and then were gone, the mother and her young off the other way. "My, I love this country," she exclaimed, holding out her arms, rubbing the inside of one and then the other, where the excitement flowed.

"But your doctoring'll fall off to nothing in the winter, when the travel slows down."

"The country will still be here."

"With thirty-five below zero, and a blizzard wind—"

They returned through the evening sun that lay orange along the far ridges of the northeast. But there was a chill at the river. Two antelope grazed beside the trail, tamer than all summer, and soon the sky would be full of geese going south.

At her place Tris drew his team off the trail and stopped up beside her little creek dam. Morissa sat quiet, holding herself ready for the complaints against her, the protests and the anger. But the rancher looked down along the little ditch to the golden-leafed young cottonwoods of the yard, some already as tall as the low sod house, and to the flower beds, browned, except the asters and the petunias, that had started again since the frost, with bright green grass around them.

"Water makes a lot of difference in this country," he said.

"Yes, all this wide valley could be fruitful as—"

"I know, fruitful as the Nile. But it would mean the end of cattle here, the finest business in the world."

And to this Morissa had no reply. It didn't matter, for today was like a home-coming, with Tris back.

There was a little Indian scare when the lightning of a fall storm showed a pack of Indians fording the river, or at least one man thought so and rode like a leather-chapped Revere through the bridge settlement, yelling, "The redskins are out!"

Private Charley Adams hurried to get Morissa but she had a typhoid patient and couldn't leave him, certainly not with Indians around. So the troopers brought a litter and carried him through the chilly rain to the blockhouse beside the bridge. Morning dawned clear and undisturbed, and there was nothing except the half-obliterated tracks of unshod ponies, mounted horses, the station master said. Probably horse thieves.

But it might have been Indians, perhaps fleeing trouble, for two days later word came that Chief Red Cloud had been caught sneaking his people away north to Crazy Horse and the entire band was disarmed and dismounted by the troops. Eddie Ellis came down, making the news an excuse for a visit. He told Morissa he had gone with the scouts that swept away the pony herd at dawn, before the Indians knew they were surrounded. Red Cloud's wife even had her chickens along; he heard the rooster's crow just before they struck the pony herd. Got them all, even the Chief's parade horse given him by the government. A few were turned over to the military at Robinson but most just got lost on the way there, up some draw or down a canyon. Eddie laughed. "I got six myself. They didn't belong to nobody any more."

The whole kaboodle of Indians was driven back to the agency afoot, carrying the bundles they could, losing most of the rest. Morissa guessed that the new post surgeon would have a lot of sick children and adults too on his hands, with winter close and no shelter or blankets for thousands of Indians. She said something of this to Lorette but the little breed woman only drew her blanket up over her bowed head and held her Siouan silence.

That evening Morissa and Eddie saw two men shot in a drunken brawl at Etty's, the outcome of an old trail herd grudge, it was said. She was touched with the way Eddie threw himself before her when the first bullet buried itself in the sod wall.

Truly the bright October weather, the finest Morissa had ever seen, was no time of tranquillity here, nor in herself. During the summer the sand bars of the river had pushed their impatient backs up through the tepid waters, most of their nakedness soon covered by a furring of water-sprouted cottonwoods. More and more travel had avoided the toll by fording the wide, sandy Platte, derisively described as half a mile wide and an inch deep in the wry humor common to the more precarious regions of man. It was curious how Morissa already felt herself tied to this stream, first in the turbulent gray anger of May, and in the placid summertime, too, even to the newer sand bars that were only thin layerings over quicksand, all potential buffalo springs, as the cowboys called them, waiting just under the yellowish surface.

"The water'll come boilin' up if you take a few fast steps in one spot, the sand shakin' under your heels—" one told Morissa and took her to an empty new strip to demonstrate. Almost at once the gray sandy water boiled up about his boots as it had the hoofs of the great herds of buffalo all the summers that the Platte went dry, their water-hungry noses drawing them to mill around on the empty bed of the river until the water came, welling up in buffalo springs.

How close her own turbulence lay under the smooth sand bars of her existence Morissa realized the day she saw a man get out of the coach and stand, back to her, so like Allston Hoyt that her heart knocked against her ribs once and seemed to stop. She had turned and hastened away without her mail and afterward she did not know if she had really hidden in her dusky sod house, or merely retreated there to await the lover. But Allston did not come, no one came, and the stage with fresh horses thundered over the long bridge and away northward past her place. In the despondent time afterward she recalled the doctor at medical school who denounced women in public life, all public life. They were too weak to resist the pressing lover and must have the constant presence and protection of a strong male hand, father or husband. So it had happened to her mother, and so it could have happened to her today, not at fifteen, as to Lorna Kirk, but at twenty-five, and with a worldly training.

By late fall the leading stage company of the Cheyenne-Black Hills trail seemed convinced that the time for romanticizing in their business was over. With the Indians sold out of the Hills, the prospects justified a practical, long-range approach. So the stage owners moved many of their coaches down to the safer and shorter Sidney trail, using Clarke's facilities. Morissa saw their first coach draw up at the bridge and watched the awe and envy too for the guards, these veteran shotguns who had fought their way regularly through the Robbers Roost country.

Winter cut down the adventurous travel and outside of a few accidents and a little pneumonia, influenza, and smallpox, Morissa had time to study and to carry on a correspondence with doctors longer on the frontier. Tris was away much of the time but there was skating with the Lieutenant, sometimes with his friends from Fort Robinson or the

101

Sidney post, a big fire burning on the bank, the red reflected on the glassy ice of the river, and an occasional dance with Tris. But mostly people said, "Don't you find it very dull?" waiting for the tenderfoot lady doc to pull out. Even Robin and Jackie said it Christmas time, the two days she spent with them in a bleak little hotel in the middle of the state. "We're a family; we have to spend at least part of the holidays together—" she told them gaily. But Robin knew it was to forget last year and the happiness with Allston Hoyt.

The winter was a mild one even to the Easterners. The coaches ran on schedule and with the range open the bulls worked through instead of giving way to the horses and mules that could paw snow for feed and, with a little grain, usually kept the freight moving. There was a little St. Patrick's dance planned at Clarke's but Morissa missed it. She was far away, near the place where Sid Martin's herd stampeded last June. A note had come by stage saying a man was dying of pneumonia in a soddy along the north side of the big flat there. Morissa was uneasy about starting out alone, with the morning sun so curiously white, but at the blockhouse she found that Charley Adams was off with a scouting party for some Indian herds reported stolen.

So she left a note asking him to keep an eye on her convalescents and got ready to go out alone, but she drew on a heavy pair of woolen pants of Robin's instead of a skirt, and high overshoes. She put his old buffalo coat into the buggy and a sack of provisions, too, in case the man was out of groceries, with no ranch or trail anywhere near. Then, with her rifle and her compass she settled the bays into their steady little trot up the worn trail, watching for the angle-off into the sandhills. The day was mild and dusty, the bull trains plodding as thick as midsummer, the men walking beside them in short sheepskin coats thrown open.

By the time Morissa left the trail the sun was gone and a thin rain had started. By two o'clock it had frozen to sleet and the sharpening wind veered toward the northwest. The sleet became fine sharp snow that searched out every crack of the buggy curtains and ran about the horses' feet, piling into long trailing drifts. Morissa shook the snow from the buffalo coat, wishing she had come horseback.

Gradually all the holes and little washouts were covered over and the buggy lurched and swayed in the rising blizzard. As the snow deepened to the hubs, the horses began to plunge to get through, jerking against the light doubletrees that Morissa knew might go any moment. Twice they refused a drift and the doctor had to wallow out into the powdery snow and, with the buggy whipstock to plumb the loose depths, lead Nellie around gullies that would have swallowed buggy and team. Finally she had to stay at the heads of the horses to keep them moving at all, floundering breathlessly in the buffalo coat, hip deep.

When the whipping blizzard was so thick that she could hardly breathe standing still, she stopped at what seemed a sheltered little hollow and unhitched. She rolled the provisions and her rifle into the buggy robe, and fastened the pack on Kiowa the best she could with the lines and tugs. Holding her pill bag and her lantern, and very bulky in her buffalo coat, she climbed on the gentler Nellie and started away into the roaring storm, leading Kiowa by his hitching rope tied to Nellie's hames. All Morissa could hope to do was hold the horses in the general direction of the wide flat that she had found once before, but in bright sunlight, and somehow locate a new little sod house built near the seepage springs. If she missed it—but she wouldn't think about that now, for that one little shack was the last in all the empty region of the sandhills ahead of her, and a sick man was alone inside, probably too weak to keep a fire going.

Even so she tried to turn back to the trail once, hoping somehow to strike a storm-corraled bull train with covered wagons, or even a wagon of gold seekers. But no amount of whipping would hold the horses into the stinging blizzard. Then she remembered that the team had been up at Sid Martin's temporary cowcamp, so she took the desperate chance that she must; she let Nellie have her head, particularly when she saw that the young mare didn't drift downwind but worked leftward, sidling into the storm. The cold was very sharp now. Morissa's foot and all her leg on the windy side was numb and wooden when the white dusk of early evening began to settle. Soon she must admit that they had passed the flat and were lost in the big sandhills, without house or tree for a hundred miles, even the buffalo and cow chips, the only fuel, deep under snow. Soon she must find a place out of the wind and hope she could tie the horses down, hog-tie them close together and crawl in between for their body heat before she was too exhausted. Even then they might be drifted over together, frozen and smothered as Robin told of whole bull trains. Why hadn't she gone with him as he asked, or to Allston, no matter if there was to be no wedding?

Twice the horses stopped and would hardly go on in spite of all her wooden kicks and urgings. Suddenly Nellie's snow-caked head seemed to come up; together the horses turned and, side by side, plunged through a breast-deep drift almost into the wind. Morissa could only turn her face from the storm and gasp for breath, letting her horses go their way. Then Kiowa whinnied and they both stopped, close up against a wall that seemed to be sod under the drifting snow, with a horse vaguely reaching a head over to sniff the newcomers.

Sobbing her relief that they had found shelter, any shelter now, Morissa slid awkwardly into the snow and, dragging the horses along, started to plow along the corral wall on her wooden feet. Against it was a soddy and Morissa pushed the door open into a dead chilliness and the smell of dreadful disease. Stiffly she tied the horses and went inside to light her lantern.

A man lay on a wall bunk, half conscious. A touch of her frozen fingers to the brow and the pulse, the thin tendons on the fleshless wrists already like cold steel wire, and the doctor could have cried again. Instead she asked about fuel. At the slow turn of the man's eyes she plunged out into the storm and found a snowy cow-chip pile against the house. With the fire going she looked at the wasted, exhausted man and tried to give him a little hot tea, a little brandy with her thawing hands that ached so as the blood returned. She was very clumsy, but he could not have swallowed at the best. The gray, opaque eyes held a sadness and an apology, the apology of the dying, and so she arranged him more comfortably and then sat half the night beside his body.

Finally when the man was like a frozen creature, she decided to put him outside for the long wait before burial, in a sort of return to the cleansing elements from his house of disease. She rolled him in the bulky buffalo robe but thin as he was she could not lift him, and so she used the old tarp from his bed instead.

When she went out to look after her team the man's two horses came to her, as though expecting a little grain. Cautiously she moved around the soddy into the blinding storm, careful not to lose touch with the wall until she found what she hoped—a wheel, a wagon up close, and under the covered bows a sack with a little ear corn. She drew out eight, and let the horses take the ears from her mittened hand, her head laid against the snowy necks for a moment in gratitude to them all.

Although still half-frozen and shaking she propped the door open a while to let the clean blizzard air sweep through the evil place, the snow popping and steaming against the stove. Then she threw out the soiled soogans and dug the contaminated earth away under the wall bunk, filling the hole with the clean, powdery gray ashes of cow chips that the man had raked from the stove as long as he had the strength.

She melted snow and boiled the tin cups and the rest, and then scrubbed the frying pan and the iron bean pot with earth until they gleamed. Afterward she fried a couple of strips of bacon and a little baking-powder bread. Finally she rolled up in her buffalo coat and slept, too weary for self-blaming, for sorrow or regret.

On the fourth day the sun came out clear. The broad flat valley was the same pure glistening white as the first time she saw it, in hail, and Sid Martin with his neck broken. Today there was no relief from the glare except the dark corral, the horses, and several deer moving in the buckbrush off eastward, plunging through the drifts to clear a few clinging dead leaves. They would be easy targets for Morissa's rifle but she did not bring it out. Prairie chickens flew over in a silvery flock toward the wind-bared ridge to the south, their cackling like busy, friendly women, loud in the frosty stillness. So she took the horses over there, too, hobbling Nellie and Kiowa with the halter ropes and turning the others loose. She would have to leave the man's team behind, but not to die in the sod corral. The horses grazed hungrily with no urge to drift, her hobbled team pawing awkwardly, and by two o'clock Morissa was glad she had given them this little time to eat for a gray wall of flying cloud was moving along the north, and little curls of snow began to run over the long drifts.

She was bundling up to go out for the bays when a herd of horses appeared along the barer ridges to the northeast, running fast, throwing the snow high. First she thought they were wild but then she saw horsebackers close, closer than any wild mustang would permit—probably one of the stolen Indian herds the troopers were looking for.

As they came up even with the four horses along the slope, one of the riders turned to wrangle them in. He whooped the unhobbled ones into a run toward the herd for all Morissa's angry shouting and waving her cap in protest. Then he turned back for the bay team and started them up the ridge too. But their hobbled movement was so slow he stopped and was surely going to cut them free, leave the doctor afoot here in the snowbound hills. Furious, Morissa ran for her rifle, steadied it against the doorjamb and put a bullet into the snow at the man's feet and then a second one before the smoke spread blue around the doorway. The man turned to look and the three driving the herd also stopped, one of them jerking something long, a rifle, from a scabbard. This was the showdown, Morissa knew, and she fired once more, this time to strike among the close running bunch of horses. Apparently it nicked one, for the herd exploded in a great burst of snow and scattered off southward, the long mustang manes and tails flying high and cloudy in the wind, the horsebackers hard after them.

But the man on the slope showed fight. He swung back into his saddle and spurred his gray horse through the drifts straight for the sod shack. Morissa had to make a quick decision. If she could put a bullet very close over his head, but without hitting him, he might decide it wasn't worth the risk. She shot, but her hand was unsteady and the charge went wide, too plainly the aim of a poor shot. The man kept coming, with a red spurt from his pistol and a bullet that splintered the doorpost beside her.

Now Morissa Kirk had to realize that this was like a desperate emergency operation, with the stake apparently a life—her life. And as in such an emergency she calmed to the task at once and aimed on the horse plunging straight for her through the deep drifts and very close. She drew a careful bead on the chest where a miss could do no more than break the man's leg, although she knew now that she might well have to kill or be killed.

So she shot. The horse pitched forward, but the man stayed with the saddle as the gray pawed himself up, reared and floundered, then recovered and ran crazily back toward the hill, plainly dying. One of the riders driving the herd had turned and was headed toward Morissa but now he spurred over the wind-blown slope to pick up the man who cowered behind his down gray in the snow. Together they whipped away on the one horse, but they emptied a warning revolver toward the soddy, one bullet making a neat hole in the stovepipe.

When they were gone Morissa leaned against the door, trembling, the stink of black powder sharp to her nose. Then it occurred to her that the men might return, come up from all sides, and so with the butcher knife she dug gun slits through the sod near each corner, watching while she dug the holes, her hands shaking even after she was done.

The house grew very cold for she didn't dare go out for fuel any more than for the horses, afraid of rifles behind every knoll. She could see Nellie moving with her hobbled jump, quieted and eating again, and after a while Kiowa was back beside her too. Now if the wind would die towards night, and the clouds stay back so she could find the team in the darkness—

As soon as dusk moved out of the low hills Morissa tramped snow into the wool of her buffalo coat to whiten it; then, with corn in her pocket and her rifle across her arm, she slipped out. The cold burned her nose; the drifts creaked under her feet, the sound like an echo from someone following. A dozen times she stopped, stooping low, but there was no shot from anywhere, no sound in the white starlight except a wolf's call and the noise of the hobbled horses, still feeding, moving in the cold. Nellie nickered softly and came forward, smelling the ear of corn Morissa held out to her.

Cautiously, walking hidden between the two horses in the dusk, Morissa returned to the soddy. It was still empty, so she brought the team inside, the protesting Nellie first, snorting at the smell of fire and death. After a while the warier Kiowa followed his teammate through the open door. With no light except the fire of the little stove, Morissa watched the gun slits, wishing she had Etty's loud barking old Blaze dog here.

The waiting depressed the weary doctor, with the poor man lying frozen beside the sod wall outside. The drive to self-preservation had carried her to a willingness to shoot, even to kill this afternoon, but now that was gone and the doubt of all her presence and premise here settled down like some dark and sooty cloud. It brought mistrust of every action, not only her stubborn decision to remain, a lone woman in the wilderness, but the impulse to come West at all, and behind that the foolish notion that she could ever have become the wife of a Hoyt. Even doubts of her decision to become a doctor gathered like dark buzzards to brood in the snowbound soddy.

But this final destruction Morissa Kirk would not entertain. No matter what else her self-hatred might attack this night, her profession was beyond question, sacred. A daughter of Aesculapius, Fish Head had called her, and the thought of the old fraud's posturing made her laugh aloud in her strain. Nellie stirred from sleep and rattled her halter as she reached toward the woman. Morissa went to her, rubbed the soft nose and Kiowa's, too, then looked all around the empty night snow and hoped that Fish Head was under cover somewhere, and that the man who had brought up the drags of the horse herd today was not Eddie Ellis even though it looked like him, a little. Morissa knew he had lost his job at the Indian agency, or given it up, probably given it up as Jackie might, with the vacillation of the unformed, and no one to advise him, to steady him as the goodness in Robin might steady his son.

Afterward Morissa wondered why she somehow always included Jackie with Eddie Ellis.

Dawn came clear, with the sliver of late moon white as ice. It took a long time to get the dead man on Nellie, shying and fractious, but finally Morissa put the frozen body into empty corn sacks with the smell of grain still in them. Then, while Nellie ate the last ears of corn in a cloud of frosty breath, the doctor eased the man across the mare's back from the corral wall and tied him awkwardly but firmly between the hames and the crupper. With her rifle handy, Morissa started away on Kiowa, leading the mare. She rode a saddle now. Just before dawn she had gone boldly out and got it from the robber's dead horse. She had looked for a brand, too, but if there was one it was on the underside.

She angled along the barer ridges toward the nearest trail station. In a snow-filled canyon she saw what looked like a whole bull train drifted with the storm, a few heads and frozen backs showing, eagles and buzzards already circling against the pale spring blue, and a wolf waiting on the ridge until she passed, his tail up like a plume.

The doctor wondered about the other outsiders in the country, tenderfeet made complacent by the easy winter and the deceptive warmth of the morning before the storm, but mostly she fought the weariness from her night of watching and the glare of the snow that blinded her eyes behind the protective smudging of soot on her cheekbones. Yet she had to keep going and by the compass, with everything strange in this white sweep of drifts. When she finally reached a little log station her throat was raw and swollen, closing as with quinsy, and she was shaking. But first she had to look at a man found unconscious by the herders hunting for their drifted bulls. He was thawed out now and in bad shape. The whole ends of both his feet were dying with gangrene and at least three fingers of one hand would have to go.

"The trail to the Platte isn't open?" the doctor asked.

"No, not even a horsebacker over it yet."

So she gave the man an opiate, took a big and not too hopeful dose of quinine for her cold, and slept for three hours to break the chills and steady her hand. When she was called, the man was delirious, so with the help of a stranded freighter who had seen a lot of blood in the Civil War, she amputated what she knew she must. "—I just can't take as much as might be advisable. I can't bear to leave a man here with no feet at all," she said, holding her voice steady as she worked swiftly, too swiftly.

And when it was done and the patient semiconscious, she set herself to watch through the night. "I'll stay the three worst days. If he seems to be making it, I'll go home and he's to be brought down as soon as the trail's open. In the meantime, if more inflammation shows up, rush him down to me any way you can, or get me and I'll take off what I have to—"

"Yeh, friend of mine had three sawin's on one leg. Finally took it off clear to here," the freighter said, his hand laid grimly across from the groin, "but I'd a rather seen him in the bone yard."

"Never rather dead," the doctor in Morissa protested. "But I have hopes for him. This is a tough, healthy country and he doesn't look like a tenderfoot."

"No, been freighting for years. Storms like this one could catch anybody, if luck ran that way. Joe here—his horse stepped in a prairie-dog hole in the snow and snapped off a front leg so he had to hoof it five miles against the wind and didn't quite make it. Could happen to anybody."

Ten days after she drove out of the north valley Morissa came riding back on Nellie, leading Kiowa—the first traveler on the trail except Clarke's express riders. Most of the ridges were baring now, dark in soggy moisture, the river a gray and ice-caked channel through the snow-drifted valley, with the yellow bluffs and the dark pines along the south, and Chimney Rock an unbelievable spire, like something from a fairy landscape.

The whole population was out to meet Morissa at the north end of the bridge, soldiers and everybody from Fish Head up, even Clarke, who had come in from Sidney horseback to count his losses. "Never go out on a long winter call alone again, my dear," he said, holding the worn, snow-burned girl in his arms a moment. "We can't have anything happen to our lady doc. Why, you know, four men, old-timers in the West, froze to death in the Sidney region alone, and no telling how many more over the country. One was out hunting the bighorns you saw in the Wild Cats—not ten miles from here."

As he talked, mostly to cover his anxiety, Morissa looked around the emotional faces, the watery eyes of old Etty, and the tear on the quiet, reticent cheek of his breed wife.

"It's like coming home from a far, far journey—" she finally said, and kissed the brown cheek of Lorette's baby. Then slowly she went to her house with the Lieutenant walking beside her to hear the story of the horse thieves. The two went along the path worn by those who cared for her stock while she was away, bluecoats from the post leading the two bays, but remaining well behind.

IX

Outlawry fattens on an increase in gold, and everybody said that 1877 would double, perhaps triple, the two million dollars taken from the Hills last year despite the many alarms of mines gone dry. All this dust had to be carried out, and by now the banks of Deadwood needed large supplies of currency, mostly brought in from their financial connections at Cheyenne. The March blizzard that isolated the Hills for two weeks, and almost starved Deadwood, was hardly reduced to dirty drifts, the dead and missing not all counted, when Sam Bass and his roadagents stopped the currency coach from Cheyenne just outside of the gulch.

Morissa knew Sam. He was around Clarke's bridge with a trail herd from Texas for over a month last summer and there the doctor saw him often after Eddie Ellis brought the man over to have a bullet cut out of his knee.

"Been in there for some time, Doc, but it's just worked up an ache on my cutting horse lately—" he said, surprisingly soft-spoken for his shaggy appearance.

But Morissa remembered the extra, the secret gun he carried, one on his hip and the other in a holster under his shirt, swinging in his armpit like a gambler's. He had offered her a very good saddle horse in payment, too large a fee, but naturally without a bill of sale. The doctor shook her head and took a couple of silver dollars, about all he had left from the cockfights—betting on a surly bird that Fish Head had carried up from Sidney in a gunny sack to pit against Etty's. When the knee was healed Sam bought the doctor a cup of coffee and fry cakes at Clarke's while she waited for the blacksmith to trim Nellie's split hoof. Sam was waiting too—for the herd to start north to Deadwood. He wanted to stay around the bridge, he said, but there were no jobs, and Eddie knew somebody up the trail—

Now there was this story of the holdup, with much laughing and slapping of thighs, even though the driver, well liked at the bridge, had been killed. Seemed Bass and the rest of his scrub, raked-together gang drove the killer out afterward because he scared the stage horses off with a bale of currency big as a bedroll and a bucketful of gold coins in the coach. So he went back to Fly Speck Billy.

It reminded Morissa of the old stories of Scottish border robbers that her mother liked to tell, always ending with the same words: "A boaster and a liar are canny kin but a highwayman will tread into a well as quick as a blind ould sow."

Sam and his ragged gang had loafed around the Deadwood saloons since the blizzard. It was suspected they were one of the outfits watching for the currency shipment from Cheyenne, but not that they wouldn't go off the doorstep for the holdup. While the coach was delayed by mud and snowbanks, Sam's straw boss managed to shoot himself in the foot. The man substituted to make the plans went out into the moonlight to the first narrow curve coming into the gulch. He took along half a case of whisky to celebrate and to keep off the chill of waiting and got drunk.

When the full moon stood almost overhead for midnight, Bass, disgusted, signaled the outfit home but just then they heard the thunder of the Concord coach on the frosty air as it came around the bend, the white horses always used on the run into town making a fine show in the moonlight, their silver trappings bright. With a gun in each hand, Sam Bass stepped out into the road and ordered the driver to halt. There was no arguing with the hardware, or with all the men in the brushy rocks and timber on each side, and so the driver yelled "Whoa!" and leaned back on the lines.

But another of the men had done a little celebrating and came crashing out of the brush with a loud roar to grab at a bit of the lead team. Frightened, the horses reared back into the others, setting them all into the air. Then they bolted and he emptied his sawed-off shotgun into the driver, who fell dead from the box as the horses thundered uncontrolled past Sam and along the narrow winding cliff trail leading into Deadwood, the high Concord rocking and swaying between bluff and canyon. A passenger riding the box grabbed the lines and got the horses together just as they were headed off a sharp turn into the tree-tops far below.

Although it was midnight, the whole town was out as usual to greet the stage. The sheriff got a posse moving at once but they found nothing except the dead driver on the frosty, glistening road. Later they picked up one of the Bass outfit in town but none of the passengers could identify him. The rest had sobered enough to hit for the canyons.

"Your old friend sure botched that job, Doc—went at it like a green-horn badman," Owen told Morissa down at Clarke's. He was at Dead-wood that night, even managed to get his stiff leg over a horse to ride with the posse, but mostly they warmed their bellies against the bar at Number 10 and talked about stringin' 'em up.

"Didn't the outlaws get any money?" the practical Gwinnie asked.

"Hell, no, but plenty fancy cussin' from Sam, I hear—"

The dead man got a fine funeral—carried to the Cheyenne cemetery in a stagecoach drawn by six white horses with silver trappings. Owen and several drivers from the Sidney trail went up with Henry Clarke. Morissa too. She wanted to see the work with the storm victims that a doctor up there was doing, saving many from amputation. He offered her a partnership and even though she had heard nothing from Tris since before the blizzard, she decided to stay at the bridge a little longer.

At Sidney Morissa went to look in on Tom Reeder. He was dead, died during the storm. "Nothing like violent weather to usher a man into the world or out of it," the surgeon said. Morissa Kirk nodded. But this was more than a patient lost; this had been her first victory in the wilderness.

When she got home the sheriff from Sidney finally came up to look at the saddle Morissa took from the dead horse up in the Snake Creek flat. She wondered why he hadn't answered her report but as she talked to the sunburnt officer tilted back in one of her chairs, Morissa discovered why he bothered to come at all: Henry Clarke and Tris Polk had complained about bullets fired on a resident of the bridge community. So he had to make a trip up but not necessarily for information. Besides, Morissa Kirk plainly did not fit into his idea of a white woman up here, with no roadranch or dance hall connections. Her doctoring he dismissed with a shift of his cud from one lean cheek to the other. "You let the sick man die, didn't you?" he demanded. "An' all the evidence you got for your story of the horse thieves is a saddle you admit you took off a horse you shot, shot from under a man what didn't lay a finger on you—"

Furious, Morissa went to the door and pushed it open. "You forget the man was dying when I arrived, and that I was shot at—"

But the sheriff did not go. Instead he teetered insolently in his chair. "Seems I recall that you fired first," he said, laughing as at a child or a half-wit, but with a threat behind it somewhere, Morissa realized, and wondered what it could be.

She realized too, now, that she was helpless. The Sidney sheriff could not be thrown out as she would Fish Head. There wasn't even a voting precinct here to help put him out election time. And although her grandmother once wrote her "Always walk with a prideful foot—" Morissa went to bring coffee cups and fresh gingerbread.

The man seemed to soften up a little; he spit out his cud and talked a long time as they sat at the pleasant window bordered with blooming geraniums. The roadagents who worked the Cheyenne route, men like Dunc Blackburn, Persimmon Bill and Big Nose George, were dangerous men. "We ain't got bad hombres like them on our trail. Them hideouts like Fly Speck and Cut Lip up 'round Red Cloud Agency there may work down to'ards Sidney but till they does they ain't my lookout."

He made it clear, however, that he kept track of what went on up there, as well as at the bridge. He heard troops from Fort Robinson had chased Fly Speck Billy last month and repossessed the Indian horses he sold to the miners without a bill of sale. "Probably was back to the agency in time to take 'nother herd south—if you seen one," the sheriff said, tipping his chair back again, his spurs anchored to the soft pine floor.

The young woman considered him as she would a puzzling patient. "I saw the herd," she said as though she hadn't just been called a liar twice. "If it's Fly Speck somebody should stop him, but I don't think he does all the stealing. I hear there's a regular thieves trail across those Snake Creek flats, the horses turned over to some ranchers down the Platte, east of here, who send them on toward Kansas. That gets it close to your Sidney—"

The sheriff pulled out his snap knife and pared a fingernail. Finally he spoke, making it mild. "Have you seen your brother Jack lately? I hear he's been up around that Red Cloud gang—"

"Oh, I don't think so," Morissa replied very quickly, needing to make the denial immediate. "He's been with his father, Robin Thomas, grading for the new railroad—" But then her face flushed as she understood the man's full meaning and his threat, and saw too his bold admiration for her rising color. Angry, she still had to remember that Robin didn't mention Jackie in his last letter and that the boy never wrote, although who could expect an affinity for ink at his age?

"Some Kearney trail outfit may have given Jack a ride up," she explained, thrown off her attack completely. "They cross White River east of Red Cloud, as you know. He likes to visit with Eddie Ellis—"

"Ah, yes, Ellis—" the sheriff said, his voice tapering off as he let the chair down, shifted his gun and went to talk to Clarke, without a word of good-by or so long.

112

When he was gone Morissa stood in the middle of the sunny room looking after his loping horse. Now finally she admitted that something must be done about her brother and she sat down to write a note to Eddie. "There's always a slice of cake or something waiting for any of Jack's friends who come past my door," she told him.

Eddie came sooner than she expected. Twice since she moved across the river she had late callers who came sneaking up from the back, out of sight of the trail, and insisted on close-curtained windows before they came into the light. Once it was a bullet that had to be dug out of a man's calf and once a ball from an old muzzleloader flattened against the scapula. The third time the patient who came out of the unidentifying darkness was her brother. Barely a week after the sheriff's questions about Jack, Eddie Ellis brought him in, riding double, Jack with his right arm tied up across his breast by a kerchief knotted around his neck. They had been running antelope, trying to rope one. Jack's horse stepped into a badger hole, snapped off a leg, and threw him over his head, breaking the collarbone.

They made a straight story of it, Eddie, as the older, around twenty-one by now, the leader in the telling, Jack nodding, saying, "Yeh, Sis—" and "Yeh, down he went—"

The story seemed a little too consistent, without differences or contradictions. Nor would Jack let his sister give him a whiff of ether, although he almost fainted when she set the bone, his face sweat-beaded and so white that his hair looked like a black hood, hanging far down behind, as long as Wild Bill Hickok's ever was, but straight.

Eddie rode away before dawn, saying he must get back to work, although Morissa knew he had lost his job at the agency long ago. But it was fine to have Jackie around for the planting again, handing her the roots with his free arm as she set out a lot of rhubarb, enough for a supply of pleasant physicking sirup, asparagus, so good for the kidneys, and also a large plot of herbs. Then the boy arranged the young lilac sprouts in a trench from which they might grow into a wall of spring purple some day, and the yellow roses in clumps along the gray sod walls.

About a week later the Bosler cowboys brought a small bunch of herd sires through. While the men wet their throats at Etty's, some of the bulls broke down Morissa's pasture fence and tolled away two of her young heifers. On Appaloosa she went to look for them, hoping that they would be down to the river for water soon although there were still ponds in buffalo wallows over the prairie. She rode out northeast the way the Bosler bulls had gone, to some high ridges that overlooked the sandhills.

It was somewhere off this way that the boys had chased the antelope, and when Morissa saw a dozen buzzards circling slowly, she went over and found the horse half-gutted by wolves. It was Robin's RT brand on the shoulder all right, but no broken leg; instead there was a bullet through the heart.

As she stood there, looking all around under her shading palm, Morissa noticed old tracks and dry horse droppings leading down the slope that funneled off toward the Platte. There was nothing more except a coyote rising from the edge of a gully, watching her over his shoulder. Morissa rode down that direction with her rifle ready across the saddle. The coyote was too wily but in a washout the earth was worn by animal pads, drawn there by another carcass, that of a man, poorly buried and now half uncovered where wolves had begun at his belly, perhaps as soon as the stink of decay overcame the man smell. Morissa scraped the earth back from the face that was bearded, with an old scar across the corner of the swollen, blackened mouth—surely the Cut Lip that the Sidney sheriff had mentioned, Cut Lip Johnson from around Red Cloud. He had at least two bullets through his stocky body, and many would say he had them coming a long, long time.

With the big knife left in Cut Lip's sheath, Morissa dug sand and sod down upon him. Then she slipped her boots and socks off and tramped the earth with her bare feet for the human smell. When she was about a mile on her way home she turned the Appaloosa back to the dead horse and cut out Robin's brand, haggling it as though wolves had been gnawing there, looking over her shoulder several times and all around the empty prairie, furious that she felt driven to such trickery.

Home without the heifers she unsaddled and went in to talk to Jackie. He was reading a fanciful story about Wild Bill Hickok in an old copy of *Harper's Magazine* but he finally broke down and admitted that Eddie's story was a lie. They had hired out to help drive some horses down to the Platte, but when they got a few miles above where his horse lay, they saw a bunch of Sioux bucks come whooping after them, shooting as they rode. One got Jack's horse, really a work mare and not fast. But the Indians whipped right past him after the herd. The man who dropped back to stand them off was killed, the rest got away, letting the horses scatter.

"Eddie came back for me when the Indians had whooped their horses off back north, and brought me in."

"Who buried Cut Lip?" Morissa demanded.

For a moment the boy looked at his sister, his young face naked in astonishment and fear. "I don't know," he finally admitted. "Eddie went down to help him, too, but he was dead. Eddie's very brave."

"Bravery is a relative thing. There's nothing brave about getting a seventeen-year-old boy in with horse thieves. You know what happens to them if they're caught. Strung up to the first tree, and anybody caught with them, too, for in a country without courts, you're as guilty as the gang you run with, and if an innocent man is hung now and then, that's the bad luck of his bad judgment."

The boy sat looking straight ahead over the arm laid across his breast, his bony young face drawn and afraid, and yet Morissa knew that her talking was futile. Jackie had understood these things long before she came to the valley, long before she complained about the man hanging at the bridge that Clarke characterized as a dead owl left out to warn others away.

"—You know I have to report this," she added slowly.

"Turn in your own brother?" the boy said angrily, flushing under the thin bearding.

No, she couldn't do that, not the only blood kin she had, and so she wrote the sheriff about finding the dead man while hunting stock and left a copy of the letter at Camp Clarke, but nothing more. The next morning she rode out with Lieutenant Larman and two of his bluecoats to bring in the body. No one seemed to care how Cut Lip was killed; the sheriff didn't come, and so another grave was added to the knoll across the river and one more name put on the cemetery plat in Clarke's office.

The next week Eddie Ellis came back to see Jack and took him out for a long ride, away from Morissa; it was then that Charley Adams said that Cut Lip had been with Sam Bass in the Deadwood holdup and so she packed Jackie off on the first coach to Sidney and bought him a ticket to his father. Eddie was going to work, Jackie protested. He had a job at Pratt's ranch up the river. The doctor put her brother on the train anyway. Soon Ed Ellis was tying a team and buggy to the hitch-rack at Clarke's, but Morissa never saw anybody in the seat beside him and nobody questioned his ownership of the outfit—the horses marked with what seemed to be an ID skillfully blotted.

The freighters looked under their curling hatbrims to the lady doc, but nobody considered stealing horses with the Indian Department brand much of a crime—mostly just good business.

When Morissa came back from the blizzard and found her cattle fed, her plants saved by the daily fire somebody had troubled to build for her, she knew she must have a hired man. One did not impose on good neighbors like that. She needed a man with a wife or sister, or even a mother—preferably a woman who knew something about practical nursing for the patients when Morissa was called away. Perhaps Tom Reeder would not have died from a perforated ulcer as he did at Sidney if she could have kept him here on a strict diet, quiet, feeling secure. It seems he got more and more afraid after the town dogs killed his antelope. No one said where the gold went.

115

Morissa knew that the couple she needed must be available, with much unemployment all over the East and wages going down again, the railroads cutting theirs a second time within six months. So she wrote her idea to Robin and to two doctors from her class. Once she thought of writing to the young Dr. Walter Reed who had spoken passionately for a medical career on the frontier. But when she sat down to write him, she was as embarrassed and humble as the time he addressed their medical group a year ago, such a long, long year ago, and so she only wrote him a greeting, a belated note of thanks for his encouragement.

The week after Jackie left the problem seemed solved. Charley Adams said he was through soldiering. Sixteen years was too much. He wanted to file on a homestead here in the valley and bring his wife up from Kansas. But his Ruth was uneasy; she knew about cattlemen warring against settlers from down there.

"I suppose she's wise to weigh that possibility. There will be difficulties here some day, but if we stick together—" Morissa said thoughtfully. "You're a crack shot; you'd be very useful then too—"

So Charley sent for his wife and built a bunk and a bureau and chairs for the little ell along the far side of Morissa's hospital room. Then he went down to enter his claim and brought back a team, wagon, and plow, and a tent that he pitched beside Morissa's pond. No use advertising his homesteading until he had to establish his residence, he said. "A man learns to keep his head down in the Army." He laid out a new garden plot at Morissa's dam and that brought enough riders to sit watching him sourly a while and then spur off to the whisky stores instead of laughing at his first breaking, which was choppy as the flooded Platte in a windstorm. But Charley soon learned to handle the bucking sod buster behind his steady-footed old gray mares.

By that time Ruth Adams got off the coach at the bridge. She turned out a plain woman with a bleakish face, perhaps from waiting sixteen years for her soldier husband to make a home for her, take her out of hired-girling. She looked at Morissa, tall, slender, and high-busted, her uncovered hair shining like a dark bay filly in the sun, and she went to live in the tent instead of the room Charley prepared for them in the house of this Doctor Kirk woman. All Morissa heard of her was the mournful settler hymn that she sang out there in the tent, about some desperate pilgrim forever crossing flooded waters and the burning sands.

But two weeks out there cooled Ruth off a little, Charley whispered to Morissa when he came back from Sidney with a load of wire fencing. Maybe it was being alone through the cold rain of late April in the tent, or perhaps that Morissa's cat went up to the pond and stayed to rub his back against the woman's gray calico skirts. Or the medicine the doctor put together for Ruth's female weakness. Who can say what little wind will veer the set of the mind?

116

When the grass was well started so that turning the sod would kill most of it, Charley went to lay out the ten acres on Morissa's timber-claim. His breaking rolled back smooth as satin bands now, with black-birds, gulls, even meadowlarks and killdeers following at his heels, peck-ing in the new-turned earth. Morissa followed him, too, working in a navy denim jumper suit and yellow sunbonnet, her hair in the thick braid hanging below her waist, tied with big pompoms of yellow and mustard-colored yarn. She carried a sack of seedling cottonwood, box-elder and ash slung under one arm, and with the spade she set them out two swinging steps apart, driving the blade deep through the sod, working it back and forth to make a little bed for the rootlets. With her gloved hands she packed earth around them, stepped a firm foot on each side, and then went on to the next, perhaps pausing to wave to a freight train heading north, or some hurrying gold seekers.

By this time the riders who stopped to slouch over their saddlehorns were more pointed in their disapproval, telling the city woman about the drought, the hail, and grasshoppers, and the range cattle running loose here.

"Oh, there's the state herd law to protect cultivation from straying stock—" she reminded them easily.

"You mean you expect the courts 'way off at Sidney to make us keep our cows up, just for your little shirttail patches here?" one of Bosler's men asked in astonishment.

"Well, I have a legal claim to the land, and that's more than you cat-tlemen can say for your range," she said, her teeth white. "But I do in-tend to fence it as soon as Charley gets the time."

The man looked down at the tall young doctor, at her brown oval face, the hazel eyes luminous with their remote glow, the red lips humorous, and the sway of her body to the spade and the planting as provocative as a dance. But a plot of growing things so close to the bridge and the trail was a serious threat to all the free-range country, and particularly attractive to every disappointed bonanza seeker dragging back down the trail.

It was the foreman of the Cradle Six, setting up a new ranch in the Snake Creek country, who finally put it straight to Morissa, and after-ward she wondered how many spoke through the usually mild-voiced man who slouched sideways in the saddle, a hand on the cantle as he talked to her.

"You remember your first day here, ma'am," he said over the impa-tient stomp of his horse, "when Clarke nailed up the dead owl to warn the others off?—hanging the first man who threatened his bridge—"

Morissa scraped at a bit of earth clinging to her spade with a chip of flint. So he knew what Clarke had told her. They all worked together. "Are you threatening me?" she finally trusted herself to ask. "Because if you are, let me tell you I'm from a breed of owls that don't scare easy."

The man grinned, showing his strong brown teeth pleasantly. "You wouldn't be no good owl to warn others off, ma'am; better at tolling 'em, I'd say," apparently still wishing to seem gallant. But only for a moment. "Why don't you grab you a man and quit this switching your skirts around?" he added.

And when Morissa was determined to laugh at that because it was funny, and discerning, he pulled his hat lower upon his sun-narrowed eyes. "Why don't you grab up the Lieutenant and go East—before your luck runs out? Be mighty easy to make a case against you here, you know. Shielding and comfort for outlaws. People have been hung for less."

Morissa noticed that he didn't mention Tris Polk for her, but she didn't overlook the threat that had been spoken so plainly. In the morning she took her rifle out to her tree planting and set it up against the tub of seedlings. It glistened there in the sun of May that was exactly like the sun of a year ago, the day she came to the valley of the North Platte with a new trousseau trunk and a silly little hat with yellow feathers like agitated birds, always trying to escape.

The next day a smooth-fingered man from Bosler's came to offer Morissa $500 for her relinquishments, and when she pointed out that the preemption was paid for, at $1.25 an acre—$200 for one of the three quarters—the man raised the price for her departure to $1,000, "providing you don't file on another place in the country—"

Morissa smiled. "I like it here—" and to this the man set his spurs. The doctor looked after him a long time. Now she understood why wolves traveled just under the crest of the ridges—where it was easy to disappear, never be a silhouetted target against the sky.

All winter there had been news and rumors of Indian battles and now Crazy Horse and the last of his hostile followers were finally driven to the reservations, not by guns so much as by the disappearance of their commissary, the buffalo. With the surrender of the Sioux, the troops began to move out and the passenger coaches from Cheyenne had to fight their way past Robbers Roost and other hideouts free to work in the open again—men like Jesse James and his gang along with the regular roadagents; escaped convicts, deserters, and the miners gone broke in the Hills. One reply to them was the steel-lined Concord coach the stage company at Cheyenne ordered made, on rush.

The blizzard that had brought famine and sky-high prices to the isolated Deadwood was followed by a cry that the mines were really done, finished. Now gold seekers coming in were held up for whatever they carried. One party was robbed of their stock and when they tracked the robbers on borrowed horses these were also taken from them, and their

118

guns, the men set afoot and unarmed far from food or water. After a while the Cheyenne trail was shortened to avoid the Roost and yet the outlawry grew until the Dakotans did a little rope work. Up near Deadwood three men being held as horse thieves were dragged out of jail by a mob and left hanging for days in the hot sun.

"More dead owls," Morissa said sourly.

The lynchings didn't seem to scare anybody. The Cheyenne coaches were still held up, the locks blown off the treasure boxes with gunshot right in the road before the passengers standing around, hands up, pockets turned out, the haul perhaps twelve, fifteen thousand dollars. Stories of a woman riding with the outlaws sifted down to Clarke's bridge, and then late one night there was the quiet but firm tap of a gun butt against Morissa's door.

In the darkness she opened the middle window a little and looked out, a man vaguely visible in the diffused light of her sign. "You have the wrong place," she said, keeping her voice down from Ruth. "What you want is available over across the bridge."

"Ain't you the lady doc?"

"Yes, I am."

Then he had come to fetch her. Sick woman off west here a ways. But when Morissa lit the lamp and held it up to look out, the man stepped back into the shadows, his face hidden between the broad hatbrim and the high collar drawn up.

For the first time here Morissa hesitated. "Who is sick, and who are you?"

Now the man made no more pretense. With his gun he motioned the young doctor outside. "Get on the horse there or I'll put a bullet through yeh—"

"And then who'll care for your sick woman?" Morissa said scornfully. "Plainly you don't want to go to Sidney, or to the post surgeon at Fort Robinson—"

"No, but if you don't come you ain't gonna be feedin' nobody no more pills—"

That made sense, and so Morissa smiled a little. "If you are afraid to let me know who you are now, what proof is there that I'll live to tell what I might find out?"

"Oh, that's easy, Sis. I'll take an' blindfold you, in 'n' out. Please hurry, ma'am, the woman's a dyin'."

"Wounded?"

"No, don't know what's ailin' her."

"In pain?"

"She's feverin', and talkin' wild, and goin' into fits—"

"Convulsions, probably."

But Morissa couldn't get anything more out of the man, and so she

119

said she wanted her own horse and would need Charley Adams, up at his tent tonight. He was a good nurse, good with ether, if it was necessary to operate.

"Operate—" the man said in sudden fear, but he was still adamant. "No, I ain't takin' nobody else."

"Then I don't come. You can blindfold him too."

So with the man slipping up to listen, Morissa woke Charley. "Need you on a call—" she said. While he dressed and came down she managed to leave an awkward little note written in the dark depths of the trunk where she pretended to dig for medicines: "Taken away with Charley to woman patient off west by threat of gun. Slight man with limp—"

Saddled up, they rode through the darkness, westward apparently. Although there were almost no stars, it was a long time before they left the smell of sweet water and the far pumping sound of the shitepokes. The doctor felt a curious familiarity with such a night ride, and then she remembered the tales her mother told her, long ago—about the Scottish highwayman who stole Morissa's great-grandmother as a girl and carried her a long, long ways in the night. It was almost like reliving the story as it seemed in her childhood, before she knew that the robber had become her great-grandfather, and paid for his adventure by an earthbound life of wife and children and blatting sheep.

Toward dawn the man stopped and ordered Morissa to blindfold Charley and then herself, perhaps as her ancestress had her eyes covered on that first ride. Soon another horsebacker met them without word or greeting, only the sound of a horse falling in behind them. When the sun had boiled down hot for hours and the lagging hoofs struck rock, the leader stopped at the sound of a murmuring creek. The Appaloosa drank deeply, and a tin cup was put into Morissa's hand, brimful of cold sweet water, with the sweet coldness of swift spring flow. Then they followed up this stream and dismounted. Morissa was led over a step into walls, a stinking shack, and told to remove her blind.

Although the door had been open, the stench of dead flesh and living putrefaction roiled even the doctor's empty stomach. As her eyes adjusted themselves to the windowless place, the awkward log walls, greasy with old smoke, came out of the duskiness and she saw a woman on a bunk, only the white skull-face clear. Swiftly Morissa counted the failing pulse and verified her sudden fears. "The man should have told me what was wrong," she said, angry to be caught so unprepared. "I should have brought things I stopped carrying in this man's country—"

The woman tried to speak. "They don't know—" she finally managed in a breathy whisper. "It was—before" her voice stopped, as though frightened by the words.

"I must know how long—" Morissa urged gently.

Four months, and took sick a week ago. She had done what a woman at Deadwood told her. "I—I was afraid, but when I come to—come here I couldn't have me a—a bastard."

Morissa felt herself grow unprofessionally angry. "Don't use that vile and dreadful word!" she commanded. "Abuse the father or yourself, but not the innocent. Someone here knew of me; why didn't you come before this was done? I would have welcomed you, cared for you both."

But the woman seemed unable to stop now, or to listen. Her voice barely above a whisper, she kept up a murmuring of talk, disjointed, but steady; driven to it, as though the presence of another woman had broken a winter of ice. Yet always her sunken, fevered eyes sought out the open doorway.

Morissa knew she must do what little she could immediately, with the abdomen hard as from peritonitis. She called for the man, who came to stand behind her, his blue neckerchief drawn up across his face when she turned to give him a note. "You better send this to my place if you won't go to a pharmacist. Get Mrs. Adams to send me what I want."

"No!"

"Yes!—Even now it may be too late. I'll do what I can in the meantime, but everything may be too late."

For a moment she saw a look of deep apprehension and misery come into the shadowed eyes, of fear and of sorrow that made the woman in the doctor feel rejected and depressed. But she could give only a passing notice to her sudden envy of this affection, and a gladness for it too. She set out the carbolic acid and her instruments on a towel spread over a stump bench and began her task, the woman no more than a girl for all the gaunt and bloated skeleton, the doctor still hoping that the distended abdomen was not from a break into the pelvic cavity. It seemed hopeless after so many days, but Morissa knew that sometimes women become resilient as barbed wire. With the strength of the strenuous, hard life here, along with nature's wise provision against a direct blood path between the mother and her nested young, a doctor could at least hope.

Twice Morissa stopped to give the girl a heart stimulant and finally it was necessary to call Charley, although the watcher outside stood against it. "—I won't have no man in there!" he commanded.

"But Charley is like a doctor." And when he still resisted, Morissa told him the rest. "Perhaps it won't matter now anyway—"

Slowly the man slid a hand down upon the grip of his pistol and then let it fall helplessly, his face convulsed behind the neckerchief mask. So Charley came into the silent shack and closed the door against the deep, choking sobs outside.

121

At last they could do no more; even the final irrigation and disinfection was completed. Morissa sat down on the stump bench, pinned her hair back and hoped that she had done no more harm than good. After a while, when the girl seemed quieter, the man outside brought in a little beef stew with onions and potatoes in it, and Morissa knew it had all been taken from freight and cattle outfits, perhaps as a sort of toll for letting the rest pass. But it was late afternoon now, a long time and a long ride since their last meal, and so Morissa and Charley ate heartily while the girl slept on the bunk, so much like a worn, wasted child. It would be almost morning before a man could return from the Platte if anyone went at all, and that would be too late, or scarcely needed, one way or the other.

They took turns beside the girl in the low lantern light, watching particularly for signs of the convulsions the man had described, but toward midnight the breathing became deeper, more regular and Morissa's hand found the forehead cooler, and moist as with a little dew of morning. At her first move, the man outside was peering in the crack of the door. She nodded reassuringly and awoke Charley to show him the change in the smoky light.

"If you stay out here long enough there will be women, families, all over the region," she said. "An old army nurse like you might as well learn to know the signs. Besides—"

Yes, besides the signs of a turn in a woman were like anybody's.

By the next afternoon it was plain that no one had been sent on Morissa's errand but, with the patient very much better, the two were blindfolded again and led away. The girl had cried softly as she clung to Morissa's hand, not speaking, and the young doctor choked back the advice that rose in her: "Go home, wherever that is" for who could see the life of young Dr. Morissa Kirk of the gold trail this moment and not say to her also, "Go home, wherever that is."

Before they left the log shack the man had laid five double eagles in her hand, heavy, glistening new gold, and when Morissa objected to the amount, he said, "Interest comes correspondingly high as the risk increases—"

"But you are an educated man!" Morissa exclaimed in surprise.

Immediately the outlaw returned to his surly, illiterate speech behind the blue cloth, with the anger of an actor who has slipped in his part. So, blindfolded again, they rode out and after a while more hoofs came, more clink of bridles until there were at least five men around them, silent, riding in the darkness of Morissa's blind. Could their silence mean she might recognize a voice? At the least an escort of this size seemed ominous, even though the man had promised their safe return— the promise of a roadagent.

Morissa heard nothing of Charley for so long that she wanted to call out to him, discover if he was still along. She coughed once, making it womanish and plain, but she got no return signal, only a sudden break into a canter, and she had to trust Appaloosa to prepare her for any sudden turn or jump as she clung to the knob of the sidesaddle with her knee until her leg was numb and her back seemed broken from the heavy bounce and jolt of the ride in total darkness. But there were worse things on her mind—with five outlaws around them, perhaps only around her, blindfolded, unarmed, alone with night surely near and the country as empty as the night.

But after a long winding stretch Morissa sensed that the hoofbeats were lessening until there seemed only one man, and Charley, if he was there. Finally the outlaw spoke. "You kin jerk the blind, Miss—"

It was dark, the big dipper out clear for early night, and the Appaloosa pulling against the bit for home now that he felt the returned assurance of his rider. Without another word the man swung away into the darkness.

"If things don't go right, make a horse litter and bring the patient to me at once—" Morissa called after him, and did not know whether he heard.

When they got home Ruth was at the stable to meet them pretending not to cry that her Charley was back. Morissa saw·a horse standing near the gate beyond, and Tris was waiting on the bench before the lighted doorway, with the night sweetness of four o'clocks and mignonette all around.

"We've been very uneasy about you, after a Wyoming outlaw was seen riding this way couple days ago by Pratt's men, and Ruth found your note—" he said sternly.

"Oh, nobody's going to hurt me," Morissa said as she stretched herself wearily on the low bench.

For a long time Tris stood against the doorjamb, silent as though listening to the comforting song of the frogs. "I ran into your heifers, up near where you left your buggy in the blizzard," he finally told her. "In with the Bosler herd. I had them brought back."

"Oh, you are kind, Tris." Morissa tried to make herself recall why she should have heifers astray but she was too worn out tonight.

The man did not seem to listen to even the little she said. "I can't have you going on like this, Morissa," he protested angrily. "Out nights, kidnaped by outlaws. Next month is the Walker horse show and you're going to marry me there."

X

Morissa was returning from a call on a small girl over beyond the mountain lion pass when she saw troopers riding across the bridge two abreast. Behind them came a row of mounted Indians, a few wagons, and a long string of people walking, many bent to the bundles on their backs—men, women, and children, and far behind these a little beef herd stirring up a dust.

She stopped and knew what it was. Three days ago Lieutenant Larman said he had an unhappy order, to help start a thousand Cheyennes on their transfer down to Indian Territory. Here they were, most of them afoot, to walk across Nebraska and Kansas and farther—all moving like dead ones, a beaten people driven from their homes, going into exile.

Suddenly the young doctor's face was scalded with tears and such a fury rose in her that she had to whip her horses, holding them close until they reared and plunged, froth flying from the bits. Then she let them out and they leapt ahead, jerking the buggy along in a lope until she got control of herself and set the whip into the stock and was ashamed. But she knew it would be a long, long time before the guilt of this was washed from the grass where their moccasins had moved.

The Indians camped south of the river, setting up a few ragged skin and canvas lodges, the rest to sleep out. The women scattered for wood, where for the last three, four years every stick and twiglet had been searched out. It was late when they returned and what wood they brought was through troopers who, in pity, had loaned them a few horses to drag it in from the bluffs. And after the evening smoke one of the men came over the bridge to Morissa with a child at his side, a shy, dark-eyed little boy, the baby she had saved last year. Evidently they had not found food in the south either, and had returned, and now must retrace the long road.

By signs the man asked permission to go to the small pasture where the Appaloosa grazed. "Talk with horse," his signs conveyed to Morissa, and she quickly smiled and nodded and he went to squat beside the animal, silent, it seemed, for a long time before he touched him at all, and held the small boy up for the horse to smell. Impulsively Morissa ran out. "I give it you—" she motioned.

The Indian smiled sadly and shook his head. "They take from me— white man take all horse—" he said, and then he touched Morissa's hand and guided it to the velvety place under the horse's jaw, moving her fingers up and down until the Appaloosa closed his eyes and stretched his head forward, like a cat rubbed on the back. But the Indian could not take the horse. It had been a trade, the horse traded for the life of his son, and he would never have that undone.

"How sensible," Morissa caught herself thinking as she went back to the house and left the man there until the night darkened and the fireflies laced the riverbank.

The next morning the doctor saw the queue start southward, and heard a thin clear keening. She wondered what death had now occurred among them. She wondered too, at some other things—notably how much fear the Crazy Horse Sioux, with a small fraction of these Indians along, had struck into the hearts of the whites when the very arms with which they fought had to come from the enemy white man. Of course it was blown up by the contractors behind the great bull trains of goods to the armies rousted out for the pursuit. But she knew that something deeper lay there—some relation between the pursued and the pursuer, the transgressor and the transgressed.

Robin's grading for the railroad was put off for the same reason that railroad employees got their wages cut again—because times were hard enough so it could be done; had to be done, the owners said. But the trainmen protested the action by a strike that spread out of the East to Chicago and St. Louis and now toward Omaha. President Hayes, insecure in his office because he won it from Tilden against the electoral vote, was in a panic. He called out the Army to put down the strike—the revolution as he called it.

Robin came back to the valley half decided to file on a homestead. Perhaps Jack, left behind to look after the equipment, would be twenty-one in time for some free land too. With nine quarters of their own, debt free, the three of them could make a living in cattle and farming, even with an occasional year of ten-cent corn, two-cent beef and nothing paid on doctor bills. He talked late into the night about this and about the boy, and while Morissa dropped a hint or two of Jack's bad associations around Red Cloud, she could not say all she knew of the horse stealing.

"Why don't you send him for a visit to your father in Kentucky?" she suggested once. "Or to school somewhere?"

Robin got up and tapped the ashes from his pipe into the hearth of the cold stove. "He won't go unless I make him, and I can't do that."

"Well, then we'll have to try it here," Morissa agreed. "Eddie Ellis has a top buggy and seemed to be looking for a girl but he's running with that Doc Middleton who used to work up at Pratt's, too, before he turned horse thief. I would prefer not to have Jackie here just now—"

Robin eased a hand over his stiff gray brush of beard and kept his silence while Morissa went to look at her patients, another cowboy with a broken leg and a gambling woman from Deadwood with summer quinsy. Next day he came hurrying back from Clarke's as soon as the stage was in, bringing news to Morissa at her tree planting. One of the new settlers down west of Sidney was found shot between the shoulders, and his little claim shack dragged into a draw with lariats. It seemed he was caught eating beef, with no cows of his own.

"Must a man die because he might have bought or begged a chunk of meat? Even if he stole it, the range stock was probably eating his grass," Morissa defended hotly. "The Boslers tolled off two of my heifers. Should I have gone out and shot the men?"

This deserved no reply and Robin gave it none. Instead he spoke of the coming rush of settlers West, with so much unemployment and the hard times. Looked to him like the homeseekers this spring were only a first spilling over at the dam. But the cattlemen would fight for their free range even if it meant war here as it did back in Custer County, near the new railroad.

Morissa told her stepfather nothing of the Bosler threats but as he talked she led him down the rows of young trees. There were a few bare streaks, the trees gone, particularly along the better end, the one reached by the little irrigation ditch. Morissa had found the fence cut several times with tracks of running horses across the plot, trees pulled out and dropped all along them, as though cowboys had leaned from their saddles and jerked them up as they spurred through. So she had drawn big skulls and crossbones with stove polish on boxboard and tacked them up on fence posts, one at each side of the patch. When she saw anyone come riding across the prairie toward the trees, she went out and put a couple more bullet holes into the skulls with her rifle. She had to steady the gun on top of the yard gatepost for that distance, but the bullet went where she wanted it.

"The lady doc's sure afixin' to be picked off on the range one a these days—" some were saying. There was still the rancher Polk on her side, Sid Martin, too, with his neck out of its leather brace now, and Clarke of the bridge as well as a dozen others who wanted the young woman out of the country as a homesteader but owed her too much as a doctor to push the matter. At least not yet.

Robin wondered how much of this the girl realized, but he would not be the one to bring it up. Before she took the homestead, yes, but now that she was committed to it, he would not be the one to make her waver, fail in this, when so much ground had already slipped under her young feet.

Tris Polk, like the other cattlemen, sent his roundup wagons to the Walker ranch for their summer horse show. He had an extra house tent brought along for his two pretty Texas cousins and their mother, furnished with cots, wolf-skin rugs for the floor and a cheval glass and dressing table as ladies required. With a little trouble he got the ranch cook into a white cap and willing to set up a folding table, with flowers beside the breakfast biscuits. Then he drove over for Morissa Kirk and, because she had Charley and his serious-faced Ruth to look after her patients now, to dispense physics and digestives or bandage a wound, she went. Appaloosa was tied beside the buggy team, Morissa's green riding habit and her plumed hat in the valise under the buggy seat. Neither Tris nor the girl spoke of last year's preliminary show, in which Morissa was to ride even though the Carlotta saddle did not arrive in time. By that show time sod had been broken on her homestead, and the rancher's horse pawed no flies at her gate but was up at Deadwood with the beef herd or carrying Huff Johnson's Gilda over the new mountain trails.

Now the rancher helped Morissa into his shining buggy. "This is a proud day for me," he said, and the young doctor smiled.

The show grounds lay on a little half-dry creek on the north Sidney table, the long scattering of log buildings and corrals among a few cottonwoods, with the shimmer of dust over it in the hot afternoon sun. Out a ways was what seemed a tent and wagon city of visitors, with a little circle of Sioux lodges, the smoke of their cooking fires twisting upward. Cowboys rode here and there, their loping horses kicking up spurts of dust. Some whooped in little herds of bulls or calves for the contests in cutting, roping, and tying. Horses were brought in, too, those for the races led in, the wild herds loose, sunfishing as they came, turning this way and that, always a fast, wily mare in the lead and quick to slip out at the slightest opening, the others close at her heels.

Morissa was welcomed almost as a betrothed and kissed with Southern exuberance by Auntie Mae and then by Li-Laurie and Li-Annie as Tris called the twins. They had gray eyes, too, but without the stormy darkness of their uncle's, lighted instead by the baby-soft fluffs of pale curls. The girls already had a following among the young men of the ranch country, one a reserved young Englishman with sun-bleached hair and very good financial connections, Li-Laurie whispered to Morissa, while the colored maid smiled softly as she laid out moon-white dresses for the girls, and Morissa's india muslin, yellow as ripe corn.

After the early supper they all moved across the slanting sunlight toward the big dance pavilion of new pine. The fiddlers and a dulcimer tuned up, and the Sioux came marching up in single file to watch. Morissa wondered once if Tris realized the story of her parentage, perhaps from Calamity Jane's remark, and thrust it from her mind as she swung from his arms to those of some young Englishman, to Colonel Walker, or to Sid Martin, whose neck turned easily enough to look after Tris's laughing Auntie Mae from Texas. Morissa danced once with young Ellis too. He didn't ask about his friend Jackie but spoke intense, angry words into her ear.

"If I was a few years older I'd trample that Tris Polk in the dust gettin' to you—"

Morissa laughed. "Ah-h, Eddie! That Texas sweet-talk seems to be catching. Why don't you try it on one of the pretty Southern girls?"

He seemed embarrassed and was silent, and afterward every time Morissa turned his way, she saw the pale, hurt eyes following her.

From the short dancing they scattered through the moonlight to the big fire at the Sioux camp, with the drumming and the songs, the feathered and painted dancers in their curious backslip steps and their leapings to the hand drums. Afterward there was the dance of the young people. The girls drew the men in as was their custom. Here and there they reached out for a white man, too, coquettish in their daring, and so Tris was swept away from beside Morissa, joining in as though he had been there often before. His aunt and the girls laughed gaily at his high-heeled boots among the soft moccasins, and then they were grabbed too and whirled along in a running, flying circle around the fire until the dancers fell apart, laughing, holding their sides, Indians and all.

After the return to the tents, Aunt Mae took Morissa's arm and led her out into the moonlight for a little walk, and when they returned past the silent wagons standing in their deep shadows, she sat down on one of the tongues, easy as any old gold trailer at eveningtime.

"—But I have been a boomer too," she protested when Morissa said this. "I was scarcely more than a bride when we went down the Santa Fe trail, Illinois to Texas, sitting on the wagon tongues a spell every night before we crept into our beds for the early morning start."

"Well, you *are* a pioneer!"

"And so are you, in this new country and also in a new field for women. I am very happy about you for Tris."

The girl's face grew warm in embarrassment. "I—there's nothing settled—" she had to say.

"I know, but you will marry. Tris is a fine man. He's had to give up, too, in his life. His father and my George were killed together the first year of the war, although our hearts were still with the North—" she paused a little, to steady her voice, and it was so much like Tris, this self-restraint, that a sudden warmth for him flooded over Morissa. But even now there was another man in her mind, his arm about her as she couldn't forget, standing beside her looking down over the golden autumn on the Missouri.

But Aunt Mae's soft voice was firm again. "—We die for our neighbors in their need, whether we know it or not, and so my husband and his brother died for our neighbors in Texas. Then Tris, the only man left of our two families at sixteen, returned from his first year study of engineering. He had to get into his chaps, round up our scattered stock from the brush, set the two ranches back on their feet. But with the war over, there was all this beef and so he started north to market with one of the first big herds. He was only a small stockman among the others, a seventeen-year-old and new to such rough men and to fighting outlaws and Indians, but he learned. When he saw all the grass up here eight years ago he located the TeePee ranch for what is left of the family—we four. He has done well for us here. Now there's that new packing house he plans to go into with Forson from Chicago. I think you met them. Tris says it may make us all rich, very rich." She stopped and in the moonlight Morissa saw the pretty woman draw her wrap about her shoulders in satisfaction, as though it were already ermine.

"I'm glad to hear this good news for you and the girls," Morissa told her. "He hasn't said much about it to me."

"You don't need money as we do, my dear. The twins and I—But don't you think that handsome young English boy is drawn to Laurie? It would be so pleasant to have good connections in England, and money helps a great deal there. Tris says the boy is from a financial syndicate but only an employee—although he is the second son of an earl," she hastened to add.

The camp stirred early, the men setting the fires in the barbecue pits at daylight to get the coals ready for the meat, a steady and clean broiling without smoke. By ten the August sun was shimmering on the Sidney table, and little heat dances played along the west. "A burning day for a lady's delicate complexion," Aunt Mae warned. "Don't go out without a good dusting of talcum, girls, and do hold your parasols low, over the eyes," she said, tipping her silly little rush of blue ruffles on a stick coquettishly sideways over a pretty brow.

They went to the race track and from there to the corrals and sat with Colonel Walker's visiting wife and young daughter-in-law under a row of military awnings. A dozen or more other women and girls were there, more than the range country ever saw together before. There was a thin scattering of pretty dresses along the fence and at the corral walls, too, just a scattering among the hundreds of men, mostly sunburnt and big-hatted, with a few paler visitors from Sidney and farther east. Everybody from the region was represented except the settlers; Morissa, as far as she could see, the one exception, but tolerated as the range's only doctor.

Although Walker had a homemade sprinkler wagon to lay the dust on the circular track, there was plenty to blow in from the dry August prairie and from the bare space inside the track, too, where running horses seemed aimlessly driven back and forth, Indians whipped their mounts into excitement, race horses were limbered up, and hazers got organized to help protect the broncho busters later. Tris was in much of this, here and there on the white-stockinged Cimarron, a single-footer in this show place, his rider sitting as easy as in a rocking chair, the nieces crying, "Oh, Uncle Tris, you are *so* handsome, you and that black, *black* horse!" until Morissa couldn't decide if it was native Texas exuberance or a little Southern scheming.

Tris laughed it off. "You wait until you see Morissa's horse—" he called back to them. But he really was a fine figure on Cimarron, Morissa had to admit, in his new pale chaps and hat, gray as silver dust, the black shirt set off by the flowing yellow silk kerchief knotted behind his neck, the fringes of his embroidered gloves barely stirring as he rode.

The show started gradually, with an easy Western casualness. Colonel Walker and his redheaded daughter-in-law led out on Kentucky mares, the Colonel riding English saddle, bringing a loud and surprised whooping from his old cow waddies. "Look at 'im! The cunnel a bobbin' up 'n down like some jack rabbit hitting for the brush!"

"Yeh, an' thet there's a mighty good horse, only cain't no horse look good under them flapjack saddles—"

But there were hearty handclappings from the special guests, and a cry of "Bravo!" Behind the Walkers came other ranchers from the region riding good Western saddles, Tris on his black between his pretty nieces in wine-colored habits on silver-maned buckskins. Businessmen from Sidney and beyond mostly rode stock saddles too, but were plainly not grown to them, although the few women with them sat their side-saddles well. There were four visiting officers in army blue, followed by the race horses, and then the bronch riders, a dozen or so. Behind them came the Mexican bullfighter, walking past in solitary grandeur in his silver embroidery, the two picadors at his heels bareback on old stove-up chore horses, each with a pitchfork held high. The Indians joined the parade, too, the men in paint, their feather headdresses blowing in the light wind, the women with their pony drags and small children in skin sacks. Finally the real backbone of the cattle business came past: a thick crowding of cowboys and ranch hands with rope and gun and branding iron, followed by the cook and bed wagons, and a calf wagon, too, with a couple of bawling dogies looking out the slats. Tris even got Eddie Ellis away from the women and up on a horse.

The calf roping began, with a couple of bowlegged cowboys trying to keep a calf away from the fence for the roper. "Awkward as a Scotsman holding a pig in an alley—" Morissa remembered her mother saying once, and she laughed with the others as the little brindle dogie dove between this pair of barreled knees and that one to escape the zinging loop. But finally the calves were all neatly footed with the intelligent help of the roping horses or caught around the neck and dragged to the branding fire anyway.

130

Then the horse races were called, with a free-for-all-comers, and Bat's Blue, the blue roan from up near Red Cloud Agency, was led out. Now the Indians became interested; one by one they got up, walked solemnly to their betting post and threw down beaded robes, shirts, pipe bags and even knives and moccasins on the blue roan to win, matched by goods and tobacco and money on the other side of the post.

"Ain't you runnin' the 'Paloosy? He's mighty fast—" one of the passing cowboys called to Morissa, his teeth white in his brown, laughing young face.

A pistol shot finally started the horses. The Kentucky stock drew out ahead, followed by the fast cowponies and then the slower-starting Blue, with a dwarfed and twisted little Indian riding him bareback, riding with only a jaw rope, riding all over the shaggy horse, whipping to both sides with the knotted end of his rope, whooping every few jumps. He was the clown of the show, and everybody laughed and then looked to the leaders, but as the laps piled up the Blue's tough distance blood began to show. Then suddenly the heels of the hunched little Indian went deep into the Blue's flanks as he lay close to the back. The horse lengthened out, too, his belly close to the ground. Running like a scared coyote for his life, he shot past the fine blooded saddlers, the race horses, and the whole band of Indians whooped to see it, as well as some of the whites.

Finished, the rider came down on the jaw rope and set the Blue on his haunches in the dust. Then he turned back to the judges to receive the applause and the ribbon that the Indian tied into the mane, one more ribbon to go with the dozen already feathering the show gear of Big Bat's wife when she rode the Blue in their ceremonial parades.

Now the Sioux came marching up in formal file to carry away their wagers and everything from the other side of the post too—the little piles of blankets, silk kerchiefs, bridles, tobacco, and gold coins thrown down there.

The other races were less fun but more fitting to Colonel Walker and his special guests. There was the star-faced Neptune, a descendant of the all-time finest, the unbeatable Eclipse, besides half a dozen others of fine blood from the ranches toward Denver and Cheyenne.

"Better watch that fancy stock here for horse thieves. They been operating right at the tracks off down in the middle of the state—" Sid Martin was telling Morissa from his horse when one of his cowboys came up, embarrassed at the need to interrupt. "A Seven U rider got a knee kicked, Boss. Mebby—"

So Sid walked over with Morissa, leading his horse, the girl holding up the long side of her green habit, the feathers of her hat blowing. Then he loped off to the tent for her little black bag. But while Morissa was kneeling beside the horsebreaker, examining what seemed a cracked kneecap, a man in a dusty frock coat came pushing through. "I am Doctor Meddows," he said importantly, and elbowed Morissa aside.

"This here is Dr. Kirk," one of the awkward cowhands managed to say. The goateed man looked up. "Ah, Dr. Kirk?—a midwife, no doubt," he said and fell to straightening out the leg, feeling the bone. Morissa walked away and later Sid came riding by to apologize. "I hate that happening, ma'am. Meddows has hung up a shingle on one of those chicken ladders leadin' up over the saloons in Sidney. Just a big blowhard, I hear."

"He's probably all right; a lot of doctors still act that way," Morissa said quietly, "but I was taught a different courtesy to a fellow physician."

They started back along the fence, past the race horses tied out to leave the corrals free for the wild stuff and the rodeo stock. Morissa wanted to stop with them a little, to look at the fine blooded animals, but a commotion arose among them. Sid spurred ahead into it as a sharp pistol shot cut the air, then more, with yells and shouting. Morissa grabbed her skirts and ducked behind the nearest horse, clinging to his mane, patting his shoulder to quiet him as she looked under the neck. Three men with bandanas drawn up across their noses, guns smoking, their horses rearing, had charged in among the racers and leaned right and left to cut them loose. As help came running from every direction, shooting too, the horse thieves swept off half a dozen of the best, firing back from their hurrying dust into the horses left behind, to set them rearing and plunging. Then they were gone down a gully, with at least twenty men hot after them, and a hundred more swinging into saddles.

But in ten minutes or so the pursuers all came back. The thieves had switched saddles to the racers leading their own, much slower horses, which they could release any time if pushed too hard, and so leave all pursuit behind, as though standing still. Besides, there were a dozen ambush places toward the Sidney breaks to think about, where the thieves could pick them off one by one.

So a man was started to Sidney immediately with the description of the horses, including the star-faced Neptune, and as much as could be ascertained about the thieves, although no two agreed on whether the men were dark or light, tall or short. Every Westerner noticed the horses carefully but they were the regular chute-run of bays and sorrels probably picked without markings to stick in the mind. No one expected to recapture the stock. The same thing had happened off East several times the last year.

Then suddenly there was another shouting out near the race horses, and a call of "Tris Polk!" In the dust beside the excited, faunching horses still rearing and kicking, Sid had found the young doctor, face down and a streak of blood in her hair.

"Morissa, Morissa—" Tris said softly, pushing the dusty bangs off the pale face.

But the girl opened her eyes almost at once, sat up groggily. "Oh, my head! Did I get kicked?" Then as her hand found a furrowed wound through her hair she exclaimed, "Why, it feels like a creasing from a bullet! —Oh, I remember now. Bullets from the horse thieves, to upset the stock."

It was true, for two horses were bleeding, neither serious—one a nicking on the hip and the other with a bullet half an inch under the skin of the belly and easy to draw out with the point of a knife while the horse was held by half a dozen willing men.

"The dirty outfit—shooting good horses like that—" a ranch hand said angrily, and was mystified by the laughing.

"You don't mind 'em shootin' Doc?—" somebody called, and the man's face grew red.

So Tris took Morissa to the tent, Aunt Mae hurrying after them, her blue parasol forgotten, suddenly once more the woman who had pioneered in Texas, quiet and capable. But except for the little hole in her hat, a headache, and the soreness where the scalp was split across the top of her head, Morissa wasn't hurt. The maid brushed the dust from her clothing and with her wound disinfected and her face washed, she went out to all the excitement over these arrogant horse thieves—a story that the Eastern and foreign guests would be telling their grandchildren fifty years from now. There was a great deal of anger too and finally even Colonel Walker spoke in favor of hanging. Any horse thief caught down here would be hanged as surely as up around Deadwood. Confronted by such bold outlawry, it was time to get together. Vigilantes, regulators—that was what they needed.

But there was still the horse show to carry on, and the colonel led his guests out to watch a little of the broncho busting. "Don't you get on any of those wild things!" Aunt Mae called to Tris as he started for the corrals. "He used to ride the most dreadful outlaws at sixteen, seventeen, and just *make* them buck!" she said to Morissa.

The girl shook her head. "I don't think he will now, unless it's necessary. At his age you leave it to the professional horse breakers and the young show-offs."

"I know," Aunt Mae nodded, still keeping her eye his way, "but with this dreadful excitement you can't tell about men—"

At the big pole corral the horses were roped, one after another, eared down and saddled. Then the gate was thrown open, and the sky broke over them as the ropes were released, the blind snapped away, and the wild horse found himself on his feet and loaded with leather and man. Now it was a fight to the finish.

There were half a dozen hazers to keep the bucking stock away from the fences and the people, with Tris Polk among those who looked after the riders, lifted them from the horses when they were through or set into a blind and dangerous run across the holes of the open prairie. Once Morissa cried out within herself as a cowboy went off an end-switching bucker and sprawled into the dust, the horse still pitching on top of the man, trying to rid himself of the saddle right there, coming down again and again, head between his knees, all four feet together, over the dark little bundle that was lying curled up motionless as a rabbit, and none could tell if this stillness was nerve or death.

After what seemed a winter's age, Tris's rope got the horse, head down and hard to snag, and jerked him away, crashed him to the ground. Once more Morissa found herself wholly the doctor, running to a patient, but then she remembered the frock coat and goatee of Dr. Meddows, and stopped as men hurried in from all directions to pick up the thrown rider. His clothing was in tatters but he was certainly the luckiest man alive, for he was not even seriously cut. Two lucky escapes today, Morissa thought, as she eased the ache of her head with a palm against her temple, but such luck must not be pushed.

So she went to the tent for a while, too nervous now to watch this risk of fine sound bodies on wild horses. Before long it was noon and the barbecue cooks were calling "Come and get it!" Everybody trooped over to the long tables of planks laid on salt barrels with stacks of tin plates, cups, and cutlery laid out, where men with long gleaming knives sliced into barbecued halves of steers, brown and fragrant. Others piled hot dutch-oven biscuits, pit-baked potatoes and beans on the tin plates, and ladled out canned tomatoes and coffee and cut the great pies of raisins and dried apple. The special guests went to the tables and benches at the shade tents, the rest sat around on the grass with no protection from the sun but their big hats, as on any other day.

Afterward there was steer roping and tying, and then more races, including the wild, whooping Indian pony free-for-all, and the relays with half-broken horses. There was the cook wagon race, too, with half a dozen ranches represented. The tail gate of the leader flew open in the wild swaying run; pots, pans, kettles, tin plates, and an open flour sack scattered out over the race track as the cook, standing at the dashboard, whipped his galloping horses with the line ends to win. There was a cow-milking contest, the winner bringing in half an inch of milk in the bottom of a beer bottle, and a cowboy foot race, the crowd whooping at the awkward bowlegged runners stumbling along on their crooked-heeled boots.

Finally it was time for the bullfight, the novelty of the day to all but the south Texans and the few Mexican trail herd riders. The bull turned out to be an old buffalo with a rope around his wooly middle,

134

the mat of hair thick over his forehead so he couldn't have seen anything even if nature had given him sharp eyes. The cowboys crowded him out into the center of the race track, where he stood sniffing the air, his bony tail up ready to run, but baffled and turning. Then he got wind of the bullfighter, not ten feet away, and charged to send him scurrying in his funnel-bottom pants. But all the man had to do was to slip sideways out of the wind as the bull passed, and then stopped in confusion when the scent was lost. The picadors came whipping up with their pitch-forks, not to jab the thick hide but to hold the dirty old red underwear fastened to the tines up where the keen-nosed old bull could get the man smell. They drew him to charge foolishly this way and that, making the range workers roar with laughter. In the meantime the bullfighter swung his cape at the poor creature until he began to bellow in frothing anger. Finally the man gave a leap and was up on the buffalo's back, hanging to the belly rope with both hands as the stiff old animal tore off across the country, clumsily kicking up his hind legs, twisting his back this way and that to free himself, the picadors pounding their old plugs along far behind until the hazers rode out and carried the bull-fighter back. The old buffalo was left a dark spot in the prairie, standing, worn out.

Now the more formal numbers of the afternoon were brought on. A new Concord stagecoach came first, the six white horses in their silver trappings, the driver maneuvering them like a turning toy, their step never broken, no trace or singletree dragging as he cut his winding circles and figure eights. Then he lashed the horses into a run as masked cowboys came in the hot pursuit of roadagents, their shooting returned by blanks from the Winchesters of the guards riding the box. The crowd, not sure now that this was only a show, sat silent as two cowboys fell, rolling off as they would from a runaway horse, to be picked up by the others at top speed the way Indian warriors rescue the fallen. When the coach had escaped the mock holdup, it stopped before Colonel Walker and his guests; the colonel's daughter-in-law and two of the handsome young Britishers stepped out, a little dizzy but laughing, to the cheers of the crowd, who were now finally reassured.

Next the colonel and his friends and the cavalry officers showed their gaited saddlers, and then the Walker cowboys lugged out jump gates and stood back while the horses took them like great birds, the hired hands from other ranches laughing their hats off their heads, but respectful too. "It cain't be easy stickin' on like that with them postage stamp saddles—"

Then there was the showing of handsome horses, but less impressive with the best of the imported stock, including Neptune, gone, and in the hands of unknown horse thieves. There was the fine Kentucky blood of the ranch owners, and the cavalry horses all freshly curried and shining. Ridden past two and two, they were turned slowly to show all sides to the crowd, their poise, their balance, their beauty of color and conformation. The Texas twins were on handsome palomillas and Tris on his stockinged black was paired with the young Walker daughter-in-law in black habit on a gleaming silver-white Arabian.

Now it was time for Morissa, but instead of being with her horse she was up at the tent, talking to a gaunt-faced man who had ridden in on a lathered old crowbait that had no place on the Walker ranch today.

At the repeated call to the show ring, she finally gathered up her skirts and ran, riding out alone on her Appaloosa with the shining silver-mounted saddle.

"Made for the Empress Carlotta of Mexico, but her whole outfit was driven out by the revolution before it was finished," Aunt Mae told everyone around her. "Finest example of Texas saddlery in the world—"

The Appaloosa was slowed to show his delicate Arabian head, his light eyes, the dark gray body with the lightish, elaborately spotted hindquarters, as though covered by some royal brocaded drapery. The ornate rose patterns of silver glistened on the black saddle leather, the young woman handsome in her dark green habit with the small gray and yellow ostrich tips on her tilted hat, her dark hair gleaming with the curious golden light against her brown skin and high coloring as she turned her dramatically beautiful horse. "Remarkable! Good seat and carriage, just after she was knocked over by a bullet, too," one of Colonel Walker's British friends exclaimed. "Carlotta would not have made a more regal appearance reviewing her regiment," he added, almost regretfully.

The Polk twins left their admiring youths and came running along the fence like children, the long riding skirts held high, crying, "Oh, lovely, lovely!" in their extravagant Southern way while their mother came sedately behind, as was proper in a chaperoning lady, but smiling her warmth.

At the corral Tris helped Morissa from her horse and held her in his arms an instant before all the grinning cowboys. "So it's settled you'll marry me at the dance tonight," he said lightly, making his voice matter-of-fact for the listeners. "There'll be two other hitchings, you know, with a cowboy preacher and all the trimmings, even a ready-made shivaree, I suspect."

Morissa looked up into the man's face, into the gray eyes, darkening like a summer storm, and for a moment he was a warm blur to the girl, everything a wavering and a shimmer like sun on moving water.

But she made herself stand away. "I can't," she said slowly looking down so her feathers hid her eyes. "The man that's waiting at the tent came for me. Typhoid's hit the trail north, one man dead and five more

136

bad cases, and several developing. I have to start home right away—don't you see, Tris? A doctor would be no wife for you."

But as the man let her turn away, there was sadness in her, as though something fine was left here, finished, cut off. And at the tent there was another horsebacker to ride up the trail with her—Eddie Ellis. Once more she was glad to see him, to have his inconsequential talk to divert her thoughts from their foolish self-concern.

XI

MORISSA'S GRAY CAT SAT ON THE DOORSTEP LICKING HIS SIDES, for the garden had drawn ground squirrels and gophers from all the dry prairie around. There was much talk and rumoring about the horse thieves who swept off the best stock at the Walker race track, with many speculations about the identity of the men. Plainly they were professionals and probably familiar with the country, Fly Speck Billy maybe, or Doc Middleton, or somebody with an accomplice among the guests there—the eyes turning toward the hitchrack at Clarke's, where Eddie Ellis had tied his buggy so often this summer. Big rewards were posted for the horses returned in good condition, and for the capture of the thieves, dead or alive, but nobody planned to get fat on a cent of this money.

Charley Adams took special precautions with Morissa's horses, as did everyone around the bridge now. "Hang a noose over the stable door an' then see that the horse ain't inside, that's my motto," he said, as he whistled the Appaloosa up for a can of oats and then took him through the darkness over into his tent for the night. Ruth worked at it too from the back door, feeding Etty's big white-faced dog Blaze in the evenings until he began to stay for the pan he got in the morning.

Morissa was too busy to know much of what was being done. Typhoid struck like heavy charges of buckshot scattered over the prairie. Even with five green hands near the Water Holes station down, people living along the trail still argued that their wells were the sweetest, coldest in the world, their creeks and spring holes, too, although a little green with August scum as happened every year. How could they suddenly be poison now?

It reminded Morissa of what Dr. Reed had said: "There is so little that we can do for the many typhoid sufferers through the frontier

137

regions—" But most of the stage passengers were carrying jugs of cold tea now or keeping to something stronger. Fortunately, too, Morissa had Charley and Ruth for her six bed patients, the one with smallpox isolated in the lean-to she added on the north for a pesthouse.

With so much driving, the doctor had another young team broken out from her growing herd, hired a driver, and tried to sleep between stops. Many of the patients were heartbreaking, men for whom little indeed could be done beyond keeping the ranch cooks from feeding them fried beef and beans. Hours of sponging reduced the fever a little, but soon the temperature crept up again, so Morissa tried to keep them in wet sheets with only the blandest food—milk, where possible, eggnog, rice water, cloth-strained oatmeal, a little beef broth perhaps, and a lot of white pudding. Once a bench-legged old cook pushed his hat back and spit into the dust when he heard this diet. Maybe he ought to serve it on a goldarn doily?

"That would be nice. Have you got one handy?" Morissa replied in her preoccupation, and then laughed aloud.

Throughout the nation, even with hospital care, one out of every four typhoid patients was dying. Morissa refused to accept such mortality; she drove and rode night and day, clinging to each man like a buffalo burr to a wooly pup, visiting the convalescing regularly to avoid foolish relapses and urging that all drinking water be boiled. "Carry a tin cup, make a grass fire—"

"Yeh, don't pay for a minute of drinking on your belly at some water hole with six months on your back—" Charley added.

The prevalence of malarial fever helped spread the typhoid panic until almost half the calls really required no more than a few quinine powders but Morissa didn't dare refuse to go. When Tris Polk returned from Chicago she was just coming into the yard from such a night call to a Bosler camp, the despised settler welcome enough now that men were dying all around. She was so worn that Tris lifted her from the buggy seat like a child; she didn't remember to ask how his packing-house deal was going, and barely to appreciate the goodness of this man. Yet was it goodness or only that he left the dirty work against the settlers to his energetic ranch foreman, Morissa wondered wearily. Either way he should be married. Surely women were not scarce back in his Texas, where so many young men had gone to war, and surely too the canny Southern girls must see the good catch the rancher was.

After Tris was gone Morissa wondered if she was taking the Texan's sweet-talk too seriously. He was a determined man; perhaps he was just getting the one settler north of the river out, even if it took marriage to do it. Or did these questionings, these doubts, rise out of some deep urge to self-destruction lying within her?

Before the doctor could settle herself to sleep there was another hurried kick at the doorjamb and once more she started out, keeping herself awake with a jug of cold tea under the buggy seat. Her driver was already gone; drank water at one of the wells and was down too. She had even tried Fish Head, but he ran off at the mouth like a gully washer and got at the brandy she carried for her patients.

Jackie didn't write, and Eddie Ellis hadn't come past when Morissa heard that one of the Sam Bass gang was shot trying to hold up the Cheyenne stage and left beside the trail. At Cheyenne the guard discovered there was a reward on the dead man's head, a thousand dollars, some said two, as one of the holdups who killed the driver of the currency coach outside of Deadwood in March. The guard rode back, located the body under a plum thicket by following the buzzards and the August flies, cut off the head, and carried it in a skin sack to Cheyenne but the reward had been withdrawn.

There was much joking about this along the rival Sidney trail. It was a dirty trick and, besides, where did the Sidney crowd get off with their laughing? So far nobody in Wyoming had let half a dozen race horses be stolen from under the nose of a whole show crowd, mostly gun-bearing.

Morissa wondered a little about Eddie and hoped he had gone back East to his family. Then one morning a man came riding for the doctor, not by the bridge, still toll-free to those seeking the doctor, but across the river far below and up through the breaks. When Morissa's yard was empty he rode by and tossed a note over her fence. It was in a large, weak scrawl on wrapping paper: "Typhoid, come get me in wagon alone. Ed." There was a sketchy map, too, but Morissa didn't realize until later how much nearer he was to Sidney, the post hospital and the railroad home.

The doctor was uneasy about Ed. Those pale-eyed, thin-skinned youths took the disease very hard this summer, with lingering intestinal ulceration, if they survived at all. She found him alone in a dugout in a deep box canyon that broke toward Lodgepole Creek, with signs of many horses held behind a brushy gate, perhaps hidden there through the daylight hours. Eddie barely recognized her and although much too weak to sit up he was still too heavy to lift into the wagon. With a shovel she always carried she sank the hind wheels almost to the hub, made a ramp with the door from the dugout, and drew Eddie up into the wagon on a blanket. Then she drove home, coming in late at night, and with Charley's help got him into bed, burning with fever, delirious, talking snatches of this and that, of a Jim and a Johnson, probably the dead Cut Lip, and of horses, but little that could be followed.

They took turns keeping him in sheets wrung out in a tub of cold water and tried to feed him a little medication in scalded milk, a teaspoonful at a time, but for three weeks Morissa was afraid to ask about him every time she returned, and every time she was awakened by Ruth or Charley in the night.

By then two of the other patients were gone, one well enough to start home, the other hauled to the railroad in a box—one out of seven in her little hospital.

The summer really had tapered off pretty thin for roadagents on the Cheyenne trail, with perhaps as little as thirteen dollars the holdups' entire haul. Passengers were searched two or three times; boots, coats, even the trousers of the men removed; the women compelled to take down their hair. One stage was robbed twice within twelve miles, and clothing and bits of choice food taken from the passengers, perhaps for the girl in the robber shack, Morissa thought, and hoped.

A troop of cavalry was assigned to special patrol and sometimes the soldiers rode the coaches. But the country was so vast, so broken, that it was safer to hold the gold back for the big bull trains or haul it on the Sidney trail. This was like a burr under the saddle blanket to Cheyenne, the newspapers demanding if there was no law in Wyoming, and no hemp for a little private stretching.

In September Sam Bass and his gang got between sixty and seventy-five thousand dollars in a Union Pacific holdup, but they did this in Nebraska, east of Sidney, not very far from the hideout where Morissa found Eddie. She wondered if typhoid had kept him out of the holdup, still refusing to believe this, yet telling herself that a nod truly is as good as a wink to a blind mare. But the sheriff wouldn't be blind when he brought a charge of harboring criminals against her, nor would those who believed in hanging any companion of horse thieves when they came kicking her door down.

There was talk that the Bass gang split up, with Sam going back to Texas, and the rest heading north toward Clarke's bridge. Morissa found signs of a night camp at her dam in the little canyon, and an old piece of canvas half sunken in the mud of the shallow reservoir. She pulled it out, a heavy leather sack with a metal slide top and padlock, evidently a registered mailbag with the federal mark cut out. She sent this down to Sidney but all she ever heard was that a sheriff from up in the Black Hills saw several of the Bass gang traveling the trail at night with a pack pony. They fled out upon the prairie and ran into some patrolling cavalry. There were seventeen thousand dollars of the Union Pacific loot in a pad under one of the saddles.

Three nights before this a man had come to Morissa's door to ask about Eddie Ellis. He slipped to the window so quietly that Blaze never awoke. Morissa let the man in, and with his hat tipped to shadow his

140

face to the bearded cheekbones, he looked down upon the gaunt skeleton on the cot. Suddenly Eddie opened his eyes. "Hello, Jim—" he said weakly, and then stopped when he saw that Morissa was there, too, holding the lamp above her head.

The man left quickly. At the door he whispered, "He's a goner," and put a roll of bills into the doctor's hand. "Have him buried right."

Afterward she went in to look down on Eddie. "If I dared move you I'd send you straight to Sidney. I don't like harboring outlaws—"

But there was still slyness in the sunken yellowed eyes. "You got no proof," he said, low and weak. "I—we made some friends up to Red Cloud, me and Jack—"

"Well, plainly you did," Morissa replied firmly and drew her hand from his clutching grasp. "I trust my brother is not involved with such men."

In late August, summer complaint had struck Etty's children and those on the trail clear in to Deadwood. Some were brought down by the hundreds of disappointed miners leaving before the winter. A party of Slavonians stopped their wagon at Morissa's place and one of the ragged, bearded men carried a small child in his arms to her, the body rigid and twisted, the eyes rolled up in convulsion. "Oh, that second summer—" the young doctor cried in pity, the men standing around with their callused hands hanging helplessly, tears slipping into the beard of the father.

Morissa worked fast with a tepid bath in the foot tub, enemas, and a very light dose of sirup of rhubarb root, until the child finally relaxed but lay with her face still as death in its shower of pale curls. Later she accepted a little scalded milk and although the convulsions returned, they were shorter, less violent, and in a few days the small girl was sitting up, her frailness a hurt in Morissa's breast. If only she could keep the child, feed her milk and eggs, set her in the window, with the sun golden on the pale hair, watch her grow strong and rosy and boisterous.

Then one day the father brought a gold nugget to lay in the doctor's palm. Morissa looked down at the man's feet in burlap sacking and wire, the thin knees out, and she returned the twisted little cherry of raw gold to him. He burst into angry speech and hurried away to begin a pounding at the wagon. Toward evening he came again and held out something shining—a new-wrought ring of soft, raw gold, worked in a skillful pattern, a stylized herald's staff and the twisted double serpents of the healer. Morissa looked into the father's face and as she met his deep-socketed eyes such a sweetness of gratitude and pride rose in them that she felt ashamed and small. So she slipped the ring to her finger and watched the ragged miner go with the lovely child in his arms.

141

Late that evening a man rode up from one of the saloons at the bridge. Doc was needed right away; a woman there had the screeches or fits, he couldn't rightly say which. Morissa found that it was Calamity Jane and screeching all right. Many of the whackers had dropped out with typhoid, or the fever to hunt gold farther north, toward the Yellowstone. Because Calamity claimed she had driven bulls and could certainly manage a deuce of empty wagons back, she was shanghaied and thrown in with the bedrolls to sleep it off. Sober, she had looked mighty sick, foulmouthed and complaining, but she could walk beside the bulls and cuss the horns off the mossiest of the outfit. Then here some fool tenderfeet tried to see how much whisky the lady wild cat of Deadwood Gulch could hold. Seems that four bits worth of Etty's snakehead whisky about did it.

Morissa got Jane quieted and over to the sodhouse. But Ruth banged her door at the sight of so dissolute a woman, and the doctor had to put the coffee on herself. Toward morning Morissa got her patient out of the ragged, stinking old rawhide suit, scrubbed and into a nightgown with embroidery at the throat and wrists, perhaps the first nightgown Calamity had worn in years. Morissa was unwilling to put her into the hospital room with the serious patients. Protecting their sleep against the tremens and the loud mouth of the woman, she told herself. But Jane got to Eddie next day, talking to him about men whose names Morissa couldn't catch because Ed kept shushing the woman, pretending later that it was because of the other patients.

In two days Morissa had Jane's hair soft and fluffy from an egg shampoo and got her into one of her dressing gowns, a rose-sprigged mull from the trousseau trunk. It was a little long for this other girl from Missouri, but it restored a hint of her winsome childhood as she came to sit in Morissa's window for a cup of tea, holding up the trailing skirts, suddenly playing the lady. Yes, she felt much stronger, strong enough to roar for a drink, it seemed. Morissa poured her a little brandy and then tried to visit with her about the Canary family and discover what might be done for their Martha Jane. But already she was Calamity again, slyly drawing the bottle into the folds of her skirts. Morissa let her, and pretended not to see as she thinned out her tea with the brandy, but listened politely to her howl of laughter at their reversed positions.

"You sure been climbin' up, Issy, settin' there big as a jaybird on a rail, callin' yourself doc an' all," she repeated several times over Morissa's protests that the framed diploma was genuine. "Remember when you was bein' passed 'round to do the dirty work, a poor-farm kid with no pa? Now you're in cahoots with them big horse thieves plain fer everybody to see, an' a ridin' pretty as a picture book behint them spankin' bays. Who'd expect it of such a hombly little bastard!"

Morissa gripped her fingers on the teacup, surprised that the handle didn't crumple like a curl of white meringue. But soon Jane slipped into her crying jag and so the young doctor gave her a golden double eagle to warm her palm, brought out the rawhide suit, washed and neat, and took her out to a bull train heading back toward Deadwood right away.

When Morissa got back to the house Ruth was cooking dinner, the first time she had come to the doctor's quarters since the night Calamity entered the place.

"I don't aim to consort with her kind," the woman said, tight-lipped, the thin cheekbones surprisingly pinkened. Charley tilted his chair back and laughed and didn't remind Ruth that one of the typhoid patients she packed and carried for night and day was from Madame Trogger's place down near Sidney.

New patients couldn't keep Morissa's mind from some of the things Calamity Jane had said, not even when Gwinnie came down with typhoid too. He asked for nothing, just lay like an emaciated young saint, his blue eyes burning in the skull holes of his face. But Eddie on the cot beside him was never quiet and kept Morissa reminded of his probable tie-up with outlaws. Certainly it was Eddie Ellis that Calamity had meant.

"If you run with horse thieves you'll be strung up for one—" Morissa had warned her brother Jack several times last spring. Now she decided that as soon as Ed was strong enough for the journey to Sidney she would take him to the hospital, the responsibility of his people, wealthy Ohioans, as she had discovered. But when she read the youth a paragraph from his father, he cried like a hysterical child. "You had no business—" he repeated over and over.

"A doctor must get in touch with a patient's relatives—"

"When he's dying!" he finished for her. "Well, I rather die here with you. I hate my father and now he's got my mother sidin' with him, too, saying she wants me to come home, go to college, be a credit to him."

"His letter sounds very kind and reasonable."

"I'll kill myself first—" Eddie sobbed, and weak yellowish tears ran unnoticed from the corner of his eyes into the pillow.

So Morissa soothed him and put the idea aside for a while. He was still too weak for the trip. When the time came to write to the father she would tell him some of the things the son felt.

The Coad ranch kept the settlers out of the broad south valley and so far none had followed Morissa across the river. When an ambitious homeseeker came looking for government corners, he was met by cold-eyed, gun-fondling men who seemed to be cowboys, but were soft-handed and with free time to see everything, like the Bosler pistoleer who came to buy Morissa out. Even so the homeseekers pushed in closer. Several cowboys who knew the country and were handy with hardware themselves homesteaded south of the Wild Cat range on little valleys too small and too remote in the mountainous hills from the adjoining ranches. But after the settler was found shot in the back below Sidney, even these men were a little uneasy and Morissa with them, for herself and for next spring's homeseekers who would surely be pushing into the valley of Coad and Bosler. They would not only be dragging trouble at their stubborn heels but finding it there, waiting.

A series of fires running through the dry prairie followed the settler killing—homesteaders, grangers, burning out the winter range, the cattlemen complained. All one windy week the south horizon bloomed in white, opalescent smoke. Men from the north ranches, even the newer ones up toward the Niobrara and the Snake Creek flats, answered the distress signal of the range country. But with all the region fighting, the flames left whole townships black as shadowed velvet, and at one ranch four horses lay charred in the ashes of a log stable. They were blooded stock and if the man who set the fire was caught he would decorate a cottonwood till the buzzards picked his eyes out. True, the same thing had been promised for the thieves who stole the race horses at the Walker show but the horse thieves were mighty small-bore trouble compared to the settlers who would wreck the whole free-range business.

There was an increase of angry talk against the grangers around the saloons and the livery stables, and at the whisky ranches along the trail. Several new men known to be fast on the draw showed up at the North Platte ranches, all riding horses conspicuously branded, but never headed toward the hard work of the cattle. Morissa remembered Tris's remark that so long as the holdups continued, the professional gunmen would sit sassy as rattlesnakes on the doorstep and everybody had to walk around them. Evidently many were ready to walk around these hired range protectors just as meekly if they kept the settlers away.

Tris was back from Omaha and had been up to the Dr. Kirk Sanitarium, as Morissa's new sign in the window now announced—an absurd, squat little sod sanitarium standing alone, without city or settlement beyond the few houses of the bridge, and in unorganized territory, a sanitarium in the wilderness.

The tall rancher was quiet the first time he saw the sign with the little vigil lights behind it, setting it off in the black darkness like a string of swamp lights.

"What would you say to a practice in Omaha again?" he asked the next Sunday as they rode up the river toward Ted Sailor's British ranch.

"You aren't going to quit running cattle?" Morissa asked, dropping into the ranch expression in her concern.

"Oh, no, but with as good a foreman as I have—" he stopped, and busied himself switching the black mane of his horse all one way and then back. "The meat-packing business that's opening up in Omaha will make money for the first comers—" It seemed somehow very serious, this that he was trying to say and yet did not. Morissa remembered his Auntie Mae and her twin daughters who needed money to make the good marriages that were fitting. Besides, the haze of smoke left by the burning prairie, perhaps set by homesteaders like herself, was still blue against Chimney Rock and Scotts Bluff ahead of them, with antelope and even rabbits thick, perhaps from the burned-over region. There was silence between them until they saw two of the Britishers from Sailor's chasing a gray wolf and just about to rope him as they all vanished over a hill.

"That wolf's slow and his tail's dragging, probably mangy," Tris said, "or sick or burned."

"Could be mangy all right. I dispense a lot of itch ointment to the humans around here," Morissa answered, and was angry at her literalness.

There was a fine ranch supper at Sailor's: grouse, but unhung and Western-fresh, so any doctor could bear to eat it; venison, too, with Sailor's ale, the product that had built the family fortune in England. Tris and Morissa planned to ride back through the early moonlight but somehow the time passed, first over the hunting stories when the young men brought in their itchy wolf, and then the discussion Morissa started by saying they should burn or bury the wolf right away and bake all their clothing and rope, take scrub baths and a good anointing with a stinking itch ointment she would be happy to prescribe.

Later a couple of breed fiddlers played for the stomp of boots, although there were only four women for around twenty-five men, including about everybody of the ranch except the bronch-crippled choreman. When they were ready to start back through the clouding night, a couple of shots down at the corrals started everybody looking out to see who had so much steam to let off.

But there was a yelling that sounded like the choreman, and so everybody pushed out the door together, like cows coming out of a corral. Scattering for leg room, they ran down the slope, Morissa and Tris too, everybody very long in the light of Ted Sailor's lantern as he came puffing along behind.

There were three, four more shots, fast, spitting bright red in the darkness, and then the running of a horse. When they reached the pole corrals everything was still, but as the light of the lantern swung around through the open gate, it fell on a man down in the dry horse dust. It was Sailor's new gun hand, Pete Shrone. Nobody else seemed around but after a while the choreman came sidling out of a stable, still cautious.

"Man come ridin' in a little piece ago, askin' for Pete," the crippled old cowboy managed to say. "So I fetches him down to where Pete likes to set nights, seein's he don't have much truck with the bunkhouse—"

"Yeh, Pete's kind don't," someone volunteered readily enough, now that the gunman was dying.

So Tris and Morissa had to stay. After the man was dead the doctor cut out a bullet that had come up diagonally through his side and almost out the opposite shoulder—a mushroomed bullet that was a gray lump just under the skin. The man had spoken no word, although he was conscious to the end. But the choreman was happy with his circle of dark, attentive faces and repeated all he knew over and over. " 'Damn your hide, Joe Barker!' the stranger yells when he finds Pete a settin' there on them corral poles. 'I been follyin' you a thousan' miles, now go fer yer gun!' Then there's two quick shots runnin' together, and the newcomer's down in the dirt. Pete ambles over to 'im, laughin' that he's got a man down to fill full a lead. But there's three shots from the ground, fast, and Pete drops, his gun blastin' off into the air. Then the man tears out fer his horse and quits the country."

"So Ladyfinger Pete got his—" the cowboys told each other, laughing a little out of the contempt and envy that the working hands had for the high-priced pistoleers.

Tris was even quieter on the slow ride home through the clouding dawn and Morissa too. At the house Eddie was crying into his pillow because the doctor had been gone so long. Gwinnie had tried to help Ruth quiet him, make him feel that he wasn't deserted. Morissa found herself impatient with the sick youth as a mother might be impatient, and as contrite and loving, too, it seemed.

But before sleeping she wrote his father a little more urgently. "I really think your son Edward Ellis should be removed to a hospital where he can receive the very best treatment and care. His condition continues most serious, mentally as well as physically." Yet instead of relief Morissa felt a loss, a sad and empty loss, as though her patient were already gone. Something like the loss she felt when Tom Reeder left, only this went deeper, deep as a scalpel's blade.

Many times in her months here at the bridge, Morissa was out when Tris came, or had to leave, and slowly she admitted to herself what she had often said lightly to him—that the wife of Tris Polk should not be a doctor. Yet he had always waited, sometimes many hours, and when she put on the gold-shot reseda or the brocade of blush pink, lovely as

146

the prairie roses of August in the evening sun, no trace of annoyance seemed to remain. Finally the Sunday after the Sailor visit he spoke of the new ranch house that was to be ready for them when they came back from Texas and Illinois. "—Unless you prefer your home in Sidney, or in Omaha."

"Oh, the ranch, certainly the ranch," Morissa said, still trying to make it light, protecting herself, not clear just from whom, but when Tris kissed her she knew he took it as acceptance. She knew, too, that now she had dared to mean it, and was just a little saddened by what seemed a curious sort of desertion of Allston Hoyt and the memory of him. Almost like a daughter going away.

The next week the stage brought up a great box of roses that Tris had sent from Omaha, with a June calendar sheet enclosed and a ribboned bit of pencil that Lorette's young daughters would receive with joy. Morissa put one of the roses into the hair of the woman from Madame Trogger's and held the armful up high for Gwinnie and the others to see, their sick eyes momentarily alight with pleasure at the flowers and the flushed face of their doctor. But when Morissa looked over to Eddie he had turned towards the plastered wall, his thin shoulder racked with his crying, so she went for a bowl of soup and fed him with a spoon, although he could sit up as well as anyone by now.

At first Morissa found herself resisting the June plans perhaps because of that other spring date set two years ago with Allston and all the humiliation and unhappiness that grew out of it. But Tris was a man of different caliber. He knew Robin was her stepfather and that Morissa had been put out on a poor-farm and surely all that Calamity Jane could tell. For it turned out that Calamity hadn't stayed with the bull train after Morissa sobered her up but wandered back to hang around Clarke's and Etty's, until she was howling again, shouting out her damning words against their lady doc who would throw a sick woman into a bull wagon to get rid of her. Morissa Kirk was nothing but a woods colt, a dirty bastard. Finally Clarke's man had her loaded on his train, to ride the bedrolls out of there, cold drunk.

Nothing of this was mentioned directly to Morissa, except that Tris seemed even more openly proud of the doctor's accomplishments, which warmed Morissa's cheeks to glowing. So she circled the twenty-sixth of June for him. "Wednesday is the best day of all," her mother once said sentimentally, and wistfully. And, "Married in the month of roses, June, life will be like one long honeymoon."

So Morissa wrote her dressmaker for fashion plates of wedding attire, perhaps a silk suit this time, more fitting than a white dress here in the valley. Besides, a woman should have only one white wedding dress and hers was already in the bottom of a trunk, folded away carefully in blue tissue paper to prevent the satin's yellowing, although why she took these precautions she could not have told.

There must be two or three cool and pretty afternoon dresses, too, for Texas, and something a little more elaborate for evening, selected to show off her brown skin. No, better two evening gowns, one yellow because Tris preferred that and one in the fashionable and delicate new shade called Georgia peach.

With this feminine planning started, she wrote a letter to Dr. Aiken about her work here and her plans, asking him to recommend a substitute for the summer, perhaps permanently. Then there was a letter to Robin and Jackie, too, and finally one for Tris's Auntie Mae. "I am a happy betrothe—"

XII

THE YEAR TURNING TOWARD FALL WAS THE FINEST MORISSA HAD ever seen, sweet and golden, fragrant as her muskmelons ripening in the sun. But she couldn't live in this mood long. On the way back from typhoid vigils up north, she rode home beside a detachment of troops that Etty had guided in a three weeks' scout around the Black Hills. More Indian trouble, Lieutenant Larman said, and told her about the Indian uprisings all over the West, particularly up north again.

"—Now the troops they chase the Nez Perce, the people who grow the fine Appaloosa horse," the usually silent Etty said. "But today they go hungry and run on foot; run over rocks with soldiers chasing."

Morissa nodded. She had heard that was why long lines of troops had been marching over Clarke's bridge this summer again, hurrying to Red Cloud, many to go on north against the Nez Perce, already being pursued with Gatling guns and howitzer. Meanwhile, although gold dust poured into the Sidney bank, discouraged placer miners had been scattering north to prospect the Little Missouri country and were attacked by a few Sioux still off the reservation. One man was shot and all the horses taken, the miners forced to make the hundred miles back afoot. Deadwood raised the bounty on Indian scalps to a hundred and fifty dollars each, and when freighting slacked off, some of the bullwhackers that Morissa knew went Indian hunting with the rest. And now, with more troops drawn away from around Red Cloud Agency it seemed Crazy Horse was ready to hit the warpath again from there, only one good ride from the bridge.

"Do you believe it this time?" Morissa asked the young lieutenant, recalling all the scares of last summer.

"I don't know—" he replied, less certain about such things now than his first year out of West Point.

But that night a courier galloped out of the darkness warning all the trail and the bridge to prepare for a siege, a Sioux uprising. Morissa replied to his call and went back to bed, but several bluecoats came to take her to the darkened blockhouse.

"And what's to become of my bed patients, five with typhoid, two smallpox?" she asked.

So the troopers went back without her. Because Charley was off at Sidney, Ruth brought Blaze into the hospital room, away from the silencing knife, the arrow and tomahawk. For the first time she consented to put her hand to the steel of a gun as Morissa showed her how to fire the Colt, the Peacemaker, the doctor very patient, remembering her own horror of its dark weight only a little over a year ago.

While they were seated at the kitchen table, the gun between them, there was a soft tap at the door, unannounced by the fat, overfed Blaze dog. Morissa looked into the frightened eyes of Ruth Adams. With a swift motion of her hand the doctor pushed the gun to Ruth and sent her into the darkened hospital room. Then, with her rifle across her arm, she swung the shielded wall lamp around so the light fell upon the door, leaving her in duskiness and called, "Come in!"

A man stood in the opening doorway, a white man, young. "I came to see how Eddie Ellis is getting along—" he said apologetically.

"Well, you picked a good time, in the middle of an Indian scare!"

Afterward Morissa discovered it was Doug Goodale, said to be an outlaw too but he visited pleasantly with them that night, sitting at ease like a man well accustomed to the parlor and the drawing room. When he left he thanked the doctor. "A very pleasant evening, Miss Morissa," he said, tipping his Western hat as though on a city street.

"He's the son of a banker," Eddie said proudly, and Morissa was pleased in his pride. That and the two girls from Sidney who had come last week to see Ed seemed good omens; perhaps this patient would yet learn to be something but a hospital infant, would become a well man. It was true that the girls had seemed a bit more interested in the bridge settlement, particularly the saloons and dance halls, and even in Gwinnie. But they were well-spoken and had evidently met Eddie at a church social.

But young Goodale's visit helped ease the night and soon after dawn Charley was back. He had heard of the Indian alarm and drove his load straight through to get in, very uneasy after he heard the death keening of Etty's wife as he passed there.

Morissa knew of no one dying, but when the sun came out hot on a

149

peaceful valley, the trail was strangely empty until stirred by the hurrying dust of an army ambulance in from the north—a bearded private of the infantry riding in lone and healthy importance inside. He was kept from the saloons and gambling houses and sent on as fast as fresh horses could be hiked to the tongue, but the story of his exploit spread even faster. It seemed Crazy Horse had plotted the assassination of General Crook at the Chief's camp outside of Red Cloud. He was captured and this soldier, William Gentles, bayoneted him through the kidney. Now the Sioux were up and so the man had to be hurried away and everyone must flee the country.

It was this keening for the dead Chief that Charley had heard at Etty's, but the stocky little Frenchman stood like a tree in his baggy old pants against any move. "I have the story from the relative come last night. He say no Indian is killing anybody up there." The government wanted to take the Sioux off their reservation, move them to a hungrier country but Crazy Horse had been promised an agency up on the Yellowstone. He would make trouble. The soldiers arrested him to be taken South, to the stone prison of Florida. When they pushed him into the guardhouse, he jumped back and was jabbed with the bayonet.

So there were two versions of this, too, Morissa thought as she saw even the most land-hungry around the bridge have a moment of regret that this wild, free man must die, as though they knew that a little of themselves had died, too, no matter how treacherous they thought the Indian.

Morissa went to work off her anger stripping ripe cucumbers and muskmelons of their seed to dry in the sun, drawing wasps and sugar ants and a cloud of blackbirds to walk over the screening that kept them off. Then she went through the growing trees of her timberclaim, a flock of quail flushing from the weeds at her feet. But she barely noticed the whirr they made, thinking of the claims that passed over this region like cloud shadows running before the wind, first the Indian, then the cattleman, and now the settler coming. She forgot entirely that soon she would be out of this, married, protected, living down below Sidney—out of this valley that had seemed as much her inevitable path now as it was to the tranquil, sandy stream already deepening toward winter.

There were two children in the little sod hospital now, belonging to a gold seeker whose wife died of typhoid in a wagon camped one day's drive up the trail. Morissa had been called at the last, when there was nothing to be done except take the two small ones, ill too, away from their miserable soogans and the lame nursing of a grieving man. The girl was five, the boy three, and although weak and scrawny as birdlings, they wouldn't eat, only sobbed softly for their mother. Finally the small Alice forgot her fierce protectiveness of her younger brother long enough to go to sleep in Tris Polk's arms and let the doctor take the boy. Over the children they talked about the plans Morissa had when she entered medical school; the alleviation of pain and sorrow for sick and lonely children, to help them be as happy and healthy as she planned her own should be some day. And now, with a woman's eye, Morissa Kirk appraised the man who was to be their father, and smiled within herself, a woman fulfilled.

Soon Fish Head discovered Alice and Georgie and almost at once he was a child with them. Morissa saw it the first time she found them together, the gray little man sitting first on one cot and then the other, giving them their turns at the set of tiddly-winks the father had sent the children. With his tongue a pink tip at the corner of his bearded lips, Fish helped Georgie to snap the little red disks into the cup, holding the boy's small hand under his, the man's very little larger and almost clean, so the scar was a bright twist. Behind them was Ruth, watching unobserved, her face mellow and warm.

Almost every day since then the Fish slipped up to the back door with the catch of his lines or more often cottontail or grouse, for a trade with Ruth. When Morissa asked how he got all the grouse he said he saved the scattered oats and corn from the trail feed grounds, although some claimed he wasn't beyond fighting the mules off. He soaked the grain in a bucket until it was fermented and then scattered the mash around that old cottonwood above the timberclaim, where grouse came to roost, so many that the tree looked silvery in the rising sun as they flew down to feed. When they started to jump around, picking at each other and tumbling over like happy gold seekers who had been at the jug under the wagon seat, he slipped up with his dipnet and caught the grouse like fish.

"The only drawback, dear lady, is the season; becoming too intemperately chill for adequate fermentation," Fish Head said wistfully.

But Ruth was not the woman to let him keep the stinking bucket in the house. She did see that he never went hungry, and that his old black broadcloth suit was cleaned and set aside for the funerals he loved, and for Morissa's wedding next June. He was no longer barefoot, but wearing a pair of boots left behind by a man who died of typhoid at the hospital in the summer, and his cowboy clothing that Ruth cut down. Even Charley had been drawn upon. In the sod fuel house hung a hammock made from an old wagon tarp. There Fish Head curled up like a bony little slug, perhaps to sleep through a whole day after he walked in from some far fish hole or a cowcamp that was free with meals.

151

There was a rush of talk against the government among the agency contractors and freight outfits around the bridge now, even from Clarke. With Crazy Horse killed before their eyes, the resistance of the Sioux was really broken and they must move, in spite of the local contractors who protested that this destroyed their business investments. The Indians complained too. There was no game on the new place over beyond the Bad Lands, no farm ground, only the whisky that ruined their young men. After a pitiful plea from the older chiefs a few were taken to see the White Father. Morissa was at the bridge with her two small patients in the buggy, showing them the names carved there when the agency wagons came down the sun-yellowed slopes of evening and wound slowly toward the river. Slowly too the Indians climbed down from the double seats. Blankets and braids gray with dust, they stood together in a forlorn little knot and finally followed a young West Pointer and the agency interpreters in to Etty's for supper. There was a smarting in Morissa's eyes as she watched old Red Cloud, who had backed the White Father's army down along the Bozeman trail, also a gold road, and with him were the sub-chiefs of Crazy Horse, still out warring only six months ago. Now the moccasins of these men followed a dapper young shavetail so humbly, men who had managed the only two complete wipe-outs of the U.S. Army—Fetterman and Custer, the latter barely fourteen months ago. How quickly a people can be brought to the ground, Morissa thought, as she impulsively purchased a tub of gingersnaps to go with Etty's coffee and tin plates of fried beef and bread, and then felt ashamed of her pitiful gift.

But the luck of the Sioux was really done. In October their agencies were packed on wagons for the move. This stopped all Indian freight over Clarke's bridge, and their beef drives too. The traders and breed roadranchers were scattering from up at Red Cloud, some going with the Indians, others to the Black Hills. One started a little sod place facing the trail just north of the bridge, across from the new whisky saloon going up there with Huff Johnson as faro dealer and general gunman, a fast hand at both. The cattlemen looked upon these new buildings north of the river with distant faces but their ranch hands kept the doors fanning, and everyone waited to see how soon Tris Polk would be in a gunfight with Johnson over Gilda Ross.

These places on a homestead across the river, together with the expulsion of the Indians, seemed a sort of bridge, too, a bridge from one era to another, and so Morissa decided to go up to see the Sioux taken away. Sid Martin had bought one of the breed roadranches to give him headquarters on the White River and was pointing a herd of cows up there to winter in the breaks. He offered to bring back the three horses Morissa was to pick up from Etty's breed relatives for medical fees. Tris came along, and two army couples from Camp Sidney, all invited to a dance at Fort Robinson. It lasted late and so it was almost noon the next day when they finally rode down to the agency. The Indians were already on the move, two troops of cavalry in the lead, then Red Cloud and his chiefs riding their ponies abreast in a short line, and the many thousands of Sioux behind them, their dragging lodgepoles stirring the dust to a thick cloud that drifted off across the broad, yellowed slopes. Then two long freight trains started with rations, and finally a big beef herd.

Morissa and Tris watched the people go along the valley of the White, sad, silent, with no joyous noise of whoops and laughter, no young men showing off in the usual way of a Sioux camp on the move. This time it was Tris Polk who could not bear to look, and for a moment Morissa caught the glint of tears in his gray eyes. But there was ready diversion: Sid Martin's cow herd coming down the slope of the southern bluffs, a dusty brown stream spreading into the valley, with the yips of the cowboys to keep them together. Tris said nothing then but later he began to talk a little, standing his stirrups as the Texan he was, while the horses, the stockinged black and the Appaloosa, jogged along abreast. Eight years ago when he first saw this White River valley on a hunt, it had been buffalo country. Then suddenly the herds were gone, even the bones hauled to the railroad, and now the Indians, too, their tracks not yet cold before the cattleman was tromping them out, the white man with his cows coming down the slope over there. And who could say how soon these too must go?

Morissa touched the man's arm comfortingly, and as he bent his head to hear her soft words above the call of the cowboys, the bawling of the herd, she kissed his smooth brown cheek. "You are a serious man—" she said.

"We are both serious people," he replied, "and so are most of our fellow men, but somehow we let the ground here be bloodied by the buffalo we destroyed, and now the Indian killed and run out. The weeds from such fertilizer should grow mighty sprangly." He spoke a little sheepishly, a little embarrassed and uneasy, as though caught out with a branding iron at midnight.

They rode down to Martin's herd and looked over the range he had laid claim to, with good water and the shelter of bluff and timbered canyon. Already other ranchers had moved in above and below him. Morissa didn't ask how long they thought their free grass would last, nor did she mention the rumors she had heard that the TeePee, Tris's place below Sidney, had hired a friend of the Pete Shrone who was killed at Sailor's not long ago. Later it proved to be the Box T, but the TeePee cowboys did turn cattle in around the granger sod houses to rub them down—big herds, a couple thousand head at a time. Tris often said he had a good foreman, and this was considered the smart way—as good a hint to the settler as a bullet through his window at night, or through his back, and the TeePee way couldn't be proved deliberate. Cattle did wander and stray.

Morissa and Tris came back from the deserted Red Cloud Agency with a black dog following them, and the ownership of a canary that an officer's wife asked the young doctor to take. They were being transferred, she said, and so Morissa put the cage on the coach and carried the bird in a Sioux grasshopper box in her overcoat pocket because this would amuse little Georgie and Alice. As they came into the North Platte valley, Morissa saw that Charley had started the soddy on his homestead, the walls up waist high. Tris didn't stop his horse at the sight, but Morissa caught his surprise, and his searching look with the gray of a far blizzard in his eyes.

"Well, that makes four moved in north of the river," he finally said, "counting the new roadhouse and the saloon. But you and your trees were the first, like the first cow to slip from the roundup herd, tolling the rest to follow her for the breaks."

Yes, Morissa admitted, smiling a little and ignoring his bitterness, but she remembered that trail herders carried guns to bring such bunch quitters down. She remembered too that one spark can set the best beard afire, and that the way to put the sow out of the parlor is before she ever gets in. Sobered, she wondered if this matter of her timberclaim, her settlement over here, was to stand between them in the wall that sometimes grows up between man and wife, a wall that becomes rock, massive and high and cold.

But the next morning there was an early tap at her door. It was Tris, starting home from Clarke's. Taking Morissa's arm he hurried her out to her little pond. There a swan floated in the early fall stillness, his reflection motionless, a pure white swan with graceful bend of throat.

Most of the neighbors of the settler shot below Sidney were gone, perhaps for the winter, most likely for good. Some who stayed fingered their lean purse strings thoughtfully and then bought a little protection, too, perhaps an old rifle or a shotgun with buckshot, to use for game until they needed it against a range guard, a range pistoleer.

But the new homesteaders along the slopes of the Wild Cats, with some former cowboys among them, were not scaring out. One of them had other worries besides soft-handed gunmen. His two children picked up black diphtheria at Sidney and Morissa's top buggy lurched across the prairie to his dugout three times in one week. She was returning sadly through a graying afternoon, with flocks of snowbirds swirling like dusty leaves in the wind, when a rider came kicking a work mare toward her buggy, the sway-backed old horse jumping washouts and gullies to head her off.

Morissa reached for her rifle as every settler did these days, but the man held up his empty hands, shouting, "Doctor! Doctor!" It seemed that John Callwin, living up one of the box canyons, got hit on the head in a well. Although the man's story was jumbled and incoherent, Morissa dared not doubt it. She turned her team and followed him, whipping her horses into a run, too, for Callwin still seemed to be down there, unconscious.

"—I— let a plank s-s-slip!" the man kept saying over and over, "I—I —let it—"

The two-by-four was one of those laid across the top of the well curbing to serve as a platform for the buckets of excavated earth, and the well was deep. Morissa got her bag and, tucking her skirts back out of the way, she went down the ladder of the curbing. The man was there, crumpled under a slanted plank, jackknifed into the wet narrow bottom with a hole in the side of his skull almost as big as her palm. But he was still alive, and with a rope tied under his arms and run up through the windlass, the two drew at the man. Slowly, heavily, with the doctor steadying big John Callwin against one rung of the ladder after another, they got him out.

By now snowflakes were sifting like chaff from the gray sky, and the frightened settler had to go home to his wife, sick and alone with a blizzard upon them, and expecting her first baby. He helped Morissa get Callwin into his little dugout and stretch him out on boards laid across nail kegs and boxes, and left apologetically. In the light of the lantern Morissa built up a fire and set to work as swiftly as she could. She laid back the skin, lifted out the skull fragments and cut away the damaged tissue, working as carefully as at the most intricate, delicate embroidery, and then at the clotted blood, too, until it became watery seepage. Somehow the man's heart still kept beating, and over and over the young doctor thanked God for this strong country, these strong men. She would not, she must not lose this patient today, not when she had just helped bury a child taken right out of her hands by the diphtheria.

When Morissa finished there was the crushed and swollen scalp to consider. It seemed alive enough to repair itself but not over a naked brain, and there was no time to send to Sidney through the storm for anything. Then she remembered the silver half dollar in her pocket that the father of the dead child had put into her cloak as a token of his indebtedness. She had that, and the memory of how her ring of raw gold was hammered from a nugget by the Slavonian miner last summer.

Quickly she tied the scalp together by knotting the hair, and with the

155

lantern she went into the thickening snow to scratch among the tools left scattered at the well for that most common piece of settler equipment, a claw hammer. At last she found it and at a wheel of the man's wagon she pounded the half dollar into an oblong silver plate, thin, and slightly curved from the shape of the iron tire. She roughened the plate carefully and punched a few smooth holes around the edges for tissue penetration, with a larger one toward each end for drainage tubes. Then she washed the plate carefully in strong carbolic solution, sewed it over the quivering brain and drew the mangled, swollen scalp together as closely as she could without damage. And still there was the marvel of the man's living.

Afterward she remembered her team. She went out to hobble them so they could not stray too far, and brought in wood from the man's great pile of it. With the fire going and a cup of coffee she sat down to watch the still face in the lantern light as the snow fell softly over the dugout.

XIII

It was a long night, this time of sitting in a little dugout beside a man with a broken head, and toward four Morissa caught herself up from a doze. Startled and afraid, she put her fingers to the man's pulse and found it almost gone. That was what had roused her, the change in his breathing, so weak it seemed to have stopped. Quickly she administered the heart stimulant laid out ready, a light dose that would not overwork a weakened organ, hopeful that it would be enough.

Then she leaned forward with the lantern turned up bright on the man's face, so white now below the bandages where wind burn had certainly lain yesterday, her fingers chafing the wrists that were thick and strong, and so remote. The stovepipe began to rattle in the wind that rose toward dawn, either for a blizzard or a clearing of the skies, and the doctor dared not go far enough from the bunk to look out the low door. Finally she had to replenish the fire with the last of the wood piled against the earthen wall. She put the coffee bucket on and when it boiled up strong in the little dugout, she saw the man stir to the sharp, familiar odor. He groaned a little, mumbling, "Oh-h, my head's busting—"

"It is busted," Morissa agreed soothingly, putting out a restraining hand to hold the man motionless. He opened his eyes at the touch,

156

tried to rub the blur from them to see the woman more clearly in the dim lantern light, and gave it up.

"Your head is busted, but it can heal—" Morissa said, laughing softly, to make it sound easy and casual and half a dream as she put a bent straw from the coffee cup to the man's lip. He sipped a little and then was gone again, either into sleep or unconsciousness, perhaps somewhere on the thin border between, and all Morissa could do was watch his retreat.

The fall snow was gone from the south slopes before the doctor dared to think of leaving the man even long enough to get word to Charley Adams that she needed the wagon and the cottonwood leaf pallet to move a patient. By then Charley had come looking for her, riding along the rocky crest of the Wild Cat range. She saw him stop here and there to search the breaks and the far slopes both ways with field glasses, the sun glinting from them as he turned.

Two days later they had John Callwin in the little hospital. There was infection in the mangled scalp and no telling how much trapped underneath the silver plate in the delicate tissues of the brain, although the fever was almost down and the drain tubes oozed only a little watery fluid. Still the man barely clung to consciousness and was very weak and pale, with curious insensate areas, and no real paralysis where it might be expected.

Morissa searched her bookcase of medical works and found no remedy except good nursing and time, so she turned to a series of cool packs for the unwounded portions of the head and tried to shut her ears to the man's groaning in the night after she had to cut off the morphine. Charley watched all this uneasily and finally wondered if leeches wouldn't help.

"Mebby with less blood—" he said, embarrassed by his presumption. "Doc Gaines was a great believer in bloodsuckers. I lugged his jar a them all through the Tennessee campaign—"

But Morissa shook her head and worked out a nourishing diet of milk, eggs, and fresh game. "We'll just have to wait and hope," she said, wondering about sending the man down to Sidney. But it was a long jolting trip and all the space there was filled by the drawn-out convalescence from typhoid and the new outbreak of diphtheria that struck even grown people. "The town just isn't equal to the rush into the country this year," Clarke told Morissa. "Not with so much gold business and all the new settlers."

When little Georgie was too restless in the night, the shy-mouthed Gwinnie liked to have the boy brought to lie beside him a while as though beside his father. But Ed was troublesome about the children, complaining over the attention they got, the noise they made. He hid their big ball when it rolled his way and sneered at Fish Head to drive him out. Ed's health was worse, too, with a persistent rectal bleeding and the vomiting back. Morissa hadn't dared to ask what happened the six days she was away, but the young man's return to a babyishness beyond even small Georgie's worried her, his sobbing if she left the place for even an hour, and her own foolish tendency to humor him when she recognized his jealousy very well.

Now there was a new target for Ed, his pale eyes burning feverishly toward John Callwin because Morissa had to go over him repeatedly, mapping out the insensitive regions to discover what she might of his total injury, of any changes, both for herself and for John's uncle, a doctor in Seattle. The uncle had written immediately upon her telegram, wishing he could get away. "The brain cavity is one we dare not enter with impunity; not at all unless we must. That my nephew is still alive testifies to your skill and your courage." But even as she read this, with burning face, to John, there was the cry of "Bedpan! Bedpan!" from Eddie. And Ruth wouldn't do, or Charley.

"Oh, Ed, you could get up," Morissa scolded as she put the yellow telegram under John Callwin's numbed hand for his comfort. But she went, angry that of all her Western patients, only this one didn't protest the bedpan as a shameful violation of a man's dignity. Even Gwinnie at his worst tried to get up until they had to hold him down, easily done with one hand. The two children always demanded that they be taken out, clear out to the privy behind the bare trees.

The hospital patients were down to seven now, counting Alice and Georgie. John's head wound was some better, enough so that Morissa really hoped for a healing over her silver plate, his hand-hammered pot lid, as he called it. Sometimes he could sit up without too much dizziness and nausea, and gradually it seemed to lessen the headaches.

"Drains the blood off," he said, grinning wryly under the white bandage.

But now he began to worry about his homestead. If an entryman didn't live on his claim it was subject to contest, and while there was plenty of free land around, he had a dugout and a well with a good curbing down to water sand—a place of sorts for his wife in the spring. Besides, the cattlemen might jump his place to get rid of a settler who wouldn't scare out easy. Such a contest could be won but it would take time and money and John Callwin had neither. So Morissa drove him over to spend a night or so in the dugout, with Charley along as nurse and witness, and to do a little winter-work around the place, cover the well and stack the stovewood inside.

By now the story of the silver plate had spread. John Callwin's uncle wrote of it to Dr. Jacobs of Sidney who took the stage right out to see the patient and report. Afterward he sent a letter to the Sidney paper, telling of the curious accident and the fine piece of emergency surgical work. Next time Morissa went down she found herself described as the Silver Doc of the Gold Trail by the newspaper and on the street. Several times during the winter she was called into consultation on head injuries and suspected tumors, once as far away as the middle of the state. When she returned John Callwin had a welcome for her. He moved his left arm easily, flexing his fingers to show his progress. "Your Highland grandmother was a wise woman," he said. "Truly much can be made of a Scotsman if he be caught oft an' early."

But Eddie was no better, with little interest in anything except getting childish attention, none in the pile of magazines and books on the box between him and John, or any news of the trail or the gold or even of the outlaws. The letter that came from his father was no help:

> We are anxious to do what we can for our son but, frankly, we prefer that he remain in your care. A pretty and long-awaited baby, and a handsome toddler, he was a great favorite with everyone and idolized by his mother. By way of gratitude he drove her into sorrowful seclusion. He was irresponsible, insolent and indolent as a boy; sly, thieving and vicious as a youth. He attempted to kill one of his friends and forged the signatures of a dozen relatives and my business associates. Only his flight to the frontier saved us the embarrassment of a son who was a convicted felon or worse. He is like a changeling among us, or one possessed.
>
> I speak frankly; he has brought my beloved wife into invalidism.
>
> Your Obedient Servant,
> Culver Ellis

Slowly Morissa unpinned the check, folded the letter and put it away.

The cattlemen pushed the sheriff about Pete Shrone's murderer. Finally a man suspected of shooting him was picked up in the Trail Driver's saloon at Sidney, along with at least fifty strangers there that day, all questioned because they were strangers. Jim Hobert wouldn't talk except to say he knew nobody named Pete Shrone. But a bullet from his revolver seemed to fit the markings on the one Morissa had cut out of Pete's shoulder, so he was held for spring court.

All the autumn roadagents worked the Cheyenne trail like beavers piling up young cottonwood for a hard winter. Several times Morissa tried to get Eddie to talk about his associates and the man who came to leave the roll of bills, or about Doug Goodale. Ed still seemed very weak, yet sometimes in the sunlight of the windows, under the blooming geraniums and the canary that sang for the children, it was hard to accept his sickness as real.

With no more Indian herds to run off and the trail stock guarded, horse thieves began to move in around Platte bridge and the ranchers off south, but none were so bold yet as the men who swept away the race horses at Walker's. Many still claimed that was certainly done by Doc Middleton. He knew the country and the stock. A horse he sold for the running circuits around Sioux City looked like Neptune but without the white star, unless the bluish scar with a scattering of white hair on his forehead was a tattoo.

Doors still had no locks against petty robbers around the bridge but when two horse thieves tried to run off Etty's herd, the little Frenchman sent them flying. Then he plodded over to Morissa. "Mebby horse thief he come for cut out buckshot. You let me know—" he said, patting the lock of his old sawed-off purposefully. But Morissa did not have to face this professional decision. The buckshot was taken elsewhere.

Fish Head enjoyed the outlaws' discomfiture. "Hunger will drive the wolf into the kitchen of the powder maker," he said, without much regret.

Two thieves tried to run off some horses down near Sidney. One was killed, the other shipped to Wyoming to face earlier charges. At last Cheyenne made a real effort to hold the moneyed travel that shied from holdups like horses from mountain lions. Deadwood posted an offer of two hundred dollars per outlaw, dead or alive. With hundreds of stamp mills working, placer men with gold dust in the pocket for any taking were gone. As winter closed down many of the badmen deserted the region, gone south with the geese. Even so Morissa was happy that Jack seemed safely away at school, and Ed in his hospital bed. She went to Sidney with Tris at Christmastime and came back loaded with the presents and the trimmings for a tree, a quiet one, with so many critically weak. Next year—

"Next year we'll bust the sky open!" Tris promised little Georgie.

"Shhh!" Morissa whispered, certain Eddie would be crying again.

"Send him to Sidney," Tris commanded.

Morissa laughed at his angry face and in a moment Ed seemed forgotten.

In late January several mule trains from Sidney were attacked by Indians up toward Deadwood. In one baled hay and grain had foolishly been piled on top of the rifles but the men got to them and used the bales and sacks as breastworks. Clarke's train was ready and several Sioux were set afoot. Etty spoke regretfully of this to Morissa. "These Indians have need for horses to go to Sitting Bull in Canada," he said. "They go because they are hungry; they do not come down here."

But Ruth hadn't lived through all the Indian scares here. "I ain't the one to have my switch lifted off by a redskin," she said sourly. She rolled her nightgown in a newspaper and went to sleep in the shack of the laundress at the blockhouse when Charley was away. The old soldier was furious. "I ain't havin' my wife hang out with no post chippy!"

"Chippy? She's forty-five if she's a day!" Ruth defended.

"Sure! If she was younger she'd be working Deadwood," he said, and got only a silent mouth from his wife. "I don't like her anyway," Ruth confided to Morissa later, with a flash of daring in the plain woman's eyes, "I just want to devil Charley a little."

"Any old cow'll live if she can make it to grass," the cattlemen always said in the winters, but the woman from Madame Trogger's didn't make it, her worn heart finally done. Morissa was saddened. Somehow there should be more than the fifteen years with the Madame Troggers of the world if one must die old and exhausted at thirty. A walking sky pilot preached at the grave and Ruth dropped Morissa's handful of white geranium blooms upon the pine coffin. Then Fish Head put his tall hat back into the axle-grease bucket and they all stopped for a cup of coffee at Clarke's.

By now Gwinnie could walk clear across the bridge and Alice and Georgie were strong enough to be out on sunny days. One afternoon Ruth took them to the river to see the ice break. It cracked like pistol shots under the film of water and then began to grind and tip up, throwing fans of spray as the great cakes of rotten stick ice lifted on the pushing flood. It dammed against the bridge until Clarke's old blacksmith and several hands ran out to clear it away with ice hooks and dynamite.

When the children left the house they had waved to Morissa as for a long journey and Georgie ran back awkwardly in his heavy little coat for another good-by kiss. Morissa watched them go with a catch in her throat. One of these days the father would return from Deadwood to take them away.

But soon it would be spring, and June.

The geese came north a week before their time, as though they knew the river would be open. Then suddenly none were flying, only snowbirds flocking together. The next day a blizzard struck, such a blizzard as the cowmen had never seen. It began with the usual warm day. Morissa was coming in from below the Wild Cats, her coat thrown open, the morning sun on her face. She had left a strong baby boy to take the place of the one who died of black diphtheria there last fall, and she hummed a little Scottish tune as she turned in for a look at John Callwin.

She found him cutting fence posts and it was a joy to watch him bring down the slender pines until they lay all around him. When he

161

saw who it was he set the ax against a trunk and came striding off the slope to sit on a rock, fill his pipe and talk. His wife and the baby he had never seen would arrive in May and he wanted to fence the range cattle out of a small garden plot and a patch for calico corn and pumpkins and potatoes. Soberly he pulled his stocking cap away and bent his head to the doctor. She examined the thick scarring, the hair working in from the sides and starting in little tufts through the twisted red tissue.

"Sore?" she asked as she probed here and there with her strong fingers, tested the firmness of the plate.

"Just a little stiff—It's really fine. My uncle writes me it's a remarkable recovery and that he has a place for you in his hospital any time you want to leave us here—"

But Morissa shook her head. "I've not told even Charley but I'm marrying Tris Polk in June."

Oh, the settler hadn't known; none of them had any more than guessed that it would happen eventually. Thoughtfully he drew his knitted cap back over his dark hair. "We hoped you would stay here. The railroad will be coming through the valley before many years. My wife already thinks of you as a sister."

"Oh, thank you! I do plan to keep the hospital going. I'm making arrangements now for a doctor, a man who needs to come West for his health, to take over while I'm away. He's a recovering lunger, but he has to live in a dry sunny climate. Soon there will be work enough for two here anyway."

She tried to speak with lightness, to meet the man's dark eyes squarely, but somehow the warmth of the meeting was gone. Something had come into his brown-bearded face to close away the affection and respect she had seen there, replace it with a curious anger against her, almost an urge to violence. So Morissa Kirk got into her buggy and was nearly home before she noticed that the sky had grayed out of the northwest.

Charley was away rounding up the cattle, his three cows and Morissa's little bunch of she stuff, some of the bigger heifers old enough to be calving soon. He would throw them into the draw up the little creek, where the bluffs furnished protection and prevented drifting in any storm. "Charley's sixteen years in the Army, mostly on the Plains, have given him a weather nose," Morissa told Ruth when he came in safely, but snow-caked and bent into the growing storm.

"Yes, a weather nose with a drop of sap always hangin' on the end of it—he'd oughta know when it's freezing," Ruth laughed, her plumpening cheeks still red from the wind too. She had been rounding up the stupid chickens and hunting her pair of white geese in the snow—geese that were to grow her a featherbed, a downy one from live plucking—not from dead wild ones.

Tris had planned to come up that evening, and all night Morissa found herself rousing to every sound, hoping that he had not started into the storm. For four days not even Charley went farther than the well, and always with a guide rope tied around his waist to bring him back. Then it cleared and he walked over the great frozen drifts glistening in the morning sun, the shovel on his shoulder to tunnel down to the door of his soddy. All the valley of the Platte was lost in the deep drifted snow, the bridge silent and white, only the center of the river a dark broken channel of angry water flowing. The buildings to the north seemed buried, but little curls of smoke rose from the drift-joined hummocks at the south end—the houses of Clarke and Etty and the others. Blue and pleasant, the smoke climbed over them, high into the sharp, clear air.

Morissa looked off toward the pale outlines of Courthouse Rock and the snow-hidden trail and wondered about Tris. Surely he was safe, and yet last year the old freighter whose foot-ends she amputated would have died if he hadn't been found, already unconscious.

But she must turn her mind from these things, and as she looked off northward she saw two antelope standing inside a high swirl of drifts around her stable wall, sunning themselves together not two hundred feet away. She moved to open the door behind her for the rifle and then decided against it. She needed fresh meat but not from two such trusting creatures. They reminded her of the young antelope that Tom Reeder had taken away, lost to the dogs at Sidney. Many other things seemed to have been lost since she came fleeing here with the little round-topped trunk of her trousseau. So much softness and gentleness destroyed. Soon it would be two years, and soon a hundred, with nothing from Allston Hoyt for a long time except a clipping last week announcing his engagement to a young woman of most irreproachable name, another May wedding, this one to be carried through.

Morissa was glad that she had stated her intention before that, the final commitment not the words to Tris but to the settler John Callwin. She had said nothing of it here, not with two of her hospital patients homesteaders and Charley Adams's yard fence cut several times this winter, his windows shot out. It was done in the night, when he was away, but he bought a rifle and entered a shooting match or two at the bridge to show them how an army sharpshooter placed his bullets. There had been no more damage, but the drift fences were going up between people now, everybody having to pick his side. Already Charley and Ruth were polite as enemies to the rancher Tris Polk. Besides, any hint of Morissa's engagement would bring real hysteria to Eddie Ellis.

163

He had been learning to walk again but still wept like a child at any disappointment, like a sick and forlorn child clinging to her hand and moving her in a way she knew was very foolish. Others saw it too, she noticed. Last week she overheard a couple of cowboys talking about Eddie. "Acts like one a them scrub bull calves that won't wean 'thout you shoot the cow—"

Impatiently she shook these thoughts from her, pulled on her coat and started to the bridge for news of the south trail. She was met by a man climbing over the frozen drifts toward her. Some freighters were caught out and frostbitten, and an outfit of gold seekers, too, over at Clarke's now. So, busy, the day passed, and the next morning a rider brought a note from Tris: "I regret that the severity of the storm kept me from my appointment—" as formal as the distant smoke-gray of his eyes. But Morissa Kirk knew the fire that could burn behind that grayness, the warmth and passion, and in her relief that he was safe she held the small sheet of paper between her flattened palms and a vastness as of all the prairies filled her breast.

Before the end of the week the mail was going through by special express riders. They brought stories of great loss of stock and lives: even plainsmen of long experience had died; many work animals and around fifty per cent of the range cattle had drifted and frozen. This would be a mighty fat spring for the wolves and buzzards, a spring to offend the nose, and as soon as the stench cleared away, a time to sell the ranches to Eastern and British capital by the book, by the normal estimated increase instead of actual count.

Morissa missed the worst case of frostbite. Two army acquaintances of Charley's, their discharges in their pockets, had headed south from Fort Robinson in a wagon the morning of the storm. When the wagon stuck in the drifts they left it and the team, not even taking their rifles, blankets, or food. With their two dogs following, they struck out for a ranch they thought was nearby. They never found it and were separated by the storm. Somehow one of the men survived, surely through the warmth of the two dogs. They were found thirteen days later by a cowboy, when the snow was half gone. At the cowcamp the man was given diluted whisky and soft-boiled eggs and then hurried by wagon to Clarke's bridge. "Dr. Kirk is away on a pneumonia case," Charley had to say, shaking his head after one look at the man's rotting feet, the streaks of red reaching up the swollen thighs, the fevered, skull-starved face "Get him to the post surgeon at Sidney as quick as you can."

Later Morissa saw this tough, rugged man at the post hospital, both legs off at the knee, but he was strengthening and cheerful. "A man, after he's out in the snow thirteen days, he knows it's good to go on living with whatever he's got left," the patient said, laughing a little, awkwardly. But he sobered when he had to admit there was no news of his companion. The team was found dead but nothing of the man.

"It's a hard land, this," the post surgeon told Doctor Kirk.

Yes, a hard, a beautiful and beckoning land. After the heavy snow and the rains that followed even the driest table lay green and flowered for the rush of settlers. With times hard all over the world, the Indians gone at last, and the pull of free homes almost as strong as gold and vastly more fundamental, the cattlemen saw they must work fast, cover all the watering places and the best land with filings if they would hold their free range. First they used their cowboys and then they gathered up wagonloads of bums and prostitutes at Sidney and the other towns. With plenty of refreshments along they were taken to the open range so they could swear they had seen the land they were entering, even if the spree was fifty miles from there. The ranchers paid them what they must, from twenty-five dollars up, and hauled out claim shacks the size of a backyard smokehouse, soon rubbed down by the cattle. It didn't matter; they were all empty.

Morissa remarked that there was generally no plowing on these fraudulent claims. "No, settlers're tolled up by a strip of plowing quick as a Texas cow to a corn patch," Sid Martin told her candidly.

But while the cattlemen tried to cover all the permanent waterways, most of the settlers came prepared for drylanding with spade and rope and bucket, perfectly willing to haul water for stock and for drinking and to do without for the rest until they could dig for it. They came by railroad, covered wagon, and afoot. They settled close as possible to markets, or scattered out over the region below Sidney and up along Pumpkin Seed Creek toward the Wild Cats and anywhere that an earlier granger had a toe hold. Then they moved out into the larger ranches, unaware of or in spite of the smooth-fingered range protectors.

Morissa Kirk felt herself a part of this stream, as surely a stream as the Platte water that flowed past her place, and that other current, the one to the Black Hills. But most of the homesteaders, even John Callwin and Charley Adams at her own breakfast table, were increasingly distant, withdrawn. Only Gwinnie, who took up a homestead for Clarke south of the river, seemed the same, if one could tell from his customary silence as he came in for a cup of coffee and a piece of Ruth's sorghum gingerbread. Not even the excitement of the mallards hatching made him talkative. He had carried a clutch of the dark eggs in from along the trail for the children and slid them gently out of his hat and under one of Morissa's broody hens. But as soon as they hatched they scurried for the irrigation pond, with the scolding, ruffled hen hard after them, followed by the children. There the ducklings joined a lone pair of mallards swimming among the young rushes, bobbing along behind the

165

brown mother as Alice and Georgie ran up and down the bank, crying, as foolish as the hen.

Morissa brought the disappointed children home. "Sensible reconcilement," Fish Head advised them. "What can't be cured can hang you—" But his pompous way did not deceive Georgie. He followed the little man's arm around behind him, where he was hiding a young muskrat in a cage of chicken wire, gnawing contentedly on a piece of water root.

In early June Morissa was called to the Pete Shrone murder trial. Law must be coming to the region if a man could be tried for a shooting scrape with a professional gunman. "Yeh, but makes a difference on whose payroll the pistoleer was working," a long, sunburnt granger from over at the Wild Cats said to a whole roundup camp in at Clarke's one evening. Morissa saw him stand up to them all for a while, but when he got out he never returned. And it was true that usually a little lead was considered the normal hazard of the gunman's trade, but perhaps the hanging of McCall for killing Wild Bill Hickok at Deadwood had set a precedent.

Much against his father's urgings, Morissa was taking Eddie Ellis and his valise along to Sidney and sending him home for a three months' sea cruise with his mother, to restore him in strength and balance. She saw now that somehow the cowboys who spoke of a cow and her unweaned calf hadn't been completely wrong. It was hard to send him away. Perhaps the cow, too, liked the dependency of her overage calf too much.

She thought about Jackie, back with Robin grading for the railroad that was headed across the northern part of Nebraska to the Black Hills. Long before it was completed, sunflowers would take the trail here. But Morissa hoped there would be a railroad past her door here even sooner, with settlers and schools and towns—but of course she would be gone.

Although Charley and Ruth were moving to their place when Morissa left for the wedding trip, her patients would be safe at the Sidney hospital, even Alice and Georgie. It was hard to think of giving the children up now, particularly the willful, seductive little Georgie. But Morissa would be in Texas with Tris visiting his Auntie Mae, and then in New York and back by Chicago and the Hurley Forsons. The doctor still hoped she could get Charley to care for her trees, but he was standing off like a mustang on a hill. She doubted whether the cowboy Tris was sending up to look after her stock would care if the fence was cut or the range cattle rubbed her trees down—the trees all growing so fast this fine wet spring. Yet even Tris admitted that some day the Kirk grove might be recognized as the symbol of a new era—the first irrigated planting in a great and fruitful valley.

So Morissa started off on the Sidney trail, waving good-by to the children at the yellow roses around her door. Then she let the bays out, shining and handsome in their new flynets. She dropped Eddie and his valise at the depot, the gaunt young man silent, angry-eyed, and as appealing as an unhappy child.

"I'll never go—" he said dramatically. "You'll see—"

But Morissa lifted her whip in farewell and drove away to the hotel. Tris met her there, his smoldering eyes lighting at the sight of the girl in her new linen suit, a yellow and green plaid that showed off her fine figure.

"From our trousseau—?" Tris whispered as he took her arm, and she nodded, smiling into his eyes.

Together they went down the afternoon street crowded for the court session, many in patched and faded jeans, the sunburnt faces dark and sullen, some with hands hanging over unaccustomed holsters, rifles and even shotguns out, and nearly as many cattlemen and their cowboys around, so there was almost no room to pass at all. The high feeling seemed to be over the drawn-out case that came up before the Shrone shooting—a homesteader being tried for killing a cowboy. Two ranch hands had gone to drag a homesteader's empty shack into a washout with their lariats because he was eating beef. But as the shack went over, the settler, unexpectedly home, shot from inside the toppling doorway and emptied one of the saddles. He missed the other man, who released the rope from the horn and spurred away, leaving the shack on its side like some Halloween outhouse, the cowboy dead in the grass beside it.

The settler, afraid the ranch hands around would gang up on him, walked to Camp Sidney in the night for protection. He was turned over to the sheriff, although he kicked and fought, certain that he would be dragged out of jail to a necktie party. He wasn't molested, perhaps because he went to the troops first, but there was a lot of mean talk and shooting around the jail. The sheriff promised a swift trial and now, three days later, the case was almost finished and the settler ready for the penitentiary and the hanging, or he would be strung up here to a telegraph pole.

Morissa Kirk felt the anger along the street, the settlers gathered up solid around the courthouse—tattered, gaunt, and angry men, mostly with guns over their arms, or clubs. Inside, the judge from down in the middle of the state had his two revolvers out on the pine table before him, and the cuspidor handy at his boot heel. His aim was said to be as perfect with one as the other. Because no local lawyer would go against the cattlemen, an Eastern man out for a ranch foreclosure sale had hurriedly been retained for the defense by a group of settlers, John Callwin among them, all shut out of the courtroom.

The Eastern attorney was summing up his defense before the antagonistic spectators when Tris and Morissa squeezed into the back of the hot and sweaty little courtroom and stood on a bench cleared for the

167

ranch owner. The lawyer was working up through the record of ranch violences here, beginning with the surveyor's helper hanged at Sidney several years ago by the Bosler men, to stop the government survey. Then there were the professional gunmen on the ranch payrolls, the settler shot in the back last year down near the defendant's homestead, and a neighbor whose field fence was cut to pieces, his corn eaten up, the bullet holes put through his door barely missing his wife. He and the others nearby left the country before the next sunup.

"All left except the defendant here. So he must become an example to all would-be settlers in this ranchman's paradise, his home be dragged away into a canyon. The prosecution charges that the settler was stealing calves and eating ranch beef. Then why not have recourse to the courts, have the defendant tried for theft? A man's homestead is his legal residence, his castle. He has the right, more, the obligation to defend it!" the Eastern lawyer shouted. He shouted it out loud enough to be heard in all the murmuring courtroom and through the open windows over the growing noise, the rest lost in the roar, with fights and cursings, and a shot or two, whistling high, still harmless.

Morissa felt herself caught in the trial as in the surging flood waters of the Platte, but beside her was the hard shoulder of Tris Polk, the strong arm. When the judge's gavel had restored some quiet inside, the sweating attorney wiped his face and went on. "To characterize the frequent instances when homesteader shacks are dragged away as merely a form of cowboy prankery is an impertinence to this court. That is clearly destruction of property and endangerment of life by trespassers. It is not altered by the contention that this has become an established local custom, a sort of practice in common law for dealing with suspected rustlers. Repetition of a crime does not make it a lawful act, or reduce its criminality in any sense," the attorney told the angry and defiant courtroom, so noisy now that the judge, an outsider too, had to gavel the table for silence time after time, and finally threatened to clear the room, with his guns if necessary.

The roaring outside was so great that the windows were shut against it and immediately opened again by the crashing of one pane of glass after another. "You ain't doin' no railroadin' a that man where we can't hear!" someone shouted into the room, followed by a surge of angry approval from the settlers dark around him, with replies from inside, hands seeking their holsters. Morissa tugged at Tris's arm, to get out now while they could. But the judge was already up, a gun in each hand, his eyes cold and hard upon the leading cattlemen and upon the faces crowding the windows. To the immediate silence he spit and sat down, motioning the attorney to proceed.

The outsider nodded his thanks. "All the evidence proves that the defendant shot to protect his property, his right by law and the Constitution. It was a shot fired in defense of his home, his very life, in the tumbling little house at the end of the cowboy lariats. And the reiteration that the neighboring ranches follow this custom does not serve to establish legality for what is, to repeat, patently a criminal act, even if those ranches are the powerful Scottish Glasgow Arrow and the Texas-owned TeePee!"

"The TeePee!" someone near Tris Polk whispered in astonishment at this daring. "By God, he spits it right out—the Arrow and the TeePee!"

Morissa stiffened. So people were supposed to be afraid even to mention these names! Stone-angry she turned her face from the undenying rancher standing beside her, and withdrew her hand from his arm. She saw how the case must end, with the jury made up of cattlemen or those who hung upon their favor and custom. At the best the verdict would be murder in the first degree, with the sentence pronounced later to avoid the violence breeding today. But one outspoken rancher was protesting any delay in the sentence while another joined the spreading talk of rope and a cottonwood. They would not have the prisoner hustled off on the train due here in a couple of hours, to live his life out safe in the pen.

Now Morissa could only look about the backs in this crowded room as upon strangers from a foreign country, from a strange and violent land where a man who chose to live in a wilderness in order to have a home of his own was to be hanged or at the least imprisoned in a bleak, narrow cell for life, and in this Tris Polk was certainly like the others.

Suddenly she could bear no more. Ignoring the rancher and everyone around her she pushed down from the bench and elbowed her way out into the evening street, out through the press of people awaiting the verdict too. Her hands were shaking so she had to grip them together on her little handkerchief as she hurried between the rows of sunburnt faces, the walls of them. Even at the fringe of the crowd the settlers stood away from her. Not even John Callwin with a silver plate in his head had a word of greeting for her now.

Tris Polk was right behind her, trying to take her arm as she hurried on. "Please, dear, please let's go somewhere to talk this over," he begged.

Without reply or even a turn of her head the young doctor sought an escape from the crowd, from everyone, fleeing almost like some wild thing, almost like the fox sorrel mustang mare of the horse catchers they watched destroy herself up in the sandhills. Morissa's feet took the pathway that led toward the bluff and climbed to the top overlooking the town, Camp Sidney, and the wide, sweeping valley of the Lodgepole that lay green and shining in the lowered evening sun. And with the bright light upon her passionate face, Morissa Kirk finally turned to the man behind her.

"So it's true," she said, still holding herself firm, speaking only in sorrow, "all I have been hearing. Your cowboys are tearing down people's homes too."

Tris made a motion toward her but she stood firm and distant.

"Yes, I suppose you could say that," he admitted finally. "As I've told you, I have a good foreman; I pay him to run the ranch the best way he knows how, and I don't ask questions about his methods."

Now anger came up in the girl's face again. "Have you no sense of responsibility in this at all?" she demanded.

"Oh, Morissa, would you want me to hire a Pete Shrone?—give the grangers no warning beyond finding a neighbor face down in his plowing? I don't like it either, but we drifted into this protecting our range, our investment. It's Aunt Mae's even more than mine—"

Morissa closed her eyes. There it was, a fine, strong gentlewoman like Auntie Mae, and a man like Tris.

"—You must understand me, my dear," the rancher pleaded. "I would not do those things myself. You must see that."

But his words only lifted Morissa from her moment of sorrow and weakening. "I know you wouldn't do them, Tris," she said slowly, firmly, "but they are done for you, and that seems far worse to me. Now I am to marry a man who takes this power but delegates it, and feels he need ask no questions at all."

"Morissa!"

"No, it's no use now. I can't do it. I can't marry into such a circumstance," she cried, and before Tris could stop her the doctor had gathered up her skirts and was stumbling down the steep bluff, the path blurred before her feet. Once, after they reached the shadowing tracks and the warehouses, the man tried again. "Go to Aunt Mae's for a few weeks," he begged. "I can't bear to see you like this, going home to your place alone, with Robin and Jackie away and even Charley seeming to be against you. Go to Mae. She'll welcome you like a daughter, no matter what—"

But Morissa couldn't even thank the man, no more than she could have thanked Allston Hoyt, only this time there seemed nowhere to go, certainly not to throw herself upon Robin again. No, nowhere—

As though forgotten she left the rancher standing and went up the plank steps of the little hotel, her feet wooden and awkward, to work her way through the crowded lobby to her room, to escape all these strange and alien faces. But inside the door two men in railroad uniforms were holding Eddie Ellis, pale in the early lamplight, his suit dirty and torn, his cheek bleeding. He was sobbing, trying to pull away from the men, to run. Then he saw Morissa and clutched for her arm. "Oh, don't leave me—don't, don't!"

"Throwed himself in front of the engine," one of the men said.

"Yeh, Joe here yanks him back just in time. We brung him here, seein's he claims he's your patient."

So Morissa put an arm about the young man and guided him away through the crowd, trying to soothe him, comfort him a little out of the bleakness of her own heart. "Yes, yes, you can stay with me," she was repeating over and over, dully. "You can stay with me forever—"

In an hour they were returning from Camp Sidney, married.

XIV

Looking back, Morissa Kirk always thought of this time as the Year of the Eclipse, perhaps because there was a total eclipse of the sun late in July, the strange darkness so convincing that the chickens sang a few sad and confused little evening songs and then went to climb to their perch in the henhouse. The canary settled his head under his wing, cheeping in discontent, and a rattlesnake crawled under the step of the back door. The snake was easily settled with the hoe and hung writhing over the woven fencing of the shadowed yard, but the uneasiness of a rattler so close to the house was like all the unease of that summer.

"Ah, a Scotsman's aye wise ahint the hand," Morissa had told herself as she returned from Sidney with her new husband in middle June. None was quicker than a Scotsman in detecting past mistakes, her mother often told Morissa. Only in foresight was he laggard.

Others were more pointed about her marriage. "I thought you was hitchin' up with that Polk, the cowman," one of the guards from the gold coaches told her. "Looks to me like you traded you a sound horse fer a scrub broomtail."

Morissa gave the man a tart, a bold answer, but she knew that it put no wisdom or breeding on the scrub.

They had come back in her buggy, Eddie on the seat beside her, wearing the new suit that she had paid for. He pushed the bays along in a lathering sweat. Anxious to get home, he said, to plan all the things he would do, when Morissa suggested a little stop at the creek near Courthouse Rock, to rest and cool the horses. Ed looked almost well again, curly-headed and very young with a faint line of mustache shadowing his soft lip. Everyone around the bridge told him that if a week was a fair sample, marriage was sure the range to put fat on his ribs. Then the

171

eyes would move to Morissa and if they had known they might have compared the jilted girl of two years ago with the one today and understood that there are far worse things than a public rejection from an Allston Hoyt. But they saw enough to shift their eyes quickly, and make hasty questions of what was doing in Sidney. Yes, the trial was over and Hobert was on his way to the penitentiary for killing Pete Shrone, following on the heels of the settler who shot one of the lassoing cowboys. If anybody here had heard the news of Morissa's hasty departure from the first trial with Tris Polk running after her, no one spoke of it.

"Mebby our lady doc's still again' killers," one of the freighters said before Morissa was out of earshot, "but she fetches that outlaw's hired hand to live right here 'mongst us!"

Ed planned to file on a homestead. Although not quite of age, he was entitled to one now as the head of a family. Perhaps he would take up a preemption too but Morissa must promise to see that he had the money when the time came.

"Oh, you'll have the two hundred dollars by then," she said confidently. "You're well enough to work. You should take up a timber-claim too, and we'll have the increase in value when the settlers and the railroad come in."

But Eddie met this with a pout. "You have to kiss me if I am to take orders from you," he said, and when Morissa treated such talk as a joke, his face clouded sullenly. It was over in a moment but when he went to make his filing, the land he took up wasn't even in the Platte valley but in a deep, rugged canyon fifteen miles off, on the horse thief trail.

By then Charley Adams had come to stand before Morissa, his weathered face stubborn, his hands working over each other. "I got to know where we stand, Doc. Eddie give me my time."

"You mean he paid you off?" she demanded.

"No, he ain't paid me a cent but he says I'm through workin' fer you, an' Ruth is too. Come end of July we're both through—"

Morissa's face was flushed and angry. "I'm sorry but Ed misunderstands the situation. The hospital is on my homestead, not yet patented, and so outside all a husband's claim or control. I want you to stay."

"I don't know—Doc," Charley said slowly, moving his cud around in his stubbled cheek. "I don't like workin' fer two bosses—"

"At least try it a while longer," Morissa asked, and was prepared to talk of this and some other things with Ed. But when he came home he brought her an armful of hothouse roses and a pretty white goatskin rug for the bedside. In addition he seemed content to work in the garden and the flower beds, leaning on the hoe now and then to watch the coaches swing over the bridge and away to the Hills, past the big freight

172

trains. But he seemed most interested in the herds that splashed through the July river and bawled off northward—particularly those that were young she stuff going out to stock the dozen new ranches along the White River and down the Niobrara that flowed along the north edge of the sandhills, the long-grass country.

"Why don't you sell out here, Morissa?" Ed asked. "You could buy me cattle enough to start a ranch up there too."

She laughed. "What is there to sell? Only my preemption is patented, at a dollar and a quarter an acre, and my few head of livestock. Besides, what do you know about the cattle business?"

But underneath Morissa was uneasy, and soon Eddie was spending every evening at the whisky saloons around the bridge. Once he brought back a piece cut from the Sidney paper, an interview with Doc Middleton who claimed he wasn't the leader of any organized band of horse thieves. It was true the stock they were riding belonged to a railroad man around North Platte town. "But we left other horses just as good on his place when we took them," Doc had argued. He did admit running off Indian ponies but he hadn't done any of that in six months, and never except to get money to live on.

"That's the motive of every thief, I suspect—getting money to live on," Morissa commented, rolling her full lip down.

"He wants to give up if they'll pardon him for killing that soldier at Sidney some time ago," Eddie defended. "See what it says—"

"Most murderers would do as much," Morissa said shortly, aware that she was spoiling Ed's elation.

"Oh Doc's all right," Ed replied casually. "He gave me this clipping. His outfit's camped off north a ways from my homestead. Talked about starting a ranch up there. He says he'll stake me if I go in with him."

"Into horse stealing?" Morissa demanded. "Horse thieves end up at the busy end of a rope, my darling."

She knew this was the wrong approach but Eddie was so excited by the big, the adventuresome talk, that he must be settled down immediately. So that evening after supper, while they watched the thunderhead leaning high and white-topped over the river, she told him that he might be a father by spring.

Ed had been sprawled out on one of the benches under the young cottonwoods, and Morissa busied herself arranging a bouquet for Lorette from an apronful of flowers. She announced the possibility very casually: "What would you say to a son along about the first of April?"

Eddie sat up like a lazy young animal stretching, and grinned a little. "You can't bring me no squalling brat," he said, as though to some worn-out joking threat, a threat, for instance, to turn a suck-egg dog loose in the henhouse. "I'm your curly-headed boy. Your time and love

173

all belong to me." Then his young face changed a little. "Oh, I just about forgot. I wrote Ira Marker up in Deadwood to come get the two brats you already got here."

Morissa stopped with her hands full of pinks and nasturtiums. "You are getting to be a real tease!" she laughed. But she had to go look for the children, anxiously shading her eyes against the evening sun with a flower-filled hand as though the father might have come to steal the two away. They were both with Fish Head, coming down along the bank of the cloud-reddened stream, helping him catch frogs with the little dipnets he had made for them.

"It's bedtime—!" she called, to cover her anxiety. "Alice! Georgie! Bedtime!"

In a week Morissa had to tell Eddie that she was mistaken about the son, but by then she knew he really had written to Ira Marker, for Ira drove his wagon down from the Hills. He stood helpless before his children, embarrassed that they had grown so much since he saw them, and looked so healthy; yet happy too that this was so.

"I know I been neglectful, Miss Doctor," he said, "but there wan't steady work 'round the mines fer my kind—not with so many hard-rock miners comin' in. I—I guess I just got to send them to a orphanage someplace."

But this was like talk of violence to Morissa. "No! No orphanage!" she exclaimed. "We'll be glad to keep them until you can have them with you. Anyway, you should be marrying again soon—"

"They ain't no motherly kind a woman loose in the Hills, but back home—I mebby could there," the father said slowly, rubbing the stubbles of his face in thought. He stayed overnight, but in the morning he was out very early, and without a thank you or a pleasant word to the doctor he started down the trail with the children. Young Alice sat quietly beside her father trying to comfort the small brother she held between her knees. Georgie had clung to Morissa's skirts and then to Ruth's, but his fingers were pried loose.

"There's the end of childhood for Alice," Morissa said as the wagon drew away south. With her face bleak and angry she walked past Charley and Ruth, and past Ed, too, knowing now that he had gone to the man in the night and ordered that he take the children away. From the edge of her growing patch of trees, the doctor looked back and saw her young husband heading for the bridge, and knew he wouldn't be back until morning, to stumble in, violent and drunken, or perhaps not for days, the bills he made coming later. Last week it was a gambling IOU for three hundred dollars that she refused to pay, and now he wanted a race horse, talking of it until she wanted to cry out "So you have to have one, too, with your horse thief friends stealing them everywhere!" Truly, as her grandmother wrote her once, a woman betrayed is a woman

174

cast into sorrow, but the one who makes a quick and bad marriage she gang to the de'il with a dishclout on her head. Aye, the dishclout of sorrow and humiliation.

In furious self-contempt Morissa strode down the rows of her trees, most of them far above her head, some fifteen, sixteen feet tall, where the bit of irrigation water reached. The soft August rustle of the leaves was a comfort, and even the grasshoppers that rose in dusty waves before her sturdy shoes. She looked off along the river and recalled how this valley had moved her the first time she saw it, with its stories of all the thousands who passed on the trails westward seeking homes, and all those who died in their search, mostly from the scourges, particularly cholera, their graves all along here, unknown, unmarked. Hardship was not the killer of man, but disease, and that included the sicknesses of the mind and the heart as well as of the body—the unhealth produced by ill-advised, incautious exposure to the infections of impulse, pique, and injured vanity, and by the bloodied spur of self-hatred, as surely as from indulging a thirst with impure water, or a hunger at a prostitute's crib.

Three days later Eddie came back with a new buggy and team, a long-barreled Kentucky racer trotting nervously alongside. The man with him stayed in the buggy while Eddie came out to look for Morissa. She was at the well, filling her jug with safe drinking water to take out on a call to a new typhoid outbreak. He tried to kiss her boyishly, his hands as clumsy as his walk, his breath heavy with rotgut.

"Bought me a running horse, Morissa, and a team and buggy. Come see."

"I can see all I want to know from here," she said, feeling hard as the infuriated mother at a children's poor-farm, but helpless.

"You gotta come, to pay the man."

"What gives you the impression I could pay for these things if I wished?"

"Oh, I got it all fixed. Just sign the little mortgages on the preemption and our cows and horses—"

Morissa walked beside him to the new buggy, her step firm. "I think you should know that we have no funds for race horses, and one buggy is all we need," she told the man.

Eddie began to bluster angrily, reaching for the buggy whip. "By God, I'll show you who's boss—" he shouted.

But Morissa took the whip from him as from the clutching hands of a child and put it back into the whip stock. Motioning the man toward the road, she went back to her task.

"I'll kill you!" Eddie shouted after her. "The damn bitch! I'll kill her, the bastard!"

But Morissa was already the doctor again. Charley brought up her team and she took the lines, got in, tucked the dust robe over her knees and let the bays have their heads. The next issue of the *Sidney Telegraph* carried a small, hastily composed advertisement that many noticed or were referred to when Morissa returned their bills:

I will not be responsible for any debts incurred or any agreements or contracts entered into by my husband Edward Elton Ellis.

Dr. Morissa Kirk Ellis.

That was the last time she intended to use the name of Ellis as long as she lived.

The lady doc of the gold trail no longer stopped her buggy or her Appaloosa at Clarke's or Etty's for a little visiting when she passed. She was aware of the contempt she had brought upon herself. A good man can have a bad wife, but no wife is better than her spouse. The cattlemen seemed less uneasy about her now, and the settlers were friendly enough again, too, but with a sort of patronizing familiarity that was very different from their attitude of last summer. John Callwin came and stayed a couple of hours one afternoon, to walk through the garden and the little grove on the timberclaim with Morissa.

"You sure did make a good start here—" he said, letting his voice trail off into a sort of transparent regret. He said nothing of the silver plate in his head, or his uncle in Seattle, who once urged Morissa to come to his hospital staff—so swiftly is good work destroyed. But a few people were unchanged. Gwinnie of Clarke's store brought the mail over to save her embarrassment at the station, and offered to drive her on late night trips, or in storms when Charley had to stay at the hospital.

"—Just give me a sign," he said once. "Shall we say two shots fired in rapid succession?"

"That would keep you running almost every night, with the cowboys and the gold seekers celebrating so often—" Morissa laughed, a little alarmed to hear herself.

But she was grateful, even though Gwinnie would always be the earnest young patient to her, with boyish, black-fringed blue eyes and drake-tail curls at his temples—shining little tails. Then there was Sid Martin. He overtook Morissa going up the trail to see about her typhoid patients, and rode beside the Appaloosa for a couple of miles. He made no pretense of good wishes either, nor spoke sour words of blame. "I think maybe you busted my chances with Aunt Mae down in Texas," he laughed ruefully. "You know I had half a mind to make me some business down there, after fall roundup."

"Oh, why not? She liked you, and I can recommend you as an excellent risk physically. A man who can come through a stampede and a broken neck—"

But few of her acquaintances were as natural. Then in the midst of this August time Robin was suddenly there, walking over from the stage, and Morissa, for the second time in a little over two years, buried her miserable face against the shoulder of her stepfather.

"You never wrote me—" he scolded softly.

"I couldn't, Robin. It seemed too shameful. As soon as it was done I realized how shameful."

Slowly the man nodded, his face grieved for the girl. "Tris came to see me. Hunted me up on the job. He said you maybe needed me."

"Tris! Oh—" and now at last Morissa began to cry. Ruth, coming to greet the visitor, saw her and slipped away to leave the two together, Robin holding this daughter he had taken to his heart a long time ago.

During the summer Buffalo Bill came through again, talking about a bigger and better show and bragging up his great scouting and marksmanship to some Easterners. Morissa regretted that he was losing the outdoor look. But with his hair still falling over his shoulders like Custer and Wild Bill Hickok, he was the handsome showman and grew expansive before the admirers at Clarke's, and a little drunk too. He had paid Morissa a pretty compliment as she stopped for her mail but soon turned to the more responsive newcomers. They shouted down the sour questions of an old freighter about Cody's scouting and Indian fighting. But everybody admitted that the holdup of the Deadwood coach Buffalo Bill had in his show was still true enough.

"Yeh, still workin' the trails, an' even when them outlaws gets nabbed they gets away. I just seen the Deadwood jail, busted wide open," the freighter said.

That evening Charley Adams told Morissa about a deserter from the Army who had been working the Cheyenne route. "Come down as far as the bridge here today. Lookin' for a new hideout. Some place that might pass for a little cow outfit—" Charley said, and suddenly Morissa understood his meaning.

It was true that the fever of lawlessness seemed as catching as measles lately. Everybody at the bridge had known Lame Johnny, the bookkeeper of the big Homestake mine, a peace officer at Deadwood and a man of some culture and education. Several times, while down to oversee the transporting of heavy mine machinery, he had supper at Morissa's with Robin and Jackie. Later he stopped by several times to see Eddie, and the doctor had been pleased, but now suddenly she saw all this in a different light, for Johnny, too, had pulled his bandana up over his face and stopped the Sidney stage. One of his companions was shot in the

177

holdup but Johnny got away and hid out with Red Cloud, back and with a new agency at Pine Ridge, east of the trail. For a while he ran off Indian horses and then one day he was seen walking along the gold trail alone, like any man looking for a ride. He denied being in the holdup but was handcuffed anyway and thrown into the treasure coach. The next day a bull train found Johnny hanging from a tree. Some claimed he was innocent but plainly he was not innocent of suspicion.

Morissa listened carefully but none of Lame Johnny's accomplices were named. The next week, returning from a call, she saw new horse droppings on the thieves trail where she had shot at the man taking her team that first winter. She stopped the Appaloosa on the ridge and recalled the blinding sun on the snow that day. The dugout where Eddie was struck by typhoid was down this trail, too, far down below the Platte. Yet with this knowledge she had still married him. Perhaps Dr. Aiken was right; perhaps a woman needed the close rein of a father or husband every moment of her years and should be kept out of all public life, most certainly out of the practice of medicine. Morissa had admitted a little of this to the doctor when she canceled her request for the young lunger to take over her practice during the summer. "A woman's foolish whim—" she wrote, much ashamed.

Eddie hadn't been around the bridge since Robin came to visit those two days. Morissa suspected that he had warned Ed to keep away, although what power he might have used she couldn't guess unless it was one of the many things men managed to keep to themselves. But it didn't last. Eddie Ellis came, brought back by a bullet in his foot. "Gun went off this morning. Hurts bad—" he said to Charley as he sank miserably down to the bench against the rosebush and marigolds beside the door. The two men with him put spurs to their horses and headed north, leading his saddler, a good one.

Morissa came out to see, and was at once the doctor. She cut out the bullet, cleaned the wound of some bone fragments, set in a couple of tubes for drainage and put a temporary cast on the foot.

"You say that your gun went off this morning," she told Eddie when he was out of the little ether they had given him. "This wound is at least two days old and the bullet came from some distance or it would have gone clear through. Besides, it entered from the heel of the foot, probably from behind you while in the saddle."

Eddie grinned wryly up at her, his light curly hair in a tangle, his thin face white from ether sickness. "You're getting pretty again, like the day I married you—"

Morissa held her anger. "I've taken care of the foot well enough to get you to Sidney. Charley will see you meet the down stage."

Then she went to make her report of the gun wound for the sheriff at Sidney. She could hear Eddie rebelling outside, but Charley, who had handled much bigger patients, got him into the buggy, and with Ruth driving took him away.

Morissa sat over her report a long time. Two days ago the Cheyenne treasure coach had been held up at the Canyon Springs station, which was set in a narrow, timbered cut of the western foothills. There the invulnerable ironclad was robbed. It seemed the station keeper had been tied up and as the driver jerked to a stop for the change of horses that he could see standing harnessed and ready, the robbers began to shoot from the buildings and the brush. One of the five guards with the ironclad fell dead, another was seriously wounded, while a third ran for the timber to shoot from its shelter. He brought down a couple of the road-agents but the rest used the driver as a shield and ran him out of rifle range. Then they forced the coach and the treasure box and rode away loaded down with gold estimated at from forty thousand to two hundred thousand dollars. Among the roadagents was the Doug Goodale who visited Eddie several times last winter and helped make the night of the big Indian scare endurable—another polite and polished young man who took to robbery.

Nothing came of Morissa's report to the sheriff about Eddie's foot, but some of the gold bricks from the Canyon Springs robbery were found in a bank window in Iowa. The banker said proudly that his son Douglas had brought them from the Black Hills. Sold a mine and took the gold in pay. But on each brick was the mine imprint: HOMESTAKE, and scratched on each was a serial number—all numbers in the plunder taken from the ironclad. The son was arrested, but he escaped from a train window down in the middle of Nebraska and was not recaptured.

"Got money enough to back you, nobody needs go to the pen—" Owen, the treasure guard, told Morissa sourly. Nobody had been caught for his shattered leg.

Now that Morissa had taken a public stand against Eddie and sent him away, even while wounded, the bridge and its community softened toward her, became more friendly. Even Etty's Lorette walked over for a cup of tea and a little visit. She was pregnant again but without the heavy dullness of the last time.

"You stay here with us— It be many peoples soon, my Ettier he say," the woman told Morissa, showing her white teeth in a shy smile. "Your Eddie man he bad. Ettier he see him with other woman—"

Morissa brushed this aside with the crumbs she swept into her napkin. "I don't care if he is with a dozen. I've been wondering about your children. They'll soon be old enough for school."

"Aha, yes. He send—"

"Soon there will be enough children for a school somewhere near. Alice and Georgie may be given back to me. Yellow fever struck them all and the father isn't recovering well, nor Alice either. But perhaps she could grow stronger in our pure air. It's that or an orphanage. One of the settlers over near the Wild Cats has a sister coming who has taught. Maybe next fall we'll have a school."

Gradually, too, the freighters began to stop at Morissa's again with their small complaints, perhaps a carbuncle, a bull-tromped foot, or a general dosing. In a few weeks it was almost like before her marriage, except that it wasn't at all. She couldn't go anywhere that required an escort. In a region where women are very scarce no husbandly claim, even of an absent one, could be ignored.

Several times Morissa did go to a dance with Charley and Ruth, first just to look on a while at Etty's. There were two music-making settlers in the region now, a hoe-down fiddler and a dulcimer man who played sitting on a bench up on a table or on planks laid across empty whisky barrels so he could call the changes if there was nobody else to holler the set.

Morissa went clear up to Sailor's for their fall dance with a whole crowd of horsebackers from Camp Clarke and the region around. Charley stayed behind to look after the patients, and in case Eddie tried to return. But Ruth was along, looking nice in the new wine-colored riding habit that Morissa had her dressmaker send out. Besides, she was rapidly forgetting her Methodist feet, as Charley called them, and dancing gay as a pullet.

When they returned Etty brought news of Morissa's man. He was in trouble with some gamblers down in Sidney. "The sheriff, maybe he come get your property, your stock—" the old trader said uneasily, Lorette standing beside him to shake her neat braids solemnly in concern. A bad man was a very bad thing.

"You like I send your horses away to my pasture, hide from sheriff?"

Morissa was grateful to Etty, but she kept her horses out in plain sight. The sheriff didn't come, perhaps because of the Indian scare. All through September there had been stories of the Cheyennes raiding northward from Indian Territory toward the Yellowstone, headed right through the North Platte country. It was hard to believe these reports while the Army was escorting another band of Cheyennes over the bridge from the Yellowstone toward the Territory. Because there must be no junction with the raiders, they were held up at Camp Sidney where Morissa saw them sitting against the buildings, men, women, and children waiting, silent.

Then early in October a rider came spurring down the deserted trail shouting that Red Cloud's Sioux had jumped their new reservation and were headed south to join the raiders. "Hit for the railroad!" the man shouted as he came around past Morissa's yard. "The Indians are up!"

Ruth ran out with her apron up over her shoulders to hear, but the

180

man was already off to Clarke's, where Morissa had gone for the news. She saw the man set his sweated, bloody-jawed horse to his haunches in the dust. For one moment a thin line of fear for her patients, for them all, ran through the doctor's arms, until she got a whiff of the man's breath as he pushed past her.

But there was no doubting that the Cheyennes taken to the Territory last year were heading north, and Morissa wondered if the man who gave her the Appaloosa might be with these starved-out Indians, as General Dodge called them. Morissa had talked against alarm to the settlers, with fewer than three hundred Indians, men, women, and children, out, and the trails running black with troops sent to intercept them at every creek, river, and railroad. Their tents had spread out white down at Sidney, their iron hoofs hard on Clarke's bridge, their number gathering dark as buffalo herds up around Red Cloud at Pine Ridge to watch his thousands of sullen warriors. Besides, the Cheyennes had remained rather peaceful in spite of the pursuing troops until they reached north Kansas, where three years ago many of their relatives had been killed. Suddenly now they struck the settlers and left thirty, forty men dead in one bloody massacre.

As this news spread, even people long on the frontier fled toward Sidney and the other towns, all preparing for attack, siege. Freighters and travelers gathered at the blockhouse of Camp Clarke, too, several hundred wagons, and settlers came dusting in on work mares or running afoot. For days the bridge lay like a fall caterpillar dozing in the yellow sun, idle, silent, nothing moving upon it except a few tardy soldiers and the galloping couriers, or perhaps stockmen hurrying orders to save their herds up in the sandhills and off along the rivers. Yet certainly General Crook's forces, with a special train ready to make interception sure, would capture the Cheyennes wherever they struck the Platte. Then there was word that the Indians had eluded these troops, too, and were loose among the river settlements.

In the midst of this the sky clouded over in smoke from far prairie burning, the valley thick and blue enough to sting the nose and eyes, the sun blood-red at evening. Sioux burning out the ranchers and the troops up north, the couriers and telegrams to Camp Clarke reported. Then a call came for Morissa. A man over northeast in the sandhills was dying of a gun accident. Charley, Gwinnie, and the new lieutenant at Camp Clarke would not let her go into the path of the bloodthirsty Indians. But Clarke's old station keeper spit out his cud and said she'd be all right. He had lived around these Cheyennes for twenty years, never knew them to hurt a woman. "Wasn't no women killed so far's I heard in that massacree down there in Kansas, was they? —But you better ride the 'Paloosy."

Morissa had known she must go, and gratefully she led out the spotted

181

horse, kept up close with the rest of the stock against any skulking Indians. He almost pulled her arm out with his eagerness to run. Then suddenly he shied and there, in the end of a snakehead draw before her, were half a dozen Indian women and one old man, all afoot, burdened with small children and packs on their backs. The moment they saw Morissa they were gone like quail in a coolie, but the tracks they left were bloody from their feet.

Farther on a hatless rider, an Indian, stood on a hill awhile to watch her, then he lifted a hand, the left, and was gone too. Perhaps he recognized the horse. And at the little cowcamp the man was already dead, his cheekbone and temple crushed in. Breech blown back by an overcharge of powder in an old shotgun.

Morissa thought about the walking women and children a week later when a blizzard struck with sudden midwinter fierceness and cold. Later the post surgeon at Robinson invited her to come up. Chief Dull Knife's band of the Cheyennes had been captured in the blizzard and locked up at the post. She went, to see the cast the Indians had made for a bullet-shattered thigh. The man had ridden with it from the southern border of Kansas, fleeing night and day before the soldiers. The cast was of green horsehide sewed around the bone-punctured leg, with holes for the reeds used to drain the wound, and had become bone-hard in the drying, holding the femur straight and true. Morissa was astonished. Natural-born bone men, these Indians. But it was the misery of the people that touched her—emaciated, half-naked, frostbitten, many still shaking with malaria, particularly the children, some with unhealed gunshot wounds weeks old. "They say they will die before they will go back," the doctor told Morissa as he showed her around. He said it objectively, impersonally, but he did not meet Morissa's anxious eyes.

When the Indian scare seemed over, the sheriff finally came. It wasn't the same man who sat in Morissa's soddy last year and pared his nails, but he seemed as antagonistic. What he had to say was private so Morissa nodded to Ruth and watched her go out and over to the bridge on an errand. Then, seated beside the kitchen table, an elbow on it, the sheriff spoke of Eddie Ellis. "You ain't made a home for your husband like a good wife should."

"You know the kind of man Eddie is."

"But as a patient a yours all winter his character might have been known to you."

Yes, it was, and his father had written her of their difficulties with the boy, a truant, in bad company, a thief, a forger, and dangerously violent.

"Well, he's forged Henry Clarke's signature this time."

"Oh!" Morissa exclaimed. Her father's employer, her benefactor, and all the region's. "He's never done such a thing before, not out here so far as I know."

"His mother probably paid up, or it would have been the penitentiary faster than by holdup or murder."

"I won't pay this; I won't buy off a forger."

"You might try bein' a wife to Ellis."

No, that she couldn't do. She had nothing but contempt for the youth. She admitted she had little more than that when she married him, some compassion perhaps, and a curious and morbid attachment, but nothing beyond that.

"Then you went into this thing for spite, an' him just a kid. Now you oughta try to make a marriage of it. Take him away from the gamblers and outlaws here, go East somewheres."

Morissa thought about this, made herself think about it, but Ed's family had already failed there when he was younger, and more malleable, a child. Yet she was guilty; perhaps she had used him as an instrument of spite, certainly of self-debasement.

"You better do like I say. It'd be mighty easy to make out a case against you here, harborin' criminals—" the sheriff reminded the young woman, his eyes bold upon her helplessness.

For a moment Morissa stared at him, the badge shining on the dark flannel shirt, the cartridge belt sagging over his chaps, his hatbrim drawn down upon his eyes. And before these things the young doctor's hands felt heavy, numb in her lap.

"All right," she said slowly. "If Ed will be content to live on his homestead I'll go there with him, give him a trial."

"Well, that's better. Mebby I can work out a parole to you," the sheriff replied, standing a moment to look down at Morissa, his thumb hooked into his cartridge belt, his eyes humid with contempt, and desire, too, desire to overcome this woman. In that moment Morissa saw how helpless she could be against him unless perhaps she were willing to kill, and as her glance went to the man's gun, gauging its position and her chance to reach it if he made a lunge, she saw his eyes film over with caution, become impersonal. Without a word he turned and went out of the door. Not until he was in the saddle did he speak. "I'll be holdin' you to your word!" he called out, as Fish Head came up around the house with a gleaming string of trout for the frying pan.

Morissa didn't wait for supper. All that evening she walked through the white frosty moonlight of November, knowing that the agreement would be the end of Dr. Morissa Kirk, that it was surely intended so. She couldn't decide if the sheriff was trying to drive her out of the country or destroy her here, whether for the cattlemen or for his own satisfaction. Perhaps he was actually so sentimental as to believe that a perverse infant like the one who lived in the body of Eddie Ellis could ever grow

183

into an acceptable man. Indeed, it did seem a possession, as Eddie's father had written, an evil possession, augmented by the invalidizing of a long bed illness.

The night was a bleak one, even though the November moon sparkled on all the rime-touched grass and bushes, on the bare, lean, adolescent growth of Morissa's young trees. It was a long, chill night of trying to understand how one born a bastard could have been so stupidly unguarded, act so irresponsibly when she knew the long pay-time one foolish moment could extract from a life. Perhaps the narrow moralists were right: Man born in sin was like a stream and could never rise above his source; she, Morissa Kirk, born in shame, could never hope to escape the shameful existence.

The next morning she rode out very early on the Appaloosa to have one last day of freedom on the tawny fall prairie, riding him hard into the wind, letting her hairpins scatter to the bunchgrass as her braid slipped from under her cowman's hat and whipped out behind her. At night they returned, worn out together, and as she unsaddled and rubbed the dried sweat from under the pad, she determined to find out if the man who gave her this horse was still alive, or his son, the boy she treated in infancy. If so, she would return the Appaloosa. Such an animal belonged to her first two years here; to the fine discovery of a new land, a new people; to her doctoring and her pride in it; to the many happy times when she rode beside Tris Polk, and the day she sat his silver saddle in the Walker horse show. But mostly the Appaloosa belonged to the brave, to people like the man who left him here beside her fence.

Before Morissa went into the house she slipped up to a window. But she couldn't see Eddie Ellis. No one was at the open fire except Ruth and young Hilda Gray, an expectant mother come in early because her settler husband was away earning a little track-laying money.

Cautiously Morissa pushed the door open and stood blinking in the lamplight shaded upon a pile of mail on the table. On top was a letter from a friend in the state medical association. Morissa's name was being put up for vice president at the winter meeting and he hoped she could give them a talk on surgery along the gold trail, about the broken neck and particularly about the Callwin head injury, of which they had heard a great deal.

Morissa lifted her tired eyes from the page and saw Ruth and the young woman watching her, the sorrow, the concern over the letter plain on their faces, and suddenly the young doctor's throat filled with gratitude.

"Oh, darlings, it's all right! This is good news!" she cried. And then she started to laugh and the other two, not knowing just why, joined in, all three laughing very hard together until the canary awoke to cheep under his cover and in the hospital room a patient moved.

"Aye, it takes so little to make a Scotsman, or a Scotswoman, happy," Morissa said, wiping her eyes. "But let's not laugh Hilda's son into the world before he's ripe and ready."

XV

EDDIE DIDN'T COME, BUT FINALLY THE STORY OF THE SHERIFF'S visit got out and the promise he extracted from Morissa: that she would leave, take her husband away.

"You mean leave the valley?" the old station keeper asked, and fell silent over his slack cud.

"Leave the trail?" a bullwhacker asked. "Why, just seein' Doc's place with them flowers of a summer, an' knowin' there's geraniums bloomin' in there winter times shortens up them long pulls to the Hills—"

"Yeh, an' her a flyin' along on that 'Paloosy horse makes a man feel good after he's been walkin' mebby a thousand miles an' his boot tacks is burnin' his feet, er his ears is dropping off from the cold."

But several drifting cowboys were standing around the bar too, out of the storm. "This here country ain't no place fer a woman," one of them said, not looking over toward Morissa's house, or toward her team impatient at the hitchrack outside. Instead, he busied himself pulling at the Durham string with his teeth, and spread the tobacco along the paper with his thumb to roll it. "This country's fer cactus, rattlers, 'n' mebby cows, when it don't get too cold," he said, after the paper was licked.

So for a little while the emphasis shifted from the place north of the river with its thriving ten acres of trees, the slope of vegetable garden, its wall of growing lilac bushes, and the flower beds that drew the hopeful eye of every homeseeker. The sly remarks now were still of Eddie but not as a weapon to remove Morissa, rather against him as a man and a husband, and without her notice these dropped off. Yet each time that she had to defend him in her mind she wondered if he might not write, let her know how his foot was, and he himself, for Ed was truly not a strong man. There were stories about Goodale, the bullion-stealing son of a banker, now in the Colorado mine country with some blond, curly-headed kid who used to hang around Red Cloud Agency. That must be Eddie, but Morissa could see no way to reach him. She was still paying

185

off the first debts he made, and had had to write Henry Clarke in embarrassment to apologize for his forgery. "I am grieved that your favors have been so illy repaid."

Clarke answered in a quiet little note from Omaha. "The check, unhonored, is put away as an effective bit of evidence for some future time, when you may need it desperately." Morissa knew this was wise and still she wanted to beg that it be destroyed. Truly a woman's mind and the winter winds blow this way and that.

Yet Ed was in very bad company, and as his wife she was legally responsible in many things. Besides, people were weary of lawlessness. A group of masked men had dragged two prisoners, roadagents, from the Cheyenne coach and left them swinging from an old cottonwood on the riverbank. One of Doc Middleton's hideouts off along the Niobrara River was raided by a sheriff and seventeen, eighteen men. They got a herd of cattle and a dozen horses, and found signs of probably fifty men running stock east and west along the river from one robbers' camp to the next. Four of the outfit were captured there, but not Doc Middleton. He got away.

"Yeh, Doc's one of them quiet, wily birds," a Bosler wagon boss said. "Remember when he worked up to Pratt's? Nobody thinking him anything but a scrub cowhand till he shoots that soldier to Sidney in a fight and troops come chasin' him, so he has to take a horse from Callwin's neighbor to get away. Not all them soldiers, mad as hell, catches him. Nobody catches Doc Middleton. And he sent a hundred dollars back to pay for the granger's horse he took."

Morissa stayed to hear it all, and the retelling, although those around the station surely suspected why, perhaps even knew where Eddie hung out. But she couldn't ask, and so she had to watch for every word of outlawry, always afraid and yet hopeful. And every time the sheriff or a deputy came as far as the bridge she wanted to gather up her skirts and run for the shelter of her thickened grove.

Banks had been failing all over the East, with trouble at Sidney too. The bank there had been shaky in the middle of the town's gold boom, through greed and mismanagement, Clarke told Morissa. Then new people took it over and put their new money in the window. But times must still be hard, for although this was the coldest winter since the Indians had the country, homeseekers kept coming, measuring off bleak and snow-covered acres by scraping the snow to the frozen section corners, and then stepping off distances or driving a wagon with a rag tied to a spoke, the turns counted at so many to the mile.

Some who came late in the summer or had their crops eaten up by range cattle lived on pretty thin soup this winter, with no jobs, more than half of the regular ranch hands laid off until spring with cattle prices so low. Any settler who had a gun and ammunition could kill all the meat he wanted, small game, deer, antelope, even elk in the breaks and moving thick into the sandhills from the north. But meat demands bread or potatoes, at least for children, and for women too if they are not to do foolish things, perhaps slash a wrist with a piece of broken glass, or walk to the trail begging to be taken away, leaving their men, dark and angry, behind. Sometimes the men, particularly the bachelors, left, too, and one blew the top of his head off with a shotgun, muzzle in his mouth. There was talk that some of the settlers were eating slow elk, stolen ranch beef this cold weather, and of threats against them for it, but nothing like the hanging and burning of two homesteaders by the Olive cattle outfit down the Platte. Not yet.

Morissa got so she dug into her root cellar every time she started on a call, taking along perhaps cabbage, or turnips, or carrots and potatoes, setting the sack beside her hot footstone under the buffalo robe, letting the sirup bucket of milk freeze to ice in the buggy box behind. Toward Christmas she had sent word around that there would be a big dinner at the hospital, everybody welcome, with a little something extra for the children, and dancing in the evening. Even Fish Head helped, gathering red rose hips wherever the snow blew off, to string for the tree. Ruth knitted late, her steel needles flying, making black mittens with small rosebuds on the backs for the girls, little yellow dogs for the boys, until she had a dozen pairs in varying sizes.

"But if more come?" she asked anxiously.

"We'll have other things in reserve—" Morissa promised. Her uneasiness was that there might be no one. A year ago she would have been gaily confident, with Tris beside her. But as the wife of the shadowed Eddie Ellis—the forsaken wife of Eddie—

To this her bastardy seemed as nothing. "Rub your face in the hog's trough and your old reek's sweet as heather," Morissa's mother once told her, and how truthfully.

But just before Christmas word of guests coming poured in, many wanting to help. One woman was bringing a jar of pickled ground cherries, another preserved prickly pears from the bull-tongue cactus. One from a ranch over on Pumpkin Seed Creek would make the little dip candles for the tree, with chopped pine needles in the tallow for fragrance. John Callwin offered to run the barbecue pit and make the sauce, if there was room for his Nancy and the little boy overnight.

Christmas morning the thermometer was down below zero, the crusted snow still deep, but by ten o'clock black dots were moving here and there into the bleak valley, many with bobsleds or with wagon beds spiked to runners of slim pine poles, the beds full of quilts, robes, or soogans and perhaps hay, those from the Wild Cats bringing big loads of pine boughs for trimmings, and extra wood for the fireplace. Some

187

came horseback and others afoot over the hard snow, but Hilda Gray and her Dick were not among them at all, and it was really for them that Morissa had planned the dinner. One of nature's dreadful accidents had happened to that gay and energetic young couple. Their child was born a lump, squat-bodied and brown, with a thick, dull face and slanted eyes.

"It's the Indian scare what done it, marked the baby!" some said darkly, even after Morissa tried to explain that mongolism could happen anywhere. She grieved with the parents and tried to assure them that the next child would surely be fine. But they had put the baby into the wagon in silence.

And now the Grays didn't come, although it seemed almost everybody else was there. Tables were laid through the long sod hospital room, pleasant with the big blaze in the fireplace, the patients moved out into Ruth's quarters. But there was some uneasiness among the women in the kitchen and elsewhere, too. "I hear Ed Ellis was in Sidney this week. I figger he'll come hornin' in here," one of the men said out at the barbecue pit.

"Never no pot boiled but a little scum didn't rise to the top," Clarke's old blacksmith agreed. "But if he's the scum that's risin' around here today I could kill 'im with my peen hammer and throw 'im in some washout fer the buzzards."

They had fat venison and a half of a young beef that Sid Martin sent, with the barrel of apples that his freight hands dropped off before the last cold snap, and a wooden pail of hard candy from Owen, the coach guard. There were dishpans full of watercress salad with bits of smoked bacon in the vinegar dressing; potatoes baked in coals raked from the barbecue pit, beans, mashed turnips; several kinds of pickles, wild plum and sandcherry preserves, wild grape and chokecherry jelly, and buffalo berry, too, quivering and shining orange-red in the light. There were pumpkin pies big as a woman's arms could circle, baked in tub and bucket lids over in the Camp oven.

Finally the people were gathered, standing around with their hands awkward, at least five men to every woman. Then Morissa got them seated at the three long tables, an extra one put up with more barrels and planks the last minute, and preparations made for the latecomers. The children's table was over near the kitchen where Ruth and two of the shier mothers could look after them. Then Morissa had the cots of her patients brought in for a little while, and planned to ask John Callwin to say grace, but Clarke's old blacksmith spoke up ahead of her. "Miss Morissy, I want to get my ante in the pot first. I'm throwing Fish Head in to ask the blessin'."

It was Christmas and no feelings must be hurt, so Morissa tried to stop it, to save the little man the jibes and laughing, but he was already on his feet, standing no taller than a twelve-year-old boy, just a shoe peg of a man. He smoothed his gray beard a little and moved his watery eyes benignly around the tables. Then quietly, earnestly, he started, and Morissa realized once more how well this man could use his voice, the quality of it, the shadings, the rise and fall. And before he said two dozen words, not in his usual pompous way, but slowly, simply, an earnestness crept into the bent faces. "—We are here in a sort of double thanksgiving, Dear Father, thankful for a Savior born and for a new world created to our use. Around these laden tables are men and women who have come here seeking homes for themselves and their children, setting the plow to Your virgin prairie, turning their faces to a life as new as when You first gave Adam and Eve the earth and its promise for their toil, the promise of rain and sunshine, of seeding time and harvest—"

As the man's words spread over them, Morissa found her face wet, and when he finished and gravely sat down, other eyes had to turn to their plates to hide from the glinting firelight.

"By golly, Fish, you'd oughta been a preacher—" one of the freighters roared out, to cover his softness, and from the sudden flush on the little man's bearded face Morissa knew that once more a pretender had been caught. Somewhere, sometime, Fish Head had been a preacher.

Afterward was the children's time, fifteen of them here, counting the three infants Morissa had delivered and a fourteen-year-old boy, almost a man but shy. A closet door was opened and inside the duskiness stood a Christmas tree. Four men lifted the box base a little and drew the tree carefully out into the big room, barely swaying the strings of popcorn and rose hips. Then, with the shades drawn, the fragrant little candles were lit. The big gilt star on the top glistened, the four silken-winged angels that pointed their horns out each way, too, and the gilded walnuts and the sugared boy and girl cookies as well as the little red cheesecloth sacks of candy and the presents for the children. The faces of the young ones, some from dugouts, some barefoot, were a joy to see. "I wish Alice and Georgie could have been here," Morissa whispered to Ruth and Lorette, and when her back was turned the young breed woman moved a finger across her throat in the typical Sioux gesture. "I like do so to this Eddie who send them away—"

There was Sid's barrel of apples, too, a tub of popcorn balls, and a big gunny sack of roasted peanuts for everyone to dip into. Then a Pole from over on the breaks, a stranger "with the few English" as he expressed it, set his bright red accordion on his knee and bent his head to it, crying a little as the others sang, for this was his first Christmas in a far country. And as the early gray of evening came, the teams and horse-backers started away, the chilled horses stomping, fighting the bits, eager to run. Morissa looked anxiously into the northwest sky, and hoped that the storm would hold off until everyone was home. She looked away toward the trail from Sidney, too, and then north, but no one had seen anything of Eddie yet, and only Tris had sent no greeting, not Tris nor Allston Hoyt, the two men for whom her wedding garments lay folded, unworn, in the bottom of the round-topped trunk.

Before dark those who stayed for the dance were joined by the early evening guests, the Sailor ranch hands the first. It was a gay night, with music and stomping boots, and flight of calico and worsted skirts. During the midnight lunch there was a whirling Cossack dance by the Pole, a slip-shoe routine by the fiddler, and then a Southern jig by the dulcimer man. And suddenly Fish Head was moved to get up, too, in his rusty broadcloth, to start a sort of eccentric dance, a boneless series of little hops and jumps, slides and sways and slow falls until Charley took him away to his soddy to sleep off the whisky from the flask somebody had sneaked to him.

Finally dawn came to light the way home and when Morissa had answered the last good-by she went slowly in for a cup of coffee alone, and now she admitted to herself that this, her first community get-together, would be her last. No more of this in her ambiguous state, when even a polite compliment from the Englishmen had to seem tinged with a shameful meaning because she was no longer a girl, or single to be wooed openly, but a married woman, without the dignity of a husband by her side.

And Ed—he hadn't come to the first Christmas of their marriage at all.

All the next week Morissa planned. Then she rode the Appaloosa out through the frosted valley and the Wild Cats and pounded on Gray's dugout, the sod chimney smoking peacefully in a little nest of pines that were white-needled with rime in the snow. There was a long cold wait before the door opened and she was finally asked to come in. She was not shown the baby at all, even when its peculiar cry arose and Dick moved his foot to sway the cradle, so close in the dark little room. After a while Hilda listened to the request the doctor had come to make. To the plea in the man's sorrowful eyes, the wife finally nodded agreement, and so Morissa went back home and wrote a dozen copies of a letter offering three months of schooling at her place, to begin March first. Any child from six through fifteen would be welcomed by Hilda Gray, an experienced rural teacher from the state of Michigan. The children could board the five days of each week at the sanitarium, or the entire seven. "As pay I hope you will trade me one day's work, man and team, if you have it, for each week, payable next summer, when I hope to erect an extensive log addition to my hospital," Morissa wrote.

With the letters off, she went to the medical association meeting in Omaha, her talk neatly written out. Robin had caught a train down from his work, stopped by the frozen ground anyway, and was at the depot to meet her. The tall, neat-haired, and red-cheeked youth beside him turned out to be Jackie, and Morissa flew at them both, in her leaf-brown cloak with beaver tippet and muff. She was very happy to see Robin, but Jackie—Jack now! She could barely take her eyes from him, so fine had he grown. He was poised, and talked of being a doctor too.

"Oh!" she turned to Robin, who nodded. "Why, that's wonderful!" she cried, her eyes a golden hazel in her joy.

Yes, he was taking the prep course now and planning on medical school next fall, if he could make it. They had kept it as a surprise for her. "I have permission to go sit in on the meetings tomorrow," he said boyishly.

It was very difficult for young Dr. Morissa Kirk to stand up before the roomful of bearded men, with only three or four women among them, more probably wives than physicians. It was much more difficult than to get an unconscious settler out of a well and keep him alive while she extracted the crushed bone and cleared away the damaged tissue, hammered out the silver plate and sewed it into place. "But one does what one must—" she said.

Finally the paper was finished and she sat down with her knees still shaking, wondering if she had shamed young Jack, and if the applause was anything more than just good manners toward a weak female. Then the door opened and John Callwin was brought in, very brown and tall here, and a little embarrassed.

"I had to go show my mother-in-law anyway," he apologized to Morissa. "Uncle Bob thought it would be nice if I stopped off here for a few hours today—" But Morissa couldn't hear for the pounding of her heart.

Afterward there were three men waiting outside the door for Morissa, Tris Polk standing tall between Robin and Jack. For a moment Morissa wanted to run because his face seemed almost the same as when she left him standing on the hotel steps in Sidney last June—with all the hurt and disbelief, the guilt too and the admiration, all the things in it that she had been too distraught to realize then. Yet now he stood here as though none of the things since had happened, and that she could take up from that moment.

But they had happened, and now Morissa must greet him, passing off her flushed excitement as from the paper that she read and the election —vice president of the association. She touched the back of a hand to her cheek. "Feverish, decidedly feverish, I'd say," she laughed. "It's just been too much for this simple country.girl—"

191

Together they went along the street and once more Morissa found herself falling into such easy step with this man, her hand tucked into the long-known crook of his arm as though she had come home from far away.

They were together several times the next two days, talking over Tris's new plans, plans that seemed as beautiful and unreal as Chimney Rock in snow. He was sending an engineer out to the North Platte valley toward spring, pretending to be looking for a ranch site along the river somewhere. "What I want to know is how practical large-scale irrigation would be out there. Have you ever been up the river into Wyoming? There are several good sites for dams, although the best seems to be far up at the Narrows, where the river boils out through a deep rocky cut. There's the place for a dam and a great reservoir behind it." The man's face glowed as he talked, his gray eyes not smoky now, but like spring clouds, like April with sun spilling through.

"You're still the engineer!" Morissa exclaimed. "Your Aunt Mae said you were planning to be one when your father was killed in the war—"

"You always remember the roots, the beginnings, of everything, don't you? What a wife you would have made for a scientist—or an engineer—" he said, carried along by embarrassment. But the sudden shadowing of Morissa's face made him stop. "I—I guess there's a lot of money in the packing business here," he added lamely, "but I can't make slaughtering my life work."

"You're a rancher too—"

"No, I'm selling my interest in the ranches. Part of the money is going into the railroad that's to come through the valley. That won't bring much return for some time, but what I put into the packing business, that will pay. Anyway, I'm getting out of ranching."

"Oh, that's too bad. You belong out in that region," Morissa said, and felt ashamed of her part in this decision, ashamed that there was so much to separate them now—all the occurrences of the last year and before that too. Yet it was only of such things as packing houses and railroads that they could speak, not of the feeling between them.

They were together again after that, she married to a boy called Eddie, Tris rumored affianced to Yevette Forson, daughter of his partner, and ten years younger than Tris—a gay, irresponsible child, but with a doting father and money enough to buy anything she wished, and with enough brunette beauty, too, Morissa had to admit.

Charley Adams met Morissa at the Sidney depot and took her to the hotel. "Hurry, Doc, we're goin' to the Fireman's Masquerade. Ruth's there already and I couldn't drag her away," he said ruefully. "She shure is takin' to this here country and the good times."

There was a costume for Morissa, too, he said. Etty's Lorette had sent her mother's beaded doeskin dress and a painted mask. Morissa drew on the handsome fringed dress with winged sleeves and a wide yoke of blue and yellow beads. There were beaded moccasins, too, and long beaded bands to trail from her braids. The mask Lorette had painted was bland, round-faced, and brown. At the door of the dance hall Charley took off the black hat he wore and let down two long black horsetail braids fastened inside, drawing them over his beaded shirt. Then he tied on a dark mask, and they went inside, just one more Sioux couple.

The dancers were going strong, the fiddlers on a high platform sawing and sweating, the stomp and swing of the quadrille raising a thin dust from the floor cracks. As they entered a woman suffragette with glassless specs on the long nose of her mask came hurrying over, switching her bustle and spouting verbiage in a thin, high voice. It was Fish Head and with him was Calamity Jane, except that from under the soot-smeared mask came the whispered voice of Ruth. She tried hard to be Calamity, reeling a little, even letting out an experimental whoop and a little howling, but Ruth was not the woman to throw back her head and let 'er rip. There were other, more socially acceptable characters around, several satin-garbed princes, a bishop who ran a livery stable, a general who had been a Reb, a fairy queen mask hiding a rancher's pretty wife, and Hamlet a swamper from the Trail Drivers' saloon. There was a Columbia in stars and stripes, too, and some Colonials, Old Mother Hubbard and her dog, and an Antony and Cleopatra, who were Huff Johnson and Gilda Ross, who still attracted Tris, as well as a Satan, and a Red Tape representing a businessman's satire on slow-coach government. There were Negro minstrels with red, sunburnt ears, and some dancing girls with bony, saddle-bowed knees hanging out. Many here might be real holdups ready to go into action and so even the rope-haired Texas Belle had his gun ready under his coquettish skirts.

It was while dancing with one of the cowboys, a slightly foreign version, that Morissa finally let herself be drawn into conversation. "You're one of our many visiting Englishmen," she ventured.

Aha, that was very acute of her, yes, he was a cousin of the Sailors. Come to take up ranching too, perhaps, but it was very lonely business for a bachelor here, where there were so few young ladies.

"Seems there are plenty ladies here tonight," Morissa said.

Yes, true, but some were deucedly awkward, if he might be permitted to say so. One he had danced with, the old Texas Belle with the curious yellow curls, most certainly had cowboy boots on under her crinolines.

"Oh, how daring of you to know!"

"Yes, and I know too that you *are* a woman, one who would be a prideful helpmeet in the wilderness," he said with mock gallantry. "A cultured lady of good breeding and family."

Now Morissa found herself saying something she could never have anticipated. "Oh, kind sir, you are mistaken. I am of no breeding at all; I am a bastard."

The eyes behind the man's mask twinkled and finally the laughter came to the surface. "At home in England some of our best blood comes by the backstairs, you know. Our good queen's consort is a bastard himself, it is said."

"Ah, so I have one qualification for a good British bride, but I'll whisper something you can't pass off so lightly, my young Lochinvar. I have a husband."

"Oh, dear lady, I am disappointed. Which is the lucky man of so gracious an Indian princess?"

"He's not here, at least I doubt it. We don't live together. So there's still hope for you."

Ah, but not for a good member of the Church of England, he said, and there was no fun in his eyes, nor did he return for another dance. Instead he stood off against the wall firm in his height above the other stags and watched her. After the unmasking he still didn't come for a pleasant word, and made no move from his station even when the great trays of cold venison, antelope, grouse, and wild turkey were carried in, the cakes and coffee. Morissa ate with the post doctor and his wife and Sid Martin. Charley and Ruth came to join them, Ruth flushed and pretty now that the soiled mask of Calamity Jane was off, blushing deeper as Charley teased her about her birthday, thirty-eight today, and still acting like a pullet. But Fish Head was lost. He had to retire. Too many men tried to see if the woman suffragette was as dead set against liquor as might be expected of one of her noble persuasion.

If Eddie Ellis was there, he had not danced with Morissa, and did not stay for the unmasking here where the sheriff held a warrant for his arrest for forgery.

Even with all the sadness of seeing Tris so short a time, and the uncertainty about Eddie that underlaid even the masked ball, the new year had promised to be a good one. But now she heard about the Cheyennes, scattered dead over the snow up around Fort Robinson. The people she had seen crowded into a barracks in the fall had been ordered back to Indian Territory and refused to go. Food was cut off, then fuel with the weather far below zero, and finally water, too, and so at night they strapped their children to their backs and poured out of the barrack windows into the guns of the troops, preferring to die in honor.

And they died, running across the moonlit snow. Some managed to elude the soldiers over the winter bluffs for thirteen bloody, freezing, and starving days, until the last remnant was finally cornered in a hole out on the open prairie, the guns firing until nothing moved. The few men captured were ironed for the South. A lieutenant from up there showed Morissa the half of a long scissors with which Chief Wild Hog had tried to kill himself. The widows and orphans were allowed to go to Red Cloud's Sioux, but not Hog's wife, although she was sick and half crazy from the long pursuit in which most of her children and her people were killed. If Hog died she could remain here in the North where she had been a gay, pretty girl, wooed by half a dozen men who became chiefs.

When the wagons of prisoners came slowly down to Clarke's bridge, the cold February wind blowing the capes of the troopers about their shoulders, Morissa went out to talk to Hog if she could and to estimate his injury. He greeted her by holding out his ironed wrists, the tall, broad-boned man stooped for all time now from the stab wounds in breast and belly. The interpreter said the chief remembered her coming to the barracks with the candy for the children.

"Ahh, the children—" Hog repeated the words in soft Cheyenne, and made the sign for *killed*: the right hand, almost closed, brought down and across, to rebound a little, fingers extending. But his left hand, manacled to the right, had to follow, the steel rattling.

Morissa hurried to the officer in charge. "The Indian children—are any alive up there?"

"Yes, some; mostly wounded."

"Is there anything I can do?"

"No, they were taken to Red Cloud."

Telling her errand to no one, Morissa rode up the North Platte alone the next morning, going to where she knew a few Indians had wintered in a hole in the badland slope of Scotts Bluff. She had been up that way twice before, leaving sacks with flour, coffee, and a little brown sugar, the first time with a drawing of two Indian children made by Lorette pinned to the outside. When Morissa had come back that way the sack was gone, and in its place was a little piece of rolled buckskin tied to a stake, a drawing of an Indian with his left hand up in friendly greeting to a long-skirted woman on an Appaloosa.

But now there were no horse tracks around, and when Morissa returned next day the new sack was untouched. She knew these Indians were blamed for killing a family south of the Wild Cats, and that they probably shot a man watching cattle over that way, although the old blacksmith at Clarke's doubted it. He claimed the Indians would have used arrows since they had so little ammunition. There were rumors that most of the fleeing Cheyennes who had eluded capture had wintered in the sandhills with the troops looking down into their little valley a dozen times and detecting not even a curl of smoke. By now this band was headed north for the Yellowstone, leaving two cowboys dead at a Niobrara ranch where they got some horses. Morissa looked northward and hoped for her Indians.

195

Hilda came the evening before school opened, carrying her poor help-less baby in a willow basket. Four children would be starting, with per-haps two more later. Morissa had schoolbooks, slates, and paper, and three double seats and a folding blackboard that Charley had made. They went to bed late that night, Morissa happy that Hilda was already looking better. The school would work out if no epidemics struck, no diphtheria or scarlet fever, and no calamity like fire, perhaps, or cattle-man trouble.

For once she went to sleep without thinking about Eddie or wonder-ing who was looking after him tonight. She heard that some of Doc Middleton's gang were captured at North Platte city but Doc had spurred off over the railroad bridge, a pistol in each hand, shooting both ways. It was a fine story of daring to attract a youth and Morissa was glad that Jack was safely away at school. Later more of Doc's gang were taken, and at Sidney late in April she saw Middleton hit it out of there with the sheriff and a dozen others hot after him as he dodged into the rocks of the bluffs above the town, where Morissa had gone from the trial. Bul-lets spattered all round him but he got away.

After a while the shamefaced pursuers sneaked back down a side street, although another of Middleton's gang fell later. So far Eddie Ellis was not among the captured. Nor was Doc, although a group of big cattlemen put a hundred dollars apiece on his head.

With the spring rush of settlers into the cattle country, there was great excitement over the trial of the Olives, ranchers down in Custer County, for the hanging and burning of two settlers they claimed rustled their beef. The Olives brought an armed mob of cowboys to the trial and the judge called for militia to protect the court and witnesses. This was to be an honest legal test between the settlers and the cattlemen. Sid Martin and even the Boslers called the Olives a gang of outlaws who gave the ranchers a bad name here as they had back in Texas, and yet this lynching and burning might keep out a lot more homeseekers than any threat of a bullet in the back.

The stockmen had other worries too. The winter had been the longest and coldest since '71, the range full of dead cattle. Almost as soon as the winter snow cleared off the vast, unoccupied sandhills, prairie fires sprouted in the thick long grass, perhaps set by Indians still hidden up there, or the greenhorns in the country, careless and malicious. Besides, there was always the lightning, and broken bottles focusing the sun's rays.

Morissa knew about these sandhill fires burning for weeks, driven this way and that in the wind until finally forced to feed upon their own ashes. So far she had seen only the angry rolling clouds of pearly smoke on the horizon and men hurrying toward them—dark ants running over the prairie, and later the great black patches like cloud shadows reaching toward the horizon, with perhaps here and there an extended tongue finally tapering off.

Then one April day when the wind ran in waves over the dead grass of the upper Snake Creek region, Morissa was suddenly faced by a prairie fire. It was almost upon her, the bays suddenly shying and plunging, before she even saw the smoke, a great sausage of it running across her direction. She stood up in the buggy and whipped for a gravel slope where the grass was no more than the ragged fuzz on a balding dome. Here she might hold her horses together in the face of the flames, only two, three miles away southeast now, the smoke rolling over her and splitting against the hill beyond.

Morissa tore up a grain sack to blindfold her rearing, wild-eyed team and hobbled them close. Then with her shovel she cleared off a little strip and set a back fire to burn slowly into the wind and leave the scabby earth even barer. But suddenly the wind shifted into the south and the smoke of the fire trailed straight toward a wide wet valley that Morissa knew, one with all the thick accumulation of grass since the buffalo herds disappeared. And there, in a tent out in the middle, lived a new settler, his ankle broken and not so much as a horse to carry him away. There wasn't even a well to crawl into, only a barrel sunken into a seepage spot. That and his old tent pitched in the sea of grass was all.

Swiftly the doctor hitched up again and let her faunching horses out, the top buggy bouncing and swaying down the path of the rolling smoke that choked and blinded her and the team. They galloped before the fire, across the old buffalo trails and blowouts, through buckbrush and over ridges, fleeing rabbits and even coyotes and deer visible momentarily in the smoke. They plunged into a hidden gully and were almost out the other side when a wheel caught, something cracked, and the double-trees went. Morissa pulled the frightened team to a stop, snapped the tugs up, and with her black bag pounding against her side, she rode Nellie's galloping hames toward the man's tent, anxiously glancing back into the smoke that boiled up darker, shot with red like summer lightning as the fire gained on her, the heat searing her face, the smoke tears streaming from her eyes.

But before she got to the settler she saw the Bosler fire crew race past in the smoke, first the plows, at each a rider on the nigh horse of the double team, whipping them on while two men, their feet flying high, clung to the plow handles and tried to hold the breaker bottom in the rough sod, the second plow off to the side a little, leaving a strip roughly 40 feet wide between the two. Behind them came a horsebacker dragging a long rope, the raveled end soaked in coal oil, burning, to set a line of guard fire between the two plowed furrows. He tried to keep it close to the down-wind side, with at least fifty men strung out behind to fight any little blaze that might jump the furrow and run free.

Somebody saw Morissa. "The lady doc!" he yelled, and swinging his hat to stop her, motioned her back, but she galloped her horses on. At the settler's tent she saw the man trying to escape through the smoke in a hobbling, stumbling run on his crutches as the fire topped a hill less than a mile off, the Bosler crew barely ahead of it now, still trying to overtake the blazing front, to swing around the longest tongue that leapt on in the high wind.

With the man up on Kiowa, Morissa hurried back toward the comparative safety of the burnt fireguard. Beside the Bosler crew she slid off. Waving the man on, she grabbed a fire hoe, too, to chop and beat at the backfiring wherever the plow had jumped from the earth and left no turned furrow. Twice the wind swept the fire like an express train straight upon them, with only the narrow, half-burnt guard against it, driving them straggling back, their eyebrows and lashes gone from their sooted faces, their clothing full of smoldering holes.

But each time they edged a little closer into the wind-driven fire, tapering it more and more, until the last tongue was pinched together in some broken chophills and finally headed by the plows and fighters. The smoke died until there were only the soapweeds with their hearts smoldering like sullen punk and needing to be watched for a day or so. The burnt ground reached back southeast as far as anyone could see, a great rolling mass of blackened hills shouldering away to the horizon. The furrow-edged ribbon of the new Bosler fireguard stood against it all the way, from almost at the Platte, over thirty miles of guard thrown up in the face of the wind-driven flames.

Now the men lay scattered over the prairie like old bundles of blackened rags, flat, played-out, and already the wind was whipping up clouds of soot darker than the smoke had been, eating into the sandy knobs suddenly bare and whitening.

After a while somebody remembered the lady doc and rose stiffly to look for her. Morissa opened her aching eyes to the man's call and got to her feet, her lips blistered, her brows burnt off, her bangs scorched. The cowboy laughed a little to see her, his own eyes red and the blood seeping from his blistered lips bright in the sooty face. The crippled settler was coming back along the fireguard with Morissa's team, and now she remembered her buggy off in the gully. But it was gone, burned to the axle and hub.

XVI

FOR THE FOURTH SPRINGTIME MORISSA KIRK WATCHED THE wheels lurch heavily through the mud of the North Platte valley, drop dark earth on the bridge planks, and stop to rest a while. Then they started up the gold trail that was worn and washed out now, half a mile wide in places, and much more than that when grass became short for the smooth-jawed bulls, or the water holes dried up.

The trail over Clarke's bridge had drained away so much travel from Cheyenne that finally even the much romanticized iron-clad treasure coach came, too, carrying as high as three hundred and fifty thousand dollars in gold protected by its steel lining and half a dozen armed guards. Sidney was booming, with long freight houses, many hotels, and saloons and dance halls too, one that was half a block long, and gambling everywhere. There were still around a thousand troops at the post, and between three and five thousand employees of the stage and freight companies. Payday brought roaring battles between the two groups all along Front Street and in the gambling dens, to turn into three-cornered fights when the big trail herds hit the town.

Besides, this year the colonization literature of the railroad really drew the landless. Homeseekers poured out of the emigrant cars, stiff and sooty, or came the cheaper and slower routes of horse or shank's mare. Most of them scattered to find their own land but locaters, surveyors, and deadbeats waited like buzzards for all with a little money. Advice was free around the saloons, mostly the cowmen's stories of drouth and hot winds, and prairie fires, grasshoppers like storm clouds, and winters that were one long blizzard.

But there were fewer soft-handed gunmen to keep the range clear. "Looks as hopeless as holdin' back the north wind with a wire fence," Sid Martin admitted. Besides, the notorious lynching trial of the Olives had aroused the public. Ranchers began to drift their herds north into the sandhills or clear into Dakota; some, like Tris, sold out to combines of British or Eastern money. The new Bay State outfit bought in west and north of Sidney and shipped a great handsome ranch house in sections from the East. Jack was out for a week after school and Morissa took him over that way to see the new place on Sid Martin's invitation, before the family moved in.

"They'll go broke inside of two years," Sid predicted, as the three rode along together, "unless they can keep them Eastern widow women sinking money in here."

It was a fine house, the show place of all the region, with upholstered furniture, running water and bathtubs, velvet drapes over heavy lace curtains, and a stained-glass window high up to spill color all down the white staircase.

"Someday you ought to have one like that," Jack told his sister.

"No, nothing like that here. This belongs in some fashionable colony along the seaboard, like Newport," Morissa replied. "Sod and log will do me a long time. All I ask is space enough and the best equipment I can afford."

On the way back they swung around past Sidney. The town was excited, this time over a murderer. They went up to the bluffs above the town where Morissa had seen Doc Middleton hide. There the gambler, Reed, who shot down a businessman on the street today, was captured and taken to jail although some questioned the business of the man killed. There were murmurs and threats through the town all evening but at night these grew into a roar as the noise of a blood-angry herd rises. When Morissa and the others came out of a minstrel show, several hundred masked men were headed toward the jail, a dozen lanterns swinging among them as they ran. By the time Jack got Morissa and Sid there the guard had been overpowered and Reed was being dragged out. With shouts and curses the mob hustled him along, more and more people drawn in, some carrying flaming torches of pitch, here and there a woman's loud scream rising "Hang 'im! String up the—"

Morissa and the others were swept along too, rushed on by those behind, until south of the railroad tracks the crowd seemed stopped by something, packed solid, everybody standing on tiptoe to see. In the flaring lights a ladder rose up above the lifted heads, set against a telegraph pole. Then Reed was pushed to the top of it, a rope around his neck. The end was thrown over a crossarm, snapped tight there, and the man ordered to jump.

"—Jump, you bastard, or we'll jerk the ladder!" The crowd echoed it in a roar, "Jump! Jump!" the order repeated like a swelling chant that spread outward to the farthest edges. "Jump!"

"Oh, don't," Morissa was crying, but not even her own ears could hear her plea. In the unsteady light of the lanterns and the smoking torches the man seemed to stand like a straw figure, stiff, yet swaying a little as in a wind. But finally he moved one foot, and dropped a ways on the rope, his face working, his mouth opening as though in a soundless cry, the tongue bursting from it as the roar of the crowd rose to a climax. Then his head tipped forward, his whole body hanging straight down, his hands turned palm out in that same unheeded supplication that Morissa had seen at the bridge her first morning on the North Platte. Suddenly she could endure it no longer and she tried to fight her way out through the crowd, against all the people, against all the faces that were

200

turned, so curiously empty and spent now, up to a man that had been hanged.

After they put Jack on his train Morissa sat in her room at the hotel a long time. She should go to bed, weary from the long hours in the saddle and the contrast of the imported house of the Bay State cattle company with the horror and anger of the thing she had seen done tonight. But she knew that this might as well have been Ed, Eddie Ellis caught with horse thieves, surely a thief himself, perhaps even a murderer, for that road was all a downhill pull here.

Now Morissa felt she must get in touch with him, fretting about him like a mother over a weakling son. She lost all reticence, all pride, it seemed, and began to ask about him openly. Finally she wrote to his father, who replied very tersely:

> I have no son. Twice the last year men have come looking for a youth apparently bearing my name. Once I judged them to be the kind that he has chosen in place of his respectable family and friends, and the second time they were officers of the law, seeking him in connection with some of his nefarious activities. If there ever was such a young man I have cast him from my heart and mind. I strongly urge you to the same course.

Morissa even thought of going over near Robbers Roost to Old Mam Featherlegs, who ran an outlaw hangout on the Cheyenne trail, and mothered every roadagent and horse thief. Before Morissa could get herself to do it the old woman was found shot at her well. By then more of Doc Middleton's outfit were caught, and Fly Speck Billy seemed to be rising fast, perhaps because the smarter, bolder gangs were broken up by bullet and rope and iron bars. But no word of Eddie came from anywhere.

The spring had been a very busy one for Morissa, and later she was glad that Hilda Gray wanted to take her poor baby home after only two months of teaching, for the next week smallpox broke out at the bridge. There had been a winter-long scourge of it at Deadwood where Calamity Jane, it was said, nursed the pest shacks, and it was true she went anywhere if there was a jug of whisky to keep her company. Yet if one of the school children had caught smallpox and died at Morissa's, it might have been the final bullet. Instead she could send word around that she would be happy to vaccinate everyone who came.

Perhaps the winter of smallpox had been too hard for Calamity Jane. At least she was leaving. "Shaking the gold dust of the gulch from her feet," Owen told Morissa when he came in for something to relieve the rheumatism of his injured leg in damp weather. The next day Calamity came down the trail with a couple of her kind, stopping at an invitation to wet their gullets at the roadhouse north of the bridge. She saw Morissa from the door and shouted greetings as the doctor passed.

"Hello, Issy! How're you, you little bastard!" she roared out for the bullwhackers passing. This time the word brought no blush, no anger to Morissa Kirk. Truly a bastard might seem as good as a bowstock by a time, as her grandmother had written to her long ago.

The children had done so well at their books this spring that two school districts were being organized down near the railroad, with sod schoolhouses and at least a hope of teachers. Morissa planted more trees on her homestead, the new grove a hollow rectangle open toward the south. She added some elm to the native cottonwood, hackberry, ash and boxelder, with a few pines and a row of chokecherry bushes behind the growing lilacs for more wind protection. Inside the opening she planned a large log building, E-shaped, the back section a story and a half, or perhaps two.

Many settlers who saw the doctor out with her spade came to talk about trees and went away with pieplant and horse-radish roots, and perhaps some tansy and sweet Mary to plant at the outhouse. "They're very useful herbs," Morissa said matter-of-factly. "Keep the flies away." Besides, leaves of sweet Mary dipped in egg batter and fried made a nice change in dessert, with a sprinkling of sugar—smiling a little at the flat-footed incongruity of place and use. "Take a Scotsman not as he says—"

Tris Polk wrote every few weeks now. He began with impersonal notes and the engineer's report on irrigation for the valley. These grew into friendly letters about the progress of the plans, or clippings about irrigation perhaps as far away as the Nile valley. There was still a little doubt that gnawed at Morissa like a mouse in a remote cupboard. How could she welcome this correspondence with the man she had so summarily rejected on what had seemed to her imperative ethical grounds? How much of that had been a flight, or to put it another way, a need to deprive herself? But even so Morissa kept the letters in a sweetgrass box that Lorette gave her when her last baby was delivered. The doctor thought about the little breed woman with affection, but wished she weren't so anxious to make Ed a worthless wall-eye, and to bring all that was said against him around the gambling tables and the whisky bars to Morissa's teacups.

She spoke out more directly on Memorial Day, when Morissa went with her to the graves of her children. Lorette brought wreaths of pine and yucca leaves because they would hold their green, but not as long as their adorning clusters of red and white flowers, their petals beaded on buckskin. Morissa planted a pink rambler on the grave of the small girl who died of snakebite and set out yellow rosebushes for her other patients, one for the man hung at the bridge, too, his grave without a name board, the man as nameless as so many who died more honorably on the westward trails here.

Lorette stood away from Morissa while she worked at this last grave, wrapped close in her Indian blanket. "Bad man need have the hanging," she said, with flat firmness. "Last week Ed he go through with the horse thiefs. He be hanging, too, maybe."

"Oh, Lorette! It's just gossip that he's with horse thieves," Morissa protested. But the breed woman's face was set and dark, and the doctor had to admit that it could be true.

As they drove back toward the river, they stopped to watch a big herd of cattle headed north for Montana by their Mexican trail drivers. The bridge toll on six, seven thousand head would be exorbitant and so they were held for days to let the spring flood settle a little. The foreman was uneasy at this delay and the loss of flesh on the bare pasture, but he had no experienced help. Finally he hired two cattlemen who knew the Platte to swim the herd across. They got the stock to the river and, crowding the drags upon the rest, started them in a dusty pouring over the bank. The leaders lined straight out into the stream holding their horned heads up, followed by all the herd in a wide wedge. But about the middle of the swimming river the lead steers got uneasy, wavered and started back, the herd still following.

The cattlemen and the trail boss spurred their horses into the water and tried to line the leaders across again, but this started the herd going around in mid-current, in six, eight feet of water, a tangle of horns swimming around and around, faster and faster as the desperation grew upon them—about a hundred thousand dollars' worth of beef going nowhere. The three men worked hard to break into the spin, but as the cattle milled their frantic, tightening circle, their heads barely showing, their eyes staring, the churned water began to roll up. The troughs between the waves cut down to the river bed as the crests rose higher, breaking over the men and the swimming stock. The cattle were playing out, but the loaded cowponies were too and any moment they and their riders might be drawn under the herd, men, cattle, and all, lost.

Morissa saw horsebackers hurry out, and men try to shout advice over the churning roar of the water. She started too, whipping her team into a run, the wagon bouncing over the road, the endgate going, and then the seat, although there could be nothing she might do. When here and there a brown nose went under and it seemed the next turn of wave would drown them all a few canny older cows separated themselves from the slowing herd and struck for the north bank. Almost at once the rest started to follow, the cattle unwinding, stopping in little knots in shallow water. Then heavily they climbed out upon the bank, stopped to pant a while longer, and then lay down in fatigue, the men and their horses resting among them too. At the bridge the Mexican trailers rode over dry and easy, and came loping to their herd, white teeth gleaming in their dark faces.

Morissa sat back in the wagon bed and laughed until she was weak, and even Lorette smiled a little, but she clutched her blanket close about her shoulders.

One rainy evening when the doctor came in, Gwinnie was waiting to bring her over to meet some surprise guests of Clarke's. They turned out to be the Walter Morton Company, another English troupe going to Deadwood, this one to put on *Pinafore*, traveling with so many big trunks of costumes and scenery that it was plainly their first trip to a frontier. But they seemed a gay and hardy lot, even Walter Morton himself, with his huge loose belly, the first really fine belly Morissa found this far West. But the earlier troupe had been so successful—six weeks of *The Mikado* in Deadwood—they had to try it too.

Clarke had managed to gather most of the English and Scottish ranch people within a day's drive, including the young Henry Browne who had danced so gaily with Morissa at the masquerade until she said she was married. He seemed a little apologetic now but very friendly, and the next week he rode down with an invitation to a picnic up near Hughes Island. If Morissa couldn't manage that, he wanted her to go with a party to the opening of *Pinafore*.

But the young Britisher was saved this temptation. Morissa had two serious cases of what seemed mountain fever. She had never seen this spotted fever, so barely mentioned in her medical library, and for all her bathing and dosing one of the patients died the third day, dark-mottled and terrible. The other was a little better in a week. By then a man had come for his dead brother, getting off the stage at the bridge shouting, "Where's the she-doc what lets people die? Them women docs got no business hornin' in on what's a man's job!"

Some of the cowboys standing around nodded, perhaps because half a dozen settlers had taken up land alongside of Morissa this spring, making a solid five-mile barrier between the ranches and the river front. And still nothing had been done to drive them out except a shot or two through an empty window. But not of the hospital; so far no one had dared attack the place where the sick were resting, and ailing children slept.

The new hospital wasn't started but the cured logs were there, cut last winter and spring in the Wild Cats, the last load just in when the doctor was called to a new little ranch down the south side of the river. But she wasn't allowed to see the patient, with a fever of 105 and delirious, only to treat him from beyond the door.

"Take the man to Sidney," Morissa told the men in the morning. As she let the bays out she looked back at the little log shack and the new corral almost out of sight back in a canyon. The place seemed a hangout for rustlers and horse thieves more than a ranch, but the voice of the sick man hadn't seemed to be Eddie's.

As she waited at the bridge for the toll arm to go up, she found herself staring at a familiar figure coming across the dusty morning road from the station, a figure that she had not seen here in a long time. "Tris!" she cried, and then remembered to say the name more softly the second time, with so many around to hear. It seemed he must kiss her but instead he took the hand she barely remembered to give him, holding it between his, the gray eyes dark as a thunderstorm.

"Get in," Morissa said, trying to make it casual for the early freighters. "We'll have a nice visit while Ruth gets us a late breakfast."

He had to see how much the cottonwoods had grown, the wall of lilacs that were a purpling sweetness in the spring, and the young planting of trees for the new building. They walked through the meadow, fenced for winter hay, thick and green, with tulip gentians holding dew in their blue cups. At the timberclaim Tris looked up at the fine growth a long time, and the difference one watering a summer made, for the trees were almost doubled in height by it, strong and thick-leafed.

"Well, this certainly is the place to sell irrigation to the valley someday," he said. "We have the Sailors interested. I wonder if you could get away tomorrow. We'll ride up the south side past Scotts Bluff, now that the Coads have decided there's more money in the Black Hills than in beef and are giving up their divine right to Coads' Kingdom. Dance tomorrow night at Sailor's and then back here the next day."

Now Morissa had to face it. "Oh, I can't—"

"Why not?" Tris asked, shying gravel at a bluejay like a boy. There would be at least a dozen going up. Three Sidney couples were coming in on the stage today and hiring horses from Clarke and Etty.

Looking back on that ride afterward it seemed the most ridiculous time Morissa ever spent, and something else too, something without a name. Nine horsebackers rode out into the sunrise of July. Morissa, Tris, and young Henry Browne and the three couples from Sidney. Near Chimney Rock they were met by Alf Meekly and several visiting Englishmen. Alf was in the lead on his Irish hunter, his pack of hounds, grays and stags, running around him, some of his ranch hands trailing behind. Alf seemed to be the uncle of half the Englishmen in the region, a droll man, with considerable opportunity to be droll about himself. He never rode anything except the hunter because no other horse understood that it was his duty to be wherever his rider happened to come down.

Morissa had seen Alf around Sidney so drunk he could barely stand, showing the town to anyone who looked like a visitor, as he would a village in his country seat in England. He rode unsteadily to his hunts too, running whatever started up before his dogs: wolf, coyote, deer or even antelope, taking it all on his little flat saddle, sailing over gullies and dodging through prairie dog towns. And it was true that when his horse fell on him there was neither steel fork nor cantle to break his bones.

Now, from a knoll ahead, Alf waved his hat for the rest to hurry up, his red beefeater's face shining in the hot sun. Then he beckoned his followers and let his fast horse out. Tris and Morissa and the others rode over to the river opposite an island, rushy and full of seedling cottonwoods where wild geese nested. While they watched, their horses standing together on the bank, ears up, looking too, Alf led his foreign guests into the water, plunging his hunter in and sending the dogs ahead to scare out the young geese. Almost full grown, heavy and ponderous, but not flying, they took to the water before the baying, snapping dogs, Alf and the others hard after the scattering young birds. Overhead in frantic swoops and honkings, half a dozen of the grown geese tried to fight off these enemies, flying close enough sometimes to beat the pursuers with their powerful gray wings.

The awkward, screeching young geese fled this way and that, their weak wings flapping, almost lifting the fat bodies from the water in their flight. The horses plunged and splashed, the dogs barked and then yipped in confusion as the birds, pushed too close, dove and came up perhaps a hundred yards away, the horses, drawn up short, turned over in the water, the men going off, all except Alf. Once he was so close on a young goose that he got her tail, but she left him with only a handful of feathers.

It was a fine show for those on the bank, but suddenly there was an empty horse shaking himself on the island, no rider anywhere. Alf was still after the geese but Henry managed to get him out while the others in the water dove to find the missing rider, the watchers running along the bank to help. They found the youth near the island, in less than two feet of water and carried him out to Morissa. There was the curved mark of a blow, a hoof, at the side of his head, but evidently cushioned and padded by the water, for the skin was not broken and the bone intact. In a few minutes the man began to murmur and complain, and was soon recovered from all but a headache and a sheepish look.

The party started on with less exuberance, although Morissa broke out laughing a couple of times as she watched old Alf still leading. His loose gray shirt had dried in wrinkles that puffed and sagged behind as he bobbed in the saddle like a toad about to make a big hop. He still clutched his goose feathers to show as a trophy.

They rode around the Coad buildings and stopped up under Scotts

Bluff, the great, bold yellowish wall that almost filled the west between the river and the arm of the Wild Cats. The Meekly ranch hands spread out the lunch and made coffee up under the pines while the rest went to look at the spring where the earth was scattered with old hand-wrought nails, bits of glass, and broken wagon wheels left by an old Overlander trail station.

Afterward Morissa advised the tenderfeet to rest a little while Alf slept off some of his energy, and she went with Tris and Henry to find the zigzagging way up the sheer bluff for a view of the valley both ways. As they climbed Tris told them about some trappers far up the river fifty years ago. Their canoes were upset by the flood waters, leaving them stranded among enemy Indians without provisions or powder, and Scott, one of the men, very sick. Things looked mighty hopeless until they found sign of another party not far ahead. To get out of the wilderness and back to St. Louis they must overtake this party. But Scott couldn't travel, and so they left him, evidently dying. The next summer his bones were found at the spring here, sixty miles below where he had been left.

"—Seems he had crawled all that ways."

Morissa shuddered at the suffering. "There is really no telling what men from a hard outdoor life can endure—" she said, as she stopped for breath and to look back down the river, where Chimney Rock was a pale spire pointing upward, the region of the bridge and her home entirely lost on the flat valley.

From the top of the northern point they looked far down over the sloping yellow-white patch of badlands that was eating into the foot of the bluff from the river. It was the final attack on this rampart by the stream that had cut all this broad valley out of the high, flat table-land once stretching unbroken from near Sidney northward into the sandhills. Now this bluff, the torn Wild Cat range, and Chimney and Courthouse Rocks were the last outposts standing stubbornly against the roaring North Platte of springtime, the river that today flowed so placidly out of the west, where July thunderheads rode the Wyoming horizon.

"Isn't it awesome, this great conflict and the staunch resistance, with the sky so innocently blue overhead?" Morissa called to Henry, but he was occupied with the field glasses and Tris replied for him. "Yes, and here you can see how water will be brought down to make all this region fruitful, with elevations for ditches left by nature along both sides of the valley. The river carries a lot of water. Wide as it is, stories are told of an early steamboat making its way up almost this far, some say clear to the Wyoming line on a spring flood."

Morissa laughed at the apparent improbability. The broad flat river below them was choked with islands, many of them furred in young cottonwoods, and many newer sandbars rising yellow among them. By September there might be no stream beyond a thread of tepid water.

But Tris, with the enthusiasm of the convert, could not be stopped. "It's water any time it runs, and generally a lot of it, enough for great reservoirs. Remember your first day here? —when the man was swept from the wagon, and you stole my horse?"

"So I'm still a horse thief to you!" Morissa objected in mock aggravation, but in a moment her laughter was gone, for Tris had dropped his concern with these future things. "No, not a horse thief even that day," he said, without looking at Morissa, still Morissa Ellis. "Already you were the woman I loved."

It was a nice statement but it was interrupted by several fast revolver shots. Henry had climbed down on a rocky shelf and found himself in a nest of irritated rattlesnakes.

Even with her sadness that Tris must go away, there was the glow that came from the assurance of his affection. "You have the color of a prairie rose in your cheeks these days, dear lady, and the beguilement of a Sataness in your golden eyes," Fish Head said to her.

"Then I should think you'd be very much afraid," Morissa replied, "and run for your life." The Fish took his hat out of his axle-grease can, wiped its black sides carefully with his sleeve, and put it back. "I cherish no ambitious succumbing to beguilement," he said sadly, "but I would appreciate a sprig of mignonette."

"I know," the young doctor said. "Only you don't want it for the sentimental reason you pretend but in exchange, with a little boot—say choice parts of the young grouse you snared, preferably with some of Ruth's hot biscuits and fried potatoes on the side."

"Ah, yes, indeed suitable accouterments for these splendid trophies of the hunt."

"You're a humbug, Wilmer DeQuincey Jones, and a punk actor, with a strong craving for fried cheek of trout or breast of grouse, garnished."

But most of the time Morissa was too busy for such banterings. John Callwin was laying the stone foundation for the new hospital and she hoped to get the logs up before the chinking mortar froze in the drying. She wanted the roof on the center section before snow flew, the ells to wait until spring. She was too busy to go to Clarke's for the stage, and the news and rumors it brought of roadagents and horse thieves working closer. Then one morning the Appaloosa was gone. Attractive but also very conspicuous, it seemed the horse could only have strayed, or followed some team or rider away, but there was the one boot-heel track deep under the closed wire gate. Nellie was gone, too, from another pasture. Obviously the thief knew the doctor's favorites among the horses; Eddie

Ellis, perhaps, or someone for him. Then Morissa had to consider another possibility. Perhaps someone wanted Eddie blamed.

She made the rounds of all the bridge, going in everywhere, watching the faces in the dark, bleak morning bars and out at the hitchracks. Nobody seemed to know anything, although it was plain that Eddie was suspected, Eddie or Doc Middleton. "I hear Doc's been coming through this way," Huff Johnson told Morissa at his roadhouse north of the bridge. "But you got no call to feel bad, Miss Morissa. There's finer saddlers than the Appaloosa to be had," he said, almost making an offer of it.

Morissa thanked him politely and went home. She wrote out notices to post in all the public places up and down the trail and on the bridge, too, tacking the cardboard among all the names carved there. She also had a copy inserted in the Sidney paper:

STRAYED OR STOLEN

1 Appaloosa gelding. Seven-year-old saddler with three diagonal Cheyenne tattoo marks inside left foreleg.

1 Bay driving mare, small K brand under mane on left side of neck.

REWARD for return or information leading thereto.

Dr. Morissa Kirk,
Camp Clarke, Nebr.

Then she saddled Kiowa, whom she seldom rode except in emergencies. Today she used the saddle she took from the horse thief up near Snake Creek, sitting it astride in a divided skirt, with the Winchester in the scabbard and the cartridge belt around her narrow waist.

"Our lady doc looks like somebody's gonna get lead poisonin' sure," one of the men from the bridge said as they watched her strike out for the hills, her face flushed and angry. She headed for Eddie's homestead and the old thieves trail, to examine every pocket gopher mound, every soft spot for the small and very narrow track of the Appaloosa. She was foolishly frantic, as though a child had been taken, but she had to return at night without news. Yes, there were tracks on the thieves' route but none like the Appaloosa that she could discover.

Around the station and along the trail there were reports of the two horses seen here and there; all rumors, nothing solid. Ed and Doc Middleton were still blamed and, much as Morissa wished, she could not really believe it was Doc. She recalled the shooting of his partner two days ago at the edge of Sidney. It seemed a gambler acquaintance had been sent out to toll Middleton in, promise that he could plead self-defense in the shooting of the soldier and be cleared so he could settle down to a job or to ranching, not live on the dodge, forever in the willows.

But Doc was suspicious and wouldn't go. "They're after that there reward," he had said, still mildly. Turned out an ambush all right, but instead of Middleton they got his partner, filled him full of buckshot.

The second evening after the horses disappeared, Morissa was returning from a search up the trail. She rode in from the darkening prairie and looked off toward her trees, as she always did, even in the night. This time she saw what seemed to be a handful of red embers, a hidden little fire in the grove. Drawing her rifle from the scabbard, she turned in at the gate and followed the hint of smoke into the thickest growth. The fire was deserted but she felt someone watching, and after a while a man came forward apologetically—Doc Middleton. They had tried to trick him into going to Sidney but he got away, although he was uneasy. about his partner, who hadn't returned.

"Yes," Morissa said gently, "I hear they shot him."

For a moment the soft-spoken man seemed alone in the ember glow, his face bleak. "—I hope you don't mind me usin' your timber a couple days. I got mighty wet crossing over here in the dark, so I just stayed, waitin' for Joe to catch up."

"I've not seen you, not to tell anyone. And perhaps there will be something left from supper that the birds out here should have."

"Thank ye, ma'am," the man said in his polite way, and stood with his thumb hooked over the cartridge belt at his gaunt waist, a touch of red from the fire on his face.

Morissa wondered how such a man came to be the most hunted outlaw in the entire region, more pursued than the most ruthless of killers. It seemed incredible that Doc could shoot anyone except in direct self-defense. Yet somehow he saw no wrong in taking horses, particularly from the Indians, taking their means of hunting, of hauling wood and water—stealing the one thing that made their lives endurable at all. But many who felt themselves perfectly honest were willing to cheat Indians.

The next morning the man was gone, and all sign of him, the ashes, the boot prints, even the bones from the cold roast she had left at the gate. There was nothing by which he might be traced to his hostess. Perhaps this was why he always found someone willing to put him up. She hadn't asked about Eddie Ellis but hoped for days afterward that the youth might be sent back and that the Appaloosa would appear in the pasture some fine morning.

Then Doc Middleton, the most notorious horse thief of all, was caught. Some said it was for the reward put up by the cattlemen, others thought the troopers from Camp Sidney had avenged the soldier he killed. To many the *Sidney Telegraph* seemed overfriendly to Doc:

> He was proven a gallant foeman and all we ask is that he shall
> have a fair trial, swift conviction if guilty, and justice at any rate or

210

price. There has been much bosh and a heap o' slush in this matter and the sooner the western mind divests itself of the Doc Middleton scare, the better off all concerned.

Morissa searched every story for mention of Eddie Ellis without success, although she learned that it wasn't the Sidney troops who finally caught up with Doc, but another piece of trickery. He was promised a pardon from the governor and a job with the federal marshals if he surrendered. He did, was ambushed, and wounded one of the officers in escaping. But he carried a bullet in his hip away from the fight and so was captured at last.

No one brought up the name of Eddie and there was no Appaloosa in the captured herds in Doc's hideouts. But news of Morissa's horse finally came. Fish Head had disappeared from the bridge and from Ruth's care some time ago. No one paid much attention, none beyond predicting that he'd come trotting back like a hungry hound dog to the smokehouse. The little man did return, but flat in the wagon bed with a freighter's soogan over his face, dead. Tied to the endgate behind him plodded Nellie, with the handsome Appaloosa nervous beside her.

It was an accident. A man from a station up the trail, the freighter whose gangrenous feet Morissa had bobbed off short after the blizzard two years ago, had shot him. Out hunting meat, he had seen a horsebacker leading the Appaloosa down a gully. With his rifle ready he cut off around the ridge to come out where the rider should be, to draw down on him, take the horses. But the rider was farther on, just about to slip down a long steep canyon and get away. At a yell to stop, he put the horses into a run and as they dipped out of sight, the freighter fired. When he got up close there was poor Fish Head on the ground, the two horses shying off into the hills. He dropped a loop over the Appaloosa, and with the Fish tied over Nellie's bare back, returned to the station. By then word had come down that the two horses belonged to the girls at a roadranch near Red Cloud's new agency. Seems they got the horses, including the 'Paloosy, a northerner, from a man called Eddie working at the agency but running with some of Fly Speck Billy's gang hiding out up there.

Fish Head looked like a patriarch, small size, in the coffin that Morissa ordered up from Sidney, and there were few who did not recall that the little man went to every funeral and always wept a little, with the rusty old silk hat held respectfully over his heart.

So they laid him beside the little girl who had died of snakebite. Morissa cried a little for him, for the gentle, lost little man who had died to bring back her horses, the Appaloosa that he knew she loved. Now this too must be laid to her presence in this wild country, and to that foolish hour when she married a man called Eddie.

XVII

The drop in beef prices everywhere except to contractors out of Indian appropriations had dumped many cattlemen into the hands of Eastern loan sharks. Then the hard winter of 1878 cut the heart out of the herds. The new owners, whether imported financial interests or outright receivers, seemed a little less vigilant against settlers, at least at the start. But suddenly two settlers were left dead down below the Wild Cats. The next week Charley Adams found a noose hung to his doorknob. He took to carrying his Winchester even to the henhouse, and while around the bridge some said the rope had been put there by jokesters, really a joke on the lady doc, neither Charley nor Morissa pretended that it was funny. They kept it from Ruth as long as they could, certain she would pack her dish towels and drag Charley out of the country. But when she found out she sneaked the noose over to the bridge in her market basket and hung it up in the little mail corner at Clarke's, beside the handbills offering rewards for outlaws, train robbers, and roadagents by name and description. To the noose she had pinned a card saying, "Stray taken up on Charley Adams homestead. Will be surrendered on proof of ownership and payment of two match boxes well filled. Ruth Adams."

Of course the rope and card were taken down almost immediately, but she had selected the night the fall roundup gathered at the bridge, the room was packed and every ranch outfit in over fifty miles knew about it in a minute. If anyone muttered, "Range burner," nobody let the woman hear him as she switched out of there and went home, walking bold as a longhorn in a pansy patch.

Now the doctor did laugh, particularly the next morning when the roundup passed her door, the men turning in the saddle to look after Ruth peacefully feeding her hens. Spring and fall Morissa enjoyed watching the big outfits draw away from the bridge to gather and separate the scattered stock by brand and such markings as ear and dewlap notches, and to brand and castrate the new calves.

The north river roundup started in two divisions, one to work the valley and the breaks past Fort Laramie far west in Wyoming, the other to strike north through the Snake Creek region into the sandhills and then swing around southwestward to meet the Platte River division. It was fine to see them go, the roundup foreman and the cowboys, the wagons for bedrolls and equipment, and the cooks with their chuckwagons, the great *remuda*, the riding strings, tearing along behind in a

212

rising cloud of dust. There was always a large force of reps, the representatives of each ranch that might have cattle in the district, whether by range or by drifting or dropped by rustlers. Sooner or later there were serious accidents, with the great bawling herds that had run wild all the year, and the wilder horses. Morissa was the only settler usually welcome at the chuck wagons, anywhere she saw them on the range, perhaps because Sid Martin was one of the big ramrods of the roundup. Of course she was bound to discover that they ate outside beef—beef of owners with no representatives along, preferably some settler's fat steers.

This fall typhoid hit the roundup as it had the trail in the late summer, and with greater force than ever before. It became a real scourge in Deadwood, where many thousands of people lived jammed close together, with no sewage or water system. Then late in September fire swept through the flimsy wooden structures of the gulch, and set off eight kegs of blasting powder in the supply store on the main drag, scattering the fire like seed on the wind. The best that could be done was get the people out. Ten thousand, the sick and the well, were without shelter, all huddled together for this further contamination.

Soon after the fire the Gilbert and Sullivan troupe returned to the bridge, but some of them barely made it. The first Morissa knew of their coming was the man who galloped ahead to find her, so she could prepare for all this sickness that seemed to be more typhoid. Charley was away somewhere and Ruth up on their homestead, so the doctor ran out and fired her rifle three times fast into the air to signal them both in. Then she set the long hospital room in order, drew out the center curtain across it, pushed her two typhoid patients back out of the way and put the man convalescing from mountain fever into one of the lean-tos. With a fire started in the laundry stove for the dry sterilizing heat of the pipe oven, she put on a boiler of water, too, and waited.

But the first coach was already drawing up to the yard gate with the thunder of hoof and rattle of harness. The driver leapt from the box, the lines cutting the wind with a whistle as he brought them down. He carried in a young girl whom Morissa remembered as Lola, a vivacious little brunette. Now she drooped over the man's arm, pale as tallow. "She took sick up the road a piece, an' already she's limper'n a gunny sack—" he said in alarm.

They got the others into the house, two of them very ill, the others apparently coming down too, or at least worn out by concern and fatigue. The second carriage was worse, and those in the slower wagon were unable to lift their heads, the great, loose-fleshed body of Walter Morton like a soft feather tick, his wife sitting beside him in the bouncing wagon, holding his head in her lap, the stench of the disease heavy about them.

Addie Lofts, the Little Buttercup of their *Pinafore,* had to speak for them, chattering even now for all her concern and nervousness. Deadwood did have a great deal of illness, she said, but they had tried to be cautious, and then they all went on one last picnic up into the higher fall mountains, where everything seemed so pure, the little brook sparkling as it rippled between the rocks. But even there they kept to their boiled water to be safe. So it must have been something they ate, the egg salad perhaps. And with the town burned out, there were no hospital facilities, or even a shelter from the fall rain.

"Oh—!" Morissa cried. She got everybody down on her temporary pallets of cottonwood leaves that were so easily burned and replaced, and by then Charley was in the doorway, his hat off, scratching his balding head in concern. She had him set up the cots with waterproof drawsheets, and put Ruth to scalding milk and whipping up eggnog with brandy to put a little strength and heart into these poor people. They worked straight through the next twenty-four hours, all three wishing Fish Head could be among them. How he would have bobbed around, running errands night and day, speaking his elaborate nonsense to those still able to listen as he stopped in with a bucket of quicklime, or an armful of fragrant wormwood.

With all the self-blame of the last year like a pall upon her, Morissa was increasingly unsure in that difficult and recurring medical decision she must make between the extremes in typhoid treatment. Should she stay with the bland, or accept the newer radical procedures of many eminent doctors, who advocated disinfecting the bowel tract with mammoth and frequent doses of iodine or carbolic acid? She leaned toward the bland diet and attempts to control the diarrheas and bleeding by moderate medication, with cool baths and wet sheets against the fever and some quinine in extreme temperatures if the heart seemed strong. She was afraid of the iodine and carbolic treatment, afraid of the irritation, the toxic effect.

Now once more the decision was hers to make, and on its wisdom these people might live or die. The expected mortality was still one out of every four in the large hospitals, which meant a probable two, even three, out of the troupe of eleven here at the best. The doctor closed her eyes and made her decision for blandness, setting herself against even her Dr. Aiken.

Each day, when the sick were bathed, fed, and dosed, Morissa walked softly between the cots, four women on one side, the seven men on the other, with the dividing curtains drawn back a little in the daytime for the hope and confidence it brought, the very sick kept back, quiet and inconspicuous. Swiftly she went over the fever charts, with their consistent two-degree rise from morning to evening, the next day the same, but always beginning a degree higher, climbing.

She had sent to Sidney for two nurses but there were none, with typhoid there too, smallpox and diphtheria beginning again, and an outbreak of scarlet fever. So she enlisted Henry Browne the first time he came. With his sun-raw face, yellowish brush of mustache, and the windy blue eyes he looked very clean and scrubbed in the white duck of Charley's hospital jacket. John Callwin had offered his help, too, but winter was very near and there was always danger of infection, so Morissa shook her head. She did take a moment to examine the scarred growth over the silver plate of his head.

"It's really working out fine," she said. "You're my star patient, and I want you to keep alive. What you can do for me is feed your chickens a lot of rabbit meat and all the green stuff you can manage—cabbage leaves, turnip tops and so on, to make them lay. This will be a long, long pull here. We'll need eggs and milk and this is the low season for both."

So John rode around the settlers in the Wild Cat breaks, and after that almost every one of them who went over toward the bridge, even horseback, brought a few eggs gathered up on the way, perhaps carrying them in a bucket, packed in grass or in the wadding of an old soogan.

By the middle of the week two of Morissa's patients were no more than alive. The worst was Walter Morton, head of the troupe. He had shocked Morissa by his appearance when they carried him out of the wagon to the house, the great belly of the man like an old gray comforter, laying in folds on each side of him on the cot, all the fat that had filled the skin suddenly shrunken away, the little bloat from the disease like no more than an oblong platter upside down under the arch of his ribs. His face looked small and bony with loose folds of skin laying on each side of it too, his eyes yellowed and burning with fever.

"Oh, we did do so well up in Deadwood," his wife sobbed. "Over four months without a move!—The miners, they came in from the back country with their gold dust. If only we had gone down when we planned, or even a week before we did. But everyone did so love the story of Deadeye Dick, and the skit Walter made of Gentle Alice Brown, the robber's daughter. They were delighted to hear Lola sing so sweetly and innocently of cutting up a little lad—or Walter's promise that he would have me chop Alice's lover into little bits, which I obediently did, naturally, and as a consequence pretty little Alice grew more settled and bestowed her hand on a promising young robber, the lieutenant of his band."

The woman had to sing a little of it even in her perturbation, and make coy eyes at the floor. "Oh, we really did it very well," she sighed.

But it proved to be a rising fever that made her so voluble, for by night she was hugging the cot that seemed a rocking, lurching stagecoach, and the next week she was unaware that her husband had sunken very low, with Morissa constantly at his bed, bathing, bathing, with digitalis and brandy ready for the fading moments, the stools tarry and black with hemorrhage. Grimly Morissa Kirk clung to the man, feeding him all he would swallow, which was not much, daring to try a little paragoric for all its depressing effect, anything to slow the intestinal action, cut down the bleeding, the serious danger of perforation. But with the heart fluttering like a faint and dying bird. . . .

Morissa Kirk had other patients, as far away as Pratt's and up the trail, men who were desperately ill too, one dead almost before she got to him. Once when she hurried home during Walter Morton's critical days she found Eddie Ellis there. Ruth came running out to the yard gate to warn her. "He knows Charley's away—" she cried in alarm.

Morissa found him in the kitchen helping himself. Browned and gaunt, he seemed to be aging if not older, his curly hair thinning at the temples, his lip looser. "I come to help you take care of the patients," he said to her cold silence.

"You mean you would go in to the typhoid patients with washbowl and bedpan?"

"There's other things I can do," Eddie replied with a laugh, as he opened cupboard doors, set out cold meat, "like maybe managing and ordering, turning you and Charley free for the bedpans."

"The sheriff must be hard on your tracks. Is it forgery again?" Morissa demanded. "You better get out immediately or I'll let him know where you are."

But Eddie sat down to the kitchen table and motioned for the coffeepot. He would go after a while, but first she had to make it worth his time. He needed three, four hundred dollars right away.

Morissa didn't trouble to answer. Instead she lifted her voice, "Henry!"

There was a sudden heavy tread and the big Britisher came through the low door. Eddie's hand was on his gun, but when he saw the size of the man he laughed a little, nervously. "You been movin' in here too whilst I'm away?" he asked.

"Take this man over to Huff Johnson's and buy him supper and a drink and leave him there," the doctor instructed.

Ed started to bluster. "You'll be mighty sorry—" but Henry marched him out as easily as a boy, and after a few steps Eddie seemed to like it. Untying his horse he walked intimately beside the big man toward the roadhouse.

"Oh, he's *pretty!*" the troupe's Little Buttercup exclaimed at the window, from where she reported Ed's going to the other patients well enough to be interested.

"Charley better get your stock up!" Ruth muttered. "That galoot ain't here for his well-wishings."

216

In an hour a rider from Huff Johnson's came shouting for the doctor. A man had an arm wound, just flesh but bleeding bad. Morissa hurried over. The suddenly gathered crowd parted for her as she walked toward the bar and the tall blond Gilda Ross. Johnson, with his shirt cuffs turned back as always, was standing beside Eddie Ellis, who held his right arm down, blood running from the fingertips.

There was silence in the smoky room, but if they waited for some word, some sign of animosity between the two women they had a long wait coming. "Washbasin and clean water, please," Morissa ordered and motioned the nearest man to strip Eddie's coat and shirt off as she opened her bag. The wound was a lucky one, the bullet from the front striking through the inside of the forearm, missing both of the bones and the main artery. When it was dressed and bound up, the doctor asked the first question for the report she must make to the sheriff's office: "Who shot you?"

This was plainly what the crowd waited for and with a pleased grin for them all, Eddie Ellis gave Morissa the name: "Tris, Tris Polk."

It was the night of crisis for Walter Morton, and Morissa hunched beside him all the long hours, Charley looking in now and then as he attended the others. The doctor had had no time to think of the shooting over at Johnson's, or the statement that the bullet belonged to Tris. With the patient's critical need before her she gave her every resource to it and was furious that she knew no more. But toward morning the man seemed to rally a little, and once more Morissa found herself warm with affection for this sturdy trouper and the fight he was making. As she rose from the stool beside him she stumbled a little and Henry Browne led her away to sleep.

"I've decided that it doesn't matter that you have a husband and would be a divorcee. We'll marry at any judge's—"

For a moment Morissa looked at him as upon another delirious patient, or perhaps she was the delirious and confused one. Then she remembered the masquerade at Sidney and Henry saying he didn't mind her being a bastard; it was the husband—

But she couldn't remain awake to parry his joke now, if it was a joke, and as she let herself sink into her pillow the young Englishman drew the afghan up over her and stooped to kiss her sleeping face. Then he remembered that this house of typhoid was no place for kisses, and also that Morissa had once reminded him that any maid is fair where there's none other to compare.

Toward night Charley called Morissa to look at her patients. She pulled herself from sleep and found the one they called Deadeye Dick delirious and broken out in rose-colored spots that appeared in crops, first on the abdomen, then the chest, and finally the back. The next three, four days his fever went alarmingly high, for all the bathing and all the quinine that Morissa felt she dared administer. It was for him, in desperation, that she used the strong decoction of wild wormwood that Lorette recommended, a little at a time, watching the man, not leaving the chair beside him all one afternoon and night until he finally slept, his skin moist, his body quiet at last.

By then Charley had part of the story of Ed's shooting at Huff Johnson's and some of the surmises and the gossip, too, the latter carefully withheld by the few-mouthed man. But Morissa could guess at the talk—Eddie, still her husband, shot by Tris Polk, the man she was to have married and, from appearances, had probably taken up with now. For extra spice there was the shooting at Johnson's, he the lover of Gilda Ross, who had long and willingly drawn Tris's eye, if no more.

It seemed the rancher had come down the trail and stopped for a plate of beef and beans at Johnson's while Huff was busy with a lot of freighters just down from the Hills. Eddie was fetched in for his meal just about then, but he seemed more anxious to see Tris than to eat, and started to pick a fight right away. Tris asked Huff to look after the kid but nothing was done until Ed seemed headed for gunplay. So the rancher got up, threw down the damages for his supper, and was outside almost to the hitchrack when Huff stepped up in front of him, asking if it was true that he planned to get out of the cattle business. In the meantime he nodded over Tris's shoulder to Ed, who had been following behind. Eddie said something too low to be heard far: "You're losing your wallet, Tris." The Texan was not letting himself be shot down by an old trick: get him to reach for his wallet while he, so far as the watchers could tell, seemed to be going for his gun. Instead he stopped his hand over the holster and, as Ed drew, he shot. The bullet went through the man's gun arm and sent the Colt into the dust, to an angry, high-pitched string of oaths. In the meantime Tris had leapt to his horse and was gone before anyone else could join the fight.

"Looks like somebody's sure tryin' to get Polk killed—or get him to kill Ed Ellis, using that old dodge," the blacksmith from over at Clarke's said.

Yes, it looked that way, even after a note came for Morissa, in a plain envelope. Tris apologized for causing her embarrassment, but offered no explanation. She thought about these things as well as she could with her patients so critically ill. Was Ed hired to kill the rancher, or blackmailed into it? Then by whom and why? Certainly not over the doctor of the gold trail; more probably over some conflict she neither sensed nor suspected. Could there be cattleman uneasiness about Tris getting out of the business? Or were his plans for irrigation in the valley known? Even if it was over Gilda Ross, in the use of Eddie as the killer Morissa Kirk was guilty.

Not that the doctor had much time for self-blaming, or even for uneasiness that Tris Polk did not come. Perhaps it was true, as her adviser at medical school had said, that in a crisis one was first of all a member of the human race, and only when there was time for it became introspective, or concerned with being a man or a woman. Certainly more immediate problems were pushing Morissa Kirk. In six of the Morton troupe, including Lola, the typhoid followed its regular pattern: desperate illness, with the danger of sudden turns, even collapse, far into convalescence. Morissa had sent a note to Sidney begging the post doctor to come up, and to Dr. Jacobs too. Jacobs managed to get away but he had little to offer. The treatment of typhoid was still mostly a matter of superior nursing and this her patients seemed certain to have so long as she and her small staff could last.

His words raised a thickening of gratitude in the weary young doctor's throat. They talked a little about John Callwin and his silver plate, and the brain tumor that Jacobs had removed from a cowboy, with Morissa as consulting physician. Unfortunately the malignancy had already spread and a few weeks later the patient died of cancer of the lung.

There were still two of the Walter Morton troupe without discernible typhoid symptoms but they were so impulsive they had to be watched constantly to prevent possible infection, until Morissa threatened to forbid them the hospital room entirely. Fortunately Charley had had typhoid during the war but Morissa hadn't, and now suddenly Ruth came down with fever and a headache, and so Little Buttercup was impressed into kitchen duty until a cook could be brought up from Sidney. Before one came it was clear that Buttercup wasn't without talent with the kettle and the dough pan.

"It keeps my hands occupied," she told Morissa. "Please, can't I do the kitchen for you?"

But in a few days Ruth was improved and although still weak she wouldn't stay down. "I know how I want my kitchen kept—" she said darkly, as though this Buttercup of the small white hands were a hopeless slattern.

"You are my rod and my staff," Morissa told Ruth gratefully. "Even when you weaken and bend a little, it's only temporary. But do let Buttercup help. That's curative too."

As more people moved into the Sidney-Deadwood trail region, the conflicts and urgencies increased, including more woman trouble. There was a rumor that Gilda Ross left Huff Johnson and went back to Deadwood since the shooting of Eddie, and there was more talk about Tris. Down the river one of the cowboys who danced so gaily at Morissa's last Christmas hanged himself over the daughter of the wagon boss. He rode his horse under a bare winter cottonwood, threw his lariat over a high branch, knotted the loop around his neck, and spurred the bronch out from under him. There was more news of Eddie too. A breed girl, Tona, who said she was from a roadranch up near Pine Ridge Agency came to claim the Appaloosa. Eddie Ellis had given him to her because he got her in trouble.

"Why, I've had him back a long time," the doctor exclaimed, looking sharply at the girl's slender waist as she cut one of the fresh pound cakes that Little Buttercup had baked.

Tona actually seemed to know very little about Eddie except that he had worked up around the agency office awhile. Finally she admitted that he had left the horses to pay his bills at the roadhouse.

"And what were his bills—for entertainment that you gave?"

Tona smirked at the implication, and then stammered a little and finally admitted that this was true. And for that she was now in trou— for that she accepted the horse and then somebody from here had come to steal him.

"You were given a stolen horse in the first place, or do you claim you have a bill of sale?"

As she expected, the girl knew nothing of such things, so Morissa prepared to examine her but Tona shrank back, crying, "No! Not no woman doctor!"

So Morissa Kirk sent the girl away and the next time she rode past Huff Johnson's she saw her out talking to the freighters in the cold winter wind, perhaps to get a ride back home. But Tona stayed on at the expanding roadhouse and drew her customers from the trail as the others did. Sometimes Morissa wondered why the girl had come to her at all. More blackmail, probably, or perhaps Huff Johnson had a deal planned, Huff with the bold eyes and the fine swaggering figure that drew women. Even Ruth looked after him as he let out his galloping horse. Morissa remembered his talk of a better riding animal than the Appaloosa, per- haps hers for the taking, and by now she knew that he had sent a buggy down to Sidney for Dr. Jacobs when Walter Morton seemed to be dy- ing. The man had changed teams three times on the way and so far his boss had asked nothing in return, no favor, not even let the doctor know her obligation directly.

Morissa expected more trouble with Ed, probably coming to hang around the breed girl Tona, but not even Lorette or Ruth knew it if he came. Later there was a rumor that he was with Fly Speck Billy spend- ing the winter up near Deadwood, keeping in closer to the Hills during the cold weather. Perhaps Tris was up there too now, for Morissa saw nothing of him either.

As the Morton troupe drew out of immediate danger, the three well members worked up skits and took them down to Sidney for a couple of weeks at a theater there, and on west to Cheyenne, adding three more members by then, and finally back to Deadwood to sing at the Golden Belle. But two of the men still lay gaunt and yellow-eyed in Morissa's soddy. It had been a hard winter.

It was a violent winter, too, with more shootings around Huff Johnson's roadhouse, one that ended in railroading a settler to the penitentiary for murder when he never pulled a trigger in his life. Curiously, however, Morissa was more uneasy about Eddie Ellis than about the cattlemen or any of the desperados at Johnson's, barely off her doorstep. After that stupid attempt on Tris Polk, what could she expect? Once more the doctor shot target at a sandy spot, particularly when the freight trains passed. Word traveled here, and no man with sense went against a Winchester with a pistol.

A voting precinct had been established at Clarke's, and cowboys from half a dozen other precincts came to vote—some several times to keep the grangers out of office. The settlers talked about a new county centered here on the North Platte valley, with their own courts and sheriff. This was a Presidential year, a time to stir up the voters, and Morissa started some plans one night while she rolled a basket of newly washed bandages.

But once more she was interrupted by a man riding hard, this time from up beyond Scotts Bluff. A new settler had been digging a well, got down fifty, sixty feet to water and mud and was halfway up finishing the curbing when his five-year-old daughter plummeted past him. He tried to catch her but she slipped from his hands and only the narrowness of the well kept him from falling after her. They had her out now but the doctor must come immediately. The little girl was so limp and sleeping all the time, or unconscious, they couldn't tell. Throwing up too.

Morissa pushed the Appaloosa through the night and found that although the girl was bruised and blue-skinned, she didn't seem seriously hurt. But the horror-darkened eyes of the mother watching from the shadows refused the hope that the doctor tried to give her. The girl was still vomiting, not at the periodic intervals of concussion but whenever she was disturbed or roused from her sleep. So Morissa stayed for ten hours. By that time the child was up, a little stiff in a hip and complaining that a shoulder was sore, but playing with her brother anyway. Tomorrow she would be stiffer, but without internal injuries she would be good as new.

On the way home Morissa thought about the change in four years here, from Tom Reeder and his gold belt dragged out of the flooded Platte, a man hanged from the bridge, a neck broken in a stampede, and a thigh shattered by roadagents, to a settler's small girl falling into his well. And Morissa had ridden all the way back home without seeing any wild game larger than a jack rabbit—not a deer, or an antelope, and it

221

was almost two years since anyone told of seeing a bighorn sheep in the Wild Cats, or a mountain lion except the rug before her fireplace, to glow tawny in the light.

Between the typhoid cases and the early winter there had been no time to get the new hospital up more than knee high, so Charley banked the foundation with manure and let it wait for spring. Morissa was sorry to give up the building, particularly when along in January a mother of two children came to ask if there would be school again. Morissa had let her look into the crowded hospital room, at the double rows of cots and the gaunt, blasted face of Walter Morton sleeping fitfully with the sun on him from between the geraniums.

"Oh, no, you can't have children here, with all the sick," the woman agreed regretfully. "But ours'll sure grow up like wild Indians."

"Oh, you can get a school district organized for next year, if there's another family or two, and people are coming in all the time. Perhaps you could move into some district with school for two, three months, even to a dugout of somebody who's gone East for the winter—" Morissa suggested.

Doubtfully the settler's wife bundled her fascinator about her head and climbed up on her old plow mare between the sacks Morissa had filled in the cellar, and started away into the gray wind. The woman had asked for something else: a loan on their team for shoes for the children, and food. "We just haven't even a smidgin of flour. The range cattle ate up our corn and potatoes, plants and all—"

Morissa had given her a little money, to be worked out in the spring, but she couldn't make the loans that the settlers needed to tide them over to a crop. With her own money problems, it would mean bankruptcy, for many would fail, and she could not go to a man's place and take away his only team as a bank would.

It was hard to send women back empty-handed to their children, particularly when the snowbirds were fluffed out round against the cold and so intent on feeding on the little dark spot of yard that they barely moved before Morissa's feet.

When she came home early one afternoon in April, Tris Polk was waiting there, sitting with his long legs stretched out before him, talking about Deadwood and Gilbert and Sullivan with the two patients. He rose, apologized for the way he made himself at home, meaning after so many weeks, Morissa supposed. He laughed a little with the others and finally admitted he had driven Huff Johnson away.

"Oh, Huff—Mr. Johnson was only here for some salve to put on a bad burn," Ruth said. A drunk set fire to a stall and burned one of Huff's stablehands. Ruth wanted it clear that she did not approve of even this much of the gambler around the place, although she must give his presence the best possible color before a guest.

But whatever Tris Polk came to say had to wait. Morissa had barely washed off the dust from her ride when a stagecoach rattled up to the gate and Little Buttercup and Lola and the rest tumbled out with all their normal gaiety and excitement. Before night there was a big blow-out going over at Clarke's hotel, with the Britishers coming from up and down the river and as far as Sidney for the surprise farewell party that Buttercup and the others had been planning for weeks. Now they had come to take Walter and Deadeye Dick away to prepare for a New York engagement.

It was both a happy and lugubrious evening, with even the head of the troupe weeping a little as they left for the slow night trip to Sidney and their pullmans East, everybody kissing Morissa, and Ruth, too, Charley standing stockier than ever in his outrage that his wife should be passed so freely from one to another, even to Walter Morton, a man he never intended to trust. At the last minute Deadeye tried to stay behind, and Morton offered to take Morissa along as their troupe physician. "After New York it is Kimberley, the Deadwood of the diamond seekers! You will be the Lady Doctor of the Diamond Trail," he said expansively, looking almost well again, now that he was a trouper once more.

Yes, yes, come along, the others cried. But Morissa shook her head to this foolishness, and kissed them all a second time, while those of the valley stood by, Tris, Henry Browne, and even Clarke and the Sailors, their region here somehow suddenly very tame.

Tris Polk had brought a big roll of maps, with contours and elevations and an entire irrigation plan for the valley, from Wyoming down past the bridge, with the sites for the reservoirs and even the smaller dams and ditches marked. There were plans for a big dam, too, far up the river at the Narrows. He was determined to show these to Morissa and so he stayed over after the farewell party and rode out to the north ridge with her in the morning. They stopped here and there, letting the horses stand while they looked from the outspread maps to the valley, Tris pointing out this feature and that, until Morissa was nauseous and dizzy with the grandeur and scope of the plan. Not a plan for today, Tris admitted, or even tomorrow, but in some rich, fruitful future when the valley bloomed.

But suddenly the man became quiet. "You will need to do something about Eddie," he said. "He's your legal spouse. You can't sell without him, or mortgage or commit your deeded land to any large improvement plan—"

Morissa looked down to the sheaf of maps Tris carried and she could neither speak nor even bow her serious head in hearing. Instead she pretended to struggle with the map she held, making an awkward task of it against the wind, until Tris took it from her and folded it swiftly.

"Li-Laurie's marrying the English boy she met at the Walker horse show," he said. "Second son of an earl with a ranch in Wyoming, to be theirs after the wedding. If you can't make up your mind about Ed—split the blanket as the bullwhackers around the bridge call it—I'm giving her the Carlotta saddle."

Morissa looked up from her deep engrossment with these plans and with the man who held them in his strong brown fingers. His sudden petulance was so reducing, somehow so human that a little amusement came to the corners of her full lips, to her sun-shot hazel eyes. But today Tris Polk had no patience for any possible Scotticisms. Leaving her standing there he strode to his horse, jammed the maps into the saddlebags and, gathering up the reins, swung into the seat and was gone. He was gone without a backward look or one word, not even about the shooting of Eddie, which should have been explained long ago. Two weeks later Morissa saw an item in the Sidney paper saying Tris Polk, the prominent owner of the TeePee ranch, had taken the train west with Hurley Forson of Chicago. They planned to buy a large spread up the North Platte in Wyoming.

"So maybes won't be honeybees forever!" Ruth reminded Morissa her lips tight as a snap purse.

XVIII

FOUR YEARS AGO COWBOYS SAT THEIR HORSES IN SILENCE TO watch Morissa's first soddy go up, a homesteader invading their great free-land region across the river. Now they rode by with no more than the familiar greeting, "Howdy, Doc!" on the wind as their horses dog-loped past, their casual, easy seat still the same joy to Morissa as her first sight of them had been. But when Sid Martin came along he rode up to the rising walls of the hospital, his graying hair neat over his white sun-shielded forehead as he swept off his Stetson.

"Looks like you was plannin' to run a orphanage," he said, motioning at the size of the place. But his squinted blue eyes were on the young woman, once more moving her flower beds, transplanting everything carefully. She worked in a blue denim skirt, a black and yellow calico waist with yellow rickrack, and a matching sunbonnet that was pushed back to rest against her heavy braid. And once more Sid Martin wondered at the light that ran over her dark hair and the smooth bangs, like the golden gleam of sun on a fine dark bay, with the same light caught in the depths of her hazel eyes as she smiled up to him.

"No, no orphanage. I don't like them," she said, "but I wish I could have the place good for children, make it as full of promise as that little patch of corn coming through out there—"

"Frost will take the corn before it's ripe."

"Oh, you cattlemen! Always belittling your country, when you're willing to shoot to keep it."

"Only followin' in your tracks, ma'am, you and your rifle out popping cans off the posts around your timberclaim—" Sid said, laughing, the lines of his leathery face deepening. But plainly this lightness was only a preliminary to something else, like the wind stirring up a little dust before the rain. "I hear tell," he finally said, "that you're thinking of goin' in with your brother on a practice off farther East somewhere, take on a little hospital there."

Morissa scrubbed at the earth on her gloves with the trowel. "Well, news does travel! Just this week Jack decided he would like it. He's marrying, and the girl's father has to give up his practice. Maybe it would work out better—"

But she was interrupted by one of Sid's cowhands, spurring up and setting his horse back to its haunches in the dust. "One a them red-eyed grangers back yonder's holdin' part of our herd fer damages he claims was done last night. Got a doublebarrel loaded with buckshot."

Later Morissa saw the herd come trailing into the river valley, the longhorns running and bawling as they smelled water. She watched them from the empty window holes of the new building, and then went to see about her patients—a child with yellow jaundice still a little delirious in the night and recovering very slowly, and the man with a hole in his cheek eaten out by the plasters of a cancer quack up in Deadwood, a hole bigger than a silver dollar through into the mouth. The whole side of the face had been swollen and purpled, the edges of the wound angry in proud flesh, saliva running out night and day.

When Morissa first saw this she had been so angry she could hardly hold her hands steady to ease away the wet and bloody bandages, or see through the pity that blurred her eyes. Truly man must endure a great deal from his healers.

Rem Smith couldn't talk much, but Morissa knew something about the cancer man up in the Black Hills. All spring she saw people with great lumps and sores make the hard trip up there, hopefully and desperately, some living to describe the plasters that drew the cancer out. One man told Morissa his wife had lost a lump that the doc up there

225

said weighed three pounds. "It come loose from her breast one night with feelers like a live thing hangin' on, and so I pulls it out and throws it into the fire to kill it. But we can't stop the bleedin', nor the doc neither, and so the old woman dies. It wa'n't the cancer what killed her, the doc says. It was the bleedin'."

Morissa had listened to him and to others whose wounds she treated, her little hospital a sort of dressing station on what seemed suddenly a cancer trail. Such quacks would flourish so long as the doctors failed, but Rem Smith's wound was the most pitiful of all. Apparently a well man otherwise, and not over thirty, he was left with this hole in his face, and not even certain that the small knot removed had been malignant at all. Perhaps she could clear up the wound, give it clean edges where proud flesh now turned out in the horrible naked rolls that, without the boundary the skin provided, would grow so long as life remained. Afterward perhaps she could draw the sides together like some old bachelor draws a hole in his sock together with a string. It would make a shocking, twisted cheek, and be a futile and heartbreaking trial of endurance if the growth was malignant and any of it remained. But the man might yet have a face to turn to his fellows, a trap to catch and conceal his private juices from the public gaze.

Finally the preliminary operation was done, the wound clean. Then the doctor drew the sides in close, hopefully close, with pressure bandages to push the flesh together at the cheek to avoid strain on the stitches. So much depended now on the man's patience and fortitude to endure the packing that blocked off the entire cheek inside, and the saliva drain pipe that must remain at the far corner of his lip. Because this must always be the lower corner, the doctor tied the patient on his side with strips of canvas to keep him from turning in his sleep or forgetfulness. She went in often those first three days to lay a hand on the man's shock of reddish hair and wish that she had known just how this should be done. But remembering Dr. Aiken's warning that the miscroscopic healing granules are very delicate, she was determined not to disturb her surgery by dressing or even inspection until she must.

She had to think about Jack and his offer now. If she went into practice with him, the hospital here must have a good doctor, someone who saw the valley as it could be someday, green and lush from the water that men like Tris Polk would bring. Curiously she never thought that this doctor might be a woman. Perhaps Dr. Aiken had been right there also.

With so many settlers in the region, even though mostly single men, there were increasing sociabilities, and some fights. On the Fourth of July all the valley and many from farther away gathered at Morissa's grove, almost without her realization that anyone was coming. "A grove like that belongs to the community—" John Callwin had once said, and so wagons, horsebackers, and people afoot came from all directions to spread their blankets and picnic baskets under her trees. Many cowboys rode in too, from Bosler's and Sheedy, even from the Bay State and the old Coad, for now an increasing number of ranch hands were filing on land. Besides, there were girls here; still only a few, but girls, and with families where a man could put his feet under the pine-box mahogany for Sunday dinner; girls to show off to with broncho busting and roping and fancy riding; girls to buy lady presents for.

There was a little politicking, too, with candidates and speakers for candidates. Even Tris Polk came up for a short talk a little before noon. Standing in the back of a wagon, he praised the progress of the valley since the first piling was driven for Clarke's bridge. Through Indian scares, threats of dynamiting and outlawry, blizzards, prairie fires, falling beef prices and hard times, the North Platte region had settled down, become The Valley, a place that could gather so many here today, women and children, too, where not four white men had lived until very recently. Today they celebrated in cool green shade where four years ago there was little more than prairie, and now they had stores, a hotel, daily mail, a voting precinct, a school to start again, and a doctor and her hospital.

"Saloons, too, Mr. Polk. Don't forget them, and the sinful roadhouses where you shot a man!" a stern voice called from far back.

"Looks like mebby you're runnin' fer office, Tris," one of the old TeePee punchers shouted. "Wanta be dog catcher?"

"No!" Tris answered, cupping his hand to his mouth too, "I'm trying to round up votes for Governor Nance, but mostly I'm talking for The Valley and all the new regions of the state, for a cleanup of the rustlers and outlaws, for better brand control, and for railroads and irrigation."

Morissa was late in going over from her patients, and surprised to see Tris. She had received a couple of photographs of the Narrows that he sent from Wyoming, and a note that he might be in the valley soon. Now here he was in her grove, standing up tall in the tail end of a wagon finishing a speech and saying that he must leave immediately to make another talk at Sidney that evening. Morissa was happy to see him, the first time since he rode away with his bundle of maps, hurt by her apparent lightness. Fortunately, in this crowd there was no opportunity or need for explanation and apology. Yet somehow he didn't seem the Tris Polk that she knew—more like the man who crossed the river that first day to tell her that she had done a dangerous thing in flood time, and that taking a man's horse was a hanging matter. Then the anger-darkened gray eyes had seemed a part of the strange new country where a man could drown so quickly, with thousands looking on and none to

227

restore him. But many things had changed since then and yet the Tris of that day stood beside her, looking up at the magnificent growth of her trees. Some were big enough for swings for the younger children. Amid the shoutings and cries of excitement cowboys used their lariats in a wholly new way, and children who had never seen a swing before clamored for their turn or hung back shyly until caught up and held as they flew higher and higher.

Tris and Morissa passed them, smiling, nodding, the cowboys blushing to be caught in this softness, one even stalking away but happy to be called back. Morissa drew Tris on, nodding to the people passing them back and forth, the brown faces, stranger and friend, smiling their greetings. One woman came up to them, moving vaguely and alone, as though to wander past. Then suddenly she stopped as at a discovery.

"The shade of a tree," she murmured, "—you know, the shade of a tree it lays over you like a cool and gladsome thing—" speaking as though to herself, seeming not to hear their friendly replies that followed her down between the thick, shaded rows.

Guardedly Morissa glanced at Tris and caught the softness, the understanding and compassion in his face as he watched the sad, bemused woman, and once more the young doctor had to admit the incredible and appalling realization that this was the man she did not marry.

The celebration in Kirk's grove lasted until morning, with a dance on the shining pine floor of Morissa's new hospital, a sort of impromptu housewarming. She wasn't there the latter part of the night but riding off toward Winter Creek where a man had blown a hand and an eye to pieces shooting an anvil with black powder in noisy celebration. It was bad, yet fortunately the eye was not as damaged as the man feared, the injury mostly to the brow and the lid. Barring infection the sight would be unimpaired and with luck he wouldn't lose more than some flexibility in two fingers. The thumb, however, was torn clear back to the root and might require amputation later. The hand was still swollen thick as a ham when Morissa left the next morning, but the man slept under a little morphia.

On her way in she stopped the Appaloosa to look down the rows of her trees, with the blowing papers and trash, limbs broken and torn off. But she was happy that people had come, and a little sad that Tris was so completely the partner in the fast-growing packing plant at Omaha and its real-estate subsidiary, growing rich from the new stockyards, and now apparently deep in Wyoming ranches too.

She looked at Rem Smith's cheek before she went to sleep. The wound was still purpled and very puffy, but how much was the aftereffect of the caustic plasters she couldn't decide. At least the proud flesh was gone, and the man was no longer so gagged by his mouth pack, and getting accustomed to keeping the cheek turned up, like some poor wry-necked horse trying to look across the prairie.

The trail past the bridge was as busy as ever, although the railroad pushing west toward the Missouri River in Dakota would soon bring competition for Deadwood freight. The travelers to the gold fields were more frequently substantial businessmen or hard-rock miners, professional or hoping to be. Even the women who weren't wives or relatives of Black Hillers were quieter, better looking. As the Eldorado boys thinned out there should be less violence, less work for the gravedigger, and for the doctor along the gold trail.

But Morissa's concern for the settlers was growing, most of them new to the wilderness. Few had ever laid hand to a bucking sod buster, or drawn a line over a team of bronchos, the best most of them could hope to afford here. Few had dug wells in loose, caving earth, or lived in houses of sod, or in dugouts gophered into the ground, all on land that burned in drouth and prairie fire, or was swept white by blizzard. Only a few had ever tried to live alone.

Inevitably many left the first few weeks, or months, and some were hauled out, or buried here. There was Mrs. Thacker, the woman who had wandered through Morissa's grove the Fourth, speaking of the shade that lay on her cool and gladsome, and moved Tris to such compassion. She was dead, and Morissa called over. Somehow the woman got her hands on a bottle of wolfer's strychnine, and died bent backward, the gentle bemused face drawn into a teeth-baring snarl, like a poisoned coyote. She was buried in the valley cemetery, and afterward Morissa and Callwin balled a little pine from the Wild Cats and planted it on her grave so she need never be without the shade of a tree again.

But now Joseph Thacker was left with three motherless children—four, three, and eight months, the eldest crippled from what looked like the disease being called infantile paralysis by some, one leg withered and twisted, one hand a claw. The man held the boy between his knees at the hospital after the grave was closed. "Mrs. Thacker was that way again," he said. "I guess you know. Seems she just couldn't go on. I—I—It's hard for a man, laying beside the wife he loves night after night—"

"I know," Morissa said gently.

"If we could have put it off until I got a start and got her out of that dugout. You know that snakes come crawling in for the shade? But I haven't even a team. In Chicago I kept hoping to get my position back ever since the panic of '74, until every dollar was gone. Then we had to sell Mrs. Thacker's piano and her grandmother's cherry bed and bureau for the fare West—"

Trying to draw him out of the sorrowful past into the present, Morissa asked what was to be done with the children. "That's what I want to ask you," he said. "If you could see your way clear to trust me for their keep a little while—I want to make arrangements so they won't be separated. Joey here's been like a mother to the other two since Lena's—illness."

The boy's dark eyes searched the doctor woman's face soberly for the answer to this question. When she nodded he buried his face under his father's arm a moment, and then he reached for the crutches and went to see that the baby was not crying. Morissa shook her head. "It is an amazing thing, the swift maturity that can come to a child when it must."

So the doctor kept the children, Joey with a brace now, made from wagon rods and padded hoop iron so he could get around very well outside with one crutch, and indoors he needed only a cane fastened to his forearm by a couple of iron bands. The three-year-old Elaine was already Charley's girl, and Baby Susan the special care of Morissa, the child so pale and silent, but with hair like sun on winter-rimed floss. It was a joy to see the flesh Ruth's care put on her bird-bones, and to watch the protective way of Joey, almost five now, one more eldest child become a parent before the charming dew of infancy was well dried from his cheeks.

This summer the valley had its first big wedding, the daughter of a new settler off beyond Chimney Rock, and a ranch foreman. Morissa was pleased. Perhaps they could escape real violence between the cattlemen and the settlers here, with the bridge and its community a meeting ground, and now this wedding. It was a fine one, with everybody invited on the wind, as Sid Martin called it, meaning all who heard the news. There was a minister up from Sidney who always spoke with his finger tips together, prepared for any pious moment. The bride was pretty, and afterward a keg of homemade rhubarb wine was set out in a granite dishpan with a dipper and tin cups. The groom's hired hands emptied their flasks into the pan as it was replenished so the wine got stronger and stronger until two of the cowboys played andy-over over a haystack with their loaded six-shooters.

Morissa was at her buggy talking to Sid Martin horseback, leaning over his horn, when a tipsy cowboy missed the saddle as his buckskin whirled from him. Somehow his boot speared through the stirrup, high heel and all, and the man swung out, a heavy, many-limbed weight that catapulted back against the horse. The big buckskin went wild, crazy, kicking, plunging, and bucking as few here had ever seen, trying to rid himself of this pursuer that battered at his belly, his flanks, his legs. He kicked again and again, drawing up both feet and striking out with all his power, then running, and as the weight struck his ribs kicking again, the saddle turning, everything under his belly now, to drag and pound under his wild and panicked heels.

Those outside had stood paralyzed a moment and then ran for their horses, or reached for their guns. But there were people everywhere, and the man and terrified horse constantly mixed and flung together. Before Morissa could jerk her rifle up, Sid was gone, his spurs digging, his rope down. He missed the first throw but his second loop brought the horse to the ground, heels up, body rocking, the cowboy in a sprawled, crumpled heap, his boot still in the stirrup. Then Morissa was beside him, the man somehow still alive, with a hip dislocated and broken, an arm and a leg broken, too, ribs crushed, teeth knocked out, his face horribly cut by the kicking hoofs. But apparently there was no spinal injury, as it seemed there must be, and no bright, frothing blood.

They got him to the Sidney hospital the next morning. Fortunately Morissa had her black bag along with morphia enough to make the long painful trip in the wagon endurable. At the best it would be a long hospitalization for the man, and no more bronchos for him, perhaps never any riding at all. Morissa was glad he would be at Sidney, under Dr. Jacobs instead of with her. "We would have had to watch our guns every second," she said to his foreman. "He will get pretty depressed, young, and the horse his life—"

Then, too, there was the example of several suicides among ranch hands within the last two months, and Lena Thacker. Suicide, too, could be contagious.

As inevitable as discouragement, quarreling arose among the new settlers. The first trouble that reached Morissa came one dry, dusty afternoon when horses ran from nose flies and grouse panted in the shade of the fence posts. A man came whipping his plow mare every jump, shouting for the doctor. Bud Jackson had been shot. When Morissa got there he was past dosing, killed by a neighbor over a little exchange of work. Later when people got to talking it over, more came out. Bud, it seemed, had sold his preemption to Tallent, the new rancher who claimed the range that surrounded them all. Together the settlers had managed to hold off the range cattle because they owned the unbroken water front from Morissa's place for seven miles along the river. With no water so far, few cattle even drifted past, and the settlers had taken turns riding the line.

But Jackson's deeded quarter section cut through the middle of their block of land and gave the rancher a lane down to the river, the longhorns trailing back and forth to water all the time, wearing the narrow strip into a bald and barren waste, the thousands tolled up around the unfenced crops. Now every place had to be watched day and night, for

231

no settler had the money to fence his place and no one could expect to get the state Herd Law enforced by the Sidney courts, or by the local justice of the peace. The land sale was plainly treason in the eyes of the settlers, and for that Bud Jackson had been killed.

There was a lot of riding around, dark talk out at the edges of the sod corn, and many attempts to buy wire on tick, on time. One man put up half a mile of sod wall, shoulder high, to protect his corn, and the longhorns rubbed it down the first afternoon he was away. Men stood the line with guns, and cattle died, and as soon as the grass was dry they would burn this cattleman strip clear. But Morissa and Charley and others longer in the region were against firing the range, pointing out the danger from shifting wind. They were against range burning on principle, setting man and animal in danger and in hunger, baring the grass roots to the tearing wind. They won out and instead relatives were brought in to file on land all around the rancher's quarter, cutting it off entirely and going in together to fence around it. True, the fences were cut again and again but each time cattle were shot to get even, and bad blood grew. None of this helped the man who killed Jackson.

By midsummer the corn was dry and curling and settlers looked long and hungrily at the water that ran past them on the old, old path of the river. Even a cattleman or two was going in for irrigation. Duncan, a Scotsman who bought himself a large ranch by the book last year, had discovered that much of his beef stock was bleaching bones and nearly all his range still government grass that any land seeker could legally homestead. So he turned to intensive use of what he did own, and what he and his sons could take up as settlers. In the fall some of his ranch hands cursed as they rassled plow and scraper instead of shagging over the far range and twirling their lariats. Those who complained too loudly were reminded of all the settlers hungry and eager to make a dollar. But Duncan got his diversion dams up and his ditches cut right through any knoll or hillock that stood in his way. He was proud of his place and sent word to Morissa that he would be happy to have her or Tris Polk or anyone else interested stop when up that way.

Morissa went and was pleased with what she saw. The long, low ranch house was well furnished and the cook was a good one. Afterward Thom Duncan threw his little saddle on the Irish mare he brought from overseas and rode out beside Morissa—a large ruddy man with a rawhide thong to his Stetson so he could push the hat back to his neck and buck his red face into the wind. It was wonderful how well he understood the lay of a strip of land, the dip and the rise of it. And as they rode and talked Morissa recalled how some of the ranchers laughed at such gullible tenderfeet. Yet here was one who seemed to understand just what the valley needed, and wasn't head-shy of the work.

232

"I lived in Egypt five years," he said. "Remarkable what those early boys did. Thousands of years ago they rechanneled the entire Nile, carried it out into the middle of the plain so they could draw water from both sides—"

Yes, he knew about the irrigation survey being made by Tris Polk's engineer. "Good man, Polk," he said, and Morissa couldn't tell if it was meant for her as a woman, or as a dweller in the valley.

By late October the windmill and reservoir up on the knoll north of Morissa's place were done, the running water ready when she moved into the new house. The hospital rooms were all plastered and whitewashed, along with the adjoining pharmacy and the operating room, the latter with a skylight for day, a chain draw-lamp for night work. The rest of the building was left in log, the recreation and the convalescent rooms divided by a partial wall with a double stone fireplace, one face to each room. A long reading table with magazines, newspapers, and games reached from one room to the other, with wide windows looking over the Platte and Chimney Rock above the table. In the back of the building, with a solid wall between them and with independent outside doors, were the isolation rooms—pesthouses, Charley called them—with a bath and dressing space in each.

The two alcove sections of the big E-shaped building held large sunny windows bright with geraniums and wandering Jew and five canary cages. The office in the center projection of the E had wall bookcases for the medical publications, with the framed diploma and the certificate of election as officer in the medical society hung over them, and a large picture of Morissa standing beside the mountain lion she shot.

Slowly the doctor let herself down in her desk chair the first day and tried to feel like the head of a real little hospital, but to the Morissa Kirk of the poor-farm in Missouri, to the bastard, the woods colt, it brought up such a flood of sadness, such dissatisfaction that she had to laugh. Such self-dramatization was for the patient, the very ill patient, not the doctor. She went out into the fall sunlight, to see the place as the passersby saw it. The building, of browned, sunburnt logs, seemed solid and strong, the second story built over the back of the E a sort of promise for the future. The sliding roof windows for tuberculars were already up, and eventually she would have the inside of this section finished too. Then some of those who were sent West for their lungs could come here when they needed help, as many would. She thought of this as the Lorna Kirk division of her hospital; such a place, with good food and nursing and a quiet and cheerful mind, might have saved her mother's life.

But even here in the taming wilderness the log wings were already topped by the taller of the young trees behind them, particularly the

233

cottonwoods with the evening song of the wind in their yellow fall leaves. Suddenly Morissa felt so good she went to round up Lorette and a couple of settler women trying to trade garden truck for jeans and calico. With these tea guests and two of their boys to visit Joey, Morissa Kirk opened her new place. The next day she moved the patients in.

Election day gathered the voters to cast their first national ballot in the valley at Clarke's. Many wandered over for a taste of Ruth's coffee cake and a look at the new hospital. Tris Polk was among them.

"After all your electioneering, aren't you going to vote?" Morissa asked in surprise.

"Of course; this is my precinct now too. I filed on all the land the government permits me, a homestead and timberclaim up above Scotts Bluff, along the line that our first ditches are to take."

"Oh, stay until it clears out here and celebrate!" Morissa urged, "Come see the whole place." They went through it all, little Joe trailing along behind, making his cane thump hard so they wouldn't forget to look into the children's room. There he stopped to lean his bad side against the doorjamb, his face anxious that his sisters be admired. When they were, he came shyly in and sat as close to Tris as he dared, and once he reached out to touch the man's trouser knee. It was a shy yet an unconscious thing, and Morissa saw it as she set the baby back down into her little corral. "The children miss their father very much," she said quietly, "particularly Joey—"

Tris waited until all the other visitors were gone and then sat in the pleasant west window of Morissa's parlor. "I hear that the settlers lost some horses along the river last night," he said. "Charley seemed a little uneasy when he heard the news over at the bridge this afternoon. One of Clarke's men thinks he recognized Ed Ellis."

"Oh!" Morissa cried, "Why doesn't the sheriff pick him up?" as though she had no more connection with this than any other citizen.

But Tris Polk couldn't let this evasion stand. "Didn't your Scottish grandmother ever tell you that a man should never marry a widow unless her former husband had been hanged?" He said it almost angrily, but wryly too, and Morissa had to accept the reminder without reply.

"Ed should be picked up for his own sake," the rancher finally added, "before he does something violent and wild. I hear they had him on a forgery charge couple of years ago and let him off. Still, there are people besides Ed who might want to make trouble for you and the other settlers getting dug in so deep around here."

Although Morissa gave him time, Tris Polk went no farther. Perhaps he had nothing more to say.

Soon after New Year there was a report that Fly Speck Billy was dead. A freighter on the Kearney trail who didn't know the Speck gave him a ride, even loaned him his revolver, and then was shot with his own gun. The sheriff, one of the Coads from the early ranch in the valley here, arrested Fly Speck up in the Black Hills but a mob gathered and while a dozen men sat on the sheriff, the rest strung Speck up to a pine tree on a windy knob outside of Custer City.

Morissa heard the story in relief. Even though hanging was a violent, a lawless act, and it had come to the freckled-face youth who rode the same coach that brought her to the river almost five years ago, she was relieved. True, poor Speck was to be pitied from the first, but he was better off now. Her anger, her shock at seeing a man hanging at the bridge that first morning seemed forgotten or put aside, perhaps because this would surely break up the gang Eddie seemed to be running with. If only Ed would go home, or be caught for a minor lawbreaking before he slid into real violence. Once Morissa thought of the forged check Clarke said he would keep in case she ever needed it—yet somehow the forgery seemed such a trivial thing now. What, she had to ask herself, what had this Morissa Kirk become?

Instead of rumors of a capture or departure of Eddie Ellis, she began to hear bits and fragments of another story—foreboding little rumors that were like the first drifting tufts of a gray blizzard creeping out of the horizon. They hinted at a big robbery, the biggest in the history of the Sidney gold route, bigger even than the one at Canyon Springs. This was a Fly Speck Billy holdup, it seemed, and that was why he was hanged so swiftly and silently, given no opportunity to run off at the mouth, some said.

"If he pulled such a big job, whyn't they get the loot, make 'im tell where it's stashed away?" a skeptical cowhand loafing around Clarke's station demanded as he cracked peanuts and dropped the shells about him.

After a while the story thinned out and was lost in the new excitement over the rise of gunmen in Sidney. They had been threatening to take the town over entirely, and at last local protest brought some action. Although the Sidney Regulators had strung a man up to a telegraph pole, the quieting effect hadn't lasted and in a few weeks three more were lynched and a long list of men and some women, too, were given twenty-four hours to get out of town. They scattered, to Denver, Julesburg, or Cheyenne. Some came up the gold trail, a few on their way to the Hills but mostly they stopped at the growing cluster of roadhouses and saloons north of the bridge—men and women both.

Soon there was talk that the Sidney Regulators were really controlled by a rival gang of outlaws, but Morissa was never clear about this. She had seen these strangers come up on the stage or lope in to the toll station, outlaws fleeing across the river as others skipped over a state line or to Canada or Mexico. She saw them loaf around there, fifteen, sixteen of them at one time, their narrow, unblinking eyes upon her, some with a kind of arrogant admiration, almost as though they were considering an unacknowledgeable master in their craft. Surely being the wife of Eddie Ellis didn't justify this, unless he had risen to some peculiar height among them. If it was admiration for something in this Doctor Kirk it was certainly not the woman; few such men seemed truly male. It must be for some special kind of con or gyp robbery they thought she practiced, or was it her sense of guilt they detected? They made her feel very uneasy, and also uneasy about her place that was less than one good whoop from them, or a pistol shot.

XIX

With the first signs of spring the Sidney outlaws seemed to be moving home. At least those from the bridge were back at their old stands with card, roulette wheel, or holdup pistol, prepared for the seasonal roundup of fat stuff, including the more moneyed travelers to and from the Hills, and the financial representatives out to be sold ranches where the settlers were taking up the grass. Then there would be the trail drivers in from the south, and even an occasional granger who might have a double eagle hidden in his shoe.

By then water stood on the ice of the Platte and the snowbanks were shrinking along the darkened slopes, the gullies roaring. The mud of the worn trail was hub deep and the stage passengers had to get out and help lift the wheels, even the guards of the treasure coach forced to bend their backs. The iron-clad treasure coach overtook Morissa up on Sidney table, great balls of mud flying from the hoofs of the sweating horses as Owen and the others tipped up their Winchesters in greeting to the doctor as they passed.

Morissa looked after the coach and pushed her young team along too for she was in a hurry today, going in for a consultation on another head injury—man at the post kicked by a mule. As she passed the railroad station the train came puffing in from the west, the treasure coach ready at the express office to unload its gold bricks. Morissa slowed a little, out of curiosity, but the guards waved her on. "No loitering, Doc!" Owen called as the agent came running out, shouting something to the driver.

So the doctor went on but almost immediately a rattle and pound of hoofs made her look back. The coach with its guards still riding was swinging back toward the stage station. Morissa thought nothing of it until the next day. By then all the consultations and tests were over and it was decided not to operate on the unconscious man since there was no open wound as with John Callwin. Later perhaps, but not now.

The morning's bluster of spring snow was clearing off as Morissa stopped to buy her supplies. A great shouting and running went by and Morissa gathered up her skirts and ran with the clerks. Suddenly men with guns were everywhere and a crowd pushing and milling on the board walks and between the vehicles and bull outfits of the street, all shouting, those who asked, "Was there a robbery?" getting the answer: "Three hundred thousand in gold bricks stole!"

"Where?"

"Right over to the express office—"

Yesterday the express agent had refused to accept the gold because it came in a little late, although there was plenty of time to make the transfer while the train passengers got off to eat their supper. So it was taken to the stage station and guarded all night. Today, a while before noon, the guards returned the gold to the express office, and got a receipt for the $300,000.

"No, $299,500, or something like that—"

"Amounts to the same thing! Around a thousand dollars in currency, two small bricks worth around five, six hundred each, and the rest in big bricks, not easy to lug away," one of the stage hands said glibly.

Looking about her, Morissa decided that half the men and some of the women looked capable of stealing all they could carry. Certainly Burly Slopes and Hugh Bean and a dozen others who had hidden out north of the bridge would, except that they were too weaselly for such a bold, open job as this robbery seemed to be. Morissa found herself wondering why Eddie Ellis wasn't here too, not in the big steal but hanging around like a buzzard come to another's kill, or to feed vicariously on the violence, which someday might not be enough. Then suddenly she saw him, sunburnt and lean, with two guns, and strapped low, the heavy cartridge belt outside of his short horsehide coat. Hat drawn down, and sparse-bearded, he peered from behind the high-bowed wagons of a freight outfit, probably the lookout for some holdup gang, or for some inner urging, some scheme of his own.

Quickly Morissa slipped away into the milling crowd around the express office. Those pushing up to see passed back word that the agent was hunched down in his big chair inside, near a hole that had been sawed through the floor from the cellar underneath. He kept repeating, "They got it all! Every last ounce—!"

Owen, the guard, saw Morissa and came crowding in beside her. "Damnedest thing you ever saw, Doc. The guards wanted to put the load into the big safe when they delivered it today, but the agent gave

237

them the receipts and said it was only an hour to train time, to leave it on the push truck. Then he locked the door and went out to eat. We got the town circled and there's no tracks on the fresh snow leavin', so the bricks're still here in Sidney, unless they got smuggled on the train some way—"

"That ain't likely," a man beside Morissa put in.

Owen doubted it too. The sheriff and the deputies were searching, he said, and Morissa knew that these included the former sheriff who made her promise to move in with Eddie at the homestead after his forgery and give up her doctoring. Yet nothing was ever done to Ed about that and certainly a dozen other crimes although he was openly in and out of town, free and bold as any other thief.

With the uneasiness that doubt of law enforcement officers always brings, Morissa wished she had her rifle along, or at least her Peacemaker. Suddenly she felt she must leave, start home at once. At the edge of town two men with sawed-off shotguns demanded a look through her supplies. She laughed but was angry too. "Perhaps you might look through my purse as well—" she said very sweetly. But one of the men nodded soberly, and then peered into the little satin-lined pockets of it, his big finger probing as though a gold brick might be there beside her lace handkerchief.

"We know you been shieldin' outlaws up there on the river. Could be sneakin' the bullion outa town—" one of the men said, and to this Morissa had no reply.

Before she reached home a cowboy returning to Bosler's caught up. Hell yes, he said, the robbery down to Sidney was all cleaned up. They finally gave up searching people's rigs and went back to the express station and took another look at that hole sawed in the floor between the cellar and the office. With the outside door to the cellar still padlocked, it looked like the sawing had to be done from the top, from the office down. So there was just that little coal pile in the cellar to look through. "—There they was, all them big gold bars—!"

"All the big bars of the three hundred thousand?" Morissa asked, wanting to laugh. "Such wealth hidden in a few wheelbarrows of coal!"

"Well, seems it wasn't quite as much as that, ma'am. I hear it was more like eighty thousand."

Charley Adams snorted when he heard the man tell how the big robbery blew up. Morissa wanted to join Charley's amusement, but she wondered who was accused—whether of three hundred thousand or what suddenly seemed like small potatoes, eighty thousand—and if Eddie Ellis really was only the peeping tom on criminals he seemed in Sidney today.

The next man up from town said there had been arrests. "Seems maybe the agent and a former sheriff done it with a couple of our friends from around Huff Johnson's here. Anyhow they was where they could do it—"

So the Sidney robbery seemed solved, with probably nothing more than the express agent fired for it. But almost at once that other story was whispered around again, the story of a greater bullion haul right on their own trail, up north a ways. While this apparently happened some time back, before Fly Speck Billy was hung, that was really a $300,000 haul, and so far not one bar of all that gold had been discovered anywhere.

It seemed that after the Canyon Springs robbery the banks were very cautious and individuals even more so, particularly the big businessmen and those who had accumulated more gold than the public should suspect. Because the roadagents had spies in Deadwood to watch the coaches, for a while the bullion was taken out by large freight outfits, and some by lone riders with a pack horse that looked deceptively sleepy and shaggy, with a worn old prospector's kit strapped to the side. But the larger amounts were carried on special coach runs carefully planned and masqueraded: When a stage broke down in a snowbank just outside of the Hills below Deadwood, the old trail-worn Concord was repaired on the sly there, the bricks and dust slipped into it a little at a time. Then, apparently unguarded except for two stage hands to help hold the rickety coach together, it was started to Sidney for repairs, with the body sagging as from a bad spring but actually from a deliberately unbalanced load of bullion, and the three guards inside.

But somebody must have sent word ahead, perhaps the breed called Seminole, long suspected of spying on the gold hauls. Morissa had seen him at Etty's now and then and was told he had been run out of Colorado for stealing gold dust, mostly from other thieves, and perhaps not above a little torture to get his information. According to the latest story he vanished from his Deadwood shack the day that Fly Speck Billy and four, five of his gang held up the crippled coach near the Nebraska line. The driver was shot off the box but some said it was done from below him, from the inside, so perhaps one of the secret guards was an accomplice of the roadagents. Fly Speck let the rest of the men get away to the nearest bull train and left the coach smashed up in an old washout beside the road, the gold and the two best horses gone.

Tris and Morissa had seen the coach come in toward sunset one day, creaking and swaying, awkward with one wagon wheel and three of its own, the body full of bullet holes. Certainly there was no gold in it then, for the coach was left beside the trail north of the river over a week without guard.

Now, three days after the Sidney theft of gold bricks, all these things came to Morissa's mind as she suddenly found Eddie Ellis at her door.

239

He had ridden boldly up to the new hospital in midafternoon and, without a look around, as though he actually lived there, he turned the iron knob. He had not bothered to knock and he bothered with no preliminaries when Morissa faced him as the door opened, her hand reaching out to the jamb to hold him out—not so much as a hello for the woman who was still his wife.

"I come to get you in on that $300,000 gold stole some time ago. You mebby heard nobody's found it—" he said, speaking under the wide black hat tipped over his squinting eyes, almost hiding them, really talking and acting like the outlaws of the region now, the men who came to have bullets dug out. But they always came slipping up the back and in darkness.

"—We'll be rich," he argued when Morissa made no reply. "I'll take you out of this stinking pus business, go see the world, Europe, Egypt— Scotland even," watching her slyly for pain at this reference to the past. "We'll go anywhere, a lifetime just layin' around—"

"How can you expect anyone to believe such talk?" Morissa asked curiously, the first words she had spoken.

"I know—" he said, swaggering his shoulders, and for a moment the bragging boy of five years ago was before her again, but now he turned wilier, more nervous. "I got to come in. People listen."

Morissa didn't want to be seen either, but with both Ruth and Charley away she refused to take this man even into her kitchen, so she slammed the door behind her and with her back against it, listened to the agitated Eddie Ellis.

"I heard one a the outfit spill the whole story before he got choked off," he insisted. "The man got caught ridin' one of the horses stole from the coach and was strung up at the Niobrara crossing of the trail. They packed the $300,000 of gold off down the river from the wrecked coach, he said. Even offered to take us all to the place if we let him go—" Eddie said, growing expansive.

"Who's this *he?*" Morissa asked, and to her plain disbelief Eddie became suspicious again. He hurried to the windows, one after another, plowing through the rosebushes and the young junipers to look in, and around the corners too. He came back, easing his gun back into the holster. "Oh, I know where the gold is all right, the whole three hundred thousand!" rolling the sum like a bon-bon on his tongue.

But the woman who was his legal wife only smiled a little and so he had to add details, make it stick. "I can show you! The gold's hid just below where the Niobrara cuts down into a canyon, and there's three pines standin' on the bluffs, and a little cave below—" he said, needing to talk faster and faster as a man must against an unreceptive woman, or a mother who can be softened. "The robbers stopped there through a blizzard. Nobody's knowin' how to dispose of the stuff with-

240

out gettin' caught, like Goodale did with his gold bricks in his father's bank window, so they hid the whole kaboodle until things blow over."

"Who are these men that you can't name them?" Morissa demanded.

That made Eddie cautious again. "You ain't said if you'll help me."

"And I won't. I'm no thief. And even if I were, how would I know that the gold is still there? Everybody knows the story, all the robber crew, the law, the federal deputies, and the express company detectives. That's a lot of money."

"I know it ain't gone," Ed maintained doggedly. "The law is watchin' but the man hung tellin' about it didn't come straight out. Once he said the haul had been divided and hid around. Then that it was all hid in one bunch until they had a little start in cattle and could come back together, split it up and spend it gradual-like. It ain't the stealing that gets your neck in a rope, Fly Speck always said, but the way you flash it around."

"Oh, Fly Speck?"

"Yes, yeh—at least that's what the man they were stringing up claimed."

"I never heard of that hanging but it seems Fly Speck was hanged all right, and without flashing any money. In fact he was so poor he was afoot."

"That's part of the scheme—"

"To get each other hanged? I suppose such men would try that, if the story were true," Morissa agreed.

"Get the others hanged?" Now Eddie's hand went to his gun again. "What you hinting?—getting me hanged? You plannin' that for me?"

"No, but I'm not one of the outlaws," Morissa replied sourly, wishing Charley were here, or any able-bodied man.

"You won't believe we—that they got the gold?"

From that slip, plainly deliberate, Morissa realized Eddie Ellis had not been in this robbery either, only once more wished that he had been. She told him there was talk enough about such a robbery, and some ugly rumors of more shooting down at a place called Fly Speck Billy's cave, where she heard the haul was suppose to be hidden. Some young fellows from around the bridge, Gwinnie, Henry Browne and some others, had gone there on a lark to see, but they never told what they found, although they admitted there were three trees and a cave. Later somebody who got shot at snooping around the cave said that two of the trees had been chopped down.

"Yeh, to fool people, keep off the treasure hunters—" Eddie admitted, easier again, his thumbs hooked in his cartridge belt. "The gold's still there and I got me a good scheme to turn it into cash. You just start out with the buggy—"

"Me?"

241

"Yeh, start out just like you was going on a call up past Snake Creek flats and keep going until you see Box Butte off northeast. I'll meet you there."

"And what is the rest of my contribution to this crazy scheme to be?"

"It ain't crazy. You can get some of the bricks out of the country in your buggy and smuggle them across the border into Mexico in the night."

Morissa looked at Eddie Ellis in amazement. Why, this was a crazy man, really insane. Listening for the sound of a horse, or for Ruth's footstep up the back way, she wondered how far this delusion would carry Ed. "You have it all planned so I'm the one to get shot by the officers sure to be watching the cave and the border, if your story is true."

"They won't suspect you. People think you're honest, a doc goin' about her business."

"And who's to finance this long trip to Mexico?"

"You got the money, and can borrow what more we need."

So that was the scheme, Morissa thought, get her out alone in that empty country up there, with money, and her team and buggy to sell, even a husband's share in her property here.

But Eddie Ellis was too self-concerned to see the doctor's suspicions. "You meet me at Box Butte. I'll give you until two weeks from today to get everything set. Be there—" he said, as though it were settled. And as he left he stopped to look all around the neat new building, with its trees and shrubs already growing up so well. Then he walked to the bridge and across it, leading his horse, giving everyone plenty of time to see that he had come from Morissa's, from his wife's place.

At first the busy doctor tried to ignore Ed's presence around Huff Johnson's but he rode over toward the hospital every day at dusk now, and past it, to some hideout—so late that no one could see he went on. Once more the people around the bridge began to stand away from Morissa Kirk. Once more a settler let a child die because he wouldn't call this doctor in league with outlaws.

Ruth saw the doctor's hurt face when she came in from calls, even from Clarke's for the mail, and when settlers passed with their heads turned the other way. Ruth, become so warm-hearted here, sang her mournful hymn of the desperate pilgrim forever crossing the flooding waters and the fiery sands. And once more Charley was getting angry.

Morissa did have one happy interlude during this time. Although Lorette kept out of sight now, one of her little girls came riding over clinging to her barebacked Indian pony. A friend wanted to see Doctor Kirk at the bridge. Morissa went. It was Dr. Walter Reed, looking much as he had six years ago when he started West, a little more meat on his bones, his skin almost as brown as his neat mustache, and his fine earnest eyes very alert. He was on the way to his new station at Fort Robinson. "—I just remembered your letter from here some time ago, and the report of your head surgery in the medical journals."

So Morissa took him over the bridge to cook him an antelope steak with watercress salad while the horses of his troop escort were fed and rested.

He seemed pleased with her little hospital, and stopped a moment before the flower-trimmed sampler that Lorette had worked:

If you want to be true physicians and learn to serve MAN in all his ills, go out to these far places. There each of you must be what he is, without PRETENCE, standing before everyone in all his VIRTUES and his faults, and as open to the call of every victim of the violence and the disease of the wilderness. There I think you may discover something of the NATURE of man; there I think is the WORK for me, and for YOU.

Dr. Walter Reed

"Did I say that? How appalling!"

"Yes, you said something like that to our gathering of young doctors on your way West, remember? I took it down the best I could, but without the capitals, or the flowers, of course. Those were Lorette's idea, over at the breed's stockade. The patients like it."

"They do?" Doctor Reed said, and fell silent a while. "Seems incredible now that one can be so callow—"

"Didn't you, and the rest of us, have to be callow to come out at all?" Morissa asked.

A fine smile lifted the man's eyebrows. "I suppose so, but we get humbled down out here, don't we?"

Now even the wife of the man with smallpox at the hospital hurried away if she could when she saw Morissa come. "They insist you are bringing outlaws to the river again," Rem Smith finally told the doctor, still mouthing his words a little from the scarring that drew the lips sidewise. Behind his shielding hand, the cheek was well healed and Rem was working out his bill for Morissa by helping to care for her little diphtheria patients, and, as the eldest of eighteen children, was very good at it. Morissa paid no attention to what the man said beyond noticing that her exercises for his lips were loosening them daily. By now she was scarcely aware of the black silk patch he wore over the knotted cheek, like a court beauty's patch, except that his seemed big as a quarter-section of land to him.

When Rem Smith repeated that everybody thought Morissa was bringing outlaws back to the river, she had to listen. "You mean they think I'm taking up with Ed?" she asked.

"Well, he's hanging around, and he is your husband, for all that they can see you sometimes favor Tris Polk a little."

Morissa nodded. They were right, and she should do something final about this situation. But the time Ed had set for the meeting at Box Butte was almost here, just two days off. When he saw she was not going, he would surely give up, leave.

Then that night he rode up to the door instead of passing as he had before. "Remember, day after tomorrow. Better get there!" he warned.

"You'll remember I told you I was no thief," Morissa snapped.

"You'll come!" Eddie replied softly, and in surprise the doctor saw the gun out of its holster, the small black hole of it pointed squarely upon her from across the saddle before him, and for a moment it seemed a symbolic gesture from the man who was never quite one. She slammed the door upon him and stood with her back against it, suddenly shaken with pity, pity for Eddie Ellis and even more for all the gunfighters of the wilderness, pity as from a sudden glimpse into some inferno—some bleak badlands, torn and empty and bare.

But Ruth interrupted her, running in with news that the settler putting up a house beyond Johnson's had been hauled past to Sidney. His ax slipped and sank deep into his ankle but he preferred to go right by here and all the way to Sidney because of Eddie Ellis.

A few nights later Joey's pup seemed restless and Morissa got up to look out, but there was nothing in the windy darkness, not even a coyote howling. Perhaps it was the atmospheric change before a storm, for the night lamp seemed to smell very strongly of kerosene. She wiped the bowl but it was clean and so she gave it up, slipped out of her dark dressing gown into a hospital coverall and made one more round, beginning at Ruth's end, where Joey and the others slept, and through the hospital rooms to look in on the cowboy with a broken hip and then to the diphtheria children with Rem Smith beside them in his white cotton uniform. He turned up the shaded lamp a little and gave the doctor a crooked, one-sided smile and a nod. So she went to the disinfecting room and then back to her dressing gown and her bed.

It seemed she was hardly asleep when a shot awoke her, apparently from the inside of the building. There was a running outside, and then another shot through a red light that flared up suddenly all along the front of the building. Morissa jerked the door open into a wall of flame blazing all along the foundation and up in the shingles, too, the strong south wind blowing the fire hard against the house, the smoke stinking of kerosene and pitch pine. She flung a bucket of water against the burning door so it smoldered, and went through it to pull out the hose. But when she turned the pressure on, the water squirted from a dozen places, holes hacked with a knife. The whole building seemed afire as Rem Smith burst through the door with the two sick children bundled in their blankets, mumbling his shout, "Too late, Doc! Get everybody out an' let 'er go!"

Choked by a sob Morissa ran for the rifle and fired three rapid distress shots into the air. By this time the door at Ruth's end was burning too, so the doctor threw up a back window and received Joey and his sisters as they were handed out, wrapped in blankets, then helped carry the cowboy's cot away, and sent the smallpox patient off to himself, to roll up in a buffalo robe. They carried out the surgical instruments and the new microscope, the hospital records and the drug cabinets, while Ruth kept the doors into her end shut off, flung her belongings out of the window, and finally climbed after them.

By now Rem was throwing things out the back of the center building. Morissa lugged the piles away, helped by the men who came running from the bridge and the roadhouses into the red light. Finally the smoke boiled through around Rem and they had to drag him out, his arms still full of Morissa's dresses from her closet, to throw on top of the little round-topped trunk that she had brought West.

When the doctor got some of the smoke out of Rem's lungs, they stood back and watched the roof flame up very bright the full length and then fall in, the children crying a little in fright, Ruth with Joey and his sisters, Rem with the sick ones. Morissa had moved off to the side to be alone in her loss, the dressing gown blowing about her as she watched the sturdy log walls stand against the fire inside and then finally begin to go, too, crashing inward, the low, clouded sky reflecting the blaze of light for miles, the river running red beneath it.

Then, as the last of the front walls went in under the push of the wind, and the thick smoke rolled up, Rem remembered something. Calling it out loud to the others, making the words with difficulty, he said he had seen a man set the fire along the foundation and shot at him twice, the last time as he dodged off almost to the trees. He seemed to duck down or fall just at the edge there.

With a lantern Etty and a dozen others went to search the ground in the direction Rem motioned, moving the light back and forth over the dead lawn and flower beds. Then they stopped, gathering in a dark little knot about the lantern, the trees rising naked and tall behind them. Someone called Morissa, and when she did not come, went over to touch her arm. Slowly she moved that way, looking back at her smoking hospital as though she could not leave. When she stopped to examine the man who had set the fire she saw it was Eddie Ellis, already stiff and cold.

Soon after dawn Morissa went to Clarke's to telegraph the sheriff, Ed's father, and Robin and Jack. She wanted to send a message to Tris,

245

but there was nothing that could be said. So she hurried back to prepare a place for her patients, still out in the cold morning air. Charley was in from his homestead, so she put him to whitewashing the fuel and provision soddy, with the old wagon heater set up to hasten the drying and to warm the two diphtheria children. She was alarmed at their lassitude this morning, the rise in their temperatures, and hoped too that Joey and the others had not come close enough for contagion. The cowboy and the smallpox man would have to get along in tents for now, each with a little Indian firehole in the middle for warmth. Morissa and the rest would live in covered wagons and a tent borrowed from Clarke. By night everybody seemed comfortable enough, Ruth baking bread under a canopy at the end of one of the Martin cook wagons, the same one that had protected Sid from the hail the night he broke his neck.

But it was the others who did most of this work. All day Morissa was faced with questions, inquiries, and the inquest. First there was the justice of the peace and the precinct constable, the latter an embarrassed cowboy who suddenly found the office was not the joke he thought it was. All they wanted was to get the story and see that the body wasn't moved. By noon the sheriff came galloping up, and got a coroner's jury together. Fortunately Henry Clarke was at the bridge for a few days and he took the lead, with Etty, three settlers, some cowboys, Huff Johnson, and a sergeant still around cleaning out government property from Camp Clarke.

Eddie was plainly shot in the back and Rem Smith volunteered the information that he fired two shots at him. Some noise had awakened him and as he roused himself he saw a light flare up beside the window. He ran to see, and discovered a man outside with a little burning stick stooping along the foundation, fire blazing up ahead of him. So Rem had grabbed the rifle from its nails and shot at the man, a plain target in the light of the burning roof and walls, but he moved the instant of the shot, and so Rem evidently missed. The man fled and Rem shot a second time and brought him down at the edge of the trees. By then Miss Morissa was up, and the others, too, the whole place afire.

It sounded reasonable, even to those unfriendly to the doctor, with all the coal oil, the kerosene, on Ed's pants and his boots. The storekeeper at Johnson's swore he sold Eddie five gallons of the oil in a grease bucket that evening—the oil that was spilled along the foundation and set afire with soaked corncobs, some still charred at the wall and crumbs of them in the empty bucket on the lawn.

When the sheriff started to take Rem away, Morissa clung to the man's hand in gratitude. "I'll try to get permission to watch your scar," she promised.

But Clarke stroked his beard thoughtfully and called the sheriff aside. So Rem stayed. "Stupid politician," the bridge owner whispered to

Morissa. "Outlaw like that, caught red-handed in arson and plotted murdering, with the hose cut and your sick and helpless patients, the children—"

"Hell, that Ellis he just hung around the outlaws," the sheriff told the doctor importantly. "They couldn't shake him off. Sam Bass's outfit tell how they snuk off an' left him down in the breaks where he took sick, and even Fly Speck Billy never really pulled a holdup with Ed along, like the time they followed Clarke's party on the trail to Deadwood."

Morissa nodded. She had known a long time it was Ed who had looked so familiar that day and perhaps that was why Jackie seemed so cool, so unconcerned, even with his father and sister along. How foolishly the young are trapped, all of them, most foolishly the daughter of Lorna Kirk.

"Ellis always just hung around," the sheriff was repeating. "His outlawin' was like his marryin'."

"Ed was a sick man," Morissa wanted to cry out against him, but it was Charley who couldn't hold back. "You knew he hadn't ought to been loose, Sheriff. Not a forger like him, a horse thief an' worse—"

The next day Jack rode in on a hired horse from Sidney. He was a fine, tall young man now, very serious in his new profession and his new position as protector of his sister. "I've come to take you with me," he said. "We need you as head of our hospital."

So Morissa hid her face against his dark coat a moment while he looked angrily at the ashes blowing around, and at all the people come to stand and stare, or walk to the place where Eddie had fallen, glancing back over their shoulders at Jack and the lady doc and then hurrying away.

"Jacobs at Sidney has agreed to take over your patients," Jack added.

It was fine to hear words like this, to see someone, so many people, wanting to help, even now that she was once more a desperate pilgrim with no telling what more floodwaters and fiery sands to cross. Finally the five-year-old Joey came pushing up on his crutch and braces that Ruth had saved. He stopped to motion his sister back but the little girl hesitated, her face frightened, sensing danger to them all. "You won't send us away, please—" he begged of the doctor. And Morissa could not reassure him, only kiss his uneasy cheek and start him off to Ruth.

By morning an offer of help came from Doctor Reed up at Fort Robinson, too, and in her gratitude all Morissa could do was flee to the errands with her patients, as roadhouse crowds, settlers, travelers, cowboys, and Sidneyites came, even Lorette now, all wanting to look at the ashes. They also wanted to see this Jack who had taken over the dispensary, measuring out Epsom salts, calomel, itch ointment, cough sirup, and a dozen other pharmaceuticals as they were requested, every-

247

body suddenly in need of dosing. And with their small packets in their hands many still lingered, finally daring to ask Charley or Ruth or even Rem what Morissa planned to do. No one knew, and she could not be pressed for a decision now, although it was plain that Jack had come to take her East.

Many left reluctantly, looking back, talking together as others came. Even the freighters drew their trains off the trail and walked over to stand beside the ashes and at the place where Eddie's blood darkened the earth, brown and blowing over with gray dust. Then someone noticed that a buggy drawing up carried a man from the Sidney bank. With a blue-backed paper in his hand he went into Morissa's tent and then came out with her, driving up past the grove and to a ridge where they could see all her stock and land. When they returned the banker was gesturing, the sweep of his hand including all the place.

There, with everybody watching and Jack as witness, Morissa started to sign the papers, the people standing away, but Robin Thomas was suddenly there too. Once more his shoulder was the refuge of his stepdaughter. He had brought a letter from Sidney, from Tris, waiting and very anxious but unwilling to cause Morissa more embarrassment just now. "You must know in your heart that I am ready to do anything that is within the power of a man, as though I already stood proudly beside you as your husband—"

Husband, Morissa thought, all the things around her here suddenly like the shimmering heat dance of the midsummer prairies. Husband. Not a father oversolicitous of his good name, or a warped and pitiful son seeking a mother, but a husband to stand beside her, a wife. For a moment it seemed to Morissa that she must cry right there before them all, cry out of the flooding of all her being.

But even in this moment there was no privacy—with the papers in her hand still to be completed. And as Morissa signed the last, once more a horsebacker came galloping, this time John Callwin, his plow mare heaving from the run. "Miss Morissa!" he shouted, sliding off beside her, embarrassed by his need to interrupt, but dogged in his awkward determination to have his say. "Miss Morissa, we are sorry that everything you built here is gone, all your work and your grief for nothing. So we got up a petition asking you to stay. We want you to build a good new hospital, brick, so it won't burn easy. There will be a railroad some time, and a town, but now—" he rubbed at the plate under his scalp, pushing his cap off without noticing it go, "—for now we want to help start the new building right away."

Because there was no comment from Morissa Kirk, no reply, he looked uneasily at the banker still holding the blue-backed documents, and his earnest sunburnt face turned even redder. But John Callwin was a stubborn man, a Scotsman with a purpose. Firmly, if futilely, he undid the roll of paper he carried under his arm, a strip of many sheets pasted awkwardly together. Deliberately he stretched an arm out sideways from his nose, wrist bent, and measured the curling paper off in the wind. "One, two," he counted the reaches, "three yards long! Over two hundred names, and we could get you a thousand from Sidney to White River and Deadwood if we had time. Two hundred signers and every man pledging you something, maybe only a few days work, or five dollars—all we got. But some's gone as high as a hundred dollars, a couple five hundred, and Sid Martin's put himself down for a thousand."

"Oh!" Morissa exclaimed, "I—"

"Well, Doctor," the banker interrupted cheerfully, "seems I got to you just in time!"

John Callwin's face went dark at this show of triumph, and other settlers moved in closer, their hands lifted a little, showing hard knuckles, readiness. "You ain't sold out to this land-grabbin' interest hog," one of them demanded, "leavin' us flat?"

"Oh, no, no!" the doctor cried, with blurring eyes. "The papers I just signed weren't a deed but a mortgage. I was just borrowing money to rebuild the hospital." For a moment Morissa Kirk looked around into the earnest, browned faces, from the farthest and the smallest to big John Callwin before her, and in all the crowd she missed only one.

"You can't know how proud I am, how very proud that you—you—" Then her voice broke and she turned her face away, for it was not fitting that all these people see their doctor cry.